THE DARKEST CORNERS

THE DARKEST CORNERS

KARA THOMAS

DELACORTE PRESS

Text copyright © 2016 by Kara Thomas
Jacket photograph © 2016 by Burcin Esin/Getty

All rights reserved. Published in the United States by Delacorte Press, an imprint of Random House Children's Books, a division of Penguin Random House LLC, New York.

Delacorte Press is a registered trademark and the colophon is a trademark of Penguin Random House LLC.

Visit us on the Web! randomhouseteens.com

Educators and librarians, for a variety of teaching tools, visit us at RHTeachersLibrarians.com

Library of Congress Cataloging-in-Publication Data
Thomas, Kara.
The darkest corners / Kara Thomas. — First edition.
pages cm
Summary: When her father dies, Tessa is pulled back to the small Pennsylvania town where her life came apart when her father was sent to prison, her mother went to pieces, and her beloved older sister ran away, and where her testimony and that of her now-estranged friend Callie sent a serial killer to death row—a serial killer who may be getting a new trial as long buried secrets come to light.
ISBN 978-0-553-52145-0 (hc) — ISBN 978-0-553-52146-7 (glb) —
ISBN 978-0-553-52147-4 (ebook) — ISBN 978-0-399-55294-6 (intl. tr. pbk.)
1. Serial murderers—Juvenile fiction. 2. Murder—Pennsylvania—Juvenile fiction.
3. Secrecy—Juvenile fiction. 4. Friendship—Juvenile fiction. 5. Sisters—Juvenile fiction.
6. Detective and mystery stories. 7. Pennsylvania—Juvenile fiction. [1. Mystery and detective stories. 2. Serial murderers—Fiction. 3. Murder—Fiction. 4. Secrets—Fiction.
5. Friendship—Fiction. 6. Sisters—Fiction. 7. Pennsylvania—Fiction. 8. Youths' writings.]
1. Title.
PZ7.1.T46Dar 2016
813.6—dc23
[Fic]
2015004181

The text of this book is set in 11.5-point Sabon.
Jacket design by Greg Stadnyk
Interior design by Heather Kelly

Printed in the United States of America
10 9 8 7 6 5 4 3 2 1
First Edition

FOR KEVIN THOMAS

CHAPTER ONE

Hell is a two-hour layover in Atlanta.

The woman to my right has been watching me since I sat down. I can tell she's one of those people who take the sheer fact that you're breathing as an invitation to start up a conversation.

No eye contact. I let the words repeat in my head as I dig around for my iPod. I always keep it on me, even though it's a model that Apple hasn't made for seven years and the screen is cracked.

Pressure builds behind my nose. The woman stirs next to me. *No eye contact. And definitely do not—*

I sneeze.

Damn it.

"Bless you, honey! Hot, isn't it?" The woman fans herself with her boarding pass. She reminds me of my gram: she's old, but more likely to be hanging around a Clinique counter than at the community center on bingo day. I give her a noncommittal nod.

She smiles and shifts in her seat so she's closer to my armrest. I try to see myself through her eyes: Greasy hair in a bun. Still in black pants and a black V-neck—my Chili's uniform. Backpack wedged between my feet. I guess I look like I need mothering.

"So where you from?" she asks.

It's a weird question for an airport. Don't most people ask each other where they're going?

I swallow to clear my throat. "Florida."

She's still fanning herself with the boarding pass, sending the smell of sweat and powder my way. "Oh, Florida. Wonderful."

Not really. Florida is where people move to die.

"There are worse places," I say.

I would know, because I'm headed to one of them.

• • •

I knew someone was dead when my manager told me I had a phone call. During the walk from the kitchen to her office, I convinced myself it was Gram. When I heard her voice on the other end, I thought I could float away with relief.

Then she said, "Tessa, it's your father."

Pancreatic cancer, she explained. Stage four. It wouldn't have made a difference if the prison doctors had caught it earlier.

It took the warden three days to track me down. My father's corrections officer called Gram's house collect when I was on my way to work.

Gram said he might not make it through the night. So she picked me up from Chili's, my backpack waiting for me on the passenger seat. She wanted to come with me, but there was no time to get clearance from her cardiologist to fly. And we both knew that the extra ticket would have been a waste of money anyway.

Glenn Lowell isn't her son. She's never even met the man.

I bought my ticket to Pittsburgh at the airport. It cost two hundred dollars more than it would have if I'd booked it in advance. I nearly said screw it. That's two hundred dollars I need for books in the fall.

You're probably wondering what kind of person would let her father die alone for two hundred dollars. But my father shot and nearly killed a convenience store owner for a lot less than that— and a carton of cigarettes.

So. It's not that I don't want to be there to say goodbye; it's just that my father's been dead to me ever since a judge sentenced him to life in prison ten years ago.

CHAPTER TWO

Maggie Greenwood is waiting for me at the arrivals gate. She's a few shades blonder and several pounds heavier than she was the last time I saw her.

That was almost ten years ago. I don't like thinking about how little has changed since then. The Greenwoods are taking me in like a stray cat again. Except this time I'm well fed. I'm on the wrong side of being able to pull off skinny jeans. Probably all those dinner breaks at Chili's.

"Oh, honey." Maggie scoops me to her for a hug with one arm. I flinch but force myself to clasp my hands around her back. She grips my shoulders and gives me her best tragedy face, but she can't help the smile creeping into her lips. I try to see myself through her eyes—no longer a bony, sullen little girl with hair down to her waist.

My mother never cut my hair. Now the longest I keep it is at my shoulders.

"Hi, Maggie."

She puts an arm on the small of my back and herds me out to

where she's parked. "Callie wanted to come, but she had to get an early night."

I nod, hoping that Maggie doesn't sense how her daughter's name inspires a sick feeling in my stomach.

"She has a twirling competition tomorrow morning," Maggie says. I'm not sure who she's trying to convince. I know it's all bullshit and Callie wouldn't have come if Maggie had dragged her.

"So she's still into that?" What I really mean is, *So people actually still twirl batons and call it a sport, huh?* But I don't want to be rude.

"Oh, yeah. She got a scholarship." Maggie's grin nearly cuts her face in half. "To East Stroudsburg. She's thinking of majoring in exercise science."

I know all this, of course. I know who Callie is still friends with (mostly Sabrina Hayes) and what she had for breakfast last week (cinnamon-sugar muffin from Jim's Deli). I know how badly Callie is dying to get out of Fayette (pronounced *Fay-it*, population five thousand) and that she already parties harder than a college freshman.

Even though I haven't spoken to her in ten years, I know almost everything there is to know about Callie Greenwood. Everything except the thing I desperately need to know.

Does she still think about it?

"Your grandmother told me you decided on Tampa?"

I nod and lean my head against the window.

When I told Gram I'd gotten into the University of Tampa, she said that I had better think real hard about going to college in the city. Cities chew people up and spit them out.

As Maggie gets off at the exit for Fayette, all I can think is that I'd rather be chewed up and spit out than swallowed whole.

. . .

Maggie pulls up outside a white, two-story farmhouse that was twice as big in my childhood memory. We shut the doors of the minivan, prompting the dogs next door to flip out. It's almost one in the morning; in a few hours, Maggie's husband, Rick, will be getting ready to start his bread delivery route. I feel bad, wondering if he's waiting up to make sure Maggie got home okay. That's the kind of husband he is.

My dad was the kind of husband who'd make my mom wait up, sick with worry, until he stumbled in smelling like Johnnie Walker.

The dogs quiet down once we're on Maggie's porch, already tired of barking. Neighborhoods in Fayette wear their emotions like people do. The Greenwoods' neighborhood is tired, full of mostly blue-collar families who are up before the sun. The type of people who eat dinner together seven nights a week, no matter how exhausted they are.

When I think of my old neighborhood, I think of anger. Of crumbling town houses squashed together so tightly, you can see right into your neighbor's kitchen. I think of angry old men on their porches, complaining about the cable company or the Democrats or their social security checks not arriving on time.

The Greenwoods used to live in my old neighborhood. They moved a year before I left to live with Gram, which meant I couldn't run down the street to play with Callie like I'd been doing since I was six.

Maggie unlocks the front door, and I immediately smell the difference. I want to ask her if she misses her old house as much as I do.

But of course she doesn't. And after what happened in that

house, it's the type of question that will definitely make me unwelcome here.

"Are you hungry?" Maggie asks, shutting the door and locking it behind her. "I know they don't give you anything on the plane anymore. There's some leftover lasagna."

I shake my head. "I'm just . . . really beat."

Maggie makes a sympathetic face, and I notice all the lines that weren't there ten years ago. She probably thinks I'm upset about my father dying.

The Tessa she remembers would have been upset. She would have cried and screamed for her daddy like she did the day the cops broke the front door down and led him out of the house in handcuffs.

Maggie doesn't know that the old Tessa has been replaced with a monster who just wants her father to hurry up and die so she can go home.

"Of course you are." Maggie squeezes my shoulder. "Let's get you to bed."

• • •

The sun comes up the instant I fall asleep.

I really need a shower, but I don't know where the Greenwoods keep their towels. In the old house, they had a linen closet inside the bathroom. Instead of going downstairs and asking Maggie for a towel, I splash some water on my face and pat it dry with a hand towel.

I have trouble asking people for things. I've been this way for as long as I can remember, but I think it got bad when Gram brought me to Florida. Before she turned her office into a bedroom for me, I slept on a pullout bed. There were no blinds on the windows, so every morning at six, the sunlight streamed in and I couldn't fall back asleep.

I started sleeping under the pullout bed, because it was dark there. Gram didn't catch me for more than a month. The windows in my room have blinds now, but sometimes, when I can't sleep, I find myself crawling under the bed and staring at the bedsprings like they're constellations.

I didn't even bother trying to fall asleep last night. When I'm done washing my face I find some Listerine under the sink and swish a bit in my mouth. No reason to redo the bun I slept in. What's the point? There's no way I'll look worse than my father.

Maggie is making French toast when I get downstairs. A coffeemaker gurgles on the counter.

"Milk or cream?" she asks, gesturing to the mug she's left out for me. I don't have the heart to tell her I hate coffee.

I shrug. "Either is fine."

Maggie tilts the pan and flips a slice of bread. "I tried to get Callie up, but she's not feeling well."

I sit down at the kitchen table. I heard Callie sneak in at three this morning. I'll bet anything she's hungover. Once Callie started high school, the red Solo cups in her Facebook pictures started popping up like mushrooms.

"She's missing her competition." Maggie frowns, adjusting the heat on the stove. "But I figure I'll let her slide. It's the summer."

My muscles tense up as I realize this means that Callie probably won't be able to avoid me all day. Especially not if her mother has anything to do with it.

I called Callie every day for a week once I got to Florida. Every time, Maggie answered. Callie was either at twirling practice, or riding bikes with Ariel Kouchinsky, or finishing up her homework.

Maggie's voice became more desperate and apologetic every day. She didn't want me to give up.

Eventually my calls stretched out to once a week, then once a month. Then they stopped altogether.

This past year, Maggie called on my birthday and sent us a card for Christmas. She didn't mention Callie either time.

Three years ago, I spotted Callie in the last place I thought she'd be: an online forum dedicated to discussing the Ohio River Monster murder trial. She made only one post. It was two lines, telling the other posters to shut up—what did they know about the case, they were a bunch of wannabe lawyers living in their moms' basements. She signed off with *Wyatt Stokes is a murderer* and never came back to defend herself against the swarms of people demanding, *Prove it.*

I know it was Callie; she used the same username she's used for everything since we were ten—twirlygirly23.

I created an account and messaged her. *It's me, Tessa. I've been reading this stuff too.* She never responded.

In any event, she can't be thrilled that I'm back to remind her of the worst summer of our lives.

Maggie flops a piece of French toast onto my plate. I look up and return her wan smile. We have to be at the prison by eight.

· · ·

Fayette, Pennsylvania, looks worse during the day. Worse than I remember. Maggie stops at the Quik Mart on Main Street to get gas. Half the businesses are boarded up, or are hiding behind Closed signs that are probably gathering dust.

A big part of Fayette died with the steel industry in the early nineties. Before I was born, my father worked at a mill in the next town over. Now Fayette looks as if it were clinging on for dear life. Probably because everyone here is so goddamn stubborn. No one will let Jim's Deli or Paul the Tailor go out of business.

The people who are left refuse to pack up and leave. But with any luck, their kids will.

It takes us half an hour to get to the county prison. I don't realize my leg is jiggling until Maggie puts the car in park and sets her hand on my knee.

"Honey, are you sure you want to do this?"

Of course I don't. "It's fine," I say. "We won't stay long."

Maggie flips her mirror down and puts on a fresh coat of petal-pink lipstick. I return her tight smile, and we walk side by side to the security gate. She slips her arm around my back and doesn't pull away when my muscles tense.

Gram isn't touchy-feely. For years, every night I'd linger in the hall, watching her do her crossword puzzle in the den while muttering the answers to the questions on *Jeopardy!* under her breath. I'd wait right there, like some pathetic affection beggar, until she'd finally look up at me. She'd nod and say, "Well, good night, kiddo." And that was it.

I kind of have a thing with people touching me now. Maggie doesn't seem to notice that my reaching into my bag for my phone is really my way of trying to wriggle away from her.

"They'll probably make you leave that up front." She nods to my phone. "And hospice . . . they may not let me go in with you."

I swallow away the bitter taste the coffee has left in my mouth. I guess I should be getting sad right about now, weighed down with memories of my father. Instead, I'm curious. I wonder what he looks like, whether his skin is rice-paper thin and sunken around his high cheekbones. In my memory, he was always healthy. None of us ever went to the doctor; my mom never liked them, and my dad swore that there was no affliction a shot of whiskey couldn't fix.

I don't say anything as I follow Maggie to the security desk. A woman in a gray uniform watches us from behind a glass pane.

"Are you on the approved list?" she asks, without looking up from her computer.

"I spoke with the head of hospice yesterday." Maggie's voice is clipped.

"Who are you here to see?"

"Glenn Lowell." My voice comes out dry and raspy. The guard lifts her eyes. Takes me in.

"Glenn Lowell died this morning," she says.

Maggie's jaw sets. "How is that possible?"

"People get sick, and they die," the guard deadpans. When her eyes lock on me, pity flashes in them. She sets her pen down. "He deteriorated overnight. I'm sorry."

"Why the hell weren't we notified? This is his *daughter*." Maggie's voice rises. The people waiting on the bench behind us look up from their newspapers. My finger finds the spot on the side of my jeans that's fraying.

"His daughter deserves to see him," Maggie says. "Who is your superior?"

The guard folds her arms across her chest. Her badge says WANDA. "Ma'am, I understand your frustration, but Glenn Lowell's daughter was here last night. I wasn't aware that he had two."

"Wait." My legs have gone weak. "She was here?"

I sense Maggie stiffen next to me. Without a word, the guard flips back a page on the ledger set before her. She passes it under the glass pane. My fingers tremble as I search for her name on the page.

11

"She's not on here," I say. I go to push the ledger back, but Wanda stops me.

"Six-thirty-five p.m. yesterday," she says. "I signed her in."

I slide my finger down the page until I find the time. *Brandy Butler.*

In my sister, Joslin's, handwriting.

My toes clench in my sneakers. I know it's hers—I used to make fun of the silly way she wrote her *es*, the exaggerated dip, as if it were trying to touch its toes.

Maggie puffs up, starts arguing with the guard about needing to speak with the warden.

"Glenn Lowell doesn't have a daughter named Brandy Butler," Maggie says.

"It's her."

Maggie turns to look at me.

"That's Jos's handwriting," I say.

Maggie's lips part with disbelief. There's something else in her expression—pity. I'm getting really goddamn tired of that today.

"Let's go," I tell her. "He's dead, and that's that, so can we leave?"

Maggie hesitates. My leg is jiggling again. She casts a look at the guard, as if to say, *Someone will be hearing from me about this.* Then she grabs my hand.

The gate beyond the desk buzzes. A guard appears with a clipboard propped on his forearm. He doesn't look up from it as he shouts out a name. "Edwards?"

A man in a suit stands up in the waiting area, sheepish, as if he'd just gotten called to the principal's office in the middle of class.

"Your client's ready for you," the guard says. Edwards tucks a manila folder under his arm and walks past Maggie and me with a polite nod. He doesn't know who we are.

Maggie's hand tightens around mine, and I know she recognizes him too. Maybe from the documentary about the murders, *Unmasking the Monster,* if she brought herself to watch it. Or maybe she's been following Stokes's appeal, because her niece was the last of his victims and she feels like she has to.

Either way, Maggie's nervous energy transfers to me, and I know she sees what I see: the defense attorney who has been trying for the past ten years to get a new trial for Wyatt Stokes.

Wyatt Stokes, the Ohio River Monster, who is on death row because Callie and I put him there.

CHAPTER THREE

"Come on, Tessa," Maggie barks, as if I were the one holding us up. She drops my hand, and I follow her outside.

The doors slam behind us, shutting out the darkness of the prison. The sun streams into my eyes.

Maggie is wearing the same face she had on outside the courthouse the day Stokes was sentenced to death—as if all the light had been sucked from the earth. I wasn't there for the sentencing; Joslin, my mother, and I watched the local news from our living room so we could hear the judge's decision. One of the camerapeople got a shot of Maggie and Bonnie Cawley, Lori's mother, on the steps afterward.

I didn't understand why Maggie didn't look happy; Stokes got the death penalty, just like everyone had hoped he would. Maggie wouldn't talk to any of the reporters, but Bonnie looked right at the camera and said she'd be front row at Wyatt Stokes's execution.

I'd heard Maggie explaining to Callie that Lori's murder had changed Callie's aunt Bonnie. At Stokes's bond hearing, Bonnie had waited on the steps of the courthouse until the guards had brought him in and she could tell him to his face that he was Satan's child. Bonnie hated the man who killed her daughter so much that she hadn't been able to go on living until she'd found out he was going to die.

But I look at Maggie now, and I know that hate isn't something you can put in a person's heart by taking away something they love. You either have hate in you or you don't; it hides in someone's body like a cancer, waiting for the right moment to come out.

I didn't realize I had so much hate in me until right now. I don't hate Wyatt Stokes for making us live in fear. I don't hate my father for being sent to prison, and I don't even hate him for not holding on for a few more hours when he knew I was coming to say goodbye.

It's my sister I hate. My only sister, who kissed my eyelids when I cried and let me hang on her like a monkey at night, taking up the whole bed with my tiny body. My sister, who protected me when my father went to jail and our mother unraveled in front of us. Joslin, who said she'd never leave me but ran away from home two days after my ninth birthday and never came back.

Only she did come back. Just not for me.

• • •

There was never going to be a funeral for my father, even if he'd died on enough notice. There's no money to pay for one, and I'm not sure who would have shown up if we'd held it in the prison chapel. Wanda? The other inmates? It's mortifying. Everyone who mattered to my father—and it was a short list, trust me—is

15

long gone. So I'd booked my return trip to Orlando for tomorrow night.

That was before I knew my sister is back. *Was* back. Who knows where she is now—she's had a twelve-hour head start to get the hell out of Pennsylvania.

What I can't figure out is, how did Jos know my father was dying? Glenn Lowell wasn't even her biological dad. Our mother left Joslin's father when Joslin was two; all we'd ever heard about him was that he lived in Louisiana. He and my mother had never gotten married. I never had the nerve to ask whether or not the scar on Joslin's chin had anything to do with the reason my mother left him.

Jos called my father Daddy, and there was never any mention of the Louisiana man. My dad called us both his babies, and Jos cried like I did when he went to jail for three counts of armed robbery and attempted capital murder.

I doubt that Jos found out he was dying from our mother, since I haven't heard from her in almost ten years. Gram hasn't heard from her in twice that. I'd think maybe it was Maggie who got in touch with Jos—Maggie always had an almost mystical quality of being connected to people, always knowing what everyone was up to. But she was just as surprised as I was to find out that Joslin had been to the prison last night.

And Maggie never really liked my sister anyway.

Callie and I had been friends since pre-K, but until we turned eight, Joslin was always "That sister of yours, Tessa," said with a disapproving sidelong glance. That June, Lori Cawley came to Fayette to spend the summer with the Greenwoods. Jos was about to be a senior in high school. Lori had just finished her first year at college in Philadelphia. Maggie tried to introduce Lori to girls her own age, but she met my sister when Jos dropped me off at the house, and that was that. Joslin and Lori brought Callie and me to the pool almost every day when my sister wasn't working; they'd bend their heads together over copies of *Cosmo* and talk about the things they did with boys, and if Callie and I overheard, they'd buy our silence with giant jawbreakers from the ice cream parlor.

It was also the first summer my mother let me stay over at a friend's house. The first time I slept at the Greenwoods', Callie and I watched *Mulan* twice because we didn't want to go to sleep, our mouths white from the jawbreakers. I was having so much fun, I didn't even miss having my sister in the bed with me, like I did on the nights when she snuck out to meet her boyfriend, Danny.

The last time I stayed at the Greenwoods' was the night Lori Cawley disappeared. In Fayette, we'd heard rumors of a serial killer abducting girls from truck stops along I-70. They'd found three bodies in the previous two years. All runaways, drug addicts. Girls of the night.

Girls like Lori didn't have anything to worry about. In Fayette, we were safe from the Monster, who stalked the outskirts of town in search of the next troubled, desperate girl to accept a ride from him.

That was what we thought until the police found Lori's body in a wooded area off the interstate a day after she went missing.

• • •

"Do you want me to put on some tea for us?" Maggie asks when we get back to the house. I can tell she's being nice, that she's rattled by everything that happened at the prison and just wants to be alone.

That's fine by me. "I should probably call my gram."

"Okay." Maggie leans her back against the kitchen counter. Presses her fingers to her eyelids. When she moves her fingers, she blinks as if she'd never seen me before. She catches herself and forces a smile. "Anything you need, you let me know. Anything."

I can't ask for the one thing I really need, for Maggie to drive me to Pittsburgh so I can switch my flight to tonight, because I don't know how I'm going to make it until tomorrow.

It's two days. If you survived ten years here, you can survive two more days.

I mumble a "Thank you" to Maggie before heading upstairs. My cell phone is on the nightstand charging, where I left it. I dial Gram's house and get her answering machine. While her greeting plays, I try to figure out what I'm going to say.

I can't tell Gram that my father died before I even got to see him. She'll just feel guilty, even though it's not her fault. I hang up.

I don't have an Internet plan on my cell phone. I share minutes with Gram, even though her phone is always dead, buried in the debris at the bottom of her purse. If I'd had the chance to pack for myself, I would have brought my laptop.

I swallow the lump climbing up my throat. I saw a computer in the family room downstairs.

The top step groans under my weight, and I flinch. I don't like being in an unfamiliar house, where the slightest misstep could mean drawing attention to myself. I've learned how to avoid all the spots in Gram's house like they're land mines—the creaky third step from the bottom of the staircase, the screen door around back that desperately needs its hinges oiled.

The sound of the Greenwoods' front door slamming freezes me in place.

"Callie?" Maggie calls out from the kitchen.

I don't breathe. I feel like I'm ten again—pissed off at Callie for abandoning me, but willing to do anything to catch a glimpse of her.

The first few months at Gram's, I didn't talk much. Eventually, Gram got tired of me moping; she cornered me and pulled the truth out of me, like the way my father used to chase me down and yank the baby teeth out of my mouth when he got sick of watching me wiggling them.

Gram probably expected me to say that I missed my mom or Joslin, but the truth was, I'd already accepted that they were both gone. Callie was all I had left, and Maggie couldn't even get her on the phone with me.

"Yeah?" Callie's voice is low, slightly husky. Nothing like I remember. There's the sound of something being tossed onto the couch in the foyer—a purse, probably—and her footsteps fade into the kitchen.

I grip the banister. This is ridiculous. I can't hide in the guest room for two days.

I tiptoe down the stairs. Maggie and Callie are murmuring in the kitchen. I pause in the foyer, with the sinking feeling that they're having a conversation I wouldn't have been invited to.

I catch pieces of it. Maggie's voice. ". . . know it's hard for you. She didn't have anywhere else to go."

"We're not a halfway house, Mom." Callie's voice. It's angry.

I turn to head back upstairs. The living room floor creaks underneath me. There's a loaded silence in the kitchen.

"Tessa, honey?" Maggie sounds nervous. "Is that you?"

Crap. I squeeze my eyes shut. "I just needed a glass of water."

Maggie appears next to me in the living room. "Oh, of course. I'm glad you came down, because guess who's home?"

19

She leads me through the archway. Callie looks up from the table. She's in a green East Stroudsburg University sweatshirt, her honey-brown eyes smudged with day-old eyeliner. She's beautiful, in a way that always made me feel like something that crawled out from a sewer.

Callie meets my gaze, the color draining from her face. And in that moment I see myself exactly how she sees me: Tessa Lowell, her embarrassing, white-trash childhood friend.

The reminder of the year of her childhood that was taken away by the trial.

Maggie looks from her daughter to me. Her eyes are red. I picture her sneaking off when we got home from the prison to have a good cry about seeing Tim Edwards.

"I'm so glad you girls finally get to spend some time together," Maggie says.

Callie snorts. "Yeah, because I *definitely* asked for this."

She gets up and pushes her chair in. She's gone before the shock on Maggie's face morphs to anger. Maggie turns to me, her expression strained.

"Tessa, I'm so—"

"It's okay," I say. "Really."

Maggie reaches for my hand and squeezes it. "I need to pick up a few things from the supermarket, if you want to come."

I shake my head and make an excuse about wanting to lie down, then head up to the guest room. I sit on the edge of the bed, palms on my knees, until I hear the front door shut. And then I hurry downstairs to the family room, where the computer is.

I've typed his name so many times that my fingers have memorized the strokes; they're ready once they find the keyboard.

Wyatt Stokes. He's not in the news often anymore, but the latest article is from last week. It's one I must have missed between picking up all the extra shifts to make my second tuition deposit in time.

JUDGE GRANTS MOTION TO HEAR NEW EVIDENCE IN WYATT STOKES APPEAL

I knew that he was appealing, of course. Stokes fired his first defense attorney right after he was sentenced, and replaced him with Tim Edwards. After years of trying to overturn his conviction, a judge denied Stokes a new trial, saying the first was fair enough. But Edwards said he'd take the appeal to the highest court.

This always happens, but nothing ever comes of it, my mother explained when I was worried that Stokes would get out and come after Callie and me for testifying against him. Back before I knew that, guilty or innocent, no one goes down without a fight.

I skim the article, but it doesn't say what the new evidence is. Doesn't say when the new hearing will be. It could be years; death row inmates have nothing but time. Until the day they don't.

There's a clenching in my gut, hard and furious.

Upstairs, a door slams.

Shit. I scramble to erase the article from the browsing history. I'm deleting *Wyatt Stokes* from the search bar terms when the footsteps reach the bottom of the stairs.

I launch myself out of the desk chair at the same moment Callie rounds the corner into the family room. She stops when she sees me; I picture her ignoring me, pretending I'm invisible as she flings herself onto the couch and turns on the TV.

Instead, she sucks in a breath. I think I smell booze on her. She pats at her part, smoothing down her already flat blond hair. She used to pull at it as a kid—so much that she had a bald spot for the trial.

21

We stare at each other. The room is small; she's blocking my exit.

Callie always had more of everything than I did. I was always the needy friend, always going without something. But I'm not going to stand here now and be the one without the balls to open my mouth.

"How are you?" I say.

"Not really in the mood." She flips the hood of her sweatshirt over her head and steps around me.

I suppress the urge to shove her into the wall. Rip out her hair. I didn't realize how angry I was at her until this moment.

I haven't fought anyone since the end of tenth grade. Some stupid kid, this boy everyone called Bobby Buckteeth, was mouthing off in social studies about food stamps. Regurgitating everything his mother had said about the women who came into her Stop & Shop, spending taxpayer money while flaunting their iPhones and designer purses and five kids.

I waited for him after class and asked if those kids deserved to starve. Maybe that woman was stuck with all those kids because their father dropped dead, or went to jail. He brushed past me, muttering something to his friend about how I was white trash. I chased him down and slammed his face into a locker.

When Gram picked me up from school, she grabbed my chin in front of the assistant principal, digging her fingernails into my skin. "Don't mistake my kindness for weakness, Tessa."

That was the moment when I realized that my mother was her daughter, after all. They both have a violence lurking under what looks like a harmless outer layer.

Callie draws her knees to her chest on the couch. She takes out her phone, obviously so she doesn't have to acknowledge that I'm still standing here.

"What do you want?" she says, when I make no motion to leave.

Look at me! I want you to put down your goddamn phone and stop acting like you weren't my best friend once.

But I don't have the balls to say that. I never have, and probably never will. I clear my throat.

"Don't give your mom shit about me being here right now," I say. "We were at the prison this morning."

"I know." Callie balances her phone on her knee. The screen goes dark. "I'm sorry about your dad," she adds, as an afterthought.

"We didn't— That's not why she's upset." I swallow. "It's Stokes."

Callie flinches, and for some reason, it makes me brave.

"We saw his lawyer," I say. "The one handling his appeal."

"Okay." Callie drags the word out, as if she doesn't get why I'm telling her this. But I see her digging her fingers into the arm of the couch.

I shrug. "I thought you should know. It might be in the news."

Callie's expression shifts to one I used to know well. I used to look out for that face like it was a tornado siren. Now I'm glad she's mad. I'm glad I'm the one who did it.

"Why the hell are you bringing this up?" Callie hisses, her cheeks flushed with anger.

"Because it involves us," I say.

"Not anymore. He's *guilty,* and he's never getting out." It's a phrase Maggie's drilled into Callie's head over the years, no doubt. She even looks like her mother when she says it—has the same flattened, defiant upper lip. I can't tell her that the article claims his lawyers have new evidence; Callie will demand to know what it is, and when I can't tell her, she'll give me one of those looks that level me.

23

Callie was always the one people listened to. *Eight going on eighteen,* Maggie would say. Even now that we *are* both eighteen, I feel like a stupid child around her.

"Things are different now," I mumble.

"What are you talking about?" Callie springs up from the couch. Closes the family room door. "Do *not* tell me all those lunatics from Cyber Sleuths got into your head and now you want to take back your testimony."

So she did get my message.

"Of course not," I say. "But it's been ten years. If they retest the evidence, who knows what they'll find."

Callie folds her arms across her chest. "Tessa. He stalked Lori and he killed her. You were there when he threatened her at the pool. Don't you remember?"

Of course I remember. I've remembered it every day for the past ten years. The three of us were headed to where Lori's car was parked. Wyatt Stokes was leaning against the chain-link fence, smoking a joint. The day before, Joslin had let him borrow her lighter. I don't know what Stokes said to Lori, but she got uncomfortable and ignored him.

He sucked on his joint and said, "What's red, white, and blue and floats?"

Lori pressed her hands to our backs and pushed us toward the car as he called out, "A dead bitch," and laughed to himself all the way into the woods.

I realize I haven't responded to Callie when her eyes flash. "I *saw him,*" she says, but I hear what she really means: Wyatt Stokes is the man who killed her cousin. Even to consider the possibility that it isn't true is treason.

I lift my chin so that I can meet her eyes. Callie was always taller than me. She towers over me now, though, her low-slung jeans showing off a sliver of her toned stomach.

"How can you remember what you saw?" My voice quakes. "It was dark. We were only eight."

Callie lets out an exasperated laugh and grabs the doorknob. "I'm done talking about this."

She whirls around to face me, and I flinch. Her face softens—or maybe I only imagined it, because now she's glaring at me again. "Just remember that you said you saw him too. You can't say I lied without accusing yourself of the *same thing*."

Callie slams the door behind her. The sound may as well be the period at the end of the sentence *Wyatt Stokes is guilty*.

Two more days in Fayette.

It might as well be two years.

*   *   *

We begged Lori to let us sleep in the Greenwoods' sunroom that night. Maggie had said absolutely no to our setting up Rick's tent in the backyard. She'd promised we could camp out there some other time, when she and Rick would be home and someone could stay in the tent with us.

The sunroom was the next best thing. It made Lori nervous that a screen was the only thing separating us from the outside, but Callie insisted that nothing bad ever happened in our neighborhood. Lori relented, and we dug through the camping gear in the crawl space beneath the stairs to the basement to find me an old sleeping bag. We vowed to stay up all night and watch for bears, but by ten, we were fading, cloaked in a sun-and-chlorine-soaked bliss.

I woke up to Callie shaking me, her Cinderella sleeping bag bunched up to her shoulders.

"Tessa. There's someone out there."

I don't remember being scared. I thought it was probably an animal, until we heard another twig snap. Footsteps. Callie dug her nails into my forearm. "What if it's the man from the pool?"

I shushed her, and we peered out the screen together. Callie cried out as a dark figure skulked around the side of the yard. I yanked her through the sunroom door and into the living room, where Lori was on the couch, the television muted, a book facedown in her lap.

"There's someone outside," Callie said.

Lori grabbed a flashlight. Callie started to cry.

"It's probably a raccoon," Lori told her. "Just wait in your room."

We huddled on Callie's bed until Lori came back a few minutes later.

"No one's out there," she said. "But why don't you just sleep in here tonight, okay?"

"Can't you sleep in here with us?" Callie asked her.

Lori laughed. The three of us couldn't have possibly fit in the twin bed. Lori had insisted we'd be fine in Callie's room.

Imagine if she hadn't? I heard my mother whisper to Maggie afterward. *Lori was their guardian angel.*

When Maggie and Rick got home from dinner and drinks at a friend's house, Lori wasn't in the guest room, and her bed was still made. Callie and I hadn't heard a thing. The guest room was across the house from Callie's room. Lori's killer had surprised her, probably caught her asleep on the couch after the excitement from earlier had calmed down. She'd never even had the chance to scream.

26

Callie and I had to describe everything that happened that night so many times. Eventually, it felt like *we* were the criminals; Maggie kept reminding us that the prosecutors just wanted to make sure they were able to put away the man who'd hurt Lori. They poked holes in our testimony; they looked for places where our stories didn't match up. Callie started to cry when the assistant district attorney grilled her about what we'd had for dinner. I said Maggie had made us corn to go with our hot dogs. Callie had forgotten about the corn. Any potential hole in the story had to be plugged up; the prosecution needed us to say we saw Wyatt Stokes sneaking onto the Greenwoods' property, but they couldn't risk us looking unreliable and sinking their case.

I don't remember eating the corn now. I don't remember how the hot dog tasted or which pajamas I was wearing.

Does it even matter now if Callie and I never really saw Stokes's face? Once he went to jail, girls stopped turning up dead along the Ohio River.

Marisa Perez. Rae Felice. Kristal Davis. All strangled, robbed, and left half naked like trash off the highway, down by the river. Three girls who were so different from Lori, except for their proximity to Wyatt Stokes.

Just tell us what you saw, sweetheart. There are no wrong answers.

Every now and then another answer to what happened that night sneaks in from the darkest corners of my mind. I usually squash it like a mosquito—there's no point dwelling on questions no one can answer for me.

But now that I'm here, I can't ignore certain things any longer.

There are worse things in this world than monsters, and somehow, they always manage to find me.

CHAPTER FOUR

The sun's going down when I wake up. I'm curled up on the guest room bed, my head half off the pillow. I notice that I never took my shoes off, and sit up, guilty.

Someone's knocking on the guest room door. Maggie opens it tentatively, peeking her head in. "Get some sleep?"

"I guess so." I try to think back on what I was doing a few hours ago, but my brain is fuzzy. I probably crashed from being up for more than twenty-four hours.

"It's almost dinnertime," Maggie says, over the sound of the door across the hall closing. "I was thinking maybe the four of us could go to the Boathouse."

Before she can clarify exactly who she means by *the four of us,* Callie's head appears over Maggie's shoulder. "I'm going to Em's graduation party tonight. I told you that."

Maggie's eyes flick to her daughter, then to me. "Well, it's been a long day, and it's too hot to cook, so you're more than welcome to come with Rick and me to dinner."

Rick Greenwood has said maybe ten words to me in all

the years I've known him. It's not personal; it's just how he is. He's a quiet man, the type who gets home from work and self-medicates with online poker. The stone-faced dad in the audience of Callie's baton twirling competitions who sighed and looked away every time a routine involved any sort of ass-shaking.

"She can come with me," Callie says. When she realizes that we're staring at her, speechless, she starts pulling at the ends of her ponytail. "I mean, if she wants."

I don't know whether I should be grateful that Callie's offering to rescue me from the most awkward dinner ever, or annoyed that she can't look me in the eye while doing it.

"Tessa knows Emily," Callie says, acknowledging the skeptical look Maggie gives her. "They were friends as kids."

"I wasn't invited," I cut in. They both turn to look at me, as if they'd forgotten I'm sitting right here.

"It's open house," Callie says, seeming to think that both Maggie and I need the explanation. "Half the people who'll show up probably weren't invited."

Maggie's eyebrows form a V. "I don't like the sound of that."

"Mom, her parents are throwing it for her," Callie says. "It's not gonna be a rager or anything. I want Tessa to come."

Her eyes shift to the right. So, she doesn't really want me to come to the party with her. Then why the hell invite me?

In any case, I want to go to that party even less than Callie wants me to be there. What I really want to do is stay here—so I can get onto the Greenwoods' computer again and follow the first lead I've had on my sister in years. But I know Maggie, and she'll never let me stay here alone.

I swallow and look at her. "Maybe I'll go to the party. If that's okay."

I catch the slightest frown bend her lips before she catches herself. "Of course. Just be careful, girls, all right?"

Callie rolls her eyes. "I'll text you as soon as we get there."

Maggie smiles and tells us to have fun and make sure to lock the doors before we leave. Callie gives me a funny little nod, as if to say, *Well, okay then,* and disappears back into her room.

I look down at my sweatshirt. There's a spot of grease on the sleeve from the grilled cheese Maggie made me for lunch. It'll have to do—I didn't bring enough clothes for the cool evening weather. It'll probably be too dark for anyone to see anyway.

I'm wrestling my hair into a fresh bun when Callie appears in the doorway. "Ready?"

No. "Yeah." She's changed into low-rise jeans and a cotton peasant shirt. I fold up the cuffs of my sweatshirt to hide the grease stain and follow her downstairs.

"Shouldn't we bring a card or something?" I gesture to Callie's empty hands as she locks the front door behind us.

Callie is several strides ahead of me on the driveway. "It's not a party."

"You were pretty convincing back there."

Her face reflects in the windshield of Maggie's minivan. She's glaring.

"Would you rather sit around my depressing house all night?" She unlocks the car and we climb in.

Callie doesn't know the first thing about depressing. Gram's house is full of ashtrays and tabloids from when Princess Diana died. Regardless, I don't answer her question, and she doesn't press the issue. Callie turns for the main road, and I pretend to be immersed in reading the signs at each stoplight. One advertises a spooky walk behind the firehouse—for Halloween, nine months ago.

Callie clears her throat, dashing my hopes of spending the rest of the ride in silence. When I look over at her, she gets this look on her face like she might pass out.

"It wasn't personal." She grips the steering wheel so hard that her nail beds turn white. "How I acted when you moved away . . . It was just hard for me."

If I weren't so gutless, I'd ask her exactly what she thought was so easy for me. My mother abandoning me? Having to move in with a woman I'd never met?

"It was a long time ago" is all I say.

She moves her hand from the steering wheel and tucks a lock of hair behind her ear. Her fingers linger there, as if she can't help herself. I almost feel bad for her. But not bad enough.

"Did you ask me to come with you so I wouldn't be alone with your mom?" I ask. "Are you afraid of what I'll say to her?"

Callie sets her hand in her lap. "There's nothing for you *to* say to my mom."

The uncertainty that was in her voice thirty seconds ago is gone. I loop a finger through the hole in my jeans.

"The trial almost destroyed my family," Callie says quietly. "My mom blamed herself for years—she said if she hadn't gone out with my dad that night, Lori might still be alive."

Pathos. I learned the term in my public speaking and debate class last year. *Pathos* is an appeal to someone's emotions. Callie's message is clear: if I try to dig up things that have been buried since the trial, I'll only bring the Greenwoods more pain.

I'd be causing *Maggie* pain. Maggie, who picked me up that night at the gas station and saved me from being dumped into the foster system. Maggie, who always slipped an extra sandwich into Callie's lunch box in case my father stole my lunch money from my jacket pocket while I slept.

I keep my eyes on the spot on the horizon where the sun is disappearing. I think of Lori Cawley and her hands that always smelled of lilac lotion, brushing the one unruly curl away from my forehead. I picture her body, swollen from the river and colorless except for the ring of bruises around her neck. *Only a monster could do this,* the district attorney said, pointing to the photos of the victims' bodies lined up side by side for the jury. The sick feeling in my stomach is back.

Not for the first time, I briefly envy Wyatt Stokes. Because at least if he's guilty, he doesn't have to live with himself forever.

• • •

The "not a party" is a bonfire on the outskirts of town, across the highway from a trailer park where my father occasionally played poker with his coworkers. We park in knee-high grass, trek down a beaten path, and emerge in a field. By the light of the fire, I spot a barn in the distance. The chatter by the bonfire ebbs as everyone turns around to see who's arrived.

A girl holding a brown paper bag is the first to reach us. "I thought you weren't coming." She leans in and gives Callie a peck on the cheek. I flinch, thinking she's going to do it to me too, even though obviously not. The girl takes a step back. She has brown hair that fades into blond at her shoulders.

"Holy shit," she breathes. "Tessa?"

I glance over at Callie, whose eyes bulge as if to say *The hell you looking at me for?* I clear my throat and nod. Aside from her hair, Sabrina Hayes looks exactly the same. "Hey, Sabrina."

By the fire, someone leans into the person next to them and mutters my name. I count seven people sitting in chairs and on crates by the fire. A guy in a Steelers hat turns to get a look at

32

me. Sips from his beer and turns back around, apparently unimpressed.

Sabrina ducks her head toward Callie's. "So is this why I couldn't get ahold of you all weekend?"

A guy with the hood of his sweatshirt pulled over his head emerges from the dark. He stops next to Callie and lowers his hood, running a hand over his short hair. "No one can get ahold of her. Miss College is too good for us now."

Callie's mouth forms a line. The guy smirks. His shoulder is touching Callie's—there's something weirdly intimate about it. And then it hits me: Callie has slept with this guy. Ryan Elwood, who played soccer every day at recess while Callie, Ariel, and I pulled wild green onions from the field and pretended to make soup.

Ryan used to have a floppy blond mushroom cut and a round face. He's slimmed out and muscled up in the usual manly places now, but still has awkward-boy mannerisms. Like the way his eyes never meet mine as he nods and says "Hey, 'sup."

Sabrina passes the brown bag to Callie, who shakes her head. "Brought my own."

We all migrate to the fire, Callie hanging to the side. She removes a flask from her purse and unscrews it. An actual *flask*, which is something I thought existed only in old Western movies. I shake my head when Sabrina passes the bag of mini liquor bottles to me. Someone has to get us home in one piece.

Ryan catches my eye and nods toward an upturned milk crate, as if to tell me it's okay to sit. I lower myself next to a girl in jean shorts and cowboy boots. She uncrosses her long, tanned legs and sits up to look at me. "I can't believe it's you," she says, with mild awe.

I return Emily Raymes's tentative smile. Her lower lip is

pierced, and the smooth, golden hair I was once jealous of is now bleached platinum and frayed at the ends. She sips her beer. "I'm not trying to sound rude or whatever, but what are you doing back?"

I cradle the unopened can of beer someone has passed me. "Visiting my dad."

Emily gives a polite nod, and I can't figure out if she remembers that I'm the girl with the armed robber for a father. I decide I won't tell anyone that he's dead; even if this isn't Emily's graduation party, there's probably someone here who thinks it's their night, that life can't get any better than being under a cloudless summer sky and warmed by booze right now. And I don't want to be the buzzkill.

"Has anyone heard from Ari?" Emily turns and addresses the group, looking desperate for an excuse to stop talking to me. Callie and Sabrina sit down on the last unoccupied milk crate, their backs pressed against each other's so they can both fit.

Callie's gaze flicks downward. It's one story I've never been able to piece together from her Facebook profile alone, why she and Ariel Kouchinsky don't talk anymore.

Ariel wrote me a few letters when I first moved to Florida; flowery envelopes adorned with so many Disney stickers that the mailperson could barely read my address. Ariel's parents didn't let her call me—her father was a mean bastard who always barked at us to get out of the house and go ride our bikes.

A year or so ago, I noticed that Callie unfriended Ariel. Or maybe it was the other way around.

"You invited Ari?" Sabrina takes a pull from the cigarette in her fingers, the end glowing orange. "That's awkward."

"I don't care." It's not Callie who speaks up. It's the guy in the Steelers hat. The one I don't know. Up by the fire, I can get a better look at his face. It's wide, with reddish-brown stubble up his jaw. He's heavier than most Fayette guys, and his wide mouth is unsmiling.

I realize I do recognize him from somewhere—Ari's profile pictures, before she deleted her account a couple months ago. This guy is her boyfriend. Or *was* her boyfriend. From the sound of it.

He crushes his beer can and throws it into the fire. Next to me, Emily checks her phone, her lips pinching with worry.

"Have you even heard from her, Nick?" she asks the guy. He shrugs.

"Her pops banged on my door this morning asking if she was staying with me," he says. "I guess she took off."

Emily frowns. "Took off *where*?"

"The fuck would I know?" Nick cracks open another beer and leans back in his Adirondack chair. It occurs to me that this is probably his farm, and I feel even more like an intruder now.

He catches me staring at him, and my face burns so hot, I feel as if I could disintegrate. I avert my eyes and look to the fire.

"I hope she's okay," Sabrina says quietly. Callie is still looking at the ground, bending the front part of her flip-flop. She lets it go, and the rubber thwacks against her foot.

"You know how she's always talking." Nick takes his hat off and mashes it between his hands. "Saying she's gonna leave and get her own place."

Ariel is the second oldest of five kids. Her sister Katie is only ten months younger than her; they were always fighting. Once, Callie and I went over to see the mutt that had followed their father home from work at a construction site. Ari and Katie fought until they were both in tears over what to name him. When Mr. Kouchinsky heard them screaming at each other, he got his shotgun off the mantel and went out back where the dog was tied up. Ari grabbed his pants leg and screamed until Mrs. Kouchinsky had to come downstairs and rip her off him.

When her father came back inside, he said it was a mercy because the dog had been badly starved and infested with mites and fleas. We all clung to each other on the couch, crying hysterically, while Mr. Kouchinsky walked by as if he hadn't even seen us.

I don't blame Ariel for wanting to run away. Sometimes I think I would have too, maybe, if I'd had to stay in Fayette. Followed in my sister's footsteps. But I'd be kidding myself if I thought I could survive on my own like Jos did.

My sister was the one who could weasel an invite to someone's house for dinner, while I whined through my chapped lips about how I was hungry and wanted macaroni and cheese. Joslin was the one who would fall off her bike and get right back up, while I wailed over a scraped knee. To this day I'd sooner go hungry or subsist on potato chips than work up the balls to go through the drive-through, out of fear I'll do it wrong.

Ari will never make it on her own, I think. She was even needier than I was, always breaking into tears because she forgot her lunch bag on the bus. Our first-grade teacher had to leave a box of tissues on Ari's desk because she would forget to wipe her nose, snot dripping down her face as she traced the letters in our handwriting books.

There's an ache in my chest. I wish she were here right now, clinging to me with her bony fingers and nails bit down to the cuticle.

"Ari would have told me if she was leaving." Emily plucks the tab off her beer, wincing and slipping her torn thumb nail between her lips.

Ryan speaks up, and I notice that he's not drinking his beer either. "My uncle hasn't said anything. If it was serious, her parents would have reported her missing."

An image surfaces in my mind: a photo on the front page of the county newspaper. Officer Jason Elwood, in full uniform, as one of the pallbearers at Harvey Elwood's funeral. Ryan's father. He'd been a firefighter; four other men had died with him. It had been a three-alarm at an abandoned warehouse. Almost half of Fayette's fire department had been gone in less than an hour. Ryan had been five years old.

His uncle Jay wasn't assigned to Lori Cawley's murder, but he came to the trial to support the officers who had to testify. The entire police department did.

Ryan's gaze flicks toward Callie. Something about the way he looks at her makes the smallest sliver of jealousy move through me. Danny, Joslin's boyfriend, used to look at Jos the same way.

"You love him more than you love me," I whined one night when Jos slipped under the covers after being out late, smelling of sweat and cigarette smoke and something else I couldn't place. I expected her to pinch me and say she'd always love me the most, but instead she hissed, "Knock it off. You sound like Mom," and rolled to face the wall.

I'd always thought that was the first crack, the beginning of the chasm between us. But now I think it must have started earlier—when my father was taken away and I suddenly couldn't sleep alone without waking in hysterics. Jos probably thought it was pathetic that I had to sleep in the bed with her.

Just like Callie resents being stuck with me now.

Around the bonfire, everyone slips back into their private conversations. Next to me, Callie whispers to Sabrina, "I can't believe Ari would just run away."

"Well, wouldn't you? If we weren't going to college, and had to stay here for the rest of our lives?"

Callie pulls her knees up to her chest. "I don't want to think about that."

"You don't have to," Sabrina says. "Less than two months, babes. And we can leave this place behind forever."

Callie finally looks up. She looks right at *me*. And I know exactly what she's thinking.

As long as Tessa doesn't screw everything up.

CHAPTER FIVE

Maggie is washing dishes as I pad quietly down the stairs in the morning. She looks up at me and sets her sponge down. My stomach dips. She and Rick were asleep when we got back last night. Did she figure out that I drove her minivan home because Callie got obliterated?

But she smiles. "You girls—I'm so glad you finally spent some time alone together. You have fun?"

"Yeah," I lie. "Do you mind if I take a walk? There's a couple people I want to catch up with."

"Of course not." She wipes her hands on a dishrag and turns the faucet off. "Can I drive you?"

"No, thanks," I say. "I kind of need to be alone, if that's okay."

Maggie nods absently. Everything would be so much easier if I could just ask to use the damn computer. I know I need to work on that.

It's not even that I'm afraid Maggie would say no. Of course she wouldn't. It's just that I've always found it especially difficult to accept things from the people who would give me anything.

The *person,* I correct myself.

The library is a twenty-minute walk from the Greenwoods' house, and I don't have a card to get on the computers there anyway. Much closer is a printing shop on Main Street that advertised web access, so I head there.

I use my shoulder to push open the door. A bell tinkles at the back of the store. There's a computer at the front, and a laminated sign overhead that says FOR PRINTER USE ONLY!!! Underline, underline, bold. Well, that's obnoxious. It only makes me want to ignore the sign more.

I hop onto Google and get two hits for Brandy Butler. One is a Facebook page for a middle-aged woman in Delaware who is most definitely not my sister. Jos would be twenty-six now.

The other hit is a public record for a car loan. Someone named Brandy Butler applied for it four years ago, in a town called Catasauqua. I search for *Catasauqua to Fayette,* my stomach sinking when I see that Catasauqua is just outside Allentown—about five hours from here by car. An even longer trip on the Greyhound bus. I pull up the schedule as a hairy arm drapes over the top of the computer. Its owner, a stocky man in a sweat-stained polo shirt, peers at me.

"Computer's for printing," he grunts.

I swallow and eyeball the search results. The last Greyhound to Allentown leaves in fifteen minutes, from a truck stop half an hour from here.

"Sorry." I click out of the windows and scramble off the stool.

"Hey!" The man doesn't pursue me, but I keep running anyway.

He looked familiar. It's not until there are several blocks between the print shop and me that I decide I don't know him. Everyone here just looks the same.

. . .

Now that I have less than a day left in Pennsylvania, I know that my sister is most likely in the state. After years of thinking she was nestled in the mountains of Colorado or in a straw hut in Maui, she's *here*.

It feels as if the universe were screwing with me—until I remind myself that even if I'd made it onto the Greyhound, I'd still have to be back in Fayette by five o'clock tomorrow morning. That's almost as impossible as tracking down one woman in a town of more than five thousand. Almost.

I head down the alley between the pizzeria and a smoke shop that wasn't there ten years ago, my thoughts returning to my sister. No one in town was surprised when Jos left. She was a *Sports Illustrated* model in a sea of girls with crooked teeth and flat chests. No women wanted Jos around their sons. Or their husbands. She dropped out of school her senior year, a few months before she ran away. There were rumors that she was pregnant, that our mother threw her out, or both.

And now she's back. It doesn't matter if she doesn't want to see me. She has the answers I need, and this is the closest I'll ever be to her again. I can't let her get away this time.

I can't get on that plane.

Maggie said I could stay as long as I needed. But with Callie around, it doesn't seem like a viable option. The bonfire last night showed me that I definitely don't belong here. I'm surrounded by strangers, looking for Joslin, the one person who could already be long gone.

I cut across Main Street, skidding to a halt on the sidewalk when I see them.

Cop cars. Three of them, in front of a blue town house with

a crumbling brown porch. There's a Razor scooter and a soccer ball lying on the lawn.

I know that house. Sometimes when I see a stray dog, I can hear the gunshot and Ariel's wails.

A group of teenage boys has gathered on the corner across from the Kouchinskys' house. I can't get a good look at their faces, so I don't know if I know them. *Knew* them.

"Shut up, man," one of the guys is saying.

Another one—a redhead—leans against his bike. "I'm telling you, it's her."

"What's her?"

The guys turn around, stare at me as if I were an alien. The guy with the black hair, who told the redhead to shut up, is Decker Lucas. I always got stuck next to him in elementary school because he was right behind me in the alphabet. Decker was always getting yelled at for something—forgetting his gym sneakers at home, leaving a bologna sandwich in his desk over the weekend.

Not much has changed about him, except for his face. Something is missing. *Glasses*. He blinks at me with wide blue eyes, his mouth parting. He looks like a comic book character come to life. "Whoa. Tessa Lowell."

"What happened at the Kouchinskys'?" I claw at the hole on my thigh for something to do. If I keep at it, I'm going to shred it big enough to flash everyone. But I can't stop myself. The sight of all those cops is making me anxious.

"Ariel's been missing." The redhead spits on the sidewalk, his beady eyes looking me up and down. "Cops in Mason found a body this morning."

"They don't know *whose* body," Decker cuts in. "Could be anyone. Like an old person or something."

My breath catches in my chest. I see her clinging to her father's leg again.

I see the princess stickers on the purple envelopes. *Write back!!!*

"Where in Mason was the body?" I squeak out. "Not off I-70, right?"

Decker's friend—the redhead—shrugs and hops onto his skateboard. He stands on it, wobbling back and forth as we stare at the Kouchinsky house, silent.

A beat later, there's movement on their porch. A uniformed officer escorts a gray wisp of a woman onto the porch swing—Ariel's mother. She's so much shorter, thinner than when I last saw her, as if time had eaten away at her.

She collapses into the officer's arms and lets out a splintering cry. Behind her, two small faces look out the window.

The redheaded guy spits again, maneuvering his skateboard so he doesn't roll over the wet spot. "Don't sound like it's anyone."

CHAPTER SIX

By the time the Greenwoods' house is within view, the back of my shirt is soaked with sweat and the bridge of my nose is sunburned. I ran most of the way here, because I can't wait to find out if it's true.

I hear a screen door slam; Callie barrels down the Greenwoods' porch steps, not noticing me on the sidewalk. She makes it halfway down the driveway before she stops; she buries her face in her hands, and my stomach sinks.

It's true, and Callie found out in the fifteen minutes it took me to get here.

Callie turns and heads for the backyard before I can call out to her. I lean against the mailbox and catch my breath; it feels like there are a million pinpricks in my lungs.

Everyone at the party last night thought Ariel had run away. She could have been dying while we sat around the bonfire.

When my breathing evens out, I follow the fence around the side of the house. Callie left the gate open.

She's sitting on the grass, her palms pressed to her face. I have to cough to get her to look up. Her cheeks fill with color when she sees me. "What do you want?"

"Is Ariel dead?"

Callie tears out a fistful of grass in a single, violent motion and lets the blades fall through her fingers. "They have to ID the body, but yeah, it's her."

Body. I picture Ariel, discarded by a highway guardrail. Ariel, with her scraped-up elbows and legs from falling off her bike, and her pink mouth smelling of fake strawberries, from the Lip Smacker lip balm she carried in her pocket everywhere so her sister couldn't steal it.

I realize I'm picturing Ariel as she was ten years ago. My stomach clenches. "How did she die?"

"Don't know," Callie says. Her face is still beet red. I think she's going to lose it, cry, do *something,* but instead, she takes a deep breath. And looks straight at me. "There's a vigil tonight at the high school. If you want to come or whatever."

Terrible Tessa wants to say no. Whenever someone young dies, lots of people congregate, and as a general rule, I like to avoid places where lots of people congregate. In those situations everyone is either devastated or morbidly curious, and I don't know which side I come down on. I haven't even spoken to Ari in years.

But she was my friend, and Maggie will be disappointed in me if I don't go. For some reason, that matters. Maybe because I don't have many people left to disappoint.

• • •

We get stuck in a line of cars waiting to enter the parking lot. Fayette High is small; my elementary school class had fewer than a hundred kids. Around the time I left, people started panicking about the dropout rate and started campaigning to reinstall vocational programs.

In the front seat, Maggie stares ahead, a pan of zucchini bread in her lap. "Maybe we'll drop you girls off. Daddy and I can go sit with Ruth for a bit and pick you up later."

Callie takes off her seat belt and gets out of the car without a word. Maggie tosses me a helpless glance over her shoulder. If Rick weren't here, I'd tell her what's on my mind, that I think I may have found where my sister is staying, and I need a few more days in Pennsylvania to figure it out.

Instead, I thank her for the ride and follow Callie, who is already several strides ahead of me.

"Hey," I say. "You're pretty shitty to your mom."

Callie's shoulders tense, but she doesn't stop walking. I catch up to her, smelling something acrid when she sighs.

"Does she know you have a drinking problem?" I ask.

"You sound like a pamphlet."

She stops short of the gymnasium doors, something dark eclipsing her businesslike expression. "I can't go in yet."

"Okay." We step to the side, letting the people behind us go in. I tug at the sleeves of my sweatshirt; it still smells like smoke from the bonfire.

Callie takes off around the corner of the gym, toward the auditorium, where the buses line up at the end of the day. She doesn't object when I follow her.

There's an oak tree at the back of the bus lot; beneath it are three guys. I can see the tendrils of smoke coming out of their noses from here. As Callie and I get closer, I spot Nick, Steelers-hat guy from last night. The moon gives his face a ghastly whiteness. His eyes are bloodshot.

"Fuck this, man," he says, offering Callie his joint.

She shakes her head and wraps her arms around her chest. "What else you got?"

Nick reaches into his pocket and produces an unlabeled bottle of something amber. Callie grabs it before I can voice my feelings on accepting untrustworthy-looking liquids from people. They're pretty similar to my feelings about meeting people in dark parking lots.

Callie unscrews the cap and takes a whiff. "What is this?"

"Stronger than whatever you have," Nick says. Callie tosses back half the bottle. He reaches and pulls it out of her mouth.

"Whoa, easy," he says.

Callie wipes her lips with the back of her hand. "You brought the good stuff."

"Yeah, well, not every day your ex gets killed," he mutters. The bitterness in his voice unnerves me. Nick winds up and kicks the oak tree. *"Fuck."*

Callie flinches. The two other guys—one I recognize from the bonfire last night—glance at each other and mumble something about getting inside. Callie hangs back with Nick. "I need a minute," she says.

I wait for her, stiffly, instead of going into the gym alone. A minute or so later she trots up to me. Her body seems looser. I catch her popping a piece of Trident into her mouth as we wade through the throng of people in the entrance.

At the gym doors, someone has set up an easel with an oak tag poster. It's covered in several pictures of Ariel—I'm surprised to see that I'm in a couple of the old ones. My fingers itch to tear them down and slip them into my pocket. We never owned a camera, and any family photos we'd managed to scrounge up were thrown out when my mother and I were evicted.

In the middle of Ariel's poster, someone's written a quote in silver Sharpie. *It's better to burn out than to fade away. —Kurt Cobain.* Next to me, Callie stares at it, silent.

I touch the edge of the poster. "Actually, that's from a Neil Young song," I say. "Kurt Cobain just borrowed it in his suicide note."

"God, what does it matter who the hell said it?" Callie snaps. She stalks off, and I'm reminded why I don't talk much. People don't seem to like what I have to say.

Someone nudges my shoulder, and I move so the girls behind me can get a look at the poster. There's already a collection of dollar-store teddy bears and flameless candles in votive jars at my feet. I step to the side of the gym and scan the crowd for Callie, but it seems she's disappeared.

I expected more of the people here to notice me, because I guess I'm a narcissistic little sociopath. But instead, I'm a ghost hanging in the corner, pretending I don't notice the occasional confused glance thrown my way.

I was always good at blending into the social strata of Fayette. My grades were high enough that I didn't get any notes sent home, and low enough that I was never singled out. I wore Jos's hand-me-downs, but almost all the kids at school with older siblings wore hand-me-downs. One girl in our class even wore things that had belonged to her brother.

I dig the stubs of my nails into my palms. If I don't stop biting them, the skin underneath will split and bleed. As I'm looking down at my fist, a thin, gnarled, hand covers it.

"It *is* you!" Watery blue eyes meet mine. "RAY. Come over here. It's her!"

I snatch my hand away. *Who the hell is this old woman, and why is she touching me?*

"It's you," the woman wheezes again as a thin old man with a cane hobbles over to us. There's powdered sugar at the corner of his mouth. Cookies from the table stuffed into his pocket, probably.

"It's me." I give the woman a thin-lipped smile.

"Well, don't this beat all. Tessa Lowell, in Fayette!" She peers at me. "You don't remember us, do you? It's me, Marie Durels. Marie and Ray. Your old neighbors."

"Oh." I force out the pleasantries—"Yes, how are you? . . . Rheumatoid arthritis? That sounds awful. . . . Going to college in the fall"—but my mind is elsewhere. It's on Sycamore Street, on the lawn of my old house. I'm six, in my Little Mermaid bikini, drinking water out of the hose Joslin sprayed in my face as if I were a golden retriever. Marie Durels, watching from her porch, disapproving.

"It's terrible, isn't it?" Marie clutches my shoulder and nods to the group of crying girls by the makeshift memorial for Ariel.

I nod. "I hope they find who did this to her."

"Oh, they will." Marie's grip on me tightens. "They'll find him, and they'll put him down like that animal who hurt all those other girls."

Ray bobs his head in agreement, oblivious to the smear of sugar on his face. I have to look away. I have to *get* away—out of this stifling hot gym filled with grief I have no business being a part of. Away from these people with the power to send me straight back to the brown house with the broken porch steps on Sycamore Street.

Marie bends her head to mine. Her breath is hot on my neck and smells like garlic and marinara sauce. I bet she and her husband ate at the new Italian place before coming here for the free dessert. I clench my fist as she crows into my ear: "My heart just breaks for Ruth Kouchinsky. Folks are saying Ariel was up in Mason *working,* if you know what I mean."

Mason is as far as my mother and I made it when she decided we needed to leave Fayette before people noticed we'd been living out of her car for two weeks. Not even Callie knew. Jos had been gone for four months, and Lori had been dead for eleven.

That night, when we got to a gas station, my mother left me in the car while she used the bathroom. I opened the glove compartment, searching for my favorite toy—one of those sticky hands you throw up at the ceiling and wait for it to fall back down. I found a handgun.

I ran across the highway, toward the lights of the truck stop. In the store, I asked to use the phone so I could call Maggie. I told her everything—that we'd been living out of the car, that my mother was scaring me—everything except the gun.

She and Rick were there in half an hour. I waited in the store and read an issue of *TV Guide,* praying that my mother hadn't already called the cops when she'd found me missing.

Maggie went over to the gas station alone. I don't know what happened, but she came back with Gram's phone number. I haven't seen my mother since.

Rick waited with me in the rest stop while Maggie sat on the curb outside, on the phone with her best friend, Angela. "We want to handle this without calling social services."

While Rick and I split a bag of Doritos and talked about the comet that was supposed to pass through, because I was always into that stuff, two girls came into the store. They couldn't have been much older than my sister. One bought a phone card while the other fiddled with the hem of her jeans skirt, trying to avoid looking at me and Rick. I was nine, and I knew exactly what they were doing at the truck stop.

Like most unpleasant things, I'd learned about the girls from my father. He used to talk about the girls who approached him at the stops along I-95, back in the eighties when he'd drifted, looking for work before settling at the steel mill. After the Monster murders, the government passed an initiative to crack down on prostitution at the rest stops; they knocked down the greasy convenience stores that sold beef jerky and porn magazines and put up McDonald's and Dunkin' Donuts.

I can picture Ariel working behind the counter of a Burger King. Not in some trucker's backseat. And Marie Durels is a real piece of crap for suggesting it now when people are here to mourn Ari.

I look over Marie's shoulder for an escape route. I spot Ryan Elwood coming through the hallway double doors, holding a can of soda. He walks over to the bleachers where Callie is sitting. She looks like she's going to vomit. I think of the booze in her purse and wonder if she snuck into the bathroom and finished it.

"It was nice seeing you," I lie to Marie. I shoulder my way through the sea of bodies, stopping when I see Ryan lean in and say something into Callie's ear. She jerks away from him, knocking her purse off the bleachers. Ryan bends to help her pick up her things; from here, I can see that he's still talking. The color drains from Callie's face.

I reach them as Callie stands, stumbling over her own feet. I grab her arm to stop her from face-planting. "What is wrong with you?" I hiss.

"I just need to get home," she mumbles. "Ryan's taking me. Us. Unless you want to call my parents for a ride."

I'd sooner walk than call Maggie and Rick, and I'm not about to let some guy lead Callie into his truck alone while she's completely trashed—even if it's only Ryan Elwood. I follow them out to the lot, where Ryan stops beside a red pickup truck. Callie stumbles for the door. I think she's going to vomit all over the pavement, but she climbs through to the backseat and stretches out.

I bite back my annoyance at having to sit up front with a stranger. Ryan climbs into the driver's seat and grips the wheel. After a few minutes, Callie starts snoring lightly. I relax a bit; as long as she's making noise, I don't have to worry she's going to pull a Jimi Hendrix back there.

Ryan's truck starts with a low rumble. He reaches for the radio, but pulls his hand back at the last second, probably realizing that this situation doesn't call for music.

"What did you say to Callie?" I ask.

He lifts his eyebrows. "I didn't—"

"I saw you," I say quietly. "By the bleachers. You said something to her, and it freaked her out."

Ryan massages his jaw. Unnecessarily adjusts his rearview mirror. "I didn't realize. I forgot about her cousin."

My heart goes still in my chest. "Her cousin Lori?"

"Yeah."

Ryan hits the speed bump at the parking lot exit. Callie rolls forward and lets out a small "Oof."

"Sorry," Ryan mutters. I stare at his profile until he turns his head and notices me.

"What did you *say* to her?" I ask.

Ryan scratches his nose with his thumb. Drums his fingers on the steering wheel. "I told her how Ari was killed."

Killed, not died. It feels like a punch to the stomach. *Died* means that maybe Ari got into her car in the rest stop parking lot, closed her eyes, and that was that. A heart murmur, maybe, or one of those migraines you never wake up from.

Killed means she knew exactly what was happening to her. I swallow hard, trying to shut down the sounds in my head. Ari begging for her life. Ari screaming, trying to fight back.

"How do you know how she was killed?" I ask Ryan. "They're not . . . No one's said yet how it happened."

Ryan's quiet; I think back to last night, of how he said his uncle would know if someone had reported Ari missing. His uncle, the cop. Cold sweat breaks out on my forehead, and I know whatever Ryan says is going to be true.

Ryan taps his pinky against the steering wheel, steady like a metronome. I'm going to explode.

"I was her friend," I say.

The tapping stops. Ryan hesitates. "You can't tell anybody, all right?"

"I don't have anybody to tell," I say, even though it's probably not the response he was looking for. Ryan exhales.

"She was strangled," he says. "And naked."

I swallow. That can't mean what I think it means—but obviously Ryan's noticed the connection too, or he wouldn't have said anything to Callie in the first place.

"Where did they find her?" I ask, even though I already suspect the answer.

"Off 74, not far from the truck stop. Guy pulled over to pee and saw her clothes . . . called it in, and they found her a few miles away." He swallows. "She was by the river."

Just like the other girls. I brush my hand against the side of the seat and find a space where the filling from the cushion is leaking. I imagine tearing it open and climbing inside. Never coming out.

I should never have come back here at all.

"I don't know. It just made me sick, thinking of Ari like that." Ryan's eyes flick to the rearview mirror, pointed down to reflect Callie's still face. "I don't know why I told Cal. . . . They haven't even told Ari's family yet. So please don't say anything."

I stare out the window, the streetlights zipping past the truck in rhythm, as if punctuating the names in my head. Marisa Perez. Rae Felice. Kristal Davis. Lori Cawley. And now, Ariel Kouchinsky.

"They obviously don't want the news to find out how she died," Ryan rambles on. "They'll try to spin it like there's another serial killer out here."

The pause that follows feels so long, I'm surprised Callie doesn't feel the tension and wake up.

"You don't think it's weird that she was killed the same way and in the same place that Callie's cousin was?" I ask.

Ryan runs a thumb down the side of his jaw. His mouth hangs open for a moment before he says, "The guy who killed all those girls is in jail. It's gotta be a coincidence. Or some sick fuck obsessed with the murders, maybe."

A coincidence.

A copycat.

Or a third explanation. One I don't dare say with Callie in the car, because of what it means for us.

Everything is all wrong. The police were wrong about who killed Lori and those other girls—they were wrong, and the Monster's still out there.

We helped them get the wrong guy, and Ari could be dead because of it.

From the backseat, Callie mutters something that's barely audible, but I can just make it out.

"I never got to tell her I'm sorry."

CHAPTER SEVEN

Ryan helps me get Callie into bed. Once he leaves, I slip her phone out of her pocket and text Maggie. *Didn't feel well. Tessa and I got a ride home.* I open her bedroom window to air out the room. She's starting to sweat out the poison she put into her body earlier. Outside, thick summer rain begins to fall in sheets.

I close Callie's door and shut myself in the guest room. After I change into my pajamas, I crawl under the bed and stick my earbuds in. My fingers are trembling so hard that it takes me three tries to find the song I'm looking for—Peter Gabriel's "Red Rain."

When I close my eyes, all I see is Ariel with her Rainbow Brite backpack, floating facedown in the Ohio River.

I think of Wyatt Stokes—blond ponytail, sullen, hollow eyes.

Wyatt Stokes, who strangled his victims and left them naked along the Ohio River in western Pennsylvania.

Wyatt Stokes, who couldn't have killed Ariel, because he's in jail.

Stokes was twenty-three around the time of the first murder—

Marisa Perez, a seventeen-year-old runaway. Eight months later was Rae Felice, twenty, a truck-stop prostitute.

A year later they found the remains of Kristal Davis, nineteen, a stripper and a drug addict who'd gone missing a month earlier. Someone leaked to the media that Fayette County was dealing with a serial killer. But no one was really worried. The killer was targeting the types of girls who didn't have anyone to worry about them.

Until Lori Cawley. A sophomore at Drexel. Second in her class at Lehigh Valley High School. The girl you noticed on the yearbook page because of her smile.

No one in Fayette really questioned that Stokes was the one who killed the girls. He was a high school dropout who'd spent a couple years in juvie for burning his stepmother's garage down. He had stringy hair down to his shoulders and hollow eyes. The kind of guy you'd see walking alongside the road and you'd lock your car doors.

As Charlie Volk, the detective who arrested him, said in a now infamous quote, *Wyatt Stokes just* looked *like a serial killer.*

It also didn't help that Stokes was an asshole.

He just couldn't shut up. In the interrogation room, he smiled when he touched the crime scene photos. When the cops raided his trailer, they found disturbing sketches of girls. Dead, naked girls with the word *bitch* scrawled on them over and over on every inch of free space.

Stokes granted an interview after his sentencing, saying that he'd really been subjected to "trial by the media" and that if he were black, some lawyer from the NAACP or ACLU would have taken his case by now.

So yeah, most people tended to agree that even if Stokes didn't kill those girls, he still deserved to be locked up.

The case against Stokes was never airtight. There were witnesses who placed him at the truck stops, looking for drugs or odd jobs, where the other girls had been regulars. Stokes was a creep who had threatened a slew of ex-girlfriends and ex-bosses—anyone who didn't give him what he wanted.

But the only real evidence linking Stokes to the murders was a denim fiber found on Kristal Davis's body that matched a pair of Stokes's jeans. An eyewitness placed Kristal in the Stokeses' trailer the day she disappeared, and when the police questioned Stokes, he said he hadn't seen Kristal in weeks, before changing his story and saying they'd done drugs together that morning.

It was me and Callie who put the final nail into his coffin, though. We testified via a closed-circuit TV feed on the second to last day of Wyatt Stokes's trial. We described what happened that morning at the pool and identified Stokes as the man who threatened Lori. We swore that it was the same man sneaking into the Greenwoods' yard the night Lori was murdered.

The jury deliberated for a day and found him guilty of all four murders.

Then the rest of the world forgot about Fayette, Pennsylvania, and all its dead girls.

I can't sleep or bring myself to pack for my flight tomorrow morning, so I lie in the darkness with my music, replaying in my head my entire conversation with Marie Durels, until Ariel's face blurs with Lori's.

Several songs later, I lower the volume on my iPod, sensing someone else in the room. From my spot under the bed, I can see the door cracked open. I dig my nails into my thighs. Next to my ear, bare feet pad across the carpet. The toenails are painted turquoise. I let out a sigh of relief.

"Tessa?" Callie whispers.

I flatten my body and wiggle out from under the bed. Callie's brow creases.

"Were you sleeping under there?" She looks better than she did earlier. The color has returned to her face, and she's showered. Her hair is piled on top of her head in a bun.

"I . . . What are you doing here?" I get up and sit on the bed, as if she were the one acting bizarrely. The clock on the wall says it's almost one.

"We need to talk," she whispers. She sits at the end of the bed. Delicately tucks her feet underneath her. She looks around the room, almost like she's in a stranger's house and not her own.

"About what?" I ask. I know exactly what she's here to talk about. But I need to hear her say it. We weren't supposed to discuss the trial while it was going on, so our mothers kept us apart. By the time it was over, there was some sort of seismic shift in our friendship. On the rare days when Callie felt like having me over to play, Maggie was always within earshot, hovering as if we'd disappear the moment she turned her back.

Even if I'd had the nerve to ask Callie if she'd really seen the face of the person in her yard that night, I never would have gotten her alone to do it.

"About what Ryan said in the car." Callie squeezes her eyes shut. Collects herself and exhales. "It could still be a coincidence."

"Maybe," I say quietly.

The clock on the wall ticks, filling the space between us. Callie hugs her knees to her chest. "I looked up his appeal. . . . A lot of people really believe he didn't do it."

"I know." I've known since I was old enough to search for the answers. As soon as I could use the Internet on my own, I knew that there were people who believed Wyatt Stokes wasn't the Ohio River Monster.

Callie casts her eyes down, picks at a chip in the polish on her big toe. "He could get a new trial this time. If there's a link between Ari and the other girls . . . he could *get out*."

Wyatt Stokes, out of prison. Wyatt Stokes, who knows our names.

"My parents can't afford to move again," Callie says. "I'm going to Stroudsburg, but they can't leave Fayette, and my dad's job."

"Callie," I say, her name feeling unfamiliar on my lips. "What did you really see that night?"

A tear snakes down her cheek. "I didn't lie."

"I never said you did."

We just sort of stare at each other for a bit.

"Did you really see his face?" I finally ask.

I expect her to get angry. Storm out on me. Instead, her voice goes soft, and she says, "I don't know anymore."

The silence in the room is loaded; the sound of the clock's second hand hangs in the air like a bomb ticking.

"What are you saying?"

"I'm saying I was just a little kid, and I could have been wrong about seeing his face. Of course, I *thought* I did—Stokes was like the bogeyman, and I was so scared that he'd come after Lori after what he'd said to her."

Angry tears stream down her pink cheeks. She's not looking at me anymore.

Is that why you shut me out? I want to ask. *You thought I knew you lied?*

"Even if I was wrong," Callie says, "there was evidence he killed those other girls. He didn't even get up on the stand and deny it. They had enough to convict him."

"Maybe," I say. But I don't know if I've ever fully believed

59

that. Not with the things I know about how that night really went down.

The things that the jury didn't hear. The things that Callie still doesn't know.

I swallow and bunch up the comforter in my fist.

"What did you tell them?" Callie whispers. "When they asked you what you saw?"

"I said you woke me up and said someone was outside," I say. "The person ran around the side of the yard. I had heard you say it was Stokes, and the police kept hammering it into us that our stories had to match."

I pick a pill of fleece off the comforter and flick it away. "So I said it was Stokes. Even though I never saw their face."

"*His* face," Callie says.

I'm quiet for a beat.

"You don't think Stokes did it," Callie finally whispers. Her face says what I feared, that this is the ultimate betrayal of the Greenwoods. It's one thing to question what we saw that night, but in this house "Wyatt Stokes is the Ohio River Monster" is an irrefutable fact. Y equals y.

"I just want to know what really happened," I say. The truth is, I *have* to know. Some days I think I'll explode from not knowing.

"If this means the real Monster is still out there, we have to figure out what really happened," I correct myself. "He could go after other girls. Maybe he never stopped, and the police just haven't found those girls yet."

I swallow away the sick taste in my mouth. I think of all the girls no one would miss, what's left of them washed away with the detritus from the river.

"You mean we have to take back our statements," Callie whispers. "My family would never forgive me."

"No. We can't do that unless we're absolutely sure," I say. "We have to be sure."

"How are we going to do that?" Callie wraps her arms around her middle. "It happened almost *ten years ago*. If someone besides us saw something, they would have said something back then."

The pit in my stomach grows. "Unless they had a reason to stay quiet."

"Where would we even start?" Callie says. "You're talking about finding a *murderer*."

Or murderers. I don't dare say it—that it's possible Lori wasn't killed by the Monster at all, but by someone who wanted to make it seem that way.

I wipe my palms on the knees of my pajamas. The room feels like a sauna—small, suffocating. "We were there when Lori was taken. There has to be something we missed . . . something that could help us put everything together."

"But you're going home tomorrow," Callie says.

It feels weird, hearing someone call Florida *home*. For me, it's always been where Gram's house is. A pit stop along the way in this giant circle I'm walking.

Because Fayette isn't home either. It's just the place where I started. The place I'd do anything to leave behind for good. And if Callie and I make this whole thing with Stokes right, then maybe I'll be able to.

"I'll reschedule my flight," I say.

"Okay." A breath leaves Callie in a low hiss. "So where do we start?"

"I don't know yet."

It's a lie, spun out of the truth I've been holding on to all these years. The part of the story I didn't tell the prosecutors because I didn't want her to get in trouble and get taken away from me. The part that I had almost convinced myself meant nothing, until now.

My sister knows something about that night. She knows who besides Wyatt Stokes would have wanted to hurt Lori.

I know, because an hour before we finally went to sleep that night, I heard Lori call Joslin and tell her to stay the hell away from her.

CHAPTER EIGHT

Yes, I am a liar, but there are a couple of things I feel the need to say about that.

One: I come from a family of liars. My father was probably the worst of us, calling the credit company and swearing his card had been stolen, just to get twenty bucks wiped off his bill.

My sister was a liar too. I heard her when the police came to our house asking when the last time was that she'd seen Lori. I watched Joslin stand with her hands in her back pockets and tell them she hadn't talked to Lori since the previous morning, even though I knew she'd talked to Lori the night Lori went missing.

Two: I was eight years old. I didn't know much, but I knew that lying to the police was wrong, and that if I said something about the phone call, I would get Joslin in deep shit.

So when they asked me to tell them *everything* that happened that night, I left out what I overheard Lori say to Jos on the phone.

What was I supposed to do? She was my sister, and I was terrified of her being taken away from me. I thought she'd go to jail for lying to the police. I had to keep her secret.

It wasn't until Joslin left town that something clicked for me, that I was able to entertain the possibility that my sister, who couldn't even kill a spider without feeling guilty about it, could have been involved in her friend's murder.

It was a little white lie, my not telling the police about the phone call. A little white lie that swelled into a monster of a lie that I was too scared to expose, because I was a little coward back then.

And I can't bring myself to tell Callie, because I'm still a coward now.

• • •

Maggie wakes me up at six and tells me there's breakfast in the kitchen. I throw my sweatshirt on over the tank top I slept in and meet her downstairs. There's an unsettling feeling in my stomach.

Maggie drags out the chair across the table and sits down. Her eyes are tinged with red. I take the seat across from her, where there's a plate of sunny-side up eggs waiting. I can't believe that after all these years she remembers how I like my eggs. "How was the vigil?" she asks.

"Hard." I pop an egg yolk with my fork.

The coffeemaker beeps, announcing that a full pot is ready. Maggie pushes her chair away from the table and stands up. "Do you need to use the computer to check into your flight?"

I set my fork down. "Um, I actually wanted to call and change my flight to the end of the week. So I can go to Ari's funeral. If that's okay."

Maggie looks confused, and my stomach sinks—until I hear footsteps coming down the stairs. Callie trudges into the kitchen, rubbing her eyes.

"Look who decided to join us," Maggie says. "What are you doing up so early?"

Callie pours herself a cup of coffee. Leans against the counter and shrugs.

"So, is it okay?" I ask Maggie. "If I stay a couple more days?"

She turns her attention back to me. "Of course. You can stay here as long as you want. You're going to need something to wear for the funeral, though. How about the three of us take a trip to Target?"

Callie eyes us over her mug. "Tessa was actually going to come to Emily's house with me today. She's having a hard time with everything."

"Oh." Maggie deflates a bit before putting on a smile. "Okay, maybe tomorrow."

"Sure. Tessa can wear some of my clothes until then," Callie says. She jerks her head toward the stairs. "I'll show you what I have in my closet."

No one comments on the fact that Callie is a size two and I'm a size six. It's obvious Callie's just trying to get me alone, but Maggie doesn't seem to think it's weird that her daughter was comparing me to a street urchin two days ago and now wants to play dress-up in her room.

I thank Maggie for breakfast, clear my plate, and follow Callie up to her room. The window is still open, and the boozy stench has been replaced with the wet-earth smell from outside. After it rains in Orlando, the moisture clings to the air until it's almost suffocating. Here, I smell the rain and I can almost sense how Fayette must have been before people ruined it with all of our ugliness.

Callie sits down at her desk and begins to braid her hair. "I was thinking last night—wondering why it was Ari. She's not like the other girls."

"Neither was Lori," I say.

"Okay, but Ari wasn't like Lori either," Callie says, then steels herself, as if she were trying not to be cruel. "I mean Ari was pretty, yeah, but she wasn't exactly confident. She liked to think she was street-smart, but she was kinda clueless."

Nick said Ari had wanted to leave town; maybe she just accepted a ride from the wrong man.

Or worse, I think, remembering Marie Durels's hot breath in my ear last night.

"Did Ariel have a job in Mason?" I ask Callie.

Callie gives up on the braid and sets her elastic down. "I don't think so. She babysat, in middle school, but once her mom went back to work, her dad made her watch Kerry Ann and Dave."

I stretch my legs out in front of me on Callie's bed, my knee giving a little *pop.* I don't know how to bring up what Marie told me without sounding like I'm accusing Ariel of being a prostitute. My thoughts flick to playing "hotel" in Callie's house—seven-year-old Ari as the receptionist, wearing one of Maggie's old blazers and a satin scarf and sitting patiently behind a folding table. No matter what we played, Ariel always accepted whatever role she was given.

Callie stares at me, catching me spacing out. "What?"

"At the vigil, Marie Durels kind of insinuated that Ari was, you know . . . selling herself."

Callie snorts. "Your old neighbor? Yeah, she's super-reliable. Ari wasn't a *prostitute.*"

I pull my legs in so I'm sitting pretzel-style. My calves ache from all that walking yesterday. "Marie had to hear it somewhere."

"People talk all kinds of shit in this town." Callie turns back to the mirror, opting for a messy bun instead of a braid. "High school girls don't turn tricks at the Mason truck stop."

Maybe in your world, I want to say. But I'm not going to take a dig at Callie just because I can.

"You'd be surprised," I say instead. "There was this whole story on the news about how girls at Columbia were doing it. They used Craigslist and made thousands of bucks a week."

Callie's lips part slightly.

"What are you thinking?" I ask.

"I heard her say something at lunch last year," Callie says to my reflection in the mirror. "She was asking Nick if she needed her parents' permission to open a bank account."

I examine the filthy bottoms of my socks. "Makes sense if she wanted to hide how much money she was making."

"Or because her dad is a total psycho who has to control everything." Callie's expression darkens. I know she's always been terrified of Daryl Kouchinsky. Ironically, she never seemed bothered by my father, with his chaw-stained teeth and shameless weed smoking on the front porch. Probably because for all of his yelling and threatening to beat the shit out of Jos and me, he never actually laid a hand on us.

"Did Ari say anything else weird?" I ask Callie.

She shrugs. "I haven't talked to her since the end of sophomore year."

I'm quiet as Callie pulls off the Penn State Twirl Championships T-shirt she slept in. She catches my eyes in the mirror and reddens. Maybe she forgot that we haven't changed in front of each other in ten years.

I avert my eyes as Callie puts on a tank top. "What happened between you two?" I ask.

"What are you talking about?"

"You and Ari. Last night, you said 'I never got to tell her I'm sorry.'" I can't tell Callie that I also know that she deleted Ari from her Facebook friends, not without admitting that I'm a huge creep who has been keeping tabs on her all these years.

She fusses with her bun, clearly embarrassed. "Nothing really happened. I was a bitch to her, and she eventually got tired of it, I guess."

I raise an eyebrow. "That's it?"

Callie shrugs a freckled shoulder. "After you left, she became my best friend by default, or whatever. She was just so needy, and it got on my nerves."

Callie lets out a sigh, ruffling her side-swept bangs. "Anyway, if it's true, what she was doing in Mason, she didn't tell anyone in our group. They wouldn't have been able to keep their mouths shut."

"Someone must have known," I say, frustration creeping in. I'd sooner stab my eyes out than knock on Marie Durels's door and ask who told her Ari was selling herself.

Callie looks up. Pauses. "There's one way we could find out," she says. "We could go to the truck stop. Ask around and see if anyone ever saw Ari there."

It's probably a waste of time; any other girls who work at the truck stop will clear out for fear of the cops by the time today's newspaper, with Ariel's face on the front page, gets delivered. Probably they'll all avoid the area for a few days. The ones who stay behind most likely won't talk. Definitely not to us.

But the Fayette County Penitentiary is on the way to the truck stop. When Joslin visited my father the other night, she may have left a clue there about how to find her.

"Sure," I say. "We can start there."

It takes all I have not to bounce on the balls of my feet as Callie asks to borrow Maggie's minivan. I can feel it. I'm going to leave that prison with a phone number or address for my sister. I just have to convince Callie to stop there on the way home from Mason.

Maggie tells us not to eat lunch out, since there's plenty of cold cuts she'll have to throw away at the end of the week. We wave goodbye from the driveway, and she disappears from the living room window, smiling. As I buckle my seat belt and reach into my pocket for my iPod, I catch Callie giving me the side-eye.

"You sure listen to that thing a lot," she says.

I shrug. "Helps me tune out the noise."

Callie's forehead crinkles. It's the same face she made as kids whenever I said something too dark for her tastes. One night when I was over at the Greenwoods' house, Callie was whining about me having to go home after dinner. "Why, why, why do I have to do homework?"

Maggie was losing her patience. "So you can get good grades, and get into a good college, and get a good job," she snapped.

I remember looking up from the armchair where I was tugging my shoes on. "What's the point of life," I asked, "if you go to school, then go to work, then die?"

Callie looked horrified.

I was always such a little nihilist. I blame it on my father's drunken rants. They got especially bad after he was laid off from the steel distributor he'd worked for, about six months before it closed.

Fifteen years I busted my ass for Ed, and he couldn't even tell me it to my face. Human beings ain't nothing but the shit on the heels of whoever dumped us onto this godforsaken planet.

In any case, Callie and I were raised differently, and it seems to come up every time I open my mouth.

Callie reaches for the radio. "Do you mind if I—"

I shake my head. Put my iPod away. Callie sifts through the

static until she finds an alternative rock station. I wait for a commercial break to clear my throat and speak.

"I was thinking . . . if we want to know more about what was going on with Lori that summer, we should probably find my sister."

Callie turns off the radio. "Find her?"

I look out the window. "I haven't heard from her since she left."

"That really sucks, Tess," Callie says softly. "I'm sorry."

The pity in her voice makes me wish I could shrink into the seat. I choose my next words carefully. "I think she's back in town. She visited my dad before he died."

"Really?" Callie sounds as surprised as I was. Why would Joslin come back and see my father but not the rest of us?

"So let's look her up and call her," Callie says.

"I tried," I say. "She's using a different name. I might have found her, though. I think she lives in Allentown."

Callie is quiet.

"I'm not saying let's go to Allentown," I find myself rambling. "But it's worth talking to her."

"It's not that." Callie pauses, the one being choosy about her words now. "It's just, no offense, but your sister totally bailed on you. Even if she could help us . . . she may not want to."

I can't argue with that—my sister changed her name, for Christ's sake—so I shut up and stare out the window. On the other side of the highway, there's a giant sign lit up in orange. ROADWORK: DETOUR. A quick stab of panic. We'll have to take a different way home, and we won't pass the prison.

My rehearsed lines go out the window: *Hey, since it's on the way, maybe I should see if they have Joslin's number at the prison.* Callie's already made her feelings about my sister clear.

70

I don't have time to sell her on tracking Jos down. There's the sign. FAYETTE COUNTY PENITENTIARY—NEXT RIGHT.

"Um," I blurt. "Do you mind if we stop there? I'm supposed to pick up stuff. My dad's stuff."

"Oh." Callie chews her lip. "They didn't give it to you the other day?"

"I didn't ask," I say, which isn't a lie. "Just thought it would be nice to have it."

Callie shrugs. "Okay. But you have to put the address into the GPS."

Ten minutes later, we're in the prison parking lot. I already have my seat belt undone by the time Callie puts the van in park.

"I'll just be a couple minutes," I say. "You don't have to come in."

I slam the door before she can protest. I know it'll be an empty one, anyway. I don't blame her; I wouldn't want to follow me into a prison either. Especially not a prison where Wyatt Stokes is being held.

The lobby is a ghost town compared to how it was on Saturday. The guard, Wanda, recognizes me. Sets her pen down. She looks ready to be on the defensive, probably thinking that I'm here to give her crap about my father dying ahead of schedule, like Maggie did. We do a bizarre stare-down thing, each waiting for the other one to say something first. Little does she know that I can do this all day if I have to. I've had a lifetime of practice when it comes to making people uncomfortable with my presence.

She finally cracks, her more charitable side winning out. "What's your name, hon?"

"Tessa," I say.

Wanda folds her arms across her chest, tilts back in her chair. "What is that you need, Tessa?"

"My sister visited the other night," I say, trying to figure out exactly how to phrase this. "I'm trying to find her. Did she maybe leave a phone number, or—"

"We can't give out that information." Wanda shakes her head to drive home the point.

Desperation claws at me. "She's my *sister*. I just need a phone number or something."

Wanda's face softens a bit. No doubt she remembers that I didn't get to say goodbye to my father. If she feels bad for me, I can work with that.

"Please," I say, playing the sad orphan. "I haven't seen her in ten years."

Wanda kicks off, rolls away in her chair. She maintains eye contact with me until she enters something into her computer. I stand, digging a nail into my jiggling leg. I hear the whirr of a printer, and then Wanda comes back with a piece of paper that she pushes toward me.

It's a scan of Brandy Butler's driver's license.

I make a fist to stop myself from touching the photo of her face. Even though it's not a color photo, I can tell that Joslin's hair is bleached blond. She didn't do her eyebrows to match. They're still thick, and dark—*like Brooke Shields,* Lori used to say.

Her expression is what gives her away. Her eyes are wide—too wide. Jos always blinked when the flash went off, so whenever she had to pose for a photo, she'd force her eyes open real wide in a way that always made me nearly pee myself laughing.

We never owned a camera, so my parents didn't have any baby pictures of us. My mom kept us home on picture day to avoid the embarrassment of sending us to school without a check to hand to the photographer.

But I don't need photos to know that Brandy Butler is, without a doubt, my sister.

Wanda hands me a Post-it to copy down the address. I reach for the pen attached to the desk on a chain and scribble it down: *34 E Federal Street, Allentown, PA.*

"You never saw this," Wanda says gently. I meet her gaze and nod.

"Um." I struggle to find the words. "What about Annette? Glenn's wife. Did she come to say goodbye?"

The sympathy etched on Wanda's face morphs to full-blown pity. Of course my mother didn't come.

"Annette is still listed as his next of kin," she says. "Far as I know, she hasn't been around in years. Number we tried reaching her at was a work line. Apparently, she hasn't been there in a while either."

I nod, nod, nod. I won't let on to this stranger that this is the most information I've been given about my mother in years.

My mom never talked about Gram when I was young, obviously, since she'd led us all to believe her parents were dead. When Gram heard about me, she didn't seem surprised that I existed. Or that my mother had lied.

"I'll tell you what I told your sister." Wanda leans forward. "I'm not allowed to give out details about inmates' families, but the number for Black Rock Tavern is public and all, so I can't stop you from calling yourself and asking about a former employee."

What I told your sister. My knees wobble; I picture someone coming up behind me, smacking me behind the knees with a baseball bat.

"My sister . . . asked how to find my mother?" I ask.

Wanda blinks, as if it would be the most normal thing in the world for my sister to want to see her mother. In any other family, it would be.

"You okay?" Wanda frowns at me.

"Yeah, it's just that—" Just that I'm going to vomit all over myself. "Never mind. Thanks."

It's just that Joslin hated our mother, yet she still found time to look her up. It's just that my sister knew exactly where I'd be if I came back, and she hasn't made so much as a phone call.

At the door, I remember the reason I convinced Callie I needed to stop in here. I turn around, rolling my ankle. I'm shaking. Callie was right to think my sister would only disappoint me.

"Did my dad leave anything behind?" I ask Wanda. "Like any personal effects?"

She frowns. "Mostly we just throw that stuff out unless family comes to claim it. Let me put in a call to the officer on his block."

I stuff my hands into the pockets of my hoodie to warm them. The AC is making the hair on the back of my neck stand on end. I think of Callie in the car, the midday sun beating through her windshield.

I feel bad. But not bad enough to leave here without something of my dad's, which would make her suspicious.

Wanda hangs up the phone and tells me to take a seat, the warden's coming. I reach for the cell phone in my back pocket, thinking it might be nice to text Callie and tell her I'll be a few more minutes. Then I realize I don't have Callie's number.

I turn my attention to the tiny box of a television protruding from the corner of the ceiling. The local news station is on.

It's only because I'm ignoring the vapid segment on the upcoming heat wave that I catch it, a brief headline on the news ticker across the bottom of the screen.

Federal Court of Appeals to hear new evidence in case of

Wyatt Stokes, convicted serial killer, in October. If not granted a
new trial, Stokes could be executed as early as next year.

I zip my sweatshirt up as far as the zipper will go. *October.*
That's only a few months away.

What new evidence do his lawyers have? What aren't they re-
vealing?

A buzz at the gate interrupts my thoughts, and a stocky man
with a thick beard and wearing a guard's uniform steps into the
waiting area. "Lowell?"

I stand, legs shaky. He's holding a clear trash bag.

"This is all of it." He gives me a thin-lipped smile. People in
prison shouldn't be this nice. I grab the bag and leave without
thanking him, because apparently I'm sapped of gratitude for
people who feel sorry for me today.

When I get outside, I press my back to the brick wall. Squeeze
my eyes shut. I don't want any of his shit. I don't want any physi-
cal reminders of the man who left us when the money ran out and
called once a year from prison to beg for more.

I look down at the bag. Through the plastic I can make out its
contents. There's a Bible, which is hilarious, and papers. Lots and
lots of papers, with sketches on them.

So my father took up drawing in jail. Better than his old hob-
bies, I guess, which largely consisted of abusing pills and stealing
money.

I've convinced myself I don't care what's in the bag, and that
it's sheer curiosity that makes me fish out the envelope pressed up
against the side.

There's a name scrawled in his uneven block writing.

TESSA.

I tilt my chin toward the sky, stare at the sun until the pressure
behind my eyes goes away. I am not going to get emotional over

some deadbeat who thought stealing money for booze and cigarettes was more important than being around to see his children grow up.

They caught him after he robbed the third store—the one where he shot Manuel Gonzalo in the torso. The attorney the state assigned to my father portrayed him as a family man pushed to the brink by the crumbling economy and unemployment. My father used to be a good man, a hardworking man. He never intended to hurt Manuel Gonzalo—my father panicked when he saw the cashier pull a gun from under the counter, so he shot first.

Even as a kid I could smell bullshit. My father went into that store with a gun and a plan. We all have choices, and he made his.

I turn the envelope over, running my thumb across its lip. Someone tore it open.

It's empty.

I stare into the sun again. *You're nothing but flesh and bones now,* I think, *and you've still managed to disappoint me.*

I hear the van before I see it—see *her.* Callie's glaring at me through the open passenger window, her palms up in the *What the hell are you doing?* position.

I climb into the van and set the bag at my feet. "Sorry."

"We have to go home." Her knuckles are white on the steering wheel. "My mom called. The police want to talk to me about Ari."

Everything else she says is a dull hum in my ears. I'm still reeling from what Wanda told me, and what it means.

Jos was one step ahead of me the whole time she was in Fayette. She may have seen our mother, or talked to her.

The only lead I have on Jos is my mother—the person who acted like I never even had a sister once she was gone.

• • •

Callie is so nervous, she almost forgets to put the van in park when we get back to the house. There's a single patrol car parked at the curb across the street. Through the Greenwoods' living room window, I see the back of a man's head.

"It's Ryan's uncle," Callie mutters as we climb the steps. "I'm so screwed. There's a giant handle of vodka under my bed."

"They're homicide detectives," I say. "I doubt they care about your stash."

Maggie doesn't smile as we step into the living room. A mug rests on the coffee table in front of Jay Elwood. Another detective sits on the opposite end of the couch from Maggie.

"Tessa, there's sandwiches in the kitchen," she says. "You're probably hungry."

Jay is watching me. He's late forties. Clean-shaven. He sips from his mug and sets it back down. Steel-gray eyes locked onto mine. I wonder if he recognizes me as a Lowell.

"Okay," I say. The kitchen is a stone's throw from the living room, which means as long as they don't whisper, I'll be able to hear the conversation. There's a platter of cold cuts and rolls on the counter. I fold a slice of cheese into my mouth and stand next to the fridge, where I have a partial view of the living room.

"How're you holding up?" Jay asks. No response.

"That's Pete." Jay again. "Hope it's all right we're here."

"If this is about Ariel, you should probably talk to her friends," Callie says.

"We were under the impression you two were close." Jay takes a pen out of his shirt pocket. Clicks the top once, twice.

Callie hesitates. "A long time ago. We hadn't talked in a while. . . . You'd have better luck with Emily Raymes."

Click, click. "What about Nick Snyder?"

I picture Nick, handing Callie the liquor at the vigil. His

meltdown before we went inside. I can tell Callie's thinking about it too, because she hesitates. "What about him?"

"He and Ariel dated, right?" Jay says.

"Yeah. For a couple months, but they broke up before graduation."

Click, click. "Seems he was pretty angry at her."

Pete, the officer on the couch, leans forward on his knees. "You know Nick well?"

"We hang out with the same people," Callie says.

"He get angry a lot?" Pete again.

Callie is quiet. I can tell she's unnerved by how quickly the detectives have steered the conversation toward Nick. Of course they're asking about Ariel's unstable ex-boyfriend.

Callie is murmuring something, and I lean into the doorframe to hear her better.

"You think he did this to Ari?"

The detectives are quiet. Jay is the one who finally speaks.

"We're just getting a sense of who she spent time with."

"Well, you should start with her dad," Callie says. "Ari was terrified of him. He ran that house like Nazi Germany, and she was desperate to get out."

"Callie," Maggie says. "That's enough."

There's some indecipherable murmuring. Then everyone stands up. Jay slips his pen into his shirt pocket. "If Nick knows anything, better he comes forward now before things get messy."

"What are you talking about?" Callie asks.

Jay's face is expressionless. "He's eighteen, Callie. If it was an accident and he admits it, things may go more smoothly for him."

Callie's silent. I clutch the handle of the fridge.

Jay's message is clear: Nick Snyder is old enough to be executed by the state of Pennsylvania.

CHAPTER NINE

After the detectives leave, Maggie slips out onto the patio, house phone in hand. I can tell by her voice that she's talking to Rick; people have different voices depending on who they're talking to. Maggie's Rick voice is no nonsense, even though she's obviously rattled. I can tell because she's smoking a cigarette—I haven't seen her do that since we were kids.

I slip into the living room, where Callie is texting, fingers flying across her phone screen.

"This is such bullshit," she says, not looking up at me. "They're wasting their time."

I'd had a similar thought. The police know that Ariel was killed just how the Monster's victims were. Do they really think Nick planned to kill Ari and stage her body to make it look like a Monster copycat, or are they trying to make an easy arrest?

There was nothing in the news this week about a possible link between Ariel's death and the Ohio River murders. I picture the Fayette police commissioner on the phone with the editor of the local paper, telling her not to publish anything that could reignite rumors that Wyatt Stokes is innocent.

The Fayette area had never had as high-profile a case as the Ohio River Monster, and certainly not one they could solve. One of the detectives who'd found the denim fiber on Kristal Davis became the chief of police. The prosecutor who tried Stokes later became the district attorney.

Lots of people made it to the top over the Monster case. If it all comes apart now, they'll have a very long way to fall.

We all will, I realize. If Maggie finds out that I kept the phone call a secret, she'll never look at me the same way again.

And Callie . . . I have to tell Callie. My sister doesn't need me to protect her anymore. She's done a fine enough job on her own of distancing herself from Lori's murder all these years. But Callie deserves to know about the phone call, especially now that we're searching for the truth together.

I just don't know how to explain to her why I kept it a secret for so long. At first I thought my sister would go to jail just like my father if I revealed that she'd lied to the police. I couldn't bear the thought of losing her, but when she ran away, the fear of living without her was replaced by something even worse.

What if my sister really did have something to do with Lori's death? And what if I accidentally helped her get away with it?

That would be even more unforgivable than lying about seeing Wyatt Stokes's face.

I look up at Callie, the words on the tip of my tongue. *I have to tell you something.* But her eyes are on her phone still.

"I'm going to Ryan's," she announces. "No one can even get in touch with Nick. I have to know if everything's okay."

"Okay," I echo, feeling a little awkward that Callie didn't ask me to go with her. She slips out the door, calling out that she'll be home in a little bit. Maggie comes back inside, still in her pajamas; she gives me a weak smile and says she's going to take a bath.

I'm alone.

I can use the computer now.

First, I call Gram and leave a message on her machine saying that I won't be on the 3:59 flight to Orlando this afternoon. An old friend died unexpectedly, I'm staying for the funeral, don't worry, I'm fine. Also, I've been feeding the one-eyed cat that hangs out under the porch. Sorry. There are some cans of Friskies under my bed, if you wouldn't mind. Sorry again.

Then I call Jana, my manager at Chili's, and tell her I need some more time off because of my father's death. She tells me to take all the time I need. What I really need is the money, but I take her word for it that my job will be waiting for me when I get back—even though it's Orlando and there's no dearth of Disney rejects willing to bus tables at a chain restaurant.

If there's anything I've learned about life, it's that not everyone gets to wear the Mickey Mouse suit.

I wait for the sound of water running upstairs before I turn the computer on, the same Dell the Greenwoods had ten years ago. It's been through so many system restores that the thing runs like a lobotomized patient. Rick used to have a serious Internet porn addiction. The therapist Maggie made him see suggested online poker.

When the computer sputters to life, I search for the address on my sister's driver's license: *34 E Federal Street, Allentown, PA.*

According to Google, 34 E Federal Street in Allentown is for sale. It's a foreclosure. The pictures show bare, poorly spackled walls. Carpeting that was probably beige, once. Kitchen with the appliances ripped out.

INCOME SUITE AVAILABLE! the listing boasts. There are photos of an attached one-bedroom apartment.

According to the listing, the house has been on the market for eighty-four days. Whoever lived at 34 E Federal Street has been gone for a while. Joslin could be anywhere by now.

I click through every picture anyway. The place is a shithole by most standards, but I'm so jealous of Jos, I'm practically shaking. At some point, she lived here. On her own. She probably rented the apartment.

I think of Jos and me mashed together on a twin bed upstairs in our house. I think of the chopped-up rocking chair on our old porch, an act of desperation to fill the wood-burning stove in our living room. The house always smelled of smoke, and liquor, something foul in the carpets from the previous renters.

Jos got away from all that. Away from us.

I delete *34 E Federal Street Allentown* from the search history. Then, before I can talk myself out of it, I Google *Black Rock Tavern*.

I get an address and phone number for a restaurant in Clearwater. It has an even lower average rating on Yelp than the Chili's I work at in Florida.

Anyway, it looks like my mother didn't get quite as far as Jos did. Clearwater is about a half hour north of Fayette. I dial, triple-checking each number as I punch it in. A man picks up on the second ring.

"Black Rock."

When I decided I needed to find my sister, I didn't consider the possibility that I'd need to do it through my mother—a problem for two reasons.

One: The only person from my past I want to see less than my father is my mother.

Two: I'm a pussy.

I hang up.

My father wrote me a letter from prison, once. A single page front and back, detailing my life as he remembered it. He said I was a "screamer" as a toddler, and when he'd stick the nipple of a bottle into my mouth to shut me up, Jos would say, "No, Daddy, this way," and demonstrate proper bottle use on her baby doll.

And then there were our daddy-daughter nights at the Boathouse, a restaurant on the river. We'd share a bowl of ice cream and play tic-tac-toe with the paper place mat and crayons on the table.

I remember everything differently. I remember my father shouting at Jos that she was almost ten and too old to carry a goddamn baby doll around everywhere. I remember him coming home every couple of months with a little extra money, and dragging me to the Boathouse before my mother got home from cleaning houses. He'd park me in a booth with a bowl of ice cream while he spent the rest of what was in his pocket on whatever the bartender had on tap.

And more than anything else, I remember how my mother reacted when she found the letter under my pillow, the edges stained with greasy thumbprints and the ink fading where I'd folded and unfolded the paper. She threw it into the woodstove while I sobbed for Daddy; she grabbed my shoulders and shouted, "Daddy is never coming back."

I knew even then that it was what she'd always wanted, to have Jos and me to herself. My mom always wanted to believe we were more hers than anyone else's; it's probably why she resented Joslin and my father so much. Joslin turned out just like him, despite not even being his blood. Jos and my father both liked to laugh at crass things: episodes of *South Park*, my father clipping

83

his toenails with a wire cutter while my mother shrieked about how disgusting he was.

Most of all, she hated that Joslin didn't need her. Whenever my mother panicked about us, like she often did when our cuts were deep or when one of us couldn't stop puking, my father would snap at her, "For Christ's sake, Net, pull yourself together. Kids are tougher than you realize."

I always knew that he was really talking about Joslin when he said that.

I never did get another letter from him. My mom probably intercepted them and burned them.

In any case, I'm not afraid of my mother. I'm afraid of what I'll do when I see her.

She was all I had left, and she let Gram take me away from the only home I'd ever known. Time hasn't healed that wound. Instead, time has armed me with enough anger to self-destruct and take her down with me if I have to.

Time has made me more like my father.

I inhale and redial.

"Black Rock." The man sounds annoyed this time.

"Um. Does someone named Annette work there?"

"Not in more than a year, no."

"Oh. Okay. Sorry." I tug at one of the threads in my jeans. "Do you know where she might be now?"

The Greenwoods' house phone starts ringing, nearly drowning out the man's response. I stick a finger into one ear.

". . . living over at Deer Run," he says. "But that was more than a year ago, like I said."

"Okay. Thanks."

• • •

84

Deer Run is a mobile community, located on the outskirts of Clearwater. It's got its own Walmart, which means my mother wouldn't have had to venture to Fayette, famous for its mega-store skid row.

I can't say I'm surprised Annette wound up there; you'd have to head farther north for the cozy complexes of one-bedroom apartments for rent. Around here there's just empty homes with BANK OWNED signs on the lawns, and trailer parks. Lots of trailer parks.

It's quiet downstairs in the Greenwoods' house with Maggie still in the bath. For once, maybe I can slip out without having to explain myself. I don't like lying to Maggie, but I'd rather die than tell her the truth, that my mother hasn't called, written, or come to see me once in the past ten years, and I don't even know for sure where she's living now.

There's a creaking on the stairs as I'm getting ready to leave. Maggie tightens her bathrobe and cocks her head at me.

"Are you leaving?" she asks.

"Just . . . out for a bit."

"You know, if you won't let me drive you, Callie's bike is in the garage," Maggie says. "She hasn't used it in years."

"Thanks. That would be awesome."

I detour out of the living room and make for the door off the kitchen instead. The sunflower bike she rode when we were kids hangs upside down from a rack on the garage ceiling. An adult-sized bike—baby blue and retro-looking—with a white basket is in the back corner, propped against the side of Rick's tool bench. A daddy longlegs skitters out of the basket when I touch the handlebars. I kick away the cobwebs on the wheels and walk the bike out of the garage and down the driveway.

I haven't been on a bike since I was a kid. I swing myself onto the seat, overshooting my landing and almost falling to the pavement. I really hope no one saw that.

They say "It's as easy as riding a bike" for a reason, I remind myself as I wobble down the street, willing myself into a straight path. After several pumps of the pedals I'm steadier, but I do a practice lap around the block just because I don't want to die today.

The ache in my calves and breeze on the back of my neck wake me up instantly. I'm thrilled not to be walking anymore. I raise the gears and pump harder; the chain groans beneath me, and it occurs to me that I should have oiled it if Callie hasn't ridden in years.

The light at the corner of Main Street sneaks up on me, and I skid to a stop, an unsettling *pop* sounding below me. The street is empty, but I carefully wheel the bike onto the shoulder of the road to inspect it.

"Goddamn." I let out my breath in a slow hiss. "Shit. Frigging son of a bitch. Damn it."

There's no way I'm making the twelve-mile trip to and from Deer Run with a flat tire. I'm only ten minutes away from the Greenwoods', if I want to turn around and head back. Though the gas station is a few hundred yards up the road; I could try to put air back into Callie's tires there. Maybe they're just old and need to be inflated a bit.

I wipe the sweat from my eye with the shoulder of my T-shirt. I have to get to Deer Run, and I'm not walking, so I really have one option. I step off the bike and walk it up Main Street to the Quik Mart. The guys who watched the police outside of Ari's house with me yesterday are riding their skateboards in the parking lot. Decker Lucas watches from the curb, a bag of Twizzlers in his lap.

"Hey." He waves me over with a Twizzler. "You again."

"Me again," I say.

"Whoa, how are you riding with that?" Decker nods to Callie's tires.

I accept a Twizzler from Decker as he examines the front tire. "Nice hole," he declares. "I've got a patch kit."

"You do?" I could hug him. For some reason, the desire to get to Deer Run *right now* is a throb in my chest.

"It's at my house, though," he says, and I deflate.

"Oh." I tear the candy in half with my teeth.

"I live right around the corner, behind the school," Decker says. "We can walk there."

"Great. Thanks. I'll buy you more Twizzlers, or something."

Decker laughs and waves me off. He doesn't tell his friends where he's going, and they don't seem to care. I walk Callie's bike alongside the curb as Decker takes off down the street on his skateboard.

"So, are you, you know . . . back?" Decker stops suddenly and waits for me to catch up, probably realizing that it was rude to leave me back there.

"In Fayette?" It's not a hard question, but I'm having trouble answering.

"Yeah. Are you here for good?"

"No." I pick at the rubber peeling from Callie's handlebars. "My dad was sick. I came to say goodbye."

I look up at Decker. His eyes are wide. "That really sucks," he says. "Here, we can cut across the soccer field."

I follow him, thankful to be able to leave it at that. On our right is a chain-link fence blocking off the elementary school playground. They've replaced all the equipment since I was a kid.

"I'm just across the street," Decker says. "Watch out for the geese poop."

We pick our way around the green piles like we're in a

minefield and pass through a wooded area at the edge of the soccer field. It leads to a quiet road. I follow Decker across, once a
car has passed.

His house is a ranch-style painted forest green. There's an old-
fashioned car in the driveway; when Decker undoes the padlock
on the garage door and lifts it open, I see why the car isn't parked
inside. There's no room for it. Wall-to-wall cardboard boxes rot-
ted with water stains. Stacks of old phone books. It looks like a
scene from one of those shows Gram watches where some guy
goes into a house in a hazmat suit, maybe finds a dead cat or two,
and by the end everyone is crying happy tears.

"Ah," Decker says, "my mom doesn't like to throw stuff out."

"It's cool," I say, because the tips of his ears are red.

"A lot of it's my dad's crap," he rambles. "Eleven years, and
my mom still thinks he's coming back to get it or something."

Decker taps the indent in the center of his chin, as if he'd forgotten why we're standing here. "Oh yeah! The patch kit."

I just sort of stand there, hands in my pocket, as Decker disappears into the cavern in the garage. There's some rustling, then he
emerges with a patch kit. I sit on the lawn, pulling my knees up to
my chest as he works on the bike.

"So how long are you here for?" Decker asks.

"I'm supposed to be gone by now. I wanted to stick around for
Ari Kouchinsky's funeral."

"I kinda remember you guys playing with those little plastic
bears in Ms. Brogan's kindergarten class. She said they were for
practicing counting, but you guys always made bear armies out
of them." Decker rocks onto his heels, his tongue poking out the
corner of his mouth as he moves from Callie's tire to inspect her
chain. "I can't believe she's dead. Who'd want to hurt her? She
was so nice."

88

Nice girls are always the ones who get hurt. It's like the universe gets some sort of perverse pleasure out of taking out the nice girls one by one, while the whole world watches and gets some perverse pleasure from mourning the loss of yet another nice girl.

"It was probably a random creep," I say.

Decker pumps air into both of Callie's tires. "I heard a rumor that it's the ORM again."

Decker takes my silence as confusion. "The Ohio River Monster. Sorry, I keep forgetting you moved when that was happening."

My toes curl. "Where did you hear that rumor?"

"My mom." Decker looks sheepish. "But she, like, reads a lot of stuff. Conspiracy theories about how the cops know they probably got the wrong guy but won't admit the Monster's still out there."

So Decker doesn't remember that I testified against Stokes, I realize. Or maybe he never knew. The papers never named Callie and me as witnesses, since we were minors, and the judge issued a gag order for our testimony, to protect us. A lot of people knew Callie and I were involved in the trial somehow, but most of our classmates were clueless as to why we were being taken out of class so much. Jealous and clueless.

I pick up a twig from Decker's lawn and snap it over my thumb. "I don't think it was the Ohio River Monster. The cops seem convinced it was Ariel's ex-boyfriend."

"Nick Snyder?" Decker looks thoughtful. "That guy's a tool. He punched me in the face in the tenth grade. I didn't even deserve it. That time, at least."

I feel a small smile creeping up, in spite of myself. "What did you do?"

"Nothing," Decker says, wiping his greasy hands on his shorts.

"I was just smiling to myself, 'cause I do that sometimes, and Nick saw me and said I was laughing at him. So he punched me."

My smile fades. I feel bad for Decker; it must be hard to have a spirit in this town. Everywhere you turn, there's someone who wants to kill it.

I'm light-headed as I stand up.

"Thanks, for this." I gesture to the bike and nod to Decker. He beams.

"Anytime. Hey, I might get a job at this bike shop in town. I could hook you up with new tires."

He looks so desperate to be helpful that I don't want to say that it's not even my bike. "Sure. Okay."

Decker scratches the back of his neck, his shirt pulling up to expose a sliver of pale, hairy tummy. "Where's your cell? I'll give you my number."

I fumble in my back pocket. My phone falls onto the driveway and skitters at Decker's feet. He reaches it before I can bend to pick it up, his brow furrowing as he flips it open, begins adding his info.

I want to snatch it back, just in case he sees that the Fayette County Penitentiary is in my contacts. But his expression doesn't change. When he's finished, he hands the phone back to me, its screen still flipped open.

He's put himself in my contacts as "DECKER, YOUR FRIEND^_^"

I wave goodbye and hop back onto Callie's bike. I think I'll leave his number in my phone; you never know when you can use a friend around here.

. . .

The ride to Deer Run is a straight shot south. Brown, parched earth follows me for miles on each side. *We're in need of a good soaking,* my mother would always say. Then when the rain finally does come to Fayette, it feels like it lasts for days.

The sign says WELCOME TO DEER RUN: A MOBILE COMMUNITY. Two shirtless guys, probably in their twenties, look up from playing beer pong on the lawn to stare at me.

Deer Run isn't the meth-y type of trailer park. Mostly families live here—I can tell by the clotheslines hanging outside each home. Pajama pants, cloth diapers, a Thomas the Tank Engine T-shirt.

I imagine my mother and Jos sitting in one of the trailers, like some sort of messed-up family reunion that I wasn't invited to, and I almost turn around.

I follow the noise—kids shrieking, accompanied by splashes, a radio playing a Top 40 station—to a white building labeled MAINTENANCE. Inside, a woman sits near a fan, reading a copy of *People.* She looks up when I clear my throat.

"I'm looking for Annette Lowell."

The woman's eyes flick down toward her magazine. She flips a page. "Doesn't live here anymore."

I could have figured that much out on my own. Any other day I'd duck out, embarrassed at even having opened my mouth, but I didn't ride all this way in Death Valley-ish heat to be told no.

"I need to find her." I'm shocked by how forcefully it comes out.

The woman sets down her magazine. "Yeah, well, when you do, tell her she owes two months' rent."

I clench my hand into a fist. "Fine. I'll knock on every door here until I get someone who knows where she is."

I expect her to give me more attitude, or maybe tell me it's useless, that no one here knows where Annette Lowell is. Instead, she shrugs. "Probably should start with Nicki."

"Nicki?" An awful thought strikes me: Is Nicki my mother's daughter? It's been long enough that my mother could have started another family.

"Babysitter," the woman says. "Around back."

I nod to her and go out the way I came in. I circle around the building, where there's a concrete slab with a swing set and a sandbox. A sorry excuse for a playground. Beyond it is a pool, where a group of older kids are shouting "Marco Polo" back and forth.

A little girl pushing around a stroller with a filthy blanket inside stops to gawk at me. She's in a hot-pink bikini bottom and nothing else. She slips her thumb out of her mouth in order to address me. "Hi."

"Hi," I say. "Is Nicki here?"

She points to a row of lawn chairs. A girl who can't be more than fifteen sits in one of them, her eyes glued to her phone. At her feet, a toddler in a diaper stumbles around, a dandelion clutched in a chubby fist.

I approach Nicki, suddenly unnerved. She's in a bikini top and denim jeans. Everything is harsh about her, from her brassy highlights to her eyeliner, but she's pretty. It doesn't matter that I've got at least three years on her. I feel two inches tall.

"Are you Nicki?"

She sets her phone down on her lap, annoyed. "Yeah."

"I'm looking for Annette Lowell," I say. "You know her?"

"She used to watch the kids and stuff." Nicki shrugs. "Before me."

"How long ago?" I ask.

"She was here awhile. More than a year. Phoebe got pretty attached to her."

Nicki's eyes are on the little girl with the stroller, who's adjusting the blanket with extreme care. She can't be more than five or six. I need to get out of here, away from this child who is depressing the crap out of me with her invisible baby. Did she cry when my mom left? I can't think about it.

"What about a blond girl, twenty-sixish?" I loop my finger through the hole in the side of my jeans. "Did she come looking for Annette this week?"

Nicki's eyelids flutter as she really looks at me for the first time. Hope swells in me, but she reaches for her phone. "Nope."

I hate myself for being the slightest bit disappointed. "When did Annette leave?"

"Couple months ago," Nicki says. "Said she was moving into her family's cabin. That's all I know," she adds, her eyes back on her phone. The baby at her feet crawls under the chair, and then emerges on the other side. Moving toward the music coming from the pool.

I turn to leave, then stop myself. "You should really keep an eye on the baby. The pool gate is open."

I don't wait to see Nicki's reaction. As I'm leaving, I'm stopped by a small tug on my hand.

"Is Nettie okay?" Phoebe, the little girl, stares up at me with wide, baby-blue eyes.

"I don't know," I say. "But I'm going to try to find her."

Phoebe's eyes narrow, and she pulls her hand back. I've said something to make her not trust me.

"You can't find her," Phoebe whispers hollowly. "Because she's hiding from the Monster."

CHAPTER TEN

I punch out the kickstand a little harder than necessary before hopping back onto Callie's bike. I stub my toe and curse under my breath. Jos didn't come looking for my mother here, and I'm no closer to finding either one of them.

By the time I get back onto the main road, I've convinced myself that I'm starting to hear things. There's no way Phoebe said my mother is hiding from *the Monster*. She must have said *monsters* or *a monster*. Some combination of the heat and my brain tricked me into hearing *the* Monster.

But what kind of monster? Did my mother get mixed up with an abusive man or felon at Deer Run? Did she leave to get away from him, and told Phoebe so the little girl wouldn't be sad?

Or maybe Phoebe is making shit up, because she's a kid, and that's what kids do.

But what if my mother really *did* tell Phoebe she was hiding from the Monster? Does my own *mother* know who really killed those girls?

Do she and Jos both know who he is? Is that why my mom let Gram take me away—to keep me safe from the Monster too?

My mind races, in sync with the wheels of Callie's bike. My father knew a lot of unsavory people, some of whom he owed money to. Men with sallow cheeks and cracked leather jackets. Men with rifles and red-eyed dogs in the beds of their pickup trucks. Any one of them could have killed someone.

Maybe the Monster did kill Lori, and Jos couldn't stop it. She kept her mouth shut because she knew him—maybe we all knew him. She left not because she was hiding something but because he would have come after her next.

There's nothing to prove it, but it could still be true. I think of the empty envelope with my name on it, allowing myself to entertain the wild possibility that it contained the Monster's identity.

Everyone else in my family has secrets. Why wouldn't my father have had them?

Callie is still gone when I get back to the house. I take the stairs two at a time up to the guest room, wiping the sweat from my face with the collar of my T-shirt. I smell like I slept in a barn.

The bag of my father's things is on the bed where I left it after sneaking up here earlier, before Deer Run. I sit and dump the contents onto the quilt in front of me, pick out the torn envelope.

My father had something to tell me; the envelope had my name on it. Not Jos's, and not Annette's. Maybe he figured I wouldn't come to say goodbye, so he wrote me a letter. I think of my mother standing over the woodstove in our old living room, the flames reaching hungrily toward the letter in her hand. My letter.

My chest constricts.

My mother can't be the one who opened the envelope.

According to the guard, she hadn't visited my father in years. Whoever opened it had a reason. Maybe a wayward guard who thought there might be cash inside.

Or someone who didn't want me to find out what the letter said.

My mother didn't visit my dad on his deathbed. But Joslin did.

I push the envelope away so I don't have to look at it.

I always loved my sister the most. I knew it drove my mother insane to see Jos holding me at her hip, spinning in circles around the living room, and swinging me airplane-style. Whenever my mother snapped "Put her down," there was a layer of venom in her voice; she cared less about me getting hurt than seeing Jos make me giggle until I was in hysterics.

I was afraid of my mother, that she'd one day take my sister, the person I loved more than anything else, away from me.

There was only one time I was afraid of Jos. She and my mother were arguing—once Jos turned sixteen, they fought all the time. Ugly fights that made me hide in my closet.

The biggest ones were because my mother wouldn't let Jos get her driver's license. A few months earlier, there had been a horrific accident not far from the high school. Two boys on their way home from football practice—seniors, one with a full ride to Penn State—were split open like squirrels on the pavement, the driver's truck nearly torn in two by a telephone pole. He'd been speeding. There's still a wooden cross with their names on it on the side of the road where it happened.

My mother always talked about the boys—Rob McQueen and Tyrone Williams—as if Joslin hadn't walked the same hallways as they had, hadn't cheered for them at home games. They were ghosts, cautionary tales. The reason Jos wasn't allowed behind a wheel until she turned eighteen.

I ran down the stairs that night when I heard something shatter.

I found Jos in the kitchen, holding a shard of a drinking glass in front of her, a manic look in her eyes. *Like she needed an exorcism,* my father used to joke whenever he was around to break them up. Jos was holding the shard like a weapon and shrieking, "Just back the hell away!"

When she saw me crying in the doorway, it was as if someone had flipped a switch. Jos dropped the glass and ran to comfort me. "I would never, ever hurt you, Tessa."

I hate how I always circle back to that moment when I'm trying to convince myself that Joslin never could have let anyone hurt Lori. I hate how I have to wonder what Joslin would have done with the glass in her hand if I hadn't been in the doorway to stop her.

My stomach is groaning, so I dig out of my backpack the last granola bar Gram packed me. I tear the wrapper off with my teeth as I start to sort through my dad's drawings.

I have to admit, he's pretty good. *Was* pretty good. I wonder if it's a skill he honed in prison, or if he was always a natural and I just never knew. There's a portrait of a waterfall, sketched with such detail that I can almost point out each drop of its spray.

There's something scribbled in the bottom corner. *Rattling Run, 1986.*

I sift through the other pictures—mostly scenery, portraits of nature. Except there's something oddly specific about them; the window looking out over a backyard, two girls piled onto an Adirondack chair.

Jos's birthday, summer of '01.

They're not portraits. They're memories.

I hate myself for how quickly I fly through the drawings trying to find it. I have to know if he remembered it too. Our trip to Laurel Caverns when I was five. The only trip we ever took as a family.

Halfway through the stack, I pause at a sketch of a cabin.

I hold it up to the ceiling light to get a better look, my hands trembling in spite of myself. *Shack* might be a better word for the house; it's propped up on a raised wooden foundation. There's an enclosed porch. My father even drew a tear in one of the screen windows.

Bear Creek, 1986.

I rack my brain for any memory of a place called Bear Creek, and fail. For all I know, Bear Creek isn't even in Pennsylvania. Did my father stay at the cabin as a child? Why wouldn't he have mentioned it if his family owned a house? But wait . . . didn't Nicki say Annette was moving into a cabin her family owned?

I stuff everything back into the bag and put it under the bed. A quick look out to the garage from the guest room window tells me Callie still isn't home yet. I poke my head out into the hall; her door is open a crack.

I glance into Maggie's room to confirm she isn't in there, before I slip inside Callie's. The laminated blue card is on her dresser, where I spotted it earlier. FAYETTE LIBRARY.

Downstairs, Maggie is in the kitchen, starting dinner. She's on the phone, but she doesn't have her Rick voice on this time. I slip past her, through the side door leading to the garage, where I left Callie's bike earlier.

Hey, Maggie, I need to use the computer for a sec to check flights. It would be that easy. Of course she'd say yes. But I can't take the chance of her seeing all the stuff I've been Googling. I can't answer the questions she'd be bound to ask.

. . .

The library is around the corner from Decker's house, down the road from the elementary school. When I get there, I leave the bike in a rack outside, even though I don't have a lock. There's no one around to steal it, and I'm not about to drag it inside with me.

The sliding doors open with a *whoosh,* and a blast of cold air hits my face. When I was really young, my mother used to bring us here on oppressively hot days for the free AC.

There are a lot of people here doing just that. In the aisles of the main stacks, I have to step over a toddler smacking a naked Barbie against the carpet by its hair. There's one shelf marked NEW RELEASES, boasting a James Patterson book that came out last year. I know because Gram needed my help downloading it to her e-reader.

I round the corner into the study room, where the computers are. I log on to the Internet using the bar code on the back of Callie's card.

The first thing I do is search for *Bear Creek*. The auto-fill asks me if I meant *Bear Mountain,* which is a two-and-a-half-hour drive, according to the map. Apparently, Bear Mountain used to be a ski resort before it shut down in the eighties. The town of Bear Creek had a few restaurants for skiers, but they're all closed now too.

There aren't any population statistics for the town. In fact, there's nothing to suggest that Bear Creek is even a town where actual people live. Most likely, the picture my father drew means he went skiing on the mountain and stayed in a cabin for a weekend.

My family never owned shit. I accept it now, with a small

wave of disappointment. People who own shit don't steal other people's shit.

I lean back in my chair, a bit overwhelmed by the prospect of unfettered Internet access. I wind up doing what I always end up doing when I'm by a computer, and search for Wyatt Stokes.

There's a new article from this morning, matching what I saw on the TV at the prison. The judge has set a preliminary hearing for October to decide whether the new evidence is strong enough to let Stokes's appeal move forward. No mention of what the evidence is. I rub my eyes and peer at the last paragraph.

While attorneys for Stokes have not disclosed what evidence they will be bringing to the state supreme court, many have speculated that forensic evidence omitted from the original trial will come into play. Investigators found an incomplete DNA profile under the fingernails of two of the victims, but were unable to determine conclusively whether or not the profile was a potential match for Stokes's. Rachel Steinhoff, a professor of criminal justice at Northeastern University, says that if the DNA is someday entered into CODIS, the FBI database for DNA from violent offenders, it is a strong possibility that investigators could have a new suspect on hand.

I click out of the article. I read about the DNA profile years ago, and knew that Kristal Davis and Lori Cawley didn't have the killer's DNA under their nails. Just another minor inconsistency that the prosecution explained away: Kristal and Lori didn't have any DNA under their nails because they didn't fight back.

I close my eyes and I see her. Joslin and the shard of glass.

Sometimes I think that I've inflated the gravity of that phone call over the years. Friends argue. Jos and Lori seemed like they were inseparable, but they *were* teenage girls. They were bound to get into an argument at some point, probably about something completely stupid. In this case they just never got a chance to make up.

I've tried to pinpoint even one moment before that night when it seemed that Lori was threatened by my sister—a whisper, a strange look—but trying to remember feels like searching for something in the dark.

I've made zero progress today in terms of leads on Joslin—or my mother—so I refuse to leave the library without something. Even if it's just a name. Someone who still lives in town, who I can talk to—someone who might shed light on Jos and Lori's friendship, and if they were having any problems.

I need someone who will talk to a girl who shows up on their doorstep like an intrusive reporter.

Of course. Newspapers. The local paper probably interviewed people in Fayette who knew Lori, and probably Jos.

I log out of my Internet session and make my way to the circulation desk. The librarian is a crunchy-looking woman in a poncho with dyed red hair down to her waist. When it's my turn, she eyes my empty hands. "Whatcha need, hon?"

"Old newspapers."

"We only keep the *Gazette,*" she says, as if this should be a deal breaker.

"That's fine."

The woman looks me up and down and frowns. She calls out to a man shelving books several feet away from us. "Darius, where do we keep the old *Gazette*s?"

Darius mumbles something that would be unintelligible if we were standing right next to him. The librarian shoos me with her hand. "Darius there'll help you."

"Thanks," I say to Darius, who is now at my side and looking none too pleased to abandon his cart. He leads me down to the

101

basement and mutters what sounds like "What you need news-papers for?"

I shrug. "Looking for something."

"Ain't we all?" Darius flips a light switch and starts back up the stairs. The fluorescent bulbs overhead hum as if a thousand bees were trapped inside them. I'm about to turn and tell Darius he didn't say where the newspapers are, when I see them: boxes. Stacks and stacks of cardboard boxes with dates written on the outside in marker. So basically, a slight upgrade from Decker's garage.

I spot *2004* with two other boxes stacked on top of it and think I'm shit out of luck. There's no way I can move these things, but I try anyway and exhale, relieved that they're not very heavy. I ar-range the boxes around me like a fort and sit inside, cross-legged.

The Fayette *Gazette* comes out every other Friday morning. Lori was murdered late in the evening on a Thursday, her body found on Friday night, so she missed being front-page news. In-stead, the cover story is about a home explosion in Arnold, the town to the south of Fayette. Some sort of meth lab gone wrong in the woods.

I replace the paper, and I hold my place with my thumb as I remove the next issue, dated two weeks after Lori's death.

Lori's senior photo stops me. It's on the front page next to an article. The headline sends a chill down my spine.

DREXEL UNIVERSITY STUDENT LAID TO REST
by Shana Rosenberg

A funeral service was held for Lori Michelle Cawley, 19, of Chestertown. Ms. Cawley had been staying with her aunt and uncle in Fayette, who reported her missing late Thursday evening.

The victim's father, James Daniel Cawley, was killed in an accident during a motorcycle rally last year. His last gift to his daughter, Lori, was a sterling silver necklace bearing her name. She was laid to rest in her necklace and the late Mr. Cawley's motorcycle jacket.

Authorities believe that Ms. Cawley is the latest victim of "The Ohio River Monster," a serial killer who has been stalking women in Fayette and Westmoreland counties. While the Monster has evaded capture for the past two years, police announced a break in the case this week. A Fayette resident named Wyatt Paul Stokes, 24, has been arrested in connection with the Ohio River murders. His other believed victims are Marisa Perez, 17, Rae Felice, 20, and Kristal Davis, 19.

I wonder how Shana Rosenberg knew the detail about Lori's name necklace. Before the funeral, Maggie had been worried about the media showing up, despite the fact that it was being held a hundred miles from Fayette, in Lori's hometown. The local police had promised to keep reporters out. Shana Rosenberg must have lied to get in, or maybe she waited outside the church and convinced one of the mourners to talk to her.

A whole lot of effort to work one insignificant detail into her story.

Or at least, a detail she thought was insignificant.

A murky image starts to come into focus in my memory: Lori, surfacing from the deep end after diving in, reaching for her throat to make sure her name necklace was still there. She rarely talked about her dead father, but she never took that necklace off.

If Lori was buried with her necklace, the killer didn't steal it from her.

Shit.

I roll up the newspaper and stick it up my pant leg so no one will see me take it.

• • •

This is really bad.

The stolen jewelry was never a part of the trial. For one, the police never recovered from Wyatt Stokes's trailer anything belonging to the victims. The fact that the Monster took jewelry from the victims was a detail that emerged years later, something used to embellish the documentaries and true crime books for people with boners for serial killer stories.

People who knew Marisa Perez and Kristal Davis said that the girls were missing jewelry when their bodies were recovered. But Kristal had been known to pawn her stuff for drug money; no one could prove that she'd had anything for the Monster to steal from her in the first place.

The missing jewelry detail didn't become public until a few years after Stokes was sentenced, when Rae Felice's mother said her daughter had been missing a gold locket that had belonged to her great-grandmother. Rae's mother had gone through a box of stuff from Rae's apartment and hadn't found the locket. But by then it didn't matter.

It's just a throwaway line in a Podunk local paper— *She was laid to rest in her necklace.* Shana Rosenberg definitely did not realize that that one line could indicate that Lori Cawley was killed by someone other than the Ohio River Monster.

Someone who didn't take her necklace because they didn't know they were supposed to in order to make it seem like she'd been one of the Monster's victims.

Stokes's defense team has to know about this. They would have torn apart every aspect of the case, looking for something to cast doubt on the prosecution's version of the murders.

The possibility that Lori Cawley wasn't even killed by the Ohio River Monster would turn the entire case upside down. If *two* murderers were active at the time, how could anyone be sure Wyatt Stokes was even one of them?

Is the necklace the new evidence they found? Or do they have an even bigger bombshell that could prove Stokes didn't kill Lori Cawley—bigger than the DNA?

A bead of sweat slips down my back.

Two killers. And if Stokes really *is* innocent, both of them are still out there.

Instead of leaving the library, I return to the computer I was using before. Log in again.

I open up my email and start composing a message to the Fayette County Penitentiary.

CHAPTER ELEVEN

I get back to the house in time for dinner, which pleases Maggie infinitely. She pushes a plate of roast chicken at me. No one comments on my appearance, but I catch Callie wrinkle her nose as she sits in the chair next to mine.

"Where have you been jetting off to?" Maggie asks, passing a bowl of peas to me. "I hope you're staying hydrated."

Callie eyes me over the rim of her water glass, like she's waiting to see how I'll answer the first query.

I shrug. "Forgot how much I missed riding. Too humid to do it in Florida."

"Well, it's pretty awful here right now," Maggie says, turning to Rick. "You should really put that window unit in the guest room so Tessa can have some AC."

Rick mutters something unintelligible as Callie knocks her knee into mine under the table.

My room, she mouths. *After dinner.*

I'm sweating, and not from the bike ride. I don't know how much longer I can keep everything to myself. Callie can be relentless. As kids, she was always getting me to admit to things—like when we were eight, and she had her first crush on a boy, Evan Merrill. She was convinced I liked someone in our class too, so she badgered me until I blurted a random name.

If Callie senses I know something I'm not telling her, she'll shake me until the truth falls out.

Somewhere between the air conditioner debate and Maggie saying she ran into Emily Raymes, who was behind the counter at the grocery store, I decide I have to tell Callie everything tonight. And I mean everything: the phone call, the necklace, and the nagging fear that we're not looking for just one killer but two.

Callie asks to be excused when we're finished. I'm too antsy to feel guilty about not helping clean up, and follow Callie out of the kitchen and up the stairs into her room.

"You have to see what Ryan showed me," she says in a single breath as soon as the door's closed behind us. She gestures for me to follow her to her desk.

There's a website open on her laptop—*Connect*. Simple black letters. *Discreet*.

"What is this?" I ask.

"It's a creepy site people use to find hookups in their area," Callie says. "Some of the listings are totally disgusting."

I glance over some of the links on the home page, resisting the urge to look away. *Adventurous couple looking for a third. (Philly-metro area.)*

Callie selects *Casual encounters* from a drop-down menu and adjusts the search settings. *Maximum age: 19. Area: Fayette and Somerset Counties.* A halfhearted message encouraging us to report potential exploitation of minors pops up before the results load.

Callie scrolls down purposefully, like she's been on this page before. She clicks on *Nice girl wants a man who's not afraid to get a little naughty—PICS.*

"'Nineteen-year-old brunette available for a mature guy seeking companionship,'" Callie reads. "'Let's work something out. Serious inquiries only.'"

The girl in the photo is wearing a black dress that's so tight, it may as well be painted on her body. She's standing in front of a mirror, angled so her ass is on display, and her face is cropped out of the photo. Dark brown hair falls all the way to her bony elbows.

Callie points to the girl's hand, the one that's not planted on her hip. She's holding a digital camera up to the mirror. In the area between her thumb and forefinger, there's a patch of lightened skin. The one we used to say looked like it was in the shape of Alaska.

"Ariel," I breathe.

Callie clicks out of the page before I can read the rest.

"Ryan says it's total escort language," she says quietly. "'Let's work something out.' It's how they communicate that they're selling. I just don't get why."

"Obviously so she wouldn't get busted for prostitution," I say.

"No, I mean *why* would she do this?" Callie demands. "Okay, your life sucks and you want to get out, but having sex with random creeps for money?"

Her face is splotchy and red. She pushes herself away from the desk, and before she turns away, I see that there are tears in her eyes.

Finally, Callie clears her throat. "I called her a whore."

Her voice is as small as she looks, sitting on the bed with her back pressed to her headboard and her knees to her chest. "I called Ari a whore because she hooked up with this guy I liked. I got pissed, and I said it to her face. It was two years ago. That's why we stopped talking."

I don't say anything. Mostly because I get the sense that Callie doesn't want me to.

"I had no idea," she says. "I never, *ever* should have said it. . . . I just had no clue."

For the first time since I got here, I can understand Callie. I know how she feels right now—almost as if learning the truth about Ari's other life had blown apart bits of the world Callie had thought she lived in.

It's possible to know—like, really *know*—another human being. But I'm starting to think that most of us never even want to try to know another person until it's too late to save them.

Callie wipes her eyes with a tissue from the box on her nightstand. I feel like crying too; I decide now that I won't tell Callie about Jos tonight.

I figure there's only so much we can beat ourselves up about, things we wish we'd done differently, before we're broken beyond repair.

• • •

Without Ari's computer, Callie and I don't have a way to figure out who she was meeting up with through Connect. So we decide to run with my plan to track down the people who were in Jos and Lori's circle that summer, to see if there's anyone the police may have missed talking to.

There was Danny, Jos's boyfriend. Jos was only as tall as his chest. He was as thin as a yardstick, his jeans always sagging to his hip bones. His teeth were stained with nicotine, and he said a total of five words to me in all the time I knew him. *Hands off the ride, kiddo.*

Danny could still be in Fayette. He certainly didn't have the brains or motivation to get out—at least he didn't back when he was dating my sister. Even if he doesn't know where Jos is now, he may know why she and Lori were fighting that night.

Every moment Jos wasn't with Lori, she was with Danny. *You're spending too much time with that boy,* my mother would scold her, even though Danny was a man. He was nineteen, two years older than Jos.

I'm leaving at the end of the summer. You can see him all year, I heard Lori tell Jos when Jos went to Danny's house one morning instead of to the pool with us.

I don't know what Danny will be able to tell me if I find him. I know what I *want* to hear him say—that the girls had a stupid argument over Jos blowing Lori off for him. Danny heard the whole thing, because Jos was with him just like she said she was. Jos didn't say anything about the phone call to the police because it hadn't meant anything. The Monster really did kill Lori, and my sister wasn't involved.

I lie in bed, and I let the wanting take over my body like a dull ache. And I fall asleep without my music for the first time since I landed in Pennsylvania.

• • •

I overslept. I know because the sun is streaming through the split in the guest room curtains. The sun isn't what woke me up though; my phone is ringing.

My stomach shoots into my throat when I see the first few digits. They match the number on the prison's website that I saw yesterday before sending that email.

As many ideas do, the idea that I should talk to Wyatt Stokes seems terrible now that I've slept on it. I stare at my phone like it's a grenade. I thought it would be a few days before I got this call, if at all.

I have no idea what to say to him.

I hit *answer* as the call is about to go to my voice mail. An automated voice greets me.

"This is the Fayette County Penitentiary. You have a prepaid call from—"

There's a pause. The sound of a mucous-y cough. Then a voice that chills me to my core.

"Wyatt Stokes."

Every single one of my nerve endings dulls. The automated voice is back.

"Press one to accept."

"Hello?" My voice echoes in my head, almost as if I were in a dream.

"Hello." His voice is different. It's less gravelly than I remember. Less frightening. He sounds almost bored, like he's calling only because he has nothing better to do. Which is probably true, since he's in prison.

I take a deep breath in and let out the words: "My name is Tessa Lowell. I don't know if you remember me."

"I remember you." There's a muffled sound on Stokes's end. A sneeze. "You gonna tell me why you requested to be on my approved calls list? I know it's not faith outreach."

I had to check one of the boxes stating my purpose for

communicating with an inmate. It worked. I can't believe it worked. Suddenly, my hand is sweating so badly that my phone nearly slides away. "Because I have some questions for you."

"What makes you think I'm gonna answer your questions?" Now he sounds like the man I remember. The one who infuriated the cops who interrogated him; the one the judge and prosecutor looked at with contempt. *Trailer trash. Devil worshipper. Freak. Sociopath. Monster.*

There's a scene in the documentary about the murders where the interviewer asks Stokes why he thinks the police had it out for him. He looks right into the camera and says, as if he had the answer ready, "They want to believe I did it. I don't think they're 'fraid of me 'cause I'm different; I think they're afraid of the Monster turning out to be someone who looks just like one of them."

I switch my phone to my other hand and wipe my sweaty palm on the bedspread. Listen for sounds outside my door. It's silent.

"I was close with Lori Cawley," I tell Stokes, my voice wavering just above a whisper. "I want to understand what happened to her."

"I'm not stupid," Stokes says. "The only folks who want to talk to me these days are the ones who think that I didn't do it. So either admit that we're having this conversation because you've had a change of heart, or I'm hanging up."

"I don't think you killed Lori Cawley," I say. "I don't know who killed those other girls, or if you were involved, but I think whoever killed Lori only wanted it to look like the Monster did it."

"I didn't kill those other girls."

I grip my phone. "I believe you."

And I mean it, because someone strangled Ariel Kouchinsky and left her naked body along the river. There are too many other blanks to fill in—the Monster's ten-year absence, whether or not

Ari was missing jewelry—but for once, I'm searching for answers that are in my reach and not buried in my memory of the night Lori died.

There's silence on Stokes's end.

"You know this is being recorded," he finally says.

"Yes. I know."

There's rustling on his end, like he's switching the phone to his other ear. "Well, Tessa Lowell. If I didn't kill your friend, then who did?"

For a second I think he means Ariel, but he's talking about Lori.

I wish I didn't have an answer to the question. I wish I'd never seen Joslin about to go after our mother with that shard of glass, and I wish I'd never heard the fear in Lori's voice when she yelled at my sister that night.

I thought if I stayed in Fayette, I could get enough answers to squash the doubt in my mind—the possibility I've carried with me ever since I figured out who Lori was arguing with on the phone that night. I thought I could rearrange the clues and make them fit so I wouldn't keep arriving at the same conclusion.

That Joslin doesn't just know who killed Lori; she put her hands around her friend's neck and did it herself.

CHAPTER TWELVE

I pee, wipe the gunk of out my eyes, and shuffle downstairs, where Callie, already dressed, is fixing herself a coffee. She looks up at me, her bottom lip folding under like something is off.

She heard me on the phone, I think.

My knees go weak until she says, "You slept late."

The stove clock says it's a couple minutes after nine. Normally, I'm up at seven every day, a pattern I haven't been able to break for years. At least I was never late for school.

"Guess I was exhausted." I slide into a chair at the kitchen table, where Maggie has left a paper plate with two bagels. I can't bring myself to eat; it was so, so stupid of me to talk to Wyatt Stokes in this house.

I know Callie wouldn't understand why I had to talk to him. I know she's only digging into the past with me out of fear that the police will pin Ari's murder on Nick, and the real Monster will be free to prey on more girls. She feels guilty for how she treated Ari, scared that it's our fault she's dead. All on top of us being exposed as little liars, right before we're supposed to start our shiny new lives away at college.

But she doesn't want Stokes to get out of prison. She thinks he'll come after us if he's free, get revenge on us for lying.

Is that why I felt like I had to talk to him? To convince myself he doesn't want to hurt us?

I tear off a piece of bagel. It sticks in my mouth.

Callie sips her coffee and looks at me. "I thought about what you said last night, about your sister's boyfriend. He's probably a good place to start."

I nod, swallow away what's left of the bagel in my mouth. "I don't know his last name, though."

"Maybe an old yearbook?"

I shake my head. "I don't know where he went to school, but I know it wasn't in Fayette. And he never graduated."

Callie cups her mug with both hands. "I'm out of ideas, then. I haven't seen him since that summer."

"So he could have left town not long after Jos did." I rack my brain, trying to remember if I saw Danny around in those short months after Jos left and before I went to live with Gram.

"You think it means something?" Callie looks skeptical.

"Like, do I think they planned to run off together? I don't know." I'd never considered the possibility that simpleminded Danny might have been involved in what happened that night. He'd only ever hang out with Jos alone, maybe to convince himself he wasn't dating a high school girl. He never interacted with Lori much either, except for a head nod when we all ran into him. I'd hear him and my sister on the porch sometimes, from my spot on the living room couch. Jos would nag Danny for never wanting to hang out with Lori, and he'd mutter that Lori was stuck-up.

But as far as I knew, Danny didn't hate Lori. He regarded her in the same way he regarded me, as a minor annoyance standing in his way whenever he wanted Joslin's attention.

"Didn't Jos say she was with Danny the night Lori was murdered?" Callie looks up at me. I can see the wheels in her head turning. I swallow.

"Yeah. Hey, what if we asked someone at the pool?" I say, redirecting. "Danny worked for the company that cleaned it."

My sister was never interested in high school guys, no matter how much my mother tried to beat it into her that older men were trouble. My mother never liked to talk about Jos's real father, except to say that he was twenty-one when he got Annette pregnant at seventeen, and he promised to take care of her and he didn't.

Jos met Danny on Memorial Day weekend, before Lori arrived that summer. I only remember because my mother told us we had to stay home while she was out cleaning houses, but as soon as the door clicked behind her, Jos showed me that she was wearing her bathing suit already. The Greenwoods were camping at Cranberry Run for the weekend, so it was just Jos and me at the pool.

I was practicing blowing bubbles in the shallow end, like she'd taught me, when I saw Jos staring at the guy cleaning leaves out of the pool house gutter. Danny smirked at her; Jos didn't smirk back. Instead, she got this determined look on her face like she saw something she wanted, and that was that.

Callie slides a finger across the screen of her cell phone. "The pool's open till five. Let's go."

• • •

The town parking permit stuck on the window of Maggie's minivan is expired, so we walk to the pool from Callie's house. I'm

116

weirded out by how familiar this feels, so I remind myself of all the ways this isn't the same. There are no towels slung over our shoulders. The Greenwoods' new house is farther from the pool, and we have to take a different route to get there.

The longer trip sucks because there's more time to fill with small talk. Eventually, Callie decides it's not worth the effort, and she pulls out her phone and starts texting, stopping only when we have to cross a street.

I hate myself for how much I want to fill in the blanks for her, answer her questions about what my life has become, even though she didn't ask. I want to tell her about how I'm going to Tampa in the fall and majoring in astronomy; about living in Gram's retirement community and her bastard neighbor Frank, who is always quick to point out that my presence violates the fifty-five-and-older rule; about Ariel's letters in pink envelopes and her emphatic pleas for me to *Write back!!!!!* even though I always did.

I hate myself, and I hate Callie for making me feel like a pathetic loser without even really trying. It makes me all the more sure that I can't tell her about Joslin yet—not when Callie would never be able to understand why I kept quiet.

We hear the pool before we see it—splashing, shrieking, punctuated by the lifeguard's whistle. The parking lot is full, and we have to wind through the cars until we reach the gate, a flimsy, barbed old thing posted with a set of pool rules.

The snack bar is gone, replaced with a slab of concrete and a row of lounging chairs. One of the guys who used to work there testified at the trial—Kevin, who snuck Callie and me french fries sometimes.

A man dripping sweat pushes around a cooler, halfheartedly hawking frozen Snickers and SpongeBob ice cream pops.

I catch Callie looking at a group of girls pulling jean shorts over their bikini bottoms and packing up their stuff. They're looking at us—or Callie, rather—and angling their chins over their shoulders, whispering to each other.

Callie lowers the sunglasses perched on her head. "God, I hate this place."

I don't know if she's talking about Fayette, the pool, or both. "Come on," I say, uncomfortable with the way that the girls are watching us.

The pool-house-slash-management-office is the same ugly hunter-green building it was ten years ago. A guy with an acne-scarred face sits on a stool next to a soda vending machine, flipping through today's paper. He's wearing jeans despite the heat, and he has one of those faces where he could be either thirteen or thirty.

"Hi," Callie says. "We're looking for someone who used to work here."

The guy tucks the paper under his arm. "Don't keep employee records around. Check city hall."

"He wouldn't have worked for the town," I say. "He worked for a landscaping company."

"Which one?" The guy slides off his stool to chase away a pigeon that's wandered in the open door. "The town's had contracts with four, maybe five landscapers in the past ten years."

In my head, I try to picture the pickup truck Danny used to ride off in. "Their logo was a leaf, I think."

Callie rolls her eyes, as if to say, *That's helpful.* "It was about ten years ago. Do you know which company the pool used then?"

The guy shrugs. "I didn't work here back then. Sorry."

"Thanks anyway." Callie turns to leave, but I stare at the guy. I figure he could be around my sister's age, maybe.

"Did you go to Fayette High?" I ask him.

He nods.

"Did you know someone named Joslin Lowell?"

Next to me, Callie stiffens.

"Sounds familiar." The guy folds his arms across his chest. "Think she was a couple grades younger than me."

"What about a guy named Danny?" I ask. "Really skinny, smoker, blondish hair?" The more I attempt to describe him, the less distinct his face becomes in my mind. Did he have a birthmark? Busted teeth? I can't remember.

The guy blinks at me, and Callie tugs at my arm. "Thanks anyway," she says to him, before dragging me outside.

"He might have known Danny," I say, pulling down the hem of my shirt. "It wasn't that much of a stretch."

"It's not that. I literally *cannot* be here right now."

I trot after Callie, back toward the parking lot. She lets me catch up to her. I can hear her ragged breathing near my ear. Her face is ashen. I know what's happening to her, because I've been there.

"When did you start having panic attacks?" I ask her.

Callie shrugs. "I think I was eleven. We'd been in the new house for a while, and all of a sudden I realized there were still windows I didn't know about, and a cellar door. I just freaked, I guess, because if I didn't even know all the ways into the house, how could I stop someone from getting in?"

We step onto the sidewalk, ducking under a low-hanging branch from an oak tree on the other side of the fence.

"I had them too," I say, after a beat. "When I started at my new school, and there wasn't a bathroom in the class like there was at Eagle Elementary."

I leave out the part where I wet my pants and got sent to the nurse's office; after Gram explained over the phone that I'd witnessed a murder the year before, my teacher was nicer to me, which should have made me feel better but really made me feel kind of pathetic.

Besides, I hadn't actually witnessed Lori's murder. I don't know if Gram hadn't bothered to get the story right, or if she told people this version because it was simply easier for them to process.

"I haven't been to the pool since," Callie says, her voice soft. "I was supposed to go with Sabrina in the eighth grade, but I freaked when her mom dropped us off. We had to call her to pick us up."

Callie looks at me. "I just—I want to get out of this place. I'm never going to feel safe here, and that sucks, because it's the only home I've ever known. At least you're far away from it all in Florida."

I nod and kick at a chunk of concrete that's come loose from the sidewalk. Callie's finally opening up to me after ten years, and I don't want to ruin it by telling her that she's wrong.

There's nowhere in the world that's safe. No matter how far we go to try to outrun that night, the monsters will always find us.

• • •

We can't think of an excuse for Maggie about why we're home from the pool so quickly, so we stop at the park adjacent to the pool to kill time. Callie looks up the number for the Fayette Department of Parks and Recreation and reads it to me.

The clerk in the office gives me the name of the landscaping company the town used ten years ago—Faber & Sons Landscaping—but when Callie searches for them online, we get an expired domain name. The only number the results turns up rings about a dozen times when we call it.

Callie hangs up. "Probably went out of business. Like everything else in this shit place."

I can't argue with that. I'm sure a lot of people think poorly of their hometown, but Fayette actually *is* shitty. Seriously, you can smell the cow feces when you get off at the exit for Fayette on the freeway.

This place is too suburban to be rural, too far east to be a fly-over state, too far north to be redneck country. Fayette simply exists—the type of place that no one thinks about. The type of place where people up and leave, and if you ask about them years later, it's like they never even existed.

"We'll find him," I say, more to myself than to Callie. I *have* to find Danny, and not just because he might know what really happened between Lori and Jos that night. It's not even just about Lori's murder anymore. My father is dead, my mother is God knows where, and I'm not leaving Fayette without finding my sister.

I tried to talk about Jos every now and then when I first moved in with Gram. When Gram gave me macaroni and cheese for dinner: *My sister used to make me mac and cheese.* When Gram and I sat down to watch a sitcom: *My sister liked* Friends. Gram would get this blank, pitying look on her face like I was making it all up—this *sister* of mine was a figment of my imagination. An imaginary friend I'd created to deal with the trauma of being taken from my mother.

I push back the resentment growing in my mind toward my grandmother, who never wanted to talk about my family. She hadn't ever met Glenn Lowell, or Joslin, and whenever my mother came up in conversation, Gram would get this tired look in her eyes. She was disappointed in how her only daughter had turned out, that much I could tell. It pained Gram to talk about how her relationship with my mother fell apart, so we just didn't talk about her at all.

Maybe if we had, I'd know enough about Annette to track her and my sister down. Maybe I wouldn't feel so goddamn lost in a town where I spent half my life.

Callie and I are quiet on the walk back to her house. I guess whatever force took over her earlier and made her want to talk about her panic attacks with me is gone. She doesn't talk again until she unlocks the front door to her house for us.

"Jesus," she says, jumping back into me.

Maggie is sitting in Rick's armchair in the living room, slunk back into the cushion like she's been waiting for us.

"I got tired of waiting for you to clean your room." Her voice is strange, like her words are slurring together. "So I did it myself."

There's a handle of vodka on the coffee table in front of Maggie. It's almost empty. Callie tenses; this was obviously the bottle she was worried about leaving under her bed.

I know I shouldn't be here, and I slip upstairs like a mouse being chased by a broom.

I catch pieces of their argument before I can shut myself into the guest room.

". . . not how we raised you to deal with your problems." Maggie.

"It's been a horrible week, okay? And it's not like I can talk to you about it." Callie.

"That's ridiculous, Callie. You can come to me about anything."

"Anything except Lori!"

I let go of the guest room doorknob. I press myself against the wall of the hallway, waiting for Maggie's response.

Callie is the one who talks next, though. She's crying. "You never once asked me if I *wanted* to testify."

"Of course you wanted to. You wanted to help."

"No. You made me feel like I didn't have a choice, that if I didn't say that Tessa and I saw him in the yard, he'd go free—"

"Stop it, Callie," Maggie yells. "You don't know what you're saying."

"Yes, I do," Callie cries. "I'm not eight years old anymore. I'm old enough to know that we might have been wrong and what that detective did to us was *fucked up*—"

There's a short crack. Skin on skin. I swallow. *Maggie slapped her.*

"Callie, wait. I'm so sorry—"

Footsteps on the stairs. I duck into the guest room and shut the door, but it's too late. Callie's already flying past the room. She knows I heard everything.

There's the sound of Maggie stumbling up the stairs. I suck in my breath.

"I don't know why I did that," Maggie sobs, outside Callie's door. "I just lost it. Please let me in."

No answer. I press my ear to the door just in time to hear Maggie say, "Did she say that to you? Is she trying to convince you that you shouldn't have testified?"

She, as in me. Maggie thinks I came back to Fayette and brought along the crazy idea that we didn't really see Stokes in the yard that night.

Maggie gives up, and moments later, the door to her room closes. I wait twenty minutes, until I'm sure she's not coming out, before I sneak downstairs and slip outside.

I hop onto Callie's bike and peel away from the Greenwoods' house. I follow the main road all the way to Deer Run; I circle around the trailer park, wondering what Phoebe, the little girl with the stroller, is doing right now. I wonder if Nicki is being more careful with the baby around the pool.

I ride in circles until the sun starts going down and I figure that maybe someone at the house might start looking for me.

When I get back, Maggie is still passed out in her room. Rick is home. Callie tells him Maggie doesn't feel well and has been sleeping this afternoon. Rick has Callie order a pizza for us.

After dinner, I excuse myself to the guest room. I shuffle through my father's drawings until my eyelids start to droop. I replay Maggie's words from earlier, as though if I kept turning them around in my mind, their sharp edges would dull.

Is she trying to convince you that you shouldn't have testified?

Maggie pressured Callie to say she saw Stokes in the yard that night. Callie said as much, in the hallway earlier. I'd always suspected it. Maggie had needed us to put Stokes in jail, to put away her niece's killer and stop the pain.

She needed Stokes to be found guilty. She was convinced he'd killed all those girls and that testifying was the right thing for Callie and me to do.

I used to lay awake at night sometimes, sure that all the questions I had about Lori's death and Jos's disappearance would eat at me until there was nothing left. I was terrified of the years ticking by, of eventually dying without ever knowing every detail about what really happened that night.

I always assumed that the doubt would destroy me. But now I wonder if it's the opposite of doubt that's the dangerous thing—if instead, it's the things we're so sure of that have the power to undo us.

I think of Bonnie Cawley screaming at Wyatt Stokes that he'd burn in hell for killing her baby. I think of Maggie, stone-faced, walking Callie into the courtroom, refusing to look at him.

They were always convinced that Stokes was the reason that Lori was taken from them. If he's taken away from them too, if they can't point to him as the murderer, what will they have left to hold on to?

My heartbeat falls into pace with the cuckoo clock on the wall of the guest room. I slip my earbuds in and turn up the volume on Pink Floyd's "Us and Them." My father used to play it for me once he figured out that it helped put me to sleep.

I could use the help now. Ariel's funeral is tomorrow morning.

CHAPTER THIRTEEN

It's nine-thirty, and the service starts in half an hour. I'm in the black work jeans I wore on the plane ride here, plus my T-shirt. I'll probably be mistaken for someone who works for a catering company. When Callie slips out of her room and sees me in the hallway, she sighs. She's in a black pencil skirt and a blouse. Her eyes are swollen.

She disappears into her room and comes back with something crumpled and black. A cardigan that falls all the way to my thighs. It's been doused in perfume, like Callie plucked it from the top of her dirty laundry and tried to disguise the stench.

"Thanks." I slip the cardigan on and follow her downstairs. "Are you okay?" I add, when I see that no one is in the kitchen or living room.

"Fine," Callie says, in a way that makes it clear this isn't up for debate. She pauses by the coffeepot. "She drank more than half of that bottle. I'm surprised she's alive."

We're all going to the funeral together. Rick comes down to the living room, wearing a gray suit with pants that come up to his ankles when he sits in his armchair.

gie is the last to come downstairs, o

face heavily powdered with founda

I force myself to return the s

exchange between her and Call

feeling that after the funeral, she'll

for going back to Florida.

No one speaks on the ride to the church. I'v

once before. The summer she was killed, Lori brought

me to a summer fair on the church grounds. We ate blueberry

off napkins while Lori pawed through the homemade earrings on

sale at one of the stands. Jos was at work.

Rick parks on the side, by the entrance to the Sunday school. The church looks the same, except for a new message on the board outside: SEVEN DAYS WITHOUT PRAYER MAKES ONE WEAK.

There's a line to get inside, even though we're twenty minutes early. Someone says Callie's name. I look up to see Sabrina wading through the crowd to get to us.

"You look like shit," she says. Callie looks over her shoulder, but Maggie and Rick are busy making small talk with the couple standing behind us.

"Long night," Callie mutters, and we inch up in the line.

We break away from Maggie and Rick once we're inside the church; we sit on the outer portion of a pew about four rows back from the front. I'm suffocating in Callie's cardigan. The fans overhead do little but blow around the hot air trapped in the building.

Up front is a blown-up version of Ari's senior portrait, her hair stubbornly flat from the September heat. The coffin next to it, covered in white carnations, is empty; I know because behind me, someone whispers that Ariel's body is evidence, shut up in a metal drawer at the medical examiner's office. Her burial will have to wait.

raight ahead, tuning out the sounds of grief around

king of Lori Cawley in her casket, the name necklace

cross her throat. I don't realize that my knee is jiggling

allie shoots me a look, as if to say, *Pull your shit together.*

Was Ari wearing a necklace when they found her? I want

ask, of no one in particular. Earrings, maybe, or one of those

color-changing mood stones around her thumb that she used to

love so much?

Is she missing something that the Monster took from her?

"This is horrible," Sabrina whispers, on the other side of Callie.
Both of them have their eyes on the Kouchinsky family, who are
huddled by the pulpit, greeting mourners. Ari's siblings are lined up,
as if on display—Kyle, her older brother, who is sweating through
his short-sleeved shirt; David, the youngest, who stands to the side,
running a toy micro skateboard over his knuckles. He was in diapers the last time I saw him, and he's now taller than the second
youngest, Kerry Ann, who must be almost fourteen by now. Katie,
now the oldest sister, stands next to Kerry Ann, in a plain black
dress that hangs baggily past her knees. It probably belonged to Ari.

Kyle clutches Mrs. Kouchinsky's hand, as if he were trying to
hold her upright. I can't look at them.

"Should we go talk to her?" Callie whispers. I turn my head
and realize she's talking to Sabrina, not me.

"Can we wait until . . ." Sabrina doesn't finish her sentence.
She doesn't have to.

Mr. Kouchinsky is standing on the other side of his wife. His
hand is planted on his daughter Katie's shoulder. Even from where
we're sitting, it's obvious the gesture isn't protective.

Katie is a statue beneath her father's grip. I have to blink and
remind myself I'm not looking at Ariel. Katie's the only one of
the kids who looks like Ari did. Lanky, tanned, brunette. The

other kids are round-faced, with fair skin and dirty blond hair, like their mother.

Katie and Ari have their father's coloring. Mr. Kouchinsky is tall, with angular limbs like a praying mantis. His hair is combed to the side the same way it is in photos from twenty years ago. His thick mustache does little to help the fact that it looks as though he were constantly snarling.

He has always scared the ever-living crap out of us.

"I heard he went apeshit on her," Sabrina whispers.

"Who? Ari?" Callie says.

"Katie," Sabrina says. "She covered for Ari when she snuck out. It's why they didn't report her missing until the next day."

It's about a thousand degrees in this church, yet Katie is wearing a long-sleeved dress. I picture bruises up and down her arms beneath the fabric.

The pastor taps the microphone on top of his pulpit. Feedback reverberates throughout the church, and he asks people to find their seats.

But all I can hear is Mr. Kouchinsky slaughtering that dog and the sound of Ariel's screams.

· · ·

There are refreshments in the Sunday school room after the service. As we're following Sabrina down the church hall, Callie's phone buzzes.

"My mom," she mutters. "She says she'll meet us at the car."

Maggie and Rick must have snuck out at the tail end of the service. Unease works its way into my stomach. What if Maggie is going to bring down the hammer on Callie for the vodka by sending me home tonight?

Callie shields her eyes against the late-morning sun as we step outside the church. I shrug myself out of the cardigan, praying that my shirt is dark enough to obscure the sweat stains on my back and beneath my armpits.

"Hey." A guy's voice sounds behind us. Ryan meets us at the bottom of the church steps. He shaved and put on a tie for the occasion. He's almost unrecognizable.

"Didn't see you guys in there," he mutters, slipping his hands into his pockets. "You see Nick?"

Callie glances at me; I shrug. It was so crowded in the church that I wouldn't have spotted Nick even if I'd been paying attention.

Callie hesitates. "I don't think he came."

Ryan cracks his knuckles. Glances at the throng of people pouring out of the church. "I hope you're wrong."

"It's not a big deal," Callie says. "Plenty of people didn't show up."

"Yeah, but he's the one the cops want to see." Ryan lowers his voice. "This looks *really* bad for him, Cal."

"God, you sound like your uncle," she snaps.

"Some might consider that a compliment."

Jay Elwood is standing behind us, his partner in tow. They're both in suit jackets, guns at their hips.

"Nick Snyder been in touch with either of you today?" Detective Elwood's gaze sweeps over me as if I weren't even here. Callie and Ryan both shake their heads.

"You sure about that?"

"*Yes,*" Ryan says. "Why? What's going on?"

The partner makes a guttural *hmm* sound and yanks up his pants. Jay massages the cleft in his chin, his eyes on his nephew.

"We stopped by his stepdad's house this morning," Jay says. "Looks like Nick Snyder took off last night."

CHAPTER FOURTEEN

Rick stops at the deli on the way home to get rolls for sandwiches. While he's inside, Callie and I sit silently in the backseat as Maggie fiddles with the radio, unable to look at us.

Callie nudges me and shows me her phone. She's typed a message.

He didn't do it.

I put my hand over my pocket and remember that I left my phone at the Greenwoods', charging next to the bed. I motion for Callie to give me her phone. I hesitate before I type my response.

How do you know?

Callie takes the phone back, her brow furrowing as she reads. I look over her shoulder as she erases the conversation and types out: *I know Nick.*

My mind goes to a scene in *Unmasking the Monster*. The filmmakers interviewed Wyatt Stokes's mother—not a small feat, because they had to get her sober enough to put her in front of a camera. They filmed the whole thing right in her trailer; she sat on a threadbare couch and insisted through a haze of cigarette smoke that she knew her son. He was no girl-killer.

I wonder if Callie knows Nick as well as she thinks she does, or if the way the police are treating him reminds her of how they treated Stokes and she's simply trying to rewrite history. Trying to stop the police from throwing the first creep they can find into jail just so they can say the case is closed.

Unless Nick Snyder *did* kill Ariel. I don't know anything about the guy, except for a general impression that he's not smart enough to stage his ex-girlfriend's murder to mimic a serial killer from ten years ago.

Things were different when Lori was murdered. The Monster killings were everywhere. The media released so many details about the crime scenes that they practically did the copycat's job for him.

Or her, I can't stop myself from adding.

Rick comes out of the deli, carrying a brown paper bag. I take Callie's phone and type out: *What's Nick's story?*

Rick is pulling out of the parking lot by the time Callie is done with her answer.

He used to live with his dad in North Carolina, but they didn't get along. He moved in with his mom and her boyfriend freshman year. She died two years ago. Ovarian cancer. Her boyfriend is a dick, but Nick can't get him out of her house.

When I finish reading, I respond: *What happened with his dad?*

Callie frowns. *Does it matter?*

I shrug. What I really want to say, I don't have the words for. So I tilt back against the headrest and think of my father's face on the security camera outside the convenience store after he shot Manuel Gonzalo. I think of my sister with that piece of broken glass pointed at my mother like a dagger.

I think of Bobby Buckteeth, and how slamming his head against the locker uncaged something within me. How I wouldn't have stopped if a teacher hadn't pulled me off him.

We're all capable of violence, but some of us are born with it in our blood. There were rumors my father beat a man in a bar so badly before I was born that the guy needed twenty stitches.

Nick could have it in his blood too. Sometimes all you have to do is look at the roots to see if the rest of the tree is poisoned.

• • •

Callie shuts down as soon as we get back to the house and I tell her we need to find out if Ari is missing a piece of jewelry.

"No." She shakes her head. "They didn't even bury her yet. What am I supposed to do, message Katie and ask her to go through her dead sister's shit?"

We're outside, sitting at the patio table, cradling Snapple bottles and staying out of Maggie's way while she vacuums the living room. She's probably hoping the sound will drown out the thoughts of Ari's funeral, and Lori's. Maggie wanted to be alone—I saw it in her face when we tried to clear the table after lunch and she said, "Let me get it."

I study Callie's face as she peels the label from her iced tea bottle. "Someone needs to go through her jewelry," I say. "If something's missing, it's more proof this is the Monster."

"Jesus Christ, Tessa. They haven't even told her parents how she was killed." Callie glances at the back door, but there's only the roar of the vacuum. "We're not going to be able to go through Ari's stuff, or anywhere near Katie for that matter."

I flick away a stray piece of pollen that's fallen on my knee from the tree overhead.

"Her funeral was *this morning*," Callie adds after a moment. "Can't we let her have that, at least? There's got to be something else."

I'm quiet, her message received. No bugging Ari's family or friends. It doesn't leave us with much, except for a name—Faber & Sons Landscaping, who Danny used to work for.

Callie and I couldn't find anything about Faber & Sons Landscaping online after our visit to the pool yesterday, so we plan to ask around town about them. I want to wait out here while Callie asks to take the van, but she makes me come inside with her.

We hover in the doorway a moment before Callie clears her throat. "Is it okay if Tessa and I go to Emily Raymes's? She's having people over."

Rick has retreated to the family room with a Coors Light, but he's within earshot. Maggie's face pinches.

"I'd prefer you stay here, Callie," she says. She may not have told Rick about the vodka, but she's not going to let Callie forget it, funeral or not.

Callie's face falls.

"She didn't say me," I point out when Maggie joins Rick in the family room.

"Yeah, but what are you going to do without me?" Callie whispers. "You don't even really know anyone around here anymore."

"I know people." Decker Lucas's face pops into my mind. His sad garage, and all the old boxes and phone books. His kind, crooked smile.

Phone books. Decker said his mom has kept crap from more than eleven years ago—one of those phone books is bound to have a listing for Faber & Sons. I pat my back pocket, and remember I left my cell upstairs to charge.

Callie eyes me. "What are you—"

"I'll tell you if I find it," I say, already on my way upstairs.

I grab my phone off the nightstand and scroll through the contacts. His number is right toward the top of the list, where he put it. DECKER, YOUR FRIEND^_^

Hey . . . weird question, but are any of those phone books in your garage from ten years ago? I text him, since talking on the phone is an indignity. I don't understand why society still insists on voice calls when everyone hates them so much.

Everyone except Decker. Within a minute of my sending the message, my phone rings.

"What do you need ten-year-old phone books for?" he asks.

"Just looking for someone." The guest room door is open a crack. I nudge it with my foot to close it.

"Have you tried Google?"

Jesus. I press the heel of my hand to my forehead. "Yep, tried that. It's a company that went out of business years ago. . . . If I can find their address, I might be able to find where the owner's at now."

"Gotcha," he says. "So this is like a Sherlock Holmes thing."

I know he's joking, but it makes my toes curl. If he even knew. "Would you mind if I came over and looked through the books? It'd be really quick."

"Yeah! I mean, not yeah *I mind*—"

I'm already headed for the garage to get Callie's bike.

• • •

Decker is waiting for me in his driveway, wearing the same unfortunate jean shorts he had on the other day. The fitted sleeves of his Old Navy T-shirt are loose around his arms. They're branches

135

compared to Ryan Elwood's tree trunks, suggesting that the only lifting Decker does involves his video game controller.

I don't know when I started noticing things like the width of guys' arms, but it's not in a sexual way or anything.

"Howdy," Decker says.

"Thanks for this. It won't take long."

At least, I hope it won't; Decker's garage smells like mold. He lifts a cardboard box off the top of the phone book stack. I spy a bunch of model cars inside.

"I keep telling my mom we should have a garage sale." He sounds sheepish. I remember the other day, when he told me most of this stuff is his father's.

"Do you ever see him?" I ask. "Your dad."

Decker shrugs. He fishes a mint-green convertible out of the box and runs a finger over its wheels. "Not really. He lives in Jersey now."

The phone books aren't in chronological order. I run my thumb across the spines until I find one from the year Lori was killed.

"Did you ever see your dad?" Decker asks. "You know, while he was . . ."

"In jail?" I finish. I don't look up from the phone book. "No."

I flip past headshots of ambulance-chasing lawyers, and two-for-one offers on car detailing, searching for businesses that start with *F*. I figure my conversation with Decker is over, until he says, "Why not?"

I chew the inside of my lower lip. "My mom didn't want me to."

Decker's brow furrows. "Did you want to?"

I'm surprised at how the words seem to fall out of me: "Yeah.

I really wanted to." I shrug at Decker's horrified expression. "My mom didn't think jail was a place for kids."

"Huh," is all Decker says. I clam up, not sure why I said anything in the first place. No one has ever understood what it's like to have a parent in jail. Callie never could, so why should Decker be any different?

I flip through the phone book's directory for *Services: Lawn and pool*. There's a one-inch ad for Faber & Sons Landscaping with the now defunct phone number Callie and I called yesterday, and a name: Joe Faber.

QUALITY SERVICE AND SATISFACTION GARANTEED

Too bad no one had guaranteed Joe Faber a quality copy-editing service.

I text the address to myself so I won't forget it: 312 South Township Road.

• • •

Decker offered to drive me to 312 South Township Road, but there was so much crap in his backseat and trunk that there was nowhere to put Callie's bike. And I wanted to do this on my own, anyway, and not have to explain to yet another person how estranged I really am from my family.

South Township Road is dangerous to ride on. The faded wooden cross memorial for Rob McQueen and Tyrone Williams is a silent reminder to slow down on the curves. It doesn't help that the South Township Inn, a dive bar, is along the road. People called it the STI when I was younger, and now that I get the joke, I think it's more accurate than funny.

Rumor is that Rob and Tyrone had stopped into the STI

before their deadly crash, but people always blame the curves. There's a guardrail along the road now; I stay as close to it as I can, even though there aren't many cars zipping past me. The most notable point of interest on South Township Road is the high school, closed for the summer.

312 South Township Road is nestled in the same strip as the STI. The bar caps off a row of three businesses; the one in the middle is a deli, and on the other end is the Lemon Tree Hair-cutters.

I ride up to the sidewalk to get a better look at the numbers. The deli, which is now closed, is 312 South Township Road, where Faber & Sons Landscaping used to be located.

A sign in the window says the deli closes at five p.m. on week-days. It's a quarter after. I kick the curb.

I prop Callie's bike up against the brick wall outside the Lemon Tree, where I can keep an eye on it, and head inside. My stomach clenches.

Joslin hated when my mother brushed her hair. Annette pulled too hard, was too rough with the tangles. She yanked until our scalps were raw and we'd go to bed on the verge of tears. It didn't help that she never cut our hair; she had always wanted long hair as a child, she said, like her Barbies, but Gram had kept it in a practical bob.

One night Jos decided she'd had enough, so she ducked into our closet with a pair of scissors and hacked all her hair off. My mother brought Jos to the Lemon Tree, dragging me along, so they could fix her hair.

"Walk-in?" The voice comes from the sinks, where a red-headed girl in her twenties is shampooing a man's head. It takes a moment before I realize she's talking to me.

"Um. No. I had a question."

"Okay. One sec." She rinses the man and rubs him dry with a towel. After he settles into a chair in front of the mirror, the stylist meets me at the front counter.

"Do you know of a landscaping company named Faber & Sons?" I ask. "They used to be next door."

The stylist props her elbows on the counter. "As long as I've been here, it's been the deli."

She hasn't heard the name Joe Faber either. I thank her and head outside; a sigh leaves my chest. There's music blasting from the STI's propped-open front door.

A sign in the window says THURSDAY NIGHTS: LIVE JAZZ! There're voices at the curb outside the bar. A guy and a girl come around the side of the building; he leans over and lights her cigarette with his. They talk before he goes back inside, leaving her in full view.

Emily Raymes, who was worried about Ariel during the bonfire the other night. She takes a pull from her cigarette and leans her back against the brick wall of the building. She doesn't see me at the other end of the strip. Smoke streams out of her nose as she checks her phone and pockets it before heading back around the side of the bar, disappearing behind a Dumpster.

I walk Callie's bike past the front of the bar; a bulky man inside the doorway has his back to me. I follow Emily's path around the side of the building, past the Dumpster. There's a back door propped open with a cinder block.

I poke my head in—no bouncer back here. Just the smell of bathroom and a dimly lit hallway. I slip inside.

It's just dark enough inside the bar to mask the dirty linoleum floor and seventies-style wood paneling on the walls. Toward the front, an older man with a microphone is trying to bully people into signing up for karaoke. One TV screen over the bar displays the Quick Draw numbers while another is turned to a baseball game.

Everyone in here is either male or over forty, or both—except for Emily, who's standing in a corner with the guy from outside and another guy. When they break away from her and head for the pool table, I realize they're much older than I thought they were. Early thirties, at least.

As Emily lifts her drink to her lips, I make my way to her. When she sees me, her droopy eyes snap open. "Hey. How'd you get in here?"

"Back door." *Same as you.*

"Oh." Emily nibbles on the lip of her plastic cup. "I have a fake. If you keep to yourself and don't get sloppy, Tom's cool, though."

She eyes the broad-shouldered man hanging by the doorway. He abandons his post and slips behind the bar, wiping the area under the beer tap with a rag. He's bald, except for a thick reddish-blond beard. He must be the owner-bouncer-bartender.

Emily grips her cup with both hands; they're trembling.

"You okay?" I ask.

She meets my eyes. "Yeah, I guess. Better than Ari."

Emily sips her drink and smacks her lips. "Were you there this morning?"

The funeral. It already feels like it happened ages ago, as if I'd been in Fayette weeks and not days. "Yeah."

"I really wanted to say something." Emily wipes the inside corner of her eye and checks the tip of her pinky for eyeliner debris. "I mean, I was her best friend."

The pastor gave Ariel's eulogy—two brief paragraphs written by Mrs. Kouchinsky, who was sobbing too hard to read it.

"She was just *good,* you know?" Emily takes a swig from her drink. "You couldn't get her to say anything bad about anybody. Even people who really screwed her over."

"Like Callie?" I try to sound casual, and not like I'm prying. But there might be more to Callie and Ari's fight than Callie's telling me—and it might be important.

Emily crushes a piece of ice between her back teeth, her gaze skating over me. "Yeah. What Callie did was mad sketch. But she's too good for everyone except Sabrina now that she's going to college, so . . ."

I feel an invisible tug pulling me toward Emily. I know exactly how it feels—how Callie is capable of making you feel like you're unnecessary. Something she's eager to leave behind.

At the other end of the bar, a man sings something unintelligible into a microphone. Lyrics scroll across the screen next to him. *I've got friends in low places.*

"Callie seems pretty friendly with Nick," I'm surprised to hear myself say. What I really want to ask is why Callie is so sure Nick didn't kill Ari. If Callie's keeping something from me, now is the chance to find out.

"They're not close," Emily says. "No one's really close with him. I told Ari he was shady, but I think that made her more into him. She was so naïve, you know? She wanted to be tough, but it just wasn't her."

I eye the bartender, who's filling a beer from the tap. He's watching us, his massive eyebrows knitted together. I put my hands in my pockets and angle myself away from him.

"What do you mean, 'shady'? Are you talking about the stuff with his dad?" I ask Emily quickly, because I don't know how long I have before Tom kicks me out of here.

"His dad?" Emily's nose crinkles as she squints at me, confused.

"Callie told me he threw Nick out."

"Oh." Emily lowers her voice. "You mean what happened with his little brother."

Her breath smells like sour mix and smoke. Her eyes are red.

"So messed up." Emily twirls the rhinestone stud in her nose. "No one knows what really happened, but Nick has a little half brother. His stepmom left to go, like, to the store, and when she came back, there were ambulances outside the house. Supposedly, Nick got mad that the kid came into his room, and Nick pushed him into the wall. His head hit a corner and he got a brain injury and had to live at this rehab place for a while."

My stomach turns. I don't want to think about a little boy's skull cracking against a wall.

"So messed up," Emily says again, staring off into the distance. Then suddenly she's back, shaking her head.

"I mean, it's totally different from *killing* someone," she says, her voice low. "But now everyone's saying he peaced out. Why would he leave if he didn't do anything wrong?"

Emily has obviously never seen *The Fugitive*—something I'd point out, maybe, if I weren't trying to answer the same question about my sister.

Emily looks at something over my shoulder, and then down at her drink, as if it were suddenly the most interesting thing in the world. I turn to see Tom wiping down the bar table behind us, stacking abandoned drinks on top of each other.

"So, what are you doing here, anyway?" she asks, not rudely, when the bartender moves to the next table.

"I'm trying to find someone who used to work next door," I say. "His name is Joe Faber."

"Huh. Don't know him." Emily twirls her nose ring again. "You should try Facebook. Do you have a Facebook page?"

Only to occasionally do some light stalking of my old Fayette friends. "I don't use it much," I say.

"I'll totally add you when I get home," Emily slurs. I doubt she'll even remember this conversation when she gets home.

"I've gotta get back to the boys. Happy hour's over soon." She gives me a one-armed hug and stumbles off to a bunch of guys hanging around the pool table. A large body steps in front of me as I head for the door. Tom the bartender.

"Sorry," I mutter. "I'm leaving."

"I hear you asking about Joe Faber?" he says. His voice is a scary baritone, but his face is nonthreatening. Maybe it's the leprechaun beard. I nod.

"What in God's name is a girl like you doing looking for Joey Faber?" Tom asks.

"I need to find someone who used to work for him." I wrap my arms around my midsection. "His name's Danny."

"Joe left town a while back." Tom frowns.

It could be the lack of sleep, or maybe this place is making me lose my mind, but I feel like I might crack right here. Tom stares at me, balancing the tower of empty cups in the crook of his arm.

I press the heels of my hands under my eyes. Blink hard. *Pull yourself together.* "I'm just trying to find my sister—she dated a guy who worked for Joe."

Tom's expression softens. He shifts the cup tower to his other arm and throws his rag over his shoulder. "Joe's ex-wife, Melissa, is still around. But even if she knows where he's at, I doubt she'd tell you."

It's something, though. I let myself feel a sliver of hope for the first time today. "Do you know where she lives?"

"Red house off Main Street, across from the church that burned down back in 2001. Don't say I didn't warn you, though."

"Thanks. I really appreciate it."

Tom surprises me by extending a hand. My fingers get lost in his beefy palm; it's wet from the rag.

"You know," he says, his eyes probing mine, "you look familiar."

I shrug, suddenly desperate to get out of here. "Guess I have one of those faces."

I'm not about to tell him that I'm a Lowell. He's been so nice to me, and I don't want to ruin that.

CHAPTER FIFTEEN

It's dusk by the time I get back to the Greenwoods'. The porch light is on, and Maggie's left the door unlocked for me. I tread quietly; the kitchen is dark, and there's murmuring coming from the family room. Maggie and Rick. I head upstairs.

Callie's door is closed. My legs are tingling from all the biking, and all I want to do is lie down. I'll tell her about Joe Faber's ex-wife in the morning.

When I wake up again, it's still dark out. I roll onto my elbow and grab my cell phone from the nightstand. It's a quarter to one.

The guest room window is open; outside, the porch creaks. Someone's outside.

Probably a cat, I tell myself, swallowing the lump rising in my throat. I get up and creep toward the window. Someone in a sweatshirt with the hood pulled up slinks down the driveway. By the light of the porch I can see blond tendrils of hair beneath the hood.

Callie.

I tap on the window screen. The warbling sound overhead makes Callie pause. I do it again.

She looks up at the window, like a rat trapped in a cage. I wave. She ducks behind Maggie's van, and a few seconds later, my phone vibrates once. A text, from a number with a Fayette area code. Maggie must have given Callie my number.

Just go back to bed, it reads.

Like hell I will. Is Callie really stupid enough to sneak out for a quickie with Ryan while she's already in deep doo-doo with Maggie? If she gets caught, Rick and Maggie could punish her by sending me home. I text her back.

I'm coming down.

The thin slice of moon gives enough light for me to find my sneakers. I pluck my sweatshirt off the rocking chair where I left it yesterday, realizing as I do that it's been folded. I give it a sniff. Washed too. I think of what Maggie said about me the other night—about trying to convince Callie that we did the wrong thing—and I wonder if she's being this good to me only out of pity.

Thoughts like that will get me nowhere, though. I yank everything on and open the guest room door as if it were made of glass.

I pause to see if I woke them up, but the only sound from behind Maggie and Rick's door is the hum of the air conditioner. I pull my sleeves over my hands and slip downstairs.

Callie is in the driver's seat of the van. She unlocks the passenger door and glares at me. "I don't have time for this. My dad's gonna be up in a few hours."

I hold in a snort. "Ryan needs more than a few minutes?"

Callie's lips part. "You have no idea what you're talking about."

Her fingers climb over the part in her hair. They're shaking.

"Callie. What's going on?"

"Nick," she says. "He's at a motel off Interstate 95. He texted me asking for help."

Emily said that Callie isn't close to Nick. Then what the hell is

146

she doing dropping everything and running to him in the middle of the night? "Help?"

"Just money and food and stuff," Callie says. "Until they figure out who really did this and he can come home."

In other words, aiding a potential suspect in a murder investigation. "This is a terrible idea. What if your mom finds out?"

"I'm not getting out of this van." Callie grips the steering wheel. Her knuckles are white.

I make a big show of buckling my seat belt. "Let's go, then."

"Tessa—"

"*No.*" I'm shocked at how forceful I sound. "You're not going to some seedy motel to meet some guy alone. No matter how much you think you can trust him, you just don't know."

I'm sure Callie is going to fight me, but she shuts her mouth and starts the engine. She's silent until we get onto the highway service road and she pulls into a gas station.

Callie parks and turns to me. "You coming?"

I undo my seatbelt and follow her into the convenience store, wondering what we're doing. Inside, Callie takes eighty dollars out of the ATM and disappears down one of the aisles. I hang by the news rack, glancing at yesterday's paper. The front-page story is about some senior Taliban guy being captured.

Callie meets me by the counter, setting down a bag of Cheetos, a liter of orange soda, beef jerky, and a chocolate protein bar. I want to ask her what the plan is, aside from the only obvious one I can detect, which is to give Nick diarrhea. But Callie will kill me if I say anything in front of the cashier. She just has that look on her face.

When we're settled in the van, Callie enters an address into her phone's GPS. A woman's voice tells us to merge onto the highway. Callie stares straight ahead.

I stare out the window. "Why are you so sure he didn't kill her?"

"Nick just isn't smart enough," Callie says, in a way that makes me think she's given this more thought than I realized. "Staging a crime scene to look like one of the Monster murders? Nick thought Vladimir Putin was a *Twilight* character."

There's almost a fondness in Callie's voice. I have to wonder if the lovable-moron thing is an act and Nick has his friends fooled.

The GPS tells us to stay on I-95 for ten miles.

We arrive at the Doyle Motor Inn, which is next to a Denny's and an adult store called Playtime Boutique. Nick is in room 112, below a stairwell and next to an ice machine with an Out of Order sign.

Callie knocks on the door. I stand behind her, playing with the zipper on my sweatshirt, imagining Maggie or Rick waking up to find both of us gone.

There's the sound of footsteps, then a pause. A chain rattling. Nick opens the door, his expression darkening when he sees me. "You brought someone?"

"Hi," I say. "I'm Tessa."

"It's fine," Callie says. "Just let us in."

Nick steps aside and locks the door behind us. The room smells like cigarettes. A muted sitcom is on the TV. Nick turns it off. "Did anyone follow you?"

"Who would follow me at one in the morning?" Callie shoots back.

Nick's eyes are on me, and I turn to look at the door, just to assure myself we have a clear path out if this little meeting goes south.

Callie dumps the convenience store haul onto one of the twin beds, and Nick goes straight for the beef jerky, tearing the package open with his teeth. Callie sits, runs her hand over the bed-spread, suddenly looking uncomfortable.

"Maybe we should call Ryan," she says. "See if he can talk to his uncle—"

"The hell you think I'm doing here, Callie?" Nick sounds scared shitless. "They don't wanna talk anymore. They want to throw my ass in jail."

Nick tosses the jerky bag aside. Wipes his hands down his face. "Cops asked for a DNA sample. I panicked."

"Why didn't you just give it to them?" I ask. "It would rule you out."

Nick looks up at me, like, *Who the hell are you?*

"Why didn't you?" Callie says sharply, drawing his attention back to her.

Nick cracks his knuckles. "Because she came over to my house that morning, and we had sex."

Air leaves Callie's nostrils in a low hiss. "God. You idiot. Why didn't you just tell the cops that?"

"No shit. I did," Nick snaps. "But Ari's dumbass sister told them Ari was with *her* all day. Their dad didn't want Ari seeing me anymore, and Katie thought he'd kick her ass for covering for Ari."

Nick launches himself to his feet and begins to pace. He stops, suddenly, and points at Callie. "Who do you think the cops believe? I wasn't about to hand over my DNA so they could say I raped Ari or something. Not after what happened with my computer."

"Your computer?" Callie swipes at the air in front of her face. A fly whizzes past us and smacks into the window. It doubles back and *thwack, thwack.*

"They asked me to turn it over, so I did," Nick says. "That's when they found Ari's listing on Connect. They asked how I found it, kept saying I must have been real pissed to find out that my girlfriend was making five hundred bucks a week screwing other guys."

Nick walks over to the desk against the wall. Picks up a phone book and smashes it against the window, leaving a yellowish smudge where the fly was. The bang makes me jump. Nick stares at me, blinks, like he still can't figure out why I'm here. Shakes his head.

"I knew what Ari was doing," he says, to neither Callie nor me in particular. "She showed me the site months ago."

"She showed *you*?" I ask. "While you were *dating*?"

"First off," Nick says, "we were on and off. And I wasn't about to tell her what to do. She was making five times what she would babysitting, for an hour's work."

The way he says *work* makes my stomach turn, as if Ari had been behind the fryer at a McDonald's and not in some guy's car off I-95.

"Last fall, she submitted her picture to this modeling website," Nick says. "Except she found out it wasn't a modeling site. If she wanted to get paid, she had to Skype with guys and, you know, do stuff on camera. She did it for a little while—she'd do anything if you paid a little bit of attention to her or called her pretty."

Sadness worms its way in. My gaze flicks to Callie; her eyes are on the bedspread. Ari hooked up with a guy she knew Callie liked. She lost her best friend over attention from a guy. Then one took her away forever.

Nick takes a swig of the soda. "Ari loved the money, but she hated the men. They were creeps. She started talking to this other girl on the site, who met guys off Craigslist before they shut down the adult section. This chick said the money was way better if you actually met the guys in person. And the guys weren't behind a screen, so they didn't feel like they could say or do anything. The girl told her about Connect and helped set her up. Ari would come to my house and use the computer to update her page, so her dad wouldn't catch her," Nick continues. "But the police lab saw how many times the site was in my browser history, and the next thing I know, the cops are holding me in a room for five hours, trying to get me to say *I* was the one checking her page. Like I was stalking her and planning to kill her the whole time."

Nick stops pacing. Collapses into the desk chair. "If they had her phone, they'd see all the pervs that messaged her on that site. But her killer took it. Along with the bracelet I gave her."

My heartbeat quickens. "Bracelet?"

Nick turns away from us. He wipes at something on his face. "It was just some shitty beaded thing. I'd found it in my mom's stuff, but Ari loved it, so I told her she could have it."

"How do you know the killer took it?" I ask. "Did the cops tell you she was robbed?"

"I guess." Nick rubs his eyes. "I mean, they asked what she usually had on her, and when I described her phone and bracelet, they said they didn't find any of that stuff."

I glance over at Callie. She's looking at me, lips drawn.

"The Monster robbed the other girls too," I say.

Nick's gaze snaps to me. "Who the hell is the Monster?"

"Wyatt Stokes, the serial killer," I say. "Murdered four women around Fayette ten years ago. How do you not know about him?"

"I only moved here four years ago," Nick says. "What does that have to do with Ari?"

Callie looks at me, her face clearly saying that she's thinking what I'm thinking: if Nick is lying, he deserves an Oscar for his performance.

"Ari's murder is similar," Callie says carefully.

"So why are they up *my* ass?" Nick demands. "If it's a serial killer, shouldn't they be out looking for him?"

Callie and I are quiet. She's the one who finally speaks. "You're hiding," she says. "After the stuff with your computer, it doesn't look good for you."

"You gotta believe that it wasn't me," Nicks says. "Besides, if I did it, why would I leave her off I-95 where someone would see her? My house is on four acres of land. I could have buried her under the barn."

I'm starting to see why the cops have zeroed in on Nick. "Maybe don't say that to the police," I offer.

Callie glances at her phone. "We've got to get back." She hands Nick the eighty dollars. "Don't go anywhere or talk to anyone until Tessa and I figure some stuff out. You owe me."

"I owe you my life," Nick says, walking us to the door.

Callie's face is somber under the orange glow from the streetlamps outside. "Let's hope not."

• • •

As soon as we leave the motel, I think of a million questions I didn't get to ask Nick. If Ariel told him about her clients, maybe she mentioned one in particular who creeped her out. Maybe she said something that morning about the man she was meeting with the night she was killed, a clue to who he is.

Callie's eyelids begin to droop ten minutes into the half hour drive. I nudge her arm.

"I found something in an old *Gazette* issue," I say. "An article after Lori died. . . . It said she was buried in her name necklace."

"Well, yeah." Callie turns on the windshield wipers. "She was always wearing it."

"Did she take it off before bed?" I ask.

Callie thinks for a moment. "No. She never took it off, because she was too afraid she'd lose it."

"So she would have been wearing it when she was killed."

"Yeah. I mean, it would have been weird if she wasn't."

"He didn't take her necklace," I say. "He took a trophy from all the other girls, a piece of jewelry, but he left Lori with a necklace that had her *name* on it."

The rain beats against the windshield in a steady rhythm now.

"How—" Callie stops, her mouth hanging open. "How did the cops miss something that huge?"

"They didn't," I say quietly.

Callie listens, silent, as I tell her about Rae Felice's mother coming out years later and saying Rae's locket was missing. When I'm finished, there's bewilderment etched across her face.

"Holy shit." She ups the speed on the windshield wipers and stares ahead, gripping the steering wheel tighter. "Holy *shit*."

"I mean, it never made sense that Stokes would choose Lori," I say. "Whoever killed her . . . it was personal."

"But why?" Callie whispers. "Who could have hated her *that much*?"

Stay the hell away from me.

One detail can change an entire story. A necklace. A phone call. The smallest things could mean the difference between a man's life and death.

It's not for me to decide which details matter. I understand that now.

"Joslin." I force her name out. "She and Lori were on the

phone that night. They were arguing, I don't know about what. I overheard when I went to pee. Lori kept saying 'stay the hell away from me,' and when she hung up, I redialed, and I got the answering machine at my house."

Callie is silent. In front of us, a car stops short. Callie hits the brakes. We jerk forward; when my skull slams back against the headrest, I think, *She's going to tell Maggie, and it's going to be over.*

"The police interviewed Jos," I say. "She didn't tell them about the phone call, and I thought if I ratted her out, she'd go to jail for lying to the police. The older I got, the less things about that night made sense. . . . She could have lied because she did it. She could have killed Lori."

Callie's expression is drawn. She looks like she's lost somewhere. Finally, she says, "Why didn't you tell me?"

"She was my sister, Callie. If you said anything to anyone . . . I didn't know what would happen to her. I know I screwed up, and if I'd told the truth, they would have looked at people other than Stokes. If Jos killed Lori, it's my fault that she got away with it."

"Tessa." Callie's voice is forceful. "You didn't do anything wrong."

Something within me releases. I didn't know how much I needed to hear Callie say that until she said it.

"But if Jos killed her—" I say.

Callie holds up a hand. "You're not hearing me. There's no way that happened."

"What are you talking about?"

"The guest room window," Callie says. "Stokes—I mean, whoever took Lori—they cut the screen to get inside."

I rack my brain for this piece of information; the window

154

wasn't in any of the trial transcripts that were made public. I read them all. "Are you positive?"

"Yeah, we had to get it replaced before we sold the house," Callie says. "Think about it. Joslin wouldn't have cut Lori's window to get into her room."

"Because she knew where you guys kept the spare key," I say.

The Greenwoods hadn't gotten around to making Lori her own house key, but she came and went as she pleased, using the key hidden under a rock that Callie had painted. How many times had the four of us walked back from the pool together for lunch, Callie, Jos, and me cocooned in our towels as Lori stopped to get the key and let us inside when Maggie wasn't home?

"Jos could have just waltzed through the front door if she wanted to get into my house," Callie says. "It doesn't make any sense."

It's true; a slashed window screen does make it seem like a stranger got inside Lori's bedroom.

"Why didn't Lori close the window?" I ask Callie. "She knew we'd seen someone outside. . . . Why wouldn't she have locked the window if she was sleeping on the first floor?"

"We didn't have AC in the spare bedroom." Callie curls the end of a strand of hair around her fingertip. "It would have been too hot to sleep. Maybe she just didn't believe there was someone outside."

A thought occurs to me. "Or maybe she was expecting someone."

"Like a guy?" Callie frowns. "Lori had a boyfriend back at college."

I tilt back against the headrest and close my eyes. "Maybe it wasn't like that. She could have gotten mixed up with bad people while she was here."

Callie snorts. "Like, drugs people? *Lori* wasn't like that."

There's a silent *but* at the end of her sentence. *But your sister was.*

I don't know if Joslin did drugs. It would definitely explain her behavior in the months before she left town—she was moody, thinner, and coming home at all hours. But she was grieving over Lori. Jos was hiding something about the night Lori died. I never considered that something else was eating away at her too.

"Danny could've been a dealer," I wonder aloud. "My mom and Jos fought about her dating him, since he was a dropout and everything."

Callie's quiet as she considers this. Then: "If Lori found out Danny was a dealer, she would have freaked."

And he may have killed her to keep her quiet.

"Jos was supposed to be with Danny that night," I say. "Maybe he threatened Jos to make her stay quiet about what she knew about the murder. She could have left Fayette to get away from him."

Callie's quiet again.

"What?" I say. "You don't buy it?"

"It's not that I don't buy it," she says. "That would explain a lot of things, if they were involved somehow. But if it's true, and we find Danny . . . him not wanting to talk to us will be the least of our problems, you know?"

I do. But it doesn't mean I'm going to back off. If Danny is the person my sister has been running from all these years—if he killed Lori and I can prove it, somehow—she won't have to hide anymore.

My sister didn't kill Lori. I try the idea out. I want it to be true more than I've ever wanted anything else before.

My sister didn't kill Lori.

If I find out who did, maybe she'll finally come home to me.

156

CHAPTER SIXTEEN

We arrive back at the house undetected. Not long after I fall asleep, I wake up with a fierce pounding in my bladder. The cuckoo clock says it's ten after four. Across the hall, I hear the shower. Rick, getting ready for work. I wait for the sound of the bathroom door opening and Rick padding back into his bedroom, but it doesn't come.

I can't hold it anymore. I have to use the toilet downstairs.

There's a light on in the kitchen. When I finish up in the bathroom, I see Maggie sitting at the table, her head in her hands. She looks up at me and blinks. I smell muffins. The timer on the stove ticks.

"Are you baking?" I ask her. *At four in the morning?*

Maggie rubs her eyes. The skin around them is pink and raw. "Couldn't sleep. Thought I'd get something ready to drop off at the Kouchinskys'."

I sit in the seat next to her. She covers my hand with hers, clutches me like we're teetering at the top of a roller coaster. "This brings back awful memories."

I remember Maggie shouting at Rick when they got home that night, after he knocked on Lori's bedroom door and didn't get an answer. *What do you mean Lori's* gone? I remember Maggie and Rick frantically putting together a MISSING flyer with Lori's picture on it. They hadn't even gotten the chance to print it out before the police found her body.

"Do you remember her at all?" Maggie whispers. I know she means Lori, not Ariel. I nod.

"She loved the mornings." Maggie smiles. "Couldn't sleep past six. It was inhuman."

A flicker of a memory in my head: Lori in her shiny black leggings and lime-green gym shirt. Bangs pulled off her face with a white headband. She ran every morning, even in the rain. Maggie hated that she insisted on going alone. Lori would brag about how she went jogging in Philadelphia all the time, and Philly was much more dangerous than Fayette.

And maybe that was why he chose Lori, if it really was the Monster and not someone she knew. Maybe that was why he chose all of them, and left their bodies in plain sight, to show that he'd taught them a lesson. *You think you're safe, but you're not.*

Maggie takes her hand back from me. She leans forward on the table and rests her chin on the heel of her hand. "My sister had a difficult time after her husband's death. That's why Lori started spending her summers here. The drinking . . . Our father had a problem."

She catches herself. Closes her mouth. I can tell this is the closest Maggie will get to acknowledging the incident with the vodka bottle under Callie's bed. The numbers displayed on the oven timer count down from one minute.

"I worry about Callie," Maggie says. "I know it must seem

to you like she's had an easy life, but she doesn't deal with disap-pointment well. She cried for days when you left."

I imagined hearing something like this from Maggie some day, and I always expected it to make me feel better about Callie abandoning me. Instead, I feel an inexplicable tug of longing for my own mother. She worried about Joslin and me so much that as the years went by, it seemed like her worry whittled away at her body, taking away her curves and the soft parts where I used to lay my head when I was a toddler.

I wonder if Annette worries about me still, wherever she is now, and if when I find her, there will be anything left of my mother.

• • •

I climb back into bed after my conversation with Maggie but never fall asleep. When it's a godlier hour, I head downstairs, no-ticing that Callie's door is open and her room is empty.

She's not in the kitchen either, where Maggie is arranging the now-cooled muffins on a plate.

"Morning, sweets."

"Hi," I say around a yawn. "Where's Callie?"

"On Tuesdays she works at the studio," Maggie says. "A pre-K twirling camp. She'll be home by noon."

I don't want to wait for Callie to get home before I stop by Joe Faber's ex-wife's house. I was hoping to catch the woman on her way to work—if the former Mrs. Faber works. If I miss her, I'll have to wait for her to get home.

Maggie drains what's left in her coffee mug and sets it down. "Once I shower, I'm going to bring these over to the Kouchinskys, if you want to tag along."

Something locks up in me. I think of the way I couldn't even go up to Ariel's family after the funeral, and I feel a flush of shame.

I stumble over my words. "I—I was going to call Gram back. . . ."

It's not a lie, sort of. She's left two voice mails since yesterday morning.

"Oh, good," Maggie says. "I was wondering when you'd talk to her. I'm sure she's worried about you."

I smile and head upstairs, trying not to be unnerved by the fact that Maggie noticed I haven't spoken with Gram all week. I don't want to think about what else she's noticed.

The guilt follows me as I sneak out into the garage to get Callie's bike once Maggie gets into the shower. Guilt, guilt, guilt. I feel guilty for lying to Maggie on top of everything I've been keeping from her. I'm guilty for avoiding my Gram.

Sometimes I think guilt is the only thing I'm capable of feeling.

• • •

I see the church first. It's a sad-looking old thing, its windows busted and burned at the edges. Takes a certain person to live across the street from that for fifteen years and never complain about the place not being knocked down.

Across the street from the church, there's a house with a chain-link fence that extends to the edge of the property; if you want to park in the driveway, you have to get out of the car and open the gate. There's a pickup truck with New Jersey plates parked half on the lawn, half on the gravel.

I glance inside the mailbox; on the top of the stack is a Buy 'N Bulk flyer addressed to Melissa Lawrence.

Barking. A screen door slamming. A woman screams at me from the porch. "I told you to leave the paper at the gate and be done with it."

Two very large dogs gallop toward me, their jaws flapping, drool flying everywhere. They stop short of the gate. Off to the side, there are three empty steel bowls. Two dogs. Three bowls.

I freeze, but not because of the dogs, who are throwing themselves up against the chain link. The woman is coming down the driveway, gravel crunching beneath her hunting boots.

Melissa Lawrence is, if you're polite, what you'd call "a woman who can handle herself." I'm not polite, so I'm thinking that Melissa Lawrence is the type of woman who will break your nose for looking at her the wrong way.

"Are you deaf?" she snarls at me, her dogs circling her feet. One stands on his hind legs, puts his paws on Melissa's chest. She doesn't even flinch under his weight—just pushes him down and picks up a gnarled rawhide the size of my head and chucks it across the yard. The dogs bolt after it, body slamming each other to get ahead.

Melissa looks me up and down. Doesn't see me holding pamphlets or a clipboard. Puts her hands on her hips.

"I don't know you," she says.

"I'm looking for Joe Faber," I say.

Melissa glares at me with freaky, bulging eyes. "Someone's seen him around?"

"No. I was hoping you had."

Melissa lets out a hollow, phlegmy laugh. "Joey knows not to come within ten miles of me. What's this about?"

"A guy—man—named Danny," I say. "He worked for Joe's landscaping company."

"Yeah, I knew Danny. Friends with Joe's boys." Melissa's voice has hardened. It makes me nervous, but still, there's a flicker of hope in me at having a link to Danny.

"Do you know his last name?" I ask.

"Never had reason to ask. They'd bring their girls around and head off to the barn."

"Was one of them this girl?" I unfold the picture of Lori that I clipped from the *Gazette* article. Melissa looks down at it. Her face darkens.

"You think I don't know who that is?" She gives a body-shaking cough, spits the refuse on the ground. "Yeah, I seen her before."

"Here?" I ask. "Lori was here?"

Melissa nods. "Once or twice, with that scrawny piece of jail-bait Danny was messin' around with. They were partying in the barn one night, and the blonde got upset and left. Never saw her again after that."

"The other one"—I can't bring myself to say my sister's name—"she didn't go with her?"

"She tried to get her to stay, but the blonde was all shook up," Melissa says. "Probably Tommy or Mike made a pass at her. Knowing them."

"Where are they now?" I ask. "Joe's sons?"

The look on Melissa's face says that I've worn out my welcome. "Joe moved 'em out of state. That's what I told the police, and that's all I know."

The police. They questioned the Fabers after Lori's death? As far as I knew, Wyatt Stokes was the only person of interest they ever focused on. Melissa starts to head back up her driveway.

"Please," I call out. "I'm looking for my sister. Danny's girl-friend."

I'm sure she'll keep walking and ignore me, but Melissa stops. What comes out of her mouth is even more surprising.

"Your sister's trouble," she says. "They all are. Don't come around here asking about them again."

She yells for the dogs, and they follow her inside the house. Out of the corner of my eye, I see the curtains in the window rustle. I think she watches me as I leave.

• • •

Maggie's gone when I get back, still at the Kouchinskys', I guess. I have a text from her that says she left a key on a ledge in the shed for me, with strict instructions to hold on to it once I'm inside. The house is quiet, except for the purr of the air-conditioning unit in the living room.

I pour myself a glass of iced tea and suck it down in one breath. Then I wash the glass, dry it, and put it back in the cupboard so there's no evidence I was in the kitchen, even though Maggie has told me hundreds of times I'm welcome to whatever I'd like.

I sit in the office chair and turn the computer on. As it hums to life, I take the now wrinkled picture of Lori that I tore out of the *Gazette* article out of my pocket and set it on the desk tray.

I don't have Danny's last name, but now I have two others—Tommy and Mike Faber. A search for their names and *Fayette* turns up their photographs. Or rather, mug shots.

Thomas J. Faber and Michael E. Faber of Fayette, Pennsylvania were arrested nine months before Lori Cawley's murder and served thirty days for drug-related charges. The link accompanying the photos doesn't work.

I search for both of the Faber boys' names along with Lori's name. If the police checked out the Faber family, one of the Cyber

163

Sleuths would have gotten wind of it. There would be an entire forum dedicated to dissecting Tommy and Mike Faber's pasts and possible roles in Lori's murder.

But nothing turns up—even when I search directly in the forum archives. I try Cyber Sleuths, Crime Watchers, and Justice for Stokes, a site just for discussing the Monster case, before I'm out of ideas.

The day after Lori was murdered, a bunch of tips came in about a man who lived a few blocks away from the Greenwoods'. Some people had seen him driving up and down the street that morning, as if he'd been canvassing the houses. The cops cleared him after they talked to him and found out he was searching for a cat that had snuck out.

Still, the message boards are flooded with comments that the police should have looked at the guy more. They found out his name, and that he was a registered sex offender. His freshman year of college, he'd been caught in the backseat of a car with his high school girlfriend.

He should have been a suspect, the sleuths argued. They found the number to his workplace and posted it.

The man lost his job and eventually moved away from Fayette.

So if the police questioned the Faber boys about their involvement with Lori Cawley, they managed to do it without anyone finding out.

I erase the history of my searches and shut down the computer. I suppose I really should stop being an asshole and call my grandmother.

There are some things I need to ask her, anyway.

I head upstairs as I call the condo, because the chill from the

AC on the first floor makes the hair on my arms stand on end. Gram picks up on the last ring before the answering machine would kick in. She's wheezing, like she was outside in the garden maybe and had to run to catch the phone.

I feel bad, because Gram used to be terrible at picking up her phone and would take days to call people back. Then when I got to the eighth grade, I went through this phase where I thought she was dead all the time, and it was a whole big thing.

If I got home from school and Gram wasn't home, I'd freak out and call her cell a thousand times, even though it was always either not charged or in the junk drawer in the kitchen. I'd knock on every door in the complex asking if anyone had seen her, and turn on the cable news channel in search of horrific car accidents.

One time she came strolling down the block, smiling, her pockets full of smooth white stones from the bay. She'd decided to take a walk, even though she'd never once before taken a walk in all the years I'd lived with her.

I screamed at her, "What's the point of a frigging cell phone?"

A few months after that, when I wouldn't stop sulking, she brought me to a child psychologist. The unofficial diagnosis was anxious-insecure attachment, with mildly depressive tendencies. They put me on five milligrams of Lexapro. "Not enough to knock a terrier out," I heard Gram whisper on the phone to her friend June in Albany.

"Nice of you to call back," Gram grunts, but I know she's not really mad.

"Hi," I say.

"Quiet without you here," she says, which is supposed to be funny, because I barely even make noise when I fart.

"What have you been up to?" I ask.

"Oh, nothing. I've become one of those old people who waits for the mail every day." Gram pauses. "Would have thought you'd be anxious to get home."

"I am." I pause. "Can I ask you something?"

"Sure."

I sit on the bed and pull my legs up so I'm sitting pretzel-style. "Have you heard from my mom?"

Gram's labored breathing fills my receiver. "You know I would've told you if I had. Nettie and I have our differences, but it's not my place to keep your mother from you."

I nod, even though Gram can't see me, and trace the paisley pattern on the bedspread with my finger. "What about my sister? Did she ever contact you?"

"Tessa." There's a warning in my gram's voice. "I don't think sticking around that town is good for you. Sounds like it's bringing back some painful memories that you'd be better off leaving behind."

"Ten years, Gram," I say. "Ten years and we haven't heard a thing from them. Don't you think that's weird? That maybe they're in trouble, or worse?"

"I don't know what you want me to tell you," Gram says, her voice heavy.

I grip my phone. Gather my nerve. "I want you to tell me who Joslin's father is."

"I told you, Tess. He didn't want anything to do with her."

"She came to see him," I say. "Joslin came to see Glenn before he died. I can't find her, but maybe she tracked down her real father too. He could know where she is."

Gram sighs, a heavy, *I'm too old for this* sigh. "Honey, your heart's in the right place, but it's gonna get broken if you keep this up."

166

My chest clenches. Gram rarely calls me honey—her stubborn refusal to use pet names is proof, in her own mind, that she really does love me. It's just how she is. *Honey* is not a sign of affection. *Honey* is a word of warning.

And it's not going to work on me anymore.

"I never ask you for anything," I tell Gram, even though it cuts me up inside to play that card. "Please, for the love of God, just tell me who Joslin's father is."

Gram pauses. "Hold on."

I hear her screen door slamming on the other end. There's rustling, and I can see her as I've seen her a thousand times before, sitting in her rocking chair and using one foot to push back and forth off the porch as she rifles through her carton of cigarettes.

"Annette was nineteen," Gram says. "She came to me so excited, like she was busting with good news. . . . When she said she was pregnant, I just . . . I didn't act how she'd hoped I would. I told her a baby would change her life and she better think long and hard about whether she was gonna keep it."

Gram sucks in a breath. There's a pause. I'll bet anything, she's lighting up. "The father was older. Was supposed to leave for a job on an oil rig in Louisiana. I asked your mother if that's what she really wanted in life, to be alone with a baby in a one-bedroom apartment while he spent thirteen-hour days on the rig. But she went anyway."

"You told me this," I say gently, because sometimes her memory is bad. "And that's the last time you talked to her."

Gram exhales, and I picture the smoke tendrils coming out of her nose. "Yeah, I know. Except she called me a few months after."

I freeze. This isn't the version Gram always told before. "What are you talking about?"

"She was hysterical. Wanted me to go down to see her. She'd lost the baby."

Lost. As in, died. The baby wasn't Joslin.

"I told her to come home," Gram says. "I begged, Tess, and you know I don't do that. But she wanted to make it work with Alan, even though he hadn't been happy about the baby to begin with. She was devastated, and he was relieved."

Gram sucks in a breath. "I guess when she got pregnant again, with your sister, things got a whole lot worse. By that point she was done talking to me because she didn't like what I had to say."

My mother lost a baby. I might have had another sibling—or, maybe that baby would have been enough for Annette and I never would have been born at all, had he or she lived. I always felt as if Joslin and I were never enough for our mother—that we never measured up to what my mother thought having children would be like.

But now that I know about the first baby, it seems like we never had a chance at all.

"Do you remember Alan's last name?" I ask.

"Oh, Tessa. It was twenty-five years ago. Of course I don't remember."

If she'd hesitated just half a second less, maybe I'd be able to believe her.

• • •

At ten after twelve, I hear the front door close. I head downstairs, where Callie is dumping her gym bag onto the living room couch. She's in black spandex shorts and an East Stroudsburg University T-shirt. She's always wearing ESU stuff, like the clothes are constant reminders that her time in Fayette has an expiration date.

They're reminders to me too. All of this is going to come to an end. I can't spend the entire summer in Fayette, and if we don't get answers soon, I'll be going back to Florida with more questions than I had when I came.

"Hey," Callie says after a swig from her water bottle. "Where's my mom?"

"At the Kouchinskys'," I say. "She left a couple of hours ago."

"She's probably helping Ari's mom clean the house and stuff, knowing her," Callie says. "Which probably means Daryl isn't there. He'd never allow that."

Something occurs to me as I picture Maggie scurrying around the Kouchinskys' kitchen, washing dirty dishes and taking inventory of the fridge before Daryl gets home.

"Do you think he knew about Ari?" I ask. "The online stuff."

Callie shakes her head. "Daryl would have killed—" She comes to a full stop. "That's crazy. She was his *daughter.*"

"I know," I say. "But, I mean, there had to be a reason the Monster started killing again after all these years. If he found out his own daughter was one of those girls . . ."

Callie snorts. "Daryl Kouchinsky, the Monster?"

"I don't know," I say, feeling crabby. "It's not like we have any other real suspects."

"What about Danny?" Callie takes another swig from her water. "Did you find his last name?"

"No, but I found Joe Faber's ex-wife," I say. "I saw her this morning. She still lives in town, across from the abandoned church."

Callie almost spits. "The crazy lady with the rottweilers?"

"Yeah. Her." I sit in Rick's armchair. "Do you remember two guys who may have hung around Jos and Lori? Tommy and Mike Faber. Danny's friends."

Callie shakes her head. "Lori didn't spend time around guys when she was here."

Not because the guys weren't interested in her. They were. But Lori had a boyfriend, a guy from Delaware who lived in her dorm building freshman year. An engineering major. She called him every night before bed that summer, and was always talking about how she was going to take a road trip to see him at the end of July.

"Joe Faber's ex-wife says that Lori came to their house once with Jos." I tell Callie the story about Lori leaving alone and upset. Joslin *letting* her leave alone and upset.

When I see Callie's face, the full weight of my sister's betrayal hits me. Jos chose Danny over Lori—Danny and his dirtbag friends who had done something to make Lori feel unsafe.

But it's the part about Melissa Lawrence bringing up the police that disturbs Callie the most.

"The Fabers just left town? And no one thought it was a big deal?"

"They had people covering for them," I say. Possibly, one of them was my sister. "The Fabers were arrested for drug stuff here," I continue. "Danny could have been too. I think we should go to the police station and see if it's public record."

Callie frowns. "As in, the Fayette police station."

"We won't say anything about the murders," I say. "As far as they know, we're only interested in information that can help us find a runaway."

Callie's lips part. "Joslin."

• • •

The South Fayette Township precinct is a box-shaped building the color of sand with two entrances, one for booking people who

170

have been arrested, and one for the police department. I direct Callie to park by the latter and notice that her knuckles are white on the steering wheel. The last time we were here, we sat separately in cold rooms for hours, sipping apple juice as the detectives took down our statements.

A chill creeps up my spine.

"We're just asking about my sister," I tell Callie. "You don't have to do any talking."

"Okay."

But I can't ignore the acrid taste in my mouth. If there were any way around talking to the cops, of course I'd take it.

The lobby is just big enough to serve its primary purpose—accommodating people making complaints about their asshole neighbor using a leaf blower before eight a.m., or reports about stolen car radios. It's completely nonthreatening, all white walls and linoleum. There's a map of Fayette County on the wall next to the chairs in the waiting area. And a soda machine.

I gesture for Callie to sit while I go to the desk. There's no one here. Just an abandoned Tupperware holding the soggy remains of a salad. A radio behind the desk blips, followed by unintelligible garble.

Then laughing. Two men. I turn to the corridor adjacent to the desk. The laughing is coming from a room down the hall, not the radio. A young guy wanders to the front desk, carrying a manila folder and chuckling to himself. He stops short when he sees me.

"Help you?"

"I need to talk to someone about a missing person."

"Are you here to file a report?" he says, a white piece of gum flicking over his tongue.

I hesitate. "No. I'm following up on one."

"How long ago?"

"Um. Ten years."

The guy blinks at me, not quite knowing what to do with that. Up close, I see how young he really is. Red bumps dot his jawline. He can't be more than a couple of years older than me. Whatever hope I had of finding someone who will take me seriously deflates. He's not even looking at me, but is staring over my shoulder.

"Callie?" he says, looking surprised.

I turn around; Callie has sunk so low in her seat, it looks like she's melting. Trying to disappear.

"Hey, Eli," she says, not unkindly. He's smiling. She's not.

"Long time no see," Eli says. "What're you doing here?"

"Just helping Tessa. She's looking for her sister." Callie says the last part slowly, deliberately. Eli's eyes flick back to me.

"Ah, yeah," he says. "I'm just the paperwork guy. I'll let one of the officers know you're here."

Eli disappears down the hall, and I sit next to Callie, who's flipping through a year-old issue of *U.S. News & World Report* without actually reading any of the pages. She sets it aside and takes out her phone. I'm not sure if my head is thrumming or if it's just the sound of the soda machine. I focus on reading the topics of the pamphlets positioned around the waiting room. "Rape Aggression Defense Training." "High-Risk Drinking." "Safety Tips for Students." String them all together and they tell a horror story.

"Who's Eli?" I ask Callie.

"Ryan's friend. He graduated a year before us." She doesn't look up from her phone.

"So what's the big deal?"

Callie shifts in her seat. "I don't want it getting out that we were here."

She means she doesn't want it getting back to Maggie.

There's talking in the hallway. We look up; a plainclothes officer is escorting someone to the lobby.

"Someone here waiting to see me?"

It's a booming male voice. Next to me, Callie has her head bent over her phone.

When I look up, I see why. The voice belongs to Charlie Volk, the detective who arrested Wyatt Stokes and told our parents that Callie and I could help put him in jail.

CHAPTER SEVENTEEN

Charlie Volk locks eyes on me and makes a sweeping *Come on back* gesture. His hair is white now. His dress shirt was probably white before he sweated through it. My knees feel weak in my seat. *Get up, Tessa.*

I force myself to stand and look down at Callie, who's frozen in her seat. There's no way she's moving. I follow Volk down the hall. He wheezes and tries to figure out how to navigate with the extra twenty pounds he's put on since the last time I saw him. He doesn't look back at me, and it hits me: he doesn't know who I am.

"Sit, sit." Volk herds me into his office. I sink into the chair across from his desk, my heartbeat hammering in my ears. He balls up a greasy napkin and tosses it into the Burger King bag on his desk before sweeping it aside.

I read that Charlie Volk was being forced into retirement after all the blowback from *Unmasking the Monster*. The filmmakers portrayed him as a stubborn, bumbling cop past his expiration date who couldn't admit he was wrong about Stokes.

There was something in the papers about a lawsuit—Charlie

Volk standing behind his role in the Monster case and refusing to be bullied into taking his pension and shutting his mouth. Something about a settlement . . .

. . . and Volk being relegated to desk duty.

Crap.

"So. Missing person." Volk plops into his chair, the leather giving a little *pft* under him. He reaches for his computer mouse, knocking over a picture frame with his elbow. "Damn it."

He replaces the frame, and I can't tear my eyes away. The picture is of Volk, two girls, and a woman. One of the girls is in a graduation cap and gown. The sash says *University of Virginia*.

My daughter's Lori Cawley's age. Lots of us on the force have daughters. This case is personal to us.

Suddenly, I am eight again and I can smell Charlie Volk's turkey-and-mustard sandwich breath in my face. *Just tell me everything that happened that night, sweetheart. There aren't any wrong answers.*

Except there was a wrong answer, and we knew it. Our stories had to match. If my testimony didn't match Callie's, the man who had hurt Lori would get away with it.

What about his face? Was it someone you'd seen before, Tessa? It's important that you tell us if it was.

Volk knew Callie had woken me up and told me it was the man from the pool. When one of the other officers called for a detective to question me at the station, Volk told them not to bother, he'd do it himself.

This asshole knew exactly what he was doing, using Callie and me to get an arrest warrant for Stokes.

I feel like I could vomit all over his desk.

I've been quiet for too long. Charlie Volk squints at me. "You look awful familiar."

"My name is Tessa Lowell."

Charlie Volk takes off his glasses. Wipes the sweat from his nose. "Tessa Lowell. I'll be damned."

"I'm looking for my sister, Joslin," I say.

Charlie Volk just stares at me. "Sorry. This is just a kicker, seeing you all grown up. Tessa . . . little Tessa L."

I swallow hard. "My sister?"

"Right, right." Volk shakes his mouse, and his computer hums to life. "When was the last time you saw her?"

"She ran away when she was seventeen. She'd just broken up with this guy. He may have a record," I say. "Danny something."

Volk lifts his glasses off his nose and peers at the screen. "Do you mean Danny Densing? Says here that we booked him for possession in '06."

Danny Densing. "How did you— He came up when you searched my sister's name?"

Volk scrolls down the screen. "The Arnold police had us question him about an incident over in their town. Looks like Joslin Lowell was his alibi."

Arnold. Any other day the name wouldn't have meant anything to me. All I'd ever known about Arnold was that it was a place you didn't want to be caught in alone. But the other day at the library, I saw the *Gazette* cover story about a meth house that exploded there the night of Lori's murder.

My sister told the police that Danny was with her. He must have asked her to lie for him, because he was involved in the explosion somehow.

And without knowing it, he gave Joslin an alibi for Lori's murder.

"The meth lab explosion," I say. "They think Danny had something to do with it, right?"

Volk frowns. "I can't say. It's still an open investigation. Two other persons of interest fled the state, and we don't have enough evidence to extradite them."

I'll bet everything he's talking about Tommy and Mike Faber. So it's possible the cops never looked at them for Lori's murder at all, and Melissa Lawrence assumed I was asking about their involvement in the explosion.

Had Lori found out that they were cooking the meth that caused the house to explode? Did they have to kill her to shut her up?

"Your sister was mixed up with some bad people," Volk says, echoing my thoughts. "How come no one ever reported her missing?"

The blood flowing to my head slows. "What?"

Volk frowns, runs his finger down the scroll button on his mouse. "If someone filed a report, it'd be right here."

Anger flashes through me, leaving me feeling raw and ready for a fight. I wish my mother were here right now, so I could shake her by the shoulders until she tells me why she didn't report my sister—her *daughter*—missing, after she told me that the police would find Joslin and bring her home.

Where are you two? I feel the words rising in me like bile, as if the only way I'd feel better would be to scream them out.

Where are you, and what the hell are you hiding?

•   •   •

I don't stop in the lobby for Callie; I walk right past the front desk, past Eli's limp wave goodbye, and out the front door. Callie storms out after me.

"What happened?"

"Let's go."

She trails after me. Unlocks the car. I buckle my seat belt and stare straight ahead. Callie starts the engine and blasts the AC, but stops there.

"What happened?" she asks again.

"I got his name. Danny Densing."

"You know what I mean," she says. "Did Volk remember you?"

"Yeah. But he didn't say anything about Stokes." I make a fist to stop my hand from trembling. "No one reported my sister missing."

Callie is speechless. "Have you . . . thought about trying to find your mom?"

I would rather die than tell Callie that I have tried to find her, and the only clue I have came from a six-year-old in a trailer park. I put my face in my hands.

I'm not prepared for what Callie does next—she rests her fingertips on my shoulder. The words come out of me in a single breath: "I don't like people touching me."

Callie jerks her hand away as if she's been burned. "Sorry."

She squashes her hands between her knees.

I shut my eyes. "We have to find Danny first," I say, because what's the alternative? *My mother is hiding from the Monster.*

Besides, how could my mother be helpful? The moments leading up to her driving us to that gas station ten years ago—rarely coming out of her room after my father was sentenced, not reporting Joslin missing—point to one conclusion.

My mother had been gone long before disappearing from my life.

"Joslin told the cops that she was with Danny the night Lori was murdered," I say. "They think he and the Fabers were involved in a meth lab explosion."

Callie mulls this over. "So if your sister wasn't really with Danny, then what was she doing?"

"I don't know, but hopefully Danny does." I pause. "What are the chances a guy who's evading felony drug charges is in the phone book?"

Callie snorts. The knot in my throat loosens a little. She puts the van in gear and pulls out of the parking lot. *Danny Densing.* I imagine writing the name inside my wrist with a pen, even though I could never forget it, now that I've heard it.

We make a detour to CVS, because Callie needs to pick up her prescription. While Callie waits in line at the pharmacy, I weave up and down the aisles, even though I don't need to buy anything. I'm just tired of standing around, taking up space. I make a game out of trying to guess what kind of medications Callie is on. Happy pills like the ones Gram used to have me take, maybe.

I see the girl at the cash register in the front, buying a can of that radioactive Gatorade stuff you give to little kids when they're puking their brains out. I almost think it's her, which of course it isn't, because she's dead. Ariel. Ariel, who was always red-mouthed from a cold and sniffling, obliviously touching you right after she wiped her nose.

I watch Katie Kouchinsky from the cosmetics aisle, until Callie's voice comes from behind me.

"What are you doing?" She freezes when she sees Katie. It seems like neither of us is going to acknowledge her, until Katie collects her change, turns around, and locks eyes with me.

"Hi," she whispers. Katie's voice was always the biggest difference between her and her sister. Ariel had a voice that made teachers cringe—she never seemed to realize how loud she was being, even when she was talking about something potentially embarrassing, like buying a training bra.

Katie was quiet. Still a thumb-sucker at seven, which is when I saw her last, before the funeral yesterday.

"Hey," Callie says gently. Katie looks like she's stepped into quicksand. She doesn't move as we approach her.

"I'm so, so sorry," Callie keeps talking. "I meant to tell you in person—yesterday."

"It was hard for all of us," Katie says, in a way that's obvious she doesn't consider Callie part of *us*. Callie looks hurt; I don't envy her. That's the best part of being on the outside—you never have to wonder where you stand with people.

"I've got to go," Katie says quickly. "It was nice seeing you."

"Wait," Callie says. "Did you tell the police Ari was with you the day she went missing?"

The color leaches from Katie's face. "How did you—"

Callie lowers her voice. "Nick says she was with him."

"You talked to Nick? When?"

Callie takes a step toward Katie. "You're not going to help your sister by lying."

Katie flinches. I know Callie doesn't mean to be cruel; there has always been a cold, matter-of-factness to her when she wants something. *You have to be the stepsister, Tessa, because I look like Cinderella and you don't.*

Tears dot Katie's eyelashes. "I was just doing what she asked me to. You have no idea what my dad will do if he finds out I lied about that too. I've got to go."

Callie rests her hand on Katie's forearm. Katie is limp under her touch.

"We know about the website," Callie whispers. "I know you do too. She might have told you something that could help the cops find her killer."

"But they think Nick did it." Katie blinks. "The cops were at his house this morning, searching for whatever he used to do it."

I freeze. Whatever the cops are looking for at Nick's house, it's not a murder weapon. "What did they tell you about how she died?"

"Not much." Katie wipes the area under her eye. "They can't, because it could mess up their investigation."

A weapon. Katie thinks that her sister's killer shot or stabbed her—the police haven't even told Ariel's family that she was strangled.

I open my mouth, but Callie jabs me with her elbow.

"Katie, I heard something about Ari," Callie says. "That she may have met up with a guy before she died . . . Did she tell you she was scared of any of the men from the website?"

Katie shakes her head. "She was so careful about who she picked. She said they were just lonely, and nice. One didn't even want to have sex with her."

"Did she say anything else about that guy?" Callie asks.

"No. Now I *really* have to go." Katie pulls the handle of her plastic bag tight over her wrist. "I'm not supposed to talk about Ari to strangers."

Katie pushes past us, and we watch her disappear through the automatic doors. The look on Callie's face is determined, as if Katie calling her a stranger had rolled right off her.

"You think that guy could be the Monster?" Callie asks me.

"None of the girls were raped," I say. "Think about it."

Callie is quiet as we step through the doors—just in time to see Katie getting into a pickup truck idling at the parking lot curb. The passenger window is down, giving us a full view of Daryl Kouchinsky behind the wheel.

He looks at Katie, then back at us. His jaw sets. Before he pulls away from the curb, he says something to his daughter that makes all the color drain from her face.

CHAPTER EIGHTEEN

One look from Daryl Kouchinsky has done something to Callie. Unscrewed an already loosened bolt.

"Maybe you were right about him. Katie said she's not allowed to talk about Ari," Callie says, her voice shaking. "Maybe Katie knows something about her dad—she could have been acting when she pretended she didn't know who did it."

"I don't know." I buckle my seat belt, even though Callie shows no intention of leaving the CVS parking lot. "Could be Daryl doesn't want the other kids saying stuff that might wind up in the papers. Nothing in the news said anything about Ari being an escort."

"You know he would have hurt her if he'd found out what she was doing." Callie's expression sets as she starts the car. "He can't control himself. Remember the dog?"

I nod as Callie exits the parking lot and heads home. As a kid, I often wondered if Daryl Kouchinsky had ever killed a person. Some people wear their violence like weights around their neck. It was in the slump of his shoulders, the downward curve of his back.

There are people who like to hurt, and then there are people who just need a reason to. People who will kill their own daughters are the type that I would prefer to believe don't exist.

"Katie knew something more that she wasn't saying," Callie continues. "She's trying to protect her dad."

"Or she's trying to protect herself from him."

We don't say anything more for the rest of the ride. Callie pulls into the driveway and parks. The curtains in the window rustle. Maggie knows we're home. And she doesn't look happy.

"Did you ask if we could go out?" I say.

Callie hesitates. "I thought it would be better to apologize than ask permission."

"If she thinks I'm getting you into trouble, she's gonna send me away."

"Oh please." Callie shuts the car off. "You can do no wrong in her eyes. I need to know your secret."

There's a twinge of resentment in her voice. She doesn't know that it's not true. We all have a capacity for forgiveness, and maybe Maggie's is greater than the average person's.

But the secrets I've kept from her are unforgivable.

• • •

Callie and Maggie are having a heated discussion in the family room, so I can't get on the computer to search for Danny Densing. I figure I should comb through the rest of my dad's crap from the prison, see if he's left me any sort of clue I can use to track down my mother or Jos. I head up to the guest room and fish around the bag of his drawings until I find the one I'm looking for.

Bear Creek, 1986.

I could barely fill a shoebox with the things I know about my family's history. My father was one of five kids; all but one were half siblings. I met his brother once, when I was a toddler. He stayed with us for two days, then disappeared with a box of my mother's jewelry and the mason jar of quarters that Joslin had kept on her dresser.

They found his body in a Philadelphia crack house a year later. Pneumonia or something.

My father's father is dead. My father's mother, an obese woman in a floral housecoat, died when I was still an infant. One of our only surviving photos is of me on her knee, in her home in New Castle. Shortly after the photo was taken, she and my mother got into an argument, and my mother stopped letting my father bring us up there. Grandma Lowell died a couple years later.

And that's all I know about my father's family. *My* family.

Still, it's enough that I'm convinced the Lowells weren't the type of people who owned property; and if they did, my father definitely wasn't the type of person to keep a piece of information like that to himself. He was the type of man who'd brag to the garbage guy about the size of the dump he took that morning. He bragged about me too, to the scary men who came around the house.

That's my Tessy, right there. She's the smart one.

But it's possible my dad's family *did* own a place in Bear Creek, a really long time ago. They could have sold it before he even met my mother.

There's a tightening in my chest, like a rubber band being stretched from both ends. There's so much I'll never know about him—things I might have learned eventually, if I'd gotten the chance. If he'd stayed. If my mother hadn't done everything she could to erase him from our memories once he was gone.

Now it seems like the only way to get to her is through him.

The computer room is still occupied, so I call information on my cell, even though the service is, like, three dollars and Gram will shit herself when she sees the bill. I ask to be connected to Bear Creek's town clerk office.

The operator transfers me, and I sit through two piano versions of Beatles songs before someone picks up.

"Um, hi." I've forgotten how to speak, as I often do when I have to use the phone. "I was wondering if you had public records of a house in Bear Creek. A cabin."

"What's the owner's name?"

"Glenn Lowell."

The sound of typing. A sigh. I've bored her already. "Nothing with that name."

"What about anyone else with the last name Lowell?"

A pause. A sigh.

"Look, I'm gonna tell you something," the woman says. "There isn't much up the mountain. And the people who live there . . . You won't find an address, because there isn't one."

"What do you mean?"

"Squatters," she says. "Lots of abandoned cabins from when Bear Creek was a ski resort. People living in 'em, building more of 'em."

"That's allowed?" I ask.

"Course not, but we don't have the resources to police thousands of square miles of uncharted woods. As long as they don't cause no trouble, we don't send officers up there much."

Tax evasion. Illegal homes. Sounds right up the Lowells' alley. Now we're getting somewhere.

· · ·

Dinner tonight is tacos. While the smell of the meat cooking wafts up the stairs, Callie pokes her head into my room.

"Is she mad?" I ask.

She shakes her head. "Nah, I think we're good for a while. She agrees that getting out is good for coping with what happened to Ari."

Callie steps into the room. "I couldn't find anything on Denny Densing online. But I remembered I had this." Callie sets a Fayette High yearbook on the bed. It's open to a page of senior portraits. *Class of '03* is across the top.

"Why do you have this?" I ask.

"I did photography for the yearbook committee," Callie says. "The advisor gave me a box of old editions that go back to the eighties."

Adrenaline zips to my toes. *She could be in one of the candids.* My sister, hanging around the soccer field with friends, before she dropped out of school. Callie seems to sense my thoughts.

"Anyway, look." She points to a picture of a brunette with a big smile. Big, as in, *Look at my big teeth and big gums in all their glory.*

Anne Marie Jones. The quote she selected for beneath her picture is from *Sex and the City.*

"Remember her?" Callie asks.

I didn't really know Anne Marie Jones, other than that she was as boring as her name. Joslin didn't bring her around to the house, because we never brought friends over. And Anne Marie wasn't exactly a friend. She and Joslin worked at the bakery together.

Jos loved that job, even though it got her up at four-thirty in the morning. She worked the counter, weighing out butter cookies and tying up cake boxes in twine. She hoped her boss would eventually let her help with the baking and decorating. My sister always had steady hands, like a sculptor's. In the backyard she'd make fairies for me out of twigs and leaves, tying flower petal wings to their backs with grass as easily as if it had been thread.

"She went to the movies with Lori and Joslin a couple of times," Callie says.

Yes, she did, I realize. And Joslin complained about it because Anne Marie invited herself. Jos talked about Anne Marie as if being in a room with her had been a hostage situation, but Lori never turned down the opportunity to make new friends.

"Is she still around?" I ask.

Callie nods. "Apparently, she's Anne Marie Hahn now. As in, the Boathouse Hahns. Married their son or something."

I know better than to get my hopes up; Joslin didn't tell anyone why she was leaving or where she was going, least of all some clinger she worked with at a summer job. But if Anne Marie married into money—well, Fayette's version of money—she probably considers herself important. And important people tend to know things. Or at least they think they do.

• • •

Anne Marie Hahn lives in a two-story house that's not quite the McMansion she was hoping her husband would spring for. I can tell because as soon as Callie said she was Lori Cawley's cousin, Anne Marie welcomed us inside, beaming, shamelessly pointing out that she's "done okay" for herself when we complimented her home.

Two children are screaming their brains out in the living room off the foyer.

"Ugh, be right back," Anne Marie says. "Preschool ran only until June, so I have no help for the summer."

Callie makes a sympathetic clucking sound, while I wonder what the fuck kind of help a woman who doesn't work could possibly need. I stare at the wall to keep a straight face. It's painted sky blue, adorned in black decals proclaiming *Live. Laugh. Love.* Picture frames embossed with *Family.* Almost as if Anne Marie were trying to convince herself of something.

I must snort, because Callie glares at me. "I think it's kind of nice," she says.

In the living room, Anne Marie is setting up a Wiggles DVD for the boys. A DVD. Typical Fayette. No one even uses Netflix here.

Both kids are blond. Both under five. One stares at Callie and me, his upper lip curling at the sight of a stranger. The other whines for gummy sharks, and Anne Marie snaps that he can have them after lunch.

"Yeesh." She meets us back in the hall, her smile so wide and fake, I have to look away. "Gosh, you two are so grown up. Insanity."

Anne Marie suggests we sit "out back." She drops us at a patio table and hustles inside, then comes out minutes later with a carton of Minute Maid, cups, and two water bottles.

Anne Marie sets both elbows on the table. Rests her chin on her folded hands. I can't tell if she's staring at me or at Callie. Her bulging Pomeranian eyes are unfocused.

She clearly knows who I am, since she said *You two are so grown up,* but she hasn't acknowledged me directly.

"So how are you?" She beams again, like we're old friends shooting the shit. I look at the lemonade and the cups, and I feel bad for Anne Marie.

Callie looks at me.

"My father died," I say. *Pathos.*

Anne Marie's face softens. "I'm so sorry. Is there anything I can do?"

People who are grieving hate that question, I've heard. It's nothing more than a dumb platitude. But leave it to me to be that person who follows it up with, *Well, there's one thing . . .*

I clear my throat a little. "I'm trying to find my sister."

Anne Marie frowns. "I haven't heard from Joslin since she ran away."

"No one has," Callie cuts in. "That's why we're looking for Danny."

"Danny Densing?" Anne Marie's brow furrows in confusion, and she takes a sip of her lemonade. "But he and Joslin weren't seeing each other anymore when she left."

I knew this, of course; not that my sister would ever have told us that she and Danny had broken up, but I saw it in her face. In the months before she left, Danny would come by looking for Jos, but it seemed that every time, she'd still be at the bakery. Some nights she'd come home well past ten, claiming to be bone-tired and unwilling to talk about where she'd been.

Was she avoiding him because she was afraid? Did she know he'd been involved in the Arnold explosion, or worse?

"Do you know where Danny lives now?" I ask Anne Marie.

"Oh, God no," she says. "Last I heard he was working at a car dealership somewhere."

Anne Marie hands me a cup of lemonade. Before I can raise it to my lips, a gnat flies in. I set the cup down as she pours one for Callie, who is insisting she's not thirsty.

"Honestly, I thought that Joslin would come back, eventually," Anne Marie prattles on. "I mean, she talked about getting an apartment somewhere, and I'd be like, 'Jos, do you have any idea how much it costs to live on your own?'"

So my sister *did* tell someone she planned on leaving. I pick up the lemonade to distract my hands, then remember the gnat floating in it.

"I can't believe she'd just *leave* you like that." Anne Marie covers my hand with hers, but her eyes are still unfocused. "You were just a child."

So was Joslin, according to the law. "Yeah. It was rough."

Anne Marie shakes her head. "And after everything you two had been through, with the trial."

Callie shifts in her chair. "I actually wanted to talk a bit about Lori. I don't know how well you remember her—"

"Of course I remember her," Anne Marie says. "Lori was the absolute sweetest."

I don't miss the way her eyes flick toward me, almost like an accusation. *Lori was the sweetest. Joslin was not.* It makes me wonder if Anne Marie knows something about my sister that she's not saying.

"We're just . . . trying to make sense of what happened that summer," Callie says vaguely.

Anne Marie's eyes widen. "Oh, you poor things. You're worried about him getting out, aren't you?"

She leans over and covers both our hands with hers, as if we were eight, not eighteen. "He will never, *ever* be let out. He'll never be able to hurt anyone again."

Callie offers Anne Marie a wan smile. "Oh, we know. Lori was just . . . I still miss her a lot. It's nice hearing someone other than my family talk about her."

As it turns out, hearing herself talk is Anne Marie's favorite thing. And Lori has clearly achieved saintlike status in her mind.

"She was older than us, but she acted like an awesome kid, you know?" Anne Marie smiles to herself. "This new Disney-

Pixar movie came out, and she wanted to see it at midnight, and Jos and I were too embarrassed. So Lori was like, 'Screw you guys!' and went on her own."

Callie hangs on Anne Marie's every word, a hungry look on her face. I realize she wasn't lying when she said she likes hearing people talk about Lori. I know how it feels when you're missing someone—no story anyone can tell is enough. Even if someone's willing to talk about them forever, it wouldn't be enough.

Callie clears her throat. "Did Lori and Joslin ever fight?"

Anne Marie frowns. "I can't picture Lori fighting with any-one."

"Not even an argument?" I ask.

Anne Marie is quiet for a beat. "Well— I mean, I told this to the police when they asked if Lori seemed upset about anything before she died—"

"What did you tell them?" Callie sits up. Under the table, I slam my leg into hers, as if to say, *Shut the hell up.*

"Lori came to see Jos on her lunch break," Anne Marie says. "They were out back, and I heard them a bit when I went to throw out the garbage."

Anne Marie was eavesdropping on them. I'd bet my life on it.

"I didn't know what they were talking about, but Lori was upset, and Jos wouldn't listen to her," she says. "I think it had something to do with a boy."

"Danny?" I ask.

Anne Marie shakes her head.

"What about Mike, or Tommy?"

"No, I'm pretty sure it was Steven," Anne Marie says.

I look at Callie, who shrugs.

"Who's Steven?" I ask.

"I have no idea," Anne Marie says. "Jos and I didn't go to

school with anyone named Steven, so I assumed it was someone Lori knew from home."

It definitely wasn't Lori's boyfriend. His name was Chip. I remember, because when Lori told Joslin about him, Jos laughed so hard, I thought her spleen would explode—even though Lori insisted *Chip* was short for *Christopher* and he kind of looked like Matt Damon circa *Good Will Hunting*.

"And you're sure they were arguing?" Callie asks.

"I don't know. Maybe it was more like . . . disagreeing?" Anne Marie says. "They seemed okay the next day when they came in together so Jos could pick up her paycheck."

The screen door off the kitchen slams, and the younger boy—the one with *Cars* Pull-Ups peeking over the waist of his Baby Gap shorts, the one who stared at me and Callie earlier—toddles out. He climbs into Anne Marie's lap and jibbers something into her ear.

"What's wrong, pumpkin?" she asks him. The kid bursts into tears.

Callie tries to ask Anne Marie something, but her voice is drowned out by the baby's wails.

"I'm so sorry," Anne Marie shouts. "Someone needs a nap."

"It's okay; we should get going anyway," Callie yells back.

Anne Marie walk us out the backyard gate and down the brick walkway to the curb where we're parked. The boy is curled around her neck like a spider monkey, shrieking into her ear. The goodbye is short, frazzled.

As we pull away from the curb, I can't take my eyes off Anne Marie Hahn and her son. I watch her retreat back into her world of *live, laugh, love, family* and ignore the tugging in my chest.

CHAPTER NINETEEN

"Are you sure Steven isn't one of the Faber brothers?" Callie asks when we reach the main road.

I shrug. "Joe's ex-wife only said there was Tommy and Mike."

"Maybe Steven was someone Lori knew from back home," Callie murmurs.

"Then why would Lori and Jos be arguing about him?" I ask.

"We don't even know that they were arguing," Callie says. "How is Anne Marie supposed to know for sure after ten years?"

"You didn't hear Lori on the phone, Callie." I'm feeling especially crabby after that visit with Anne Marie Hahn for some reason. "Lori was pissed."

Callie grips the steering wheel. "All I'm saying is that it's been so long. I can't remember what I was doing on this day a week ago, and you're so sure Lori was fighting with Jos that night."

I turn my head and look out the window. "Some things, you just don't forget." *Even though I wish I could.*

· · ·

When we get back to the house, Maggie is watering the hydrangea bushes that circle the porch. She lowers the hose when she sees us. "Where'd you two go?"

"Luigi's," Callie says, plucking out the name of the Italian ice place up the road from the pool. The Greenwoods used to take Callie and me there all the time; one time was after Callie's twirling competition. She freaked out and refused to get out of the car because people would see her in full costume and makeup.

"We'd have brought you something, but it would have melted," Callie adds for effect before disappearing into the house.

I wind up helping Maggie water the rest of the plants so she can finish weeding before the three p.m. sun hits. When we're done, she starts prepping dinner in the kitchen. I sneak into the family room, where I saw the latest version of the yellow pages stacked next to the user manuals for the computer.

I figure no one will miss the phone book for a few hours. I abscond upstairs with it, hoping Maggie won't be up anytime soon to ask if I've made any plans to reschedule my flight.

The guest room is stifling, so I hate to close the door. At dinner last night, Rick talked about moving the AC unit from the family room into the guest room, so I wouldn't have to sleep with the window open every night. I insisted that he not go through the trouble and said I was fine, even though it feels like I'm cocooned in the folds of Satan's ball sack every night. I crank the fan to high and sit in front of it, the phone book opened in my lap to car dealerships.

There are three pages of numbers for dealerships in Fayette County alone. The county is huge, covering about thirty different townships. If Danny Densing were smart, he would have gotten out of the county completely.

But Danny was not smart when I knew him, and in my experience, dumb people get dumber as they get older. If he's managed to avoid charges for the Arnold explosion for this long, he probably thinks he's home free. I wouldn't be surprised if he's still in the county.

I call the first dealership, Brownsville Chevrolet, and am told that no one named Dan or Danny works there. When someone finally picks up at the fifth place on the list, I ask for Danny. Someone mumbles "Hold on" and transfers me. My stomach folds into itself.

The line clicks. "This is Dani," a woman says.

I hang up.

I lie on my back, hoping the purr of the fan will distract me from feeling like a black Lab left in the backyard all day. The skin on my nose is taut and burned; no doubt, my freckles have doubled. It's a good thing I'm not vain.

I pick up where I left off on the list of car dealerships. After almost two hours, I'm running out of numbers. The smell of sautéed onions has made its way upstairs. At some point, I heard Callie take a shower across the hall. A man picks up the phone.

"Bob speaking."

"I'm looking for someone named Danny."

"Got two of 'em here."

The floor seems to fall out from beneath me. I look down at the phone book, to where I'm holding my place with a finger. Smith's Nissan.

"'Lo?" Bob asks.

"Densing," I say. "Is one of them Danny Densing?"

A click. The bastard hung up on me. I hold my phone away from me, staring at the screen in disbelief, and notice that the call is still running. I put the phone back to my ear.

Ringing. He transferred me.

The phone rings and rings until I get an answering machine.

"Hey, this is Dan. I've had to step out, but if you leave me a message and your number, I'll get back to you as soon as I can."

The tone beeps. The blood in my body stops flowing, and I suddenly feel chilled to the bone.

I have to say something before the machine cuts me off. I recite my phone number and tell Danny that I need to speak with him about buying an Altima. I say that my name is Kelly.

My hands are still shaking long after I hang up. I thought it was impossible to be sure of anything having to do with this place anymore, but I know without a shadow of a doubt that the voice on the answering machine is Danny Densing's.

• • •

Maggie watches me a lot during dinner—probably because I have one hand in my pocket the whole time, on my phone, in case it rings. Rick is covering someone's shift, so it's just the three of us. When Callie's done eating, she announces that she's going to Sabrina's.

"You barely ate anything." Maggie frowns, but Callie is already up and grabbing her keys from the counter. Her hair is straightened, and her collarbone shimmers from a fresh coat of body cream.

She's not going to Sabrina's. She's going to Ryan's, no doubt. I picture them under his sheets. I wonder what it's like, letting someone in like that. Or if Callie uses hooking up to keep Ryan where she wants him.

Then I feel like a creep, and I stop.

"I'll be back in a couple of hours," Callie says. And, almost as an afterthought, she kisses Maggie on the cheek.

Maggie lifts a hand to her face, stunned.

"No more than that!" she calls after Callie, who's at the front door. "We have to be out of here by six-thirty a.m. at the latest."

The screen door slams, and Maggie turns to me. "The girls Callie coached this year have their USTA auditions in Pittsburgh tomorrow. You're more than welcome to come."

"United States . . . Twirling Association?" I offer.

Maggie smiles. Nods. "I know it doesn't sound that exciting, and it'll be a whole-day thing, but we can grab lunch in the city, explore a bit."

I push the corn kernels and lima beans around on my plate while this sinks in. The Greenwoods will be gone all day.

"I actually . . ." I set my fork down. "I have plans tomorrow. With an old friend."

Maggie cocks her head. "Who?"

"Decker Lucas?" I want to shrink in my seat. Not only am I lying to her, because Decker and I don't have plans—not yet, at least—but she probably thinks my embarrassment means we're going on a date.

"Oh," Maggie says, blinking with surprise. "Decker's a nice boy."

Maybe I'm imagining it, but her smile seems to flicker a bit as we turn our attention back to our plates. Almost like she doesn't believe me.

• • •

When I get back up to my room, I check my phone for any missed calls or voice mails, even though there's no way I wouldn't have felt it vibrate. I change into pajamas and settle into bed, my father's drawing of the cabin in Bear Creek balanced on my chest.

If Danny calls back—if he'll even talk to me once he realizes I'm not Altima-shopping Kelly—what are the chances he's been in touch with Jos in the past ten years?

My gut tells me that Jos found our mother; she didn't go to Deer Run looking for her. Possibly because Jos knew she wasn't there.

Joslin is older than me—old enough to remember my father's drawings of the cabin in Bear Creek. Maybe she'd even been there, before I was born.

The idea of driving two and a half hours to Bear Creek on a hunch that my mom may be there is nuts. Callie would tell me it's a complete waste of time.

I find Decker's number in my phone, thankful that I didn't delete it. I send him a text.

What are you doing tomorrow? This is Tessa.

A minute later, he responds. *NOTHING. WHY?*

I gnaw the inside of my cheek. Then: *Have you ever been to Bear Creek/do you want to go?*

NO/HELL YES!!!

I can't help the smile blooming on my face. I may have found someone as crazy as I am.

CHAPTER TWENTY

Decker offers to pick me up at the Greenwoods', but I insist on meeting him at the Quik Mart. I don't want him thinking this is a date or anything.

Admittedly, I've never actually been on a date, hence all the fretting about what constitutes a date and what doesn't. The closest I ever got was in the seventh grade. Frank Tricarico sat behind me in science class. He was a full two inches shorter than me and always wore his hair gelled down with that little flip thing in the front. On Valentine's Day he shoved a piece of folded loose-leaf paper at me and mumbled, "Someone told me to give this to you."

There were pen drawings of all nine planets, with the explanation that he'd included them because we were studying the solar system. And then the message *HAPPY VALENTINE'S DAY, TESSA!!!* plus a phone number, in Frank's handwriting.

I threw it into a Dumpster behind the school before I got onto the bus, thinking I would die if Gram ever found the card. For the rest of the year I was careful never to make eye contact with Frank, even when I had to pass handouts back to him.

I've never told anyone this, but sometimes I pretend there are two shrinks arguing in my head—one looks just like Dr. Marano, the woman Gram made me see when I was younger. Dr. Marano argues that I threw the card away because of my avoidant personality and inability to form meaningful relationships; the second shrink says I just didn't like Frank back.

I like the second one better.

Before I leave the Greenwoods', I add some air to Callie's bike tires with the pump I saw in the garage the other day. Just in case. I get to the gas station before Decker, so I buy two bags of Twizzlers and a bottle of iced tea from the convenience store. When he pulls into the space out front, I wave to him and he rolls down his window. When I hold up the candy for him to see, Decker lights up like a Christmas tree. He gets out of the car and helps me shove Callie's bike in his trunk.

I pop open the door and climb into the passenger seat of the old-looking car that was in Decker's driveway the other day. The leather is cracked inside and the dashboard is faded. "What kind of car is this?" I ask.

"It's a 1992 Chevy Monte Carlo," Decker says with pride. "It was my dad's."

"Cool." I run a finger along the seam on the side of my seat, trying not to think about the odds of making it to Bear Mountain in a car that's older than we are. Decker revs it out of the gas station parking lot; we hit the curb and bounce in our seats, my head almost hitting the ceiling. I close my eyes and try to relax once the sound of the engine evens out.

"The directions I printed said we should take the interstate." Decker scratches his neck. "I think."

He gestures toward my feet, where there's an old Taco Bell bag full of garbage and a piece of paper. I unfold it and scan the route to Bear Mountain; it's the same as the one I pulled off Google and wrote down this morning.

Decker gets onto the highway, and I settle back in my seat.

"I have gas money for you," I say. Courtesy of the ATM inside the store. The number in my checking account is down to double digits, which worries me, but with any luck I'll be out of Fayette and back to work soon.

Decker waves his hand dismissively—the hand that's not submerged in the Twizzlers bag. "Man, these are my favorite, which sucks because my mom never lets me eat anything with red dye."

"What's so bad about red dye?"

"PKU," Decker says, as if that were self-explanatory. I shrug, and Decker launches into the story of his birth, and how he was diagnosed with phenylketonuria, which meant he had to be on a super-strict diet or else he'd develop seizures or mental defects.

"Anyway, no one uses Red Dye Number Three anymore, but I'm pretty sure my mom thinks I'm not going to college because of that time I had M&M's at Kevin Bishop's birthday party in kindergarten."

I don't know if I'm supposed to laugh or not, but Decker is grinning.

"So what's in Bear Creek?" Decker sticks another Twizzler between his teeth and lets it dangle there like an absurdly long cigarette.

"My mom," I say. I feel it's only fair to prepare him for the possibility that this will all be a huge waste of time, so I add: "I think. I've been looking for her since I got here, and I found this drawing. I think my family has a cabin up there."

Decker looks enraptured, and not at all disturbed that we're taking a five-hour journey, round trip, because of a drawing and a hunch. "So we're kind of being PIs, or something?"

"Yeah." I smile. It feels good. "Exactly."

"*Sweet,*" Decker says. "This is so freaking sweet."

"You really don't mind?" I ask. "I'm sure you have a hundred better things to do."

"Nah, I didn't get that job at the bike shop," Decker says. "I'm not qualified."

He puts air quotes around that last part, and I laugh in spite of the growing knot in my intestines.

Even Decker can't possibly talk for the entirety of a nearly three-hour drive, though. An hour in, he runs out of steam and turns up the radio, lowering it when I need to read him the directions. Bear Mountain and the town of Bear Creek are a straight shot up north, west of the Alleghenies. I tried to pull up satellite images of the area, but even Google Earth was like, *I got nothing.*

After two hours, the rest stops on the freeway become obsolete. Pressure builds in my ears with the increasing elevation, and the radio reception starts to sputter out. Decker shuts it off.

"Eh, I haven't seen an exit in miles," he says. "Where in tarnation are we?"

"I'm going to pretend you didn't just say 'in tarnation.'" I look over the dark, pixelated map printed below the directions. Whatever town we're in now isn't on the map. I defer to the directions.

"We're supposed to get off at Wigwam Road," I say.

"There." Decker points to a sign about a quarter of a mile ahead. "That's gotta be it."

Decker slows and exits at the sign; there are no traffic lights to help us merge onto the main road. No other cars in sight. Just a lonely stop sign. Decker turns, and within half a mile the pavement runs into gravel, then dirt. We pass an abandoned gas station, with the old-style pumps that suggest it's been abandoned for at least thirty years.

"I think we were supposed to make a left at the main road," I say, after fifteen minutes of not spotting our next turn. My toes curl at the thought of getting lost up here with no cell phone signal.

"We can ask someone," Decker says brightly, as if we were in Pittsburgh and not the freaking boondocks.

We drive for miles before we see someone—an old man in a lawn chair in front of a clapboard house, trimming his nails with a pocketknife. Decker slows down, but there's no driveway to pull into, just grass and dirt. He shrugs and parks in the dirt.

The old man sets his pocketknife in his lap as we climb out of the car. "Well, you must be lost."

His accent is thick, Appalachian.

"We're trying to get to Bear Creek," Decker tells him.

The man sits up in his chair, like this just got interesting. "The hell for?" His gaze skates over me, then back to Decker. "You get her in trouble, and hiding from her daddy?"

He's looking at my baggy T-shirt. He thinks I'm knocked up. I pull it flat across my stomach, to make a point. "We're looking for someone." I wave a cloud of gnats away from my face, noticing the half-eaten pear at the man's feet. It's swarming with black bugs. "How do we get there?"

"Back that way," he says, almost as if it were one word. *Back-thataway*. "Where the main road splits, stay on that."

"Thanks, sir," Decker says. "We really appreciate it."

As we turn to get back into the car, the man clears his throat, and we stop.

"Y'all know what Bear Creek is?" He draws up a wad of phlegm and spits, narrowly missing the pear at his feet.

"The ski resort town?" I say.

The man rocks forward and lets out a hooting laugh. "Friendly word of advice. They don't much appreciate folks casually dropping in up there. Spooks 'em."

"Because they're squatters?" I ask.

"Least of their problems," the man mutters. "If you're hidin' out in Bear Creek, usually means you got nowhere else to go."

"Whoa." Decker looks at me. "Like, criminals and stuff?"

"Some." The old man picks up his knife and goes back to trimming his nails. "Just don't ask too many questions up there."

There's a pit in my stomach as we get into the car and pull away. Questions are all I have.

• • •

We head back west on the main road.

"There." I point at the fork in the road, a little panicked at how quickly it comes up. Decker has to slow to a stop for us to creep around the fork; the road is so narrow that low-hanging tree branches graze the side of the car.

The elevation climbs, slowly. I see a sign for a cabin rental community nestled in the trees. A sign advertises VACANCY and cash deposits.

"Is this it?" Decker slows to a stop in front of the sign. He sounds almost disappointed.

I twist around to get a better look out my window. A gravel driveway disappears into the trees, and I can see a few cabins. A woman stands over a barbecue on the nearest one's deck. Her back is turned to us, but I can see that she's hugging her arms around her waist.

Goose bumps run up my arms. The pose is familiar. Too familiar. My mother stood like that, waiting for me by the flagpole, the days she got out of her housecleaning job early enough to pick me up from school.

My stomach twists. The woman turns around, glares at us, and I let out my breath. She's not my mother.

"Keep going," I tell Decker. "Look up."

Decker lifts his gaze; in the distance, a mountain looms, its two smooth peaks like humps on the back of a camel.

"Still got a ways to go," I say. "We're not even on the mountain yet."

Decker and I continue up the road, passing a rotted-out wooden sign announcing that we've entered Bear Creek. There's another sign advertising the ski resort in ten miles, the resort that closed twenty-five years ago.

The road up the mountain narrows into a concrete bridge; two men stand fishing off the side into the creek below. As Decker drives over the bridge, they stare at us. I sink lower into my seat, avoiding their gaze. I'm terrified that we're walking straight into a potential *Deliverance* situation, but Decker is bouncing in his seat with excitement.

"This is a real, serious backwoods experience right here," he says, echoing my thoughts. "And people say we're rednecks in Fayette!"

"Yeah," I say. "Just don't say that too loud."

"Right, right. Got it." We hit a dip in the road as we roll off the bridge, and we lurch forward. Decker slides forward in his seat, catches himself, and tightens his seatbelt, even though we've slowed to a crawl. There's a sign pointing up to the mountain; we're on a narrow gravel road dotted with shacks and trailers on each side.

Two women watch us from the porch of a bait-and-tackle

store. We stay on the road, because there's nowhere else to go, and creep past a saloon, a breakfast joint in an old metal trailer, and a mini-mart.

"What a cute little town," Decker says. "They even have a gas station."

Decker nods toward a slab of wood with the word *GAS* spray-painted on it outside the tackle shop.

"Let's park by the mini-mart," I say, uncomfortable with how the two women are watching us. I think of the two men fishing at the bridge and wonder if everyone travels in pairs here. I'm suddenly even more thankful to have Decker as he pulls in front of the mini-mart. I hop out of the car, kicking up a cloud of dust where my feet connect with the ground.

"Y'all lost?" The voice comes from the side of the mini-mart. A man sits on the edge of his flatbed, shucking what looks like a bucket full of crawfish. Before I can stop him, Decker steps forward.

"No, sir. Visiting family."

The man pauses, a gray, spindly creature in his grasp. My father used to say he'd never touch a fish from a Pennsylvania stream. Too much contamination from the coal plants.

"Family," the man snorts. A bit of gray dots his beard along his jaw. He's not wearing a shirt, and he has a deep suntan and broad, weathered shoulders. There's a scar on one of them, like a brown dash cutting a sentence off.

I find my voice. "Her name's Annette, but she may be going by something else. She's fair-skinned, average weight . . ." I falter, suddenly realizing I can't really remember what my mother looks like. It's as if someone had asked me to draw her, and I've come up with a stick figure devoid of details. Panic creeps in; Decker is eyeing me curiously.

"Um, she has freckled arms," I continue. "Light brown hair. And on her neck, there's like a patch . . . of discoloration."

Something flits across the man's face. Recognition, maybe. He turns his attention back to the crawfish. "Don't know nobody like that."

Decker must have seen it too—the brief second where the man looked like he knew who I was talking about—because he opens his mouth. Before I can grab the sleeve of his T-shirt, Decker says, "I think you can give us a little more than that."

The man stops cleaning the fish. "I'll give you five seconds to get the fuck out of my face, Boy Scout."

My heartbeat stalls. Decker's gaze drops to where mine is— on the knife in the man's hands. The one he's using to clean the fish.

I drag Decker into the mini-mart. "People aren't very friendly here," he mutters as the door tinkles overhead.

The mini-mart is about a thousand degrees. The fans overhead do little more than blow around the hot air. The cash register is conveniently positioned next to the icebox. A sign printed on computer paper says BAG OF ICE TWO FOR $3 in bleeding ink.

The girl behind the register barely looks up at us. Her face is youthful, but she has the type of tired skin where she could look either really good for thirty or really bad for twenty.

Decker drank all the iced tea in the car, so we head straight back for the fridge where the bottled waters are. I open the fridge door and grab one, while Decker reaches for a Coke.

"Let me handle the talking this time," I say as we approach the counter.

"Sure, sure," Decker says.

The register girl looks up and blinks at us.

"Hi there," Decker says. I elbow him.

"Hi," the girl says, slowly, tentatively, as she rings up our drinks.

"I was hoping you could help me with something," I say.

The girl tenses. "Yeah?"

"The mountain," I say. "People live up in the woods, right?"

She crosses her arms across her chest.

I lower my voice. "I'm not here to bust anyone. I'm just trying to find someone."

The girl scratches the back of her neck. Glances at the door. "Yeah, there's a lot of people livin' up on the mountain. Sheriff came and ticketed some a couple months ago, but they always find their way back."

"How many houses are up there?" I ask. "If I went to look around—"

"You go knocking on doors, and you'll be looking down the barrel of a gun." The girl's voice has a new sharpness to it—one that makes me think that she is older than me, after all. "If you found your own way up here, then you're looking for someone who doesn't want to be found."

"Not someone," I say. "My mom."

The girl's face softens a little. Next to me, Decker sticks his hands into his shorts pockets and rocks back on his heels; he has to physically hold himself back from talking.

"Is this the only place to get groceries around here?" I ask the girl.

"The next place is twenty miles south," she says.

I describe Annette as I remember her. The girl nods, a quick, almost imperceptible dip of the head.

"Yeah. She comes in here, sometimes."

The adrenaline zips to my toes. *My mother is here.* I try not to sound overeager. "When was the last time?"

She shrugs. "Last week, maybe."

My head swims. *Last week*. "If you see her, could you tell her that her daughter is looking for her?"

The girl hesitates, and nods. "Should probably leave your number for her."

She pushes a pen and an old receipt toward me. I scribble my number on the back. As an afterthought, I write *Tessa* beneath it.

"Thanks," I say, breathless.

The girl nods again, holding my gaze in a way that makes me feel like I can trust her. If my mother comes down to the grocery store, she'll know I was here, know I was looking for her.

As we leave the store, the man with the crawfish eyeballs us. He's talking to another man now, one with a shaved head and hollow black eyes. I look away.

"So what next?" Decker asks. "Should we head up the mountain and see if your mom's up there? My car can't handle that terrain, but we could hike."

"Um. I don't know." I give Decker a look that I hope he'll understand means, *Please lower your damn voice*. The men are still watching us, and they don't seem happy.

Decker glances up the mountain, shielding his eyes from the sun. Smoke rises above the trees, curling toward the mountain's peak. *That could be my mother's fire.*

"We've got a while before night falls," Decker says. "Sucks we don't have boots or long pants or a flashlight, but—"

"Decker," I say through gritted teeth. The men are coming toward us.

The guy who just showed up is as thin as a pole, hip bones jutting out over the top of his sagging jeans. I spy a swastika buried in the design of the tattoo covering his entire arm.

He's half the size of the crawfish man but ten times more terrifying. I sense Decker go completely still next to me.

"Hey, homeboy," the skinhead says, putting his face inches from Decker. "It's time for you and your bitch to get lost."

Decker puts his hands up. They're trembling. "We don't want trouble. She's just here to see her mom."

The man cracks his knuckles. Each one is tattooed with a different letter, but I can't make out the word it forms. "I don't care what y'all are doing here," he says. "You're not welcome."

I finally push the words out. "Let's go, Decker."

He doesn't object. We power walk the few steps to the car; Decker fumbles with the keys to unlock the door.

"You know," Decker says once we're locked inside, his breathing shallow, "we could go around town. Find another way to hike up the mountain."

I stare through the windshield at the expanse of woods climbing up Bear Mountain. Hundreds of square miles of the unknown. We'd have to hide the car, hike up the rest of the way. I don't know which is a worse way to die—at the hands of the skinhead and crawfish man, or getting lost on the mountain and succumbing to the elements.

"What now?" Decker says when I don't respond.

I run my finger along the side of the car door to make sure it's locked. "We get the fuck out of here."

CHAPTER
TWENTY-ONE

Decker can tell I'm not in much of a mood to talk on the ride back. He offers me one of the Twizzlers bags. I shake my head and look out the window.

"Do you think that man was a white supremacist?" Decker asks between chews.

"Yeah." And judging from his reaction to us, I'd wager he's on some sort of FBI watch list. "Sorry I almost got us killed. This was a bad idea."

"No, it wasn't," he says. "I mean, now you know your mom definitely lives there, right?"

I turn to meet his eyes; Decker gives me an encouraging smile. I smile back, and he returns his attention to the road.

I lean my head against the window and watch the mountain disappear in the side window. The surge of adrenaline from back in the mini-mart is gone, and hopelessness is working its way in. Suddenly, I'm sure that my mother won't be back to the store any-time soon.

She has to eat, I argue with myself. But my mind goes to the men fishing at the creek. I think of wild game wandering the woods on the mountain. There are ways she could fend for herself.

Yet in my heart I know that it doesn't sound like her. She could barely feed my sister and me when my father and his income were gone.

Jos was always like Daddy, the one who knew how to survive. My mother and I are lucky if we can figure out how to get by.

I consider the fact that Bear Creek has no cell service. What are the chances my mom even owns a phone?

The store has got to have a landline she can use. I saw power lines along the road.

And the one question I don't want the answer to: Will she even call me if she gets the message?

The radio signal returns about twenty minutes out of Bear Creek, when we're back on the interstate. My phone buzzes in my pocket. A single, long buzz, which means a voice mail.

I flip open the phone, not surprised there's no missed call. It would have gone straight to voice mail while we were in Bear Creek. My fingers tremble over the keys as I punch in my PIN.

"Hey, Kelly. This is Dan over at Smith's Nissan. Give me a call back so we can talk about that Altima! We've got a deal going on the—"

I tune the rest out, waiting for the callback number. It's a good thing I was always too lazy to set up a voice mail greeting. My ears are thrumming; I can't think around the Linkin Park song Decker is blasting. And drumming along to on the steering wheel.

I can't call Danny back in front of Decker. Technically, if there were someone in town I could trust, it would probably be Decker, but I can't ask Danny the tough questions about my sister in front of Decker.

If Decker knew what I suspected Joslin of being involved in—

212

if he knew the real purpose of this trip to find my mother—it would probably cut short his *Tessa and Decker, Adventuring Folk Heroes* fantasy.

We hit a few patches of traffic headed south. It's the longest ride of my life. What if Danny's not there anymore by the time we get home? I can't chase away the nagging thought that I'll be too late, that he'll catch on that something's not right before I get ahold of him. Maybe he'll replay my message and be able to tell from my voice that I'm not looking for a car.

It's after five by the time we get back to Fayette. Decker pulls into the Greenwoods' driveway; the minivan is still gone. Callie and Maggie aren't home from Pittsburgh yet.

"You should call me," Decker blurts. His ears redden. "If you hear from your mom, I mean. Let me know."

"Yeah. I will." I open the door and hop out. I poke my head back into the car. "Hey . . . thanks."

"Anytime. Remember, friends?"

Of all the things I thought would happen in Fayette, making friends wasn't one of them. But I'm glad I was wrong.

I wave at Decker and shut the door. He waves back as he pulls out of the driveway, taking the Greenwoods' recycling bin down with the bumper of his car. It's empty, so I pick it up and drag it to the garage.

I don't feel like wasting time fumbling with the front door key, so I head through the gate into the backyard. I sit down on the grass with my back pressed against the fence.

I listen to Danny's voice mail once more to make sure I have the number right, and I'm even more certain than I was yesterday that I have him. I listen to the voice mail again. I'm stalling, of course.

Stop being such a goddamn wuss, Tessa.

I dial; someone picks up on the second ring.

"Dan here." His voice is bright, bubbly. Ready for a sale. It knocks the wind out of me; the guy I knew was always mumbling around a wad of gum or tobacco in his mouth.

"Danny?" I ask, feeling two inches tall.

He pauses, like it's been a while since someone's called him that. "Who's this?"

I grab a fistful of grass to anchor myself. "My name is Tessa Lowell. Do you remember me?"

A longer pause this time. "How did you get this number?"

The friendliness has leeched from his voice. I tighten my grip on the phone. "Please don't—don't hang up." I sound like I'm out of breath.

"Look, I don't know what this is about, but I'm real busy—"

"I'm in Fayette," I say quickly. "I'm trying to find Joslin."

Danny snorts. "I sure as hell don't know what happened to her."

What happened to her, I notice. Not, *where she is.* My stomach clenches.

"I'm not trying to narc on you or anything," I say. "But I know you used her as your alibi, for the night the house in Arnold exploded. I need to know if she was really with you."

I can practically hear the gears in Danny's head turning. How much do I know? I'm shocked when he speaks instead of hanging up on me.

"No, Jos wasn't with me," he says, sighing. "I told her to say she was, because I'd gotten mixed up in some stupid shit, but that was ten years ago. I'm clean now, and I haven't heard from her since she took off."

"Do you know where she actually was that night?" I ask, feeling the hope inside me swell up like a balloon.

"No idea," Danny says. "When I called her that night to see

what she was up to, she said she was on her way to her friend's house to pick you up."

She was on her way to the Greenwoods'? That makes no sense; Jos wouldn't have picked me up in the middle of the night unless something was seriously wrong. That, and if she did come to get me, she obviously never made it.

"You there?" Danny says.

I swallow, hoping it will calm the thumping in my chest. "It's just . . . she didn't pick me up."

"I know." Danny's voice is grave. "Guess she didn't make it there in time. Jos is lucky. If she were there, it might have been her."

Lucky, maybe. Or maybe Joslin *did* make it to the Greenwoods' in time. Only it wasn't to pick me up.

The slashed screen window could have been a ruse. My sister wasn't stupid—if she had killed Lori and staged her body like one of the Monster's victims, Jos would have thought to make it look like someone had broken into the house.

"Look, kiddo, I want you to find her, but she and I were done *months* before she left," Danny says. "I'm the last person she would have told where she was going."

No. No, you're not. You don't know my mother. She's *the last person Jos would have told.*

"After Lori died—was Jos different?" I ask, hesitant to clue Danny in on *why* Jos would have been different. "Did she say or do anything . . . weird?"

"I mean, yeah, she was real bummed about Lori," Danny says.

Bummed. Like we were talking about the Eagles losing the Super Bowl. Jos was devastated after Lori's death—missing her shifts at work, unable to get out of bed to help me get ready for school. It hits me that Danny never really knew my sister at all and he's just another ghost I've been chasing.

"She did she say was fighting with her mom a lot," Danny says. "That if it weren't for you, she would have been out of there."

My eyes prick. I can't let my emotions undo me right now. "Did she say anything about her real father, or maybe going to live with him?"

"That's pretty much what she and her mom—I mean, your mom too—were fighting about." There's a low hiss on the other end, like Danny has cracked open a can. "She wanted to know who her dad was, and your mom wouldn't say, because she didn't want Jos to meet him."

Alan Something-or-other, the man my mother followed to Louisiana. The man who didn't want the baby who didn't make it, and who was abusive to my mother once Jos was born.

"Did Jos ever find him?" I ask.

"I don't know," Danny says. "But I hope she did. She deserved to know where she came from."

I wonder if that's why my mother kept Jos's father from her; she didn't want my sister to see for herself that Alan in Louisiana hadn't wanted her. Maybe Annette was just trying to protect her, and Jos was too stubborn to see it.

"Thanks, Danny," I say. "Will you—will you call me if you think of anything that might help me find her?"

"Sure. Hey, kiddo," he says gently as I'm about to press the button to hang up. "Good luck. Give Jos my best when you find her."

• • •

When I hang up with Danny, I have to run upstairs, where my cell charger is. I've got only one bar of battery left, and from here on out my phone stays with me, charged, all the time. Just in case my mother calls.

I lie on my side and watch my phone on the pillow next to me. I found Danny. Now I have to decide if I believe him.

I map out a scenario in my head. The night of Lori's murder, Danny is in Arnold with Mike and Tommy Faber, and everything goes to hell when the meth house explodes. Danny realizes he needs someone to place him in Fayette and calls Joslin. She says she's going to pick me up from the Greenwoods. She just had an argument with Lori over the phone, which she doesn't tell Danny about.

Or maybe she did, and Danny conveniently didn't tell me that part. Jos could have told Danny that Lori knew what the guys were doing in Arnold; maybe the Fabers heard, and panicked, realizing Lori could implicate them in the explosion. They decided they had to kill her and left to come back to Fayette.

But it's unlikely that Danny and the Fabers would be in any state to rush back to Fayette in time to kill Lori and move her body after their drug operation exploded. In the state they were probably in, someone was bound to notice them in the Greenwoods' neighborhood, if they were there. Three different people saw the suspicious man who was casing the neighborhood, looking for his cat that afternoon.

No one saw anything suspicious in the moments before the murder. The most likely scenario is that the killer was alone, or not suspicious-looking.

Downstairs, there's the sound of the front door opening. Then voices: Maggie's and Callie's. I freeze, as if I were an intruder. Something feels wrong about being here while they were gone.

The voices lift—they're arguing. I stick my head out the door to hear them better, but all I can make out is that it seems like Maggie's trying to calm Callie down. I inch toward the top of the stairs.

"You can't just burst in there, Callie—"

217

"He did this." Callie sounds hysterical. "Mr. Kouchinsky did this. I know it."

I can't help myself. I take the first three steps down so I'm visible. "Daryl did what?"

Maggie and Callie look up at me. Maggie hesitates.

"Katie Kouchinsky is in the hospital," Callie says. Her eyeliner is smeared. "One of her friends—a girl we drove to tryouts today—says she needs stitches."

Callie's leg jiggles so hard, it looks like it's going to give out beneath her. She turns to Maggie. "You don't understand. I have to see her—"

"I'll take you later, then," Maggie says. "I have to get dinner started."

"I have to go now. Please, Mom—"

Maggie cuts Callie off with a sigh. "You leave if Daryl's there, do you hear me? And let Tessa drive you. You're too upset."

I expect Callie to snarl something like *No way*. She turns, as if she were about to storm up the stairs, but instead she reaches over the banister and hands me the car keys.

. . .

"This is my fault," Callie says. We're on the highway, headed for Samaritan Hospital. It's not the closest hospital—that would be Fayette Mercy—but Callie thinks Mrs. Kouchinsky took Katie farther away from town to avoid questions.

Callie is slunk back in her seat, her feet resting on the dash. "He saw Katie talking to us. He must have figured out what about."

"Where is Daryl now?" I keep my eyes on the road; I've never driven the Pennsylvania highways before, so I'm on high alert. I had to pull the seat practically right up to the steering wheel; Callie's that much taller than I am.

"I don't know." Callie shifts and draws her knees to her chest. "Abby said Katie's saying she fell down the stairs. They don't want to involve the police."

My thoughts circle around each other, landing back on that dog, as they always do when I think of Ariel's father.

"What if he beat her up to keep her quiet?" Callie's words spill out a mile a minute. "People are saying he hurt her the day they found Ari, remember? Maybe it wasn't because he was angry that Katie covered for Ari but because he thinks Katie knows something about him, something that could prove who he really is—"

"Callie, slow down," I say. "It makes sense, but what are you going to do? Burst into the hospital and interrogate Katie? Accuse her father of killing Ari?" I sigh. "Katie's scared shitless of him as it is. If she knows something, she's not gonna tell us."

Callie frowns. She obviously hasn't thought that part out yet.

The emergency room parking lot is full, so I find a space in the visitors' section on the other side of the hospital. Callie barely waits for me to shut the engine off before hopping out of the car.

"Your mom is right," I say as we cross the lot. "If Daryl is there, we get the hell out."

Callie doesn't say anything. She cracks her knuckles and looks straight ahead.

"*Callie.*" I grab her elbow.

"Okay. God." She shrugs away from me as we step onto the curb by the emergency entrance.

The ER doors open with a *whoosh*. We shift to the side so two EMTs can wheel an elderly man in on a stretcher. His eyes are closed, his mouth open.

I have never been to a hospital. There were no broken bones

when I was a kid; riding my bike was the most dangerous activity my mother allowed, and still, all I got from that were some scraped elbows and a scar the length of a fingernail on my knee.

I expected chaos in the emergency room: blood, ice packs, nurses running around with crash carts. But it's quiet, except for the TV in the corner playing reruns of *Dr. Phil*. The waiting room chairs are filled, but no one is visibly sick or injured.

Callie marches to the desk and says we're here to see Katherine Kouchinsky. The nurse types something into her computer.

"She's being discharged," she says.

"I need to see her now," Callie says, doing the stubborn flat-lip thing.

The nurse sighs. "Sign in."

Callie and I take turns writing our names in the ledger while the nurse prints two visitor stickers. I grab both and follow Callie through the door adjacent to the desk after the nurse buzzes us through.

There are rows of curtains on metal racks; some of them are pulled back, exposing beds full of sick people. An elderly woman in a gown coughs and spits into a pink bowl. I've never felt more intrusive in my life, and I wish I'd insisted on staying in the car.

Callie walks straight past the patients, to the desk in the center of the room. She asks where Katie Kouchinsky is. A nurse points to a curtained-off area next to the bathroom.

"She's getting dressed," the nurse calls out to Callie's back. Callie ignores her and steps around the curtain. I follow, and find myself face to face with Ruth Kouchinsky.

"Oh," she says, stepping back. On the bed, Katie is pulling on her shirt. She stops, head halfway through the neck hole, to gape at Callie and me.

There are stitches on her lower lip. A bruise blooming on her chin. Her ankle is bound and propped up on the bed. Dizziness washes through me.

"What are you doing here?" Katie demands, yanking her shirt down the rest of the way. She winces. Mrs. Kouchinsky clutches the curtain.

"We wanted to see if you were okay," Callie says. "What happened?"

"I fell down the stairs." Katie averts her eyes to the ID bracelet on her wrist. "I'm sorry, but can you please leave?"

Katie looks at her mother to back her up; Ruth Kouchinsky says nothing, her beady eyes brimming with tears.

Callie turns to her. "There are people who can help you both." Her own voice is choked with tears. Mrs. Kouchinsky looks away. I feel sick.

The nurse from the desk pushes the curtain aside and hands Mrs. Kouchinsky a clipboard with paperwork. While she's hunched over, signing it, Callie leans in to Katie.

"If you know something—something that he doesn't want you telling people, *this* is going to get a lot worse." Callie nods to Katie's ankle. "You owe it to your little brother and sister to speak up. You owe it to *Ari*—"

"Stop," Katie says, loudly enough that her mother and the nurse look up. "You don't know anything, Callie, and you never cared about Ari before, so just *stop*."

Callie flinches in surprise, and I suck in a breath; I've never seen Katie like this before, and I can tell Callie hasn't either.

"You two need to leave." The nurse points at Callie and me.

Callie gestures to Katie, her hands shaking. "You're not going to do something about this?"

"Come on." The nurse steps behind us, herding us away from Katie. Callie stops and looks back at the curtain.

"I'll get security if I have to," the nurse says, holding up a hand.

"Callie," I whisper. "We have to go."

"She—her dad did that to her," Callie says, angry tears in her eyes. "You guys have to call the cops."

"Honey, we can't call anyone if they don't want us to."

"She's seventeen, and she—could be in danger," I cut in, suddenly annoyed by the nurse's apathy. "Isn't there a law that says you have to call?"

The nurse's face softens. "It's a sprained ankle and a cut lip. That girl very well could've fallen down the stairs," she says. "She doesn't want to press charges. We see this every day, and she's right that you're gonna make it worse for her if you try to get involved."

Callie's mouth hangs open. The nurse escorts us through the doors and deposits us at the curb. A woman rolls a little boy in a wheelchair, his arm in a sling, down the ramp past us.

Callie and I stand to the side of the doors, neither of us moving to head back to the car. A siren sounds somewhere behind us.

"That nurse had a point," I say. "If you're right about Mr. Kouchinsky, that he killed Ari and he feels like everything is closing in on him, who knows what he'll do."

There was a huge story a few years ago in Florida. It happened in a town not far from Gram's. An ex-stockbroker was about to go to jail for embezzlement, so he shot his wife and three kids before setting fire to the house and killing himself. A shudder ripples through me.

"If I'm right about him—" Callie stops midsentence. "Tess, we could have helped stop him from killing again. If we'd said we didn't see the man's face, they would have kept looking for the Monster."

"You're getting ahead of yourself," I tell her. "There's no evidence that Ari's dad is the Monster."

"Does it matter who the Monster is?" Callie starts, the words sticking in her throat. "He could be out there—Lori's killer is still out there—because of us."

I can't tell her to stop blaming herself for Ariel's death. People do this all the time, I've learned, when they're feeling guilty. They think that maybe if they'd done one thing differently, they could have stopped a chain reaction from starting.

I used to believe that it was a useless way to think. I thought that if you refused to play the role the universe has planned for you, someone else would just step up and take it. I convinced myself that if Callie and I hadn't testified against Stokes, the district attorney's office would have found someone else.

I convinced myself that Stokes would have gone to jail for the other murders even if Lori Cawley had never been killed that night. Being cast in the role of the Monster was simply the plan the universe had laid out for Wyatt Stokes.

I don't know if I believe that anymore. I don't know if I ever truly believed it at all, or if it's just the armor I invented to protect myself from my own guilt.

I never thought Callie would be the one to chip away at the armor. She was always the one who was so sure Stokes had killed Lori, the one who wouldn't even listen to anyone who suggested otherwise.

I don't feel comforted by this. I feel like I'm drifting away from a harbor at night, like someone has snapped the chain of the anchor beneath me.

I suck in a breath, and look over at Callie. "You've got to stay away from the Kouchinskys," I say. "At least for now."

"Okay," Callie says, a little too distractedly. "Can I have the keys?" she asks as we make our way back to the car. "I'm fine to drive now."

I hand them over without a fight; I'm tired, and I don't feel like navigating the dark highway again. Once I'm settled into the passenger seat, I stick my hand into my pocket and cover my phone, waiting for it to ring.

I keep it there the whole ride home.

I keep it there at dinner, eating with one hand as Callie lies to Maggie and says Katie is just a little scratched up.

When it's time for bed, I put my phone on the pillow next to me and fall asleep still waiting for my mother to call.

• • •

Vibrating. My phone is ringing, and I'm so disoriented that I knock it onto the floor.

I lean over to fish it out of the crevice between the nightstand and bed, where it's fallen. I frown when I see the number on the display.

Callie is calling me. Why is she calling me from her room? I look up at the cuckoo clock, which says it's one in the morning.

"Hello?" My voice is gravelly. I swallow twice.

"Uh, hey, Tessa?" It's a male voice. "It's Ryan."

"Where's Callie?" I sit up, suddenly awake.

"She's with me. There's kind of an issue."

"What are you talking about?" I whisper-hiss.

"Uh . . . she's in no shape to drive, but she won't leave without her car—and now she's yelling at me."

Indeed, Callie is yelling in the background. Another voice—a male's—interjects, trying to calm her down, I guess.

"Where are you?" I ask, panicked, running through the million different ways in which this could turn into a disaster.

Ryan sighs. "A motel off 80. What's it called?" he says, away from the mouthpiece of his phone.

"Doyle Motor Inn," a muffled male voice says in the background. I know who it belongs to.

"Callie is drunk in a hotel with Nick Snyder?" I hiss.

"I'll explain in person," Ryan says. "If I come get you, will you help drive her car back? I've got work at five and I can't leave my truck here."

I look at the clock. "Fine. But you better tell me *everything* that happened. Everything."

• • •

Ryan idles a few houses down from the Greenwoods', since his truck is loud. I jog down the street as soon as he texts me that he's here. I'm still in my sleep shorts, which are little more than glorified men's boxers, and I didn't bother to put on a bra.

Ryan pulls away from the curb before I even have the chance to close the passenger door.

"What the hell happened?" I ask.

Ryan rubs his chin, looking irritated. "We were hanging out around ten, me and Callie. I knew she must've known where Nick was all along; I'm not dumb." Ryan sighs, grips the steering wheel. "So I made up this story about how my uncle knew where Nick was hiding and the cops were gonna arrest him in the morning."

"She went to warn him, didn't she?" I ask. Callie is so damn predictable. It's going to get us into trouble.

Ryan rolls his window up as he merges, so he doesn't have to shout over the sound of the highway. "She led me right to his motel."

"It's not the first time," I say. "We were there the other night."

Ryan's jaw hardens, and I feel like a real dumbass for not seeing it sooner. I mean, I saw the signs—Callie calling Ari a whore, Callie dropping everything to help Nick in the middle of the night—but I hadn't actually put it together until now.

Nick was the guy Callie liked but who hooked up with Ari. Nick was the reason they weren't friends anymore.

"Sorry," I say. "I wasn't thinking. I forgot that you and Callie—"

I come to a full stop right there. I don't have a word for what Callie and Ryan are.

"It's cool," Ryan says. "We're not . . . She can do what she wants."

There's an edge to his voice, though. Before I can probe, Ryan turns on the radio. A classic rock station, WFCN, my father's favorite. His car radio, the boom box he left on the porch—both were tuned to WFCN. I knew all the words to "Stairway to Heaven" before I could read.

When I was really little, like three or four, I would bungle the lyrics to AC/DC's "Dirty Deeds Done Dirt Cheap," a song the station played at least twice a day. I thought the singer was saying *dry your nuts* instead of *drive you nuts,* which my father found hysterical. When his friends would come over, he'd shout, "Sing 'Dirty Deeds,' Tessy!" and they'd all laugh when I got to *enough to dry your nuts.* Everyone hooted, clutching their stomachs, except my mother, and I could never understand why she was so mad at me when I was making everyone laugh.

A nineties grunge song pulls me back to the present. Clearly, the definition of *classic rock* has shifted since I was a kid. Just this once, I wish something had stayed the same.

• • •

Nick lets us into the motel room. He reeks of weed, and his eyes are bloodshot.

"Come on, man," Ryan says, exasperated. "You're *asking* to get caught."

"I don't care anymore." Nick is an angry drunk. I can tell, because I've known a lot of angry drunks.

Callie sits on one of the twin beds, her back against the headboard. Her eyes are closed.

"Let's go." I shake her knee. "Before your parents wake up."

Callie groans. I resist the urge to slap her. She's risking my getting sent home over a boy. A stupid boy who makes poor decisions and isn't even that good-looking.

I use both hands to shake Callie now. "UP."

Eyes still closed, she swings one leg over the side of the bed. That's when I notice the empty bottle of Bacardi on the floor. So does Ryan.

"You let her finish it?" he practically yells at Nick.

"I don't tell her what to do," Nick says. There is the slightest emphasis on *I*, which Ryan obviously catches. He looks pissed.

"Come on," he mumbles. We both have to help hold Callie up, even though she slurs that she can walk on her own.

"Shut up," I hiss into her ear. "You've done enough, okay?"

"Yo, ease up on her," Nick says. "She's the only one who's still on my side."

I'm about to tell *him* to shut up too, but Ryan interrupts. "So I'm not on your side, because I think you should go home? Nice." His face is flooded with color.

"You want me to go to jail for something I didn't do?" Nick demands from where he's sitting on the bed. Ryan shakes his head, but he's not looking at Nick.

Nick stands up from the bed, and a chill crawls up my back.

"You think I *did* do it?" he says, getting in Ryan's face. "Is that what you think?"

Callie whimpers. I pull her away from Ryan as he returns Nick's scowl.

"I don't know what I think anymore, man," Ryan mutters. "You're sure acting like a criminal."

Nick looks like he's going to throw a punch, so I push Callie and Ryan out the door. Nick grabs the knob to stop me from closing it. My heart stops.

"You believe I didn't do it." Nick looks me right in the eye. His lids are drooping, his words a little slurred, but his voice is insistent. "I can tell. You've got to go on Connect. Find the guy."

"There was a man who didn't want sex," I say, my thoughts a rapid-fire stream in my head. "Did she talk about him?"

Nick looks more alert. "Captain. That was his username. Captain something."

"Are you sure?" I ask him.

"Yeah, she liked Captain. Said he was older and his wife just died," Nick says. "I told the cops about him, but they acted like I just made it up."

"Tessa, we've got to go," Ryan says. I look over at them and see that Callie has vomited all over the concrete.

"We have to find out who Captain is," Nick says to me. "Just get on Connect, okay?"

Before I can respond, Nick has shut the door in my face.

My stomach is unsettled as Ryan and I load Callie into the minivan. I don't realize until I'm behind the wheel that Nick said *we* have to find Captain.

I don't know when *we* happened, but I don't like it.

· · ·

Callie is passed out for the entire ride home. I lean over occasionally, to make sure she's breathing. It's a good thing I paid attention to the route Ryan took to the motel, because Callie's in no shape to help me figure out how to get home.

I nudge her awake as I pull into the driveway. She stirs and whines.

"Get it together," I hiss. "You screwed up big-time."

"Why?" she slurs.

"If we get caught, your mom will send me away," I say.

"Isn't that what you want?" she blubbers. "To go back to your nice life in Florida and forget I ever existed again?"

I'm dumbstruck. Is that really what she thinks, or is the Bacardi talking? *She's* the one who pretended *I* didn't exist anymore; she's the one who carried on with her life and her friends while I thought of Wyatt Stokes every single day for the past ten years. While Callie was numbing herself with booze and high school parties, I'm the one who went straight home every day and visited the forums, a ritual that became a prison. School, Gram's house, work, Gram's house. And not a single meaningful relationship in between.

My life became a self-imposed prison, because a prison was what I deserved. Callie has just been avoiding her sentence until now.

I can't push words out around the lump in my throat. I just want to be done with her, done with this place. I'll go back to my prison in Florida if I have to, because anything is better than this.

And of course, because I've decided that I can't possibly feel worse right now, a light goes on in the living room. Maggie is staring out the window, right at us.

CHAPTER TWENTY-TWO

Maggie doesn't look at me or speak. We silently help Callie up the stairs and into her bed. Maggie mutters something unintelligible at her, but Callie doesn't respond, her head lolling to the side.

She's blacked out.

Finally, Maggie looks up at me. "What happened?"

A lie sticks on my tongue, that we went to the STI and things got a little out of hand. But even I wouldn't go to a bar in what I'm wearing. Maggie won't buy it.

If I say I had to pick Callie up from the bar, Maggie is the type of person who will report them for serving Callie alcohol.

"I had to pick her up," I say slowly. "From a friend's."

"Which *friend*?" Maggie's voice is sharp. The whole scene—her angry face, Callie's practically lifeless body, the twirling trophies surrounding us—feels like it's falling away around me.

I can't throw Ryan under the bus for this. And it'll be even worse if I tell the truth. "She asked me not to say."

"Goddamn it, Tessa." Maggie covers her face, probably wondering when my allegiance shifted from her to Callie. "That's the thing I'd expect to hear from my daughter."

My heart squeezes. Her *daughter,* which I am clearly not. "I'm sorry."

"We'll talk in the morning. I don't want to wake Rick up." She leaves without a glance back at me.

• • •

We don't talk in the morning. When I wake up, Maggie and Rick are gone. There's a note on the kitchen counter.

Went to Nana's. Back in the afternoon. Cold cuts in the fridge for lunch.

No mention of the deep shit Callie and I are in. But in my gut, I know that without a doubt, when Maggie gets home, we're going to have a talk about how long I plan on staying in Fayette.

I'm running out of time. And all I have are random pieces that I'm not even sure fit the same puzzle.

I've seen *Unmasking the Monster* so many times, I practically have the transcript memorized, but there's always one line that sticks in my head. Something that a private investigator who took on the case pro bono after Stokes was in jail said.

I've always said that one person could blow this case apart— one person who saw something or knows something and isn't coming forward.

I pour myself a glass of orange juice and look at the clock over the sink. It's a little after ten. I head upstairs and knock on Callie's door. When she doesn't answer, I open it.

She's asleep facing the doorway, her mouth open slightly.

Snoring. It's stifling in here; no one ever turned on the AC unit in her room last night. I turn it on and shut the door behind me.

I haven't had any calls since leaving my number for my mother. I sit my phone next to me on the bed and reach behind the headboard, where I left my father's stuff.

What would I have said to him, had I made it in time? What would he have said to me?

I'm sorry, baby. That's the last thing he said to me before he went away. He cried in the courtroom, the papers said. He looked right at Manuel Gonzalo and told him how sorry he was that he would never walk again. My father played the part of the repentant convict and begged for leniency, but it didn't matter. He still got a life sentence.

After the jury announced that Stokes was sentenced to death, he smirked. They caught it on tape. The filmmakers asked him about it. He stubbed out his cigarette and looked at the camera, his pockmarked face ashy under the camera lights.

"They executed a guy on my block last week," Stokes said. "Took three guards and a Taser to get him to stop wailing like a stuck cow. I'm not going out like that."

"Then how will you go out?" the interviewer asked.

"Not quoting Matthew 6:14," Stokes said. "That's for damn sure."

I looked up the verse a while ago; it has something to do with forgiveness. I remember the Bible in my father's bag and rustle around for it. When I find it, I sit back up against the headboard and prop it open, resting it on my thighs.

As I flip to the New Testament, a square of paper falls out into my lap. A bookmark, maybe. I pick it up; a closer look, and I realize that it's part of an envelope.

There's some faded pink ink in the corner, over the stamp. I hold it an inch from my face and try to make out the name of the post office.

E-A-S-T-O. The rest is ripped off. Easton, Pennsylvania, maybe? I think there's an Easton in Lehigh Valley, not far from Allentown.

Is it possible? Did Joslin write to my father in prison?

I turn the scrap over, and there's a phone number scribbled in the corner, in my father's handwriting. No names, just a number.

I dig my phone out of the pile on the bed and dial it.

A woman picks up on the second ring. "Hello?"

Her voice is unfamiliar. My heart sinks; I allowed myself the faintest sliver of hope that Joslin or my mother would pick up the phone.

"Who is this?" the woman demands. She sounds frazzled, angry. "Who are you?"

I hang up in a panic. *Stupid, stupid.* A completely acceptable response would have been a simple, *I'm sorry. Who is this?*

I head downstairs while I work up the nerve to call back. I missed breakfast, and I figure I should eat something.

I'm rolling up a piece of turkey when my phone begins to vibrate, only the number on the screen isn't the one I just dialed a few minutes ago.

I don't recognize it—or the area code.

My heartbeat floods my ears. It could be her.

Even though I'm not ready—I'll never be ready—I answer.

"Hello?" It's a woman. Not the woman from earlier.

It's also not my mother.

"Who is this?" I ask.

There's a click on the line. "This is Agent Morgan Doherty

with the Federal Bureau of Investigation. But the real question is, who are *you*, and why are you calling the family of a missing child?"

"What? I had no idea who I was calling," I say, shocked. "I'm sorry."

There's a heavy sigh on the other end of the line. "I figured," Agent Morgan Doherty says, calmer. She sounds tired. "No one has called the tip line in years. Be more careful with your prank calls, okay?"

It wasn't a prank, I want to say, but all I can say is "I'm so sorry. I didn't know."

"It's fine," she says, and sighs again. "Just disappointing for the Stevens family, that's all."

Agent Doherty hangs up, and I nearly drop my phone.

Stevens.

CHAPTER
TWENTY-THREE

I leave the cold cuts on the counter and bolt into the family room. The computer is on—Rick abandoned a poker game. I minimize it and start a new tab to search for *Stevens missing*.

The result is instant.

Macy Stevens, last seen alive in 1991, in Tennessee. Just shy of her second birthday. The mother, Amanda Stevens, was supposed to drop Macy off at her parents' house so she could meet up with friends at a nightclub. She never showed up.

The next morning, Amanda's parents, Robin and Bernie Stevens, reported Amanda and Macy missing. An officer drove over to the apartment Amanda had been renting, and a hysterical Amanda said someone had taken the baby.

And that was when everything unraveled. The police found out that instead of driving half an hour to leave the baby with her parents, Amanda had left Macy sleeping alone in her crib while she had gone to a nightclub two miles away. Amanda said she'd gone back to the apartment twice to check on Macy, and both times had found the baby sleeping in her crib. It wasn't until

Amanda got home in the early hours of the morning that she discovered Macy was gone.

Amanda failed a lie detector test, but there wasn't enough evidence to charge her with anything but child endangerment. The FBI launched a massive search effort for Macy, but the days stretched into weeks, then months.

There's a sketch of a man in the Wikipedia entry, someone a woman in Michigan reported seeing carrying a girl who matched Macy's description, a few days after she disappeared. I exhale—a deep, relieved breath—because it can't possibly have been my father. The man was African American. And the tip was determined to be "not credible."

The vultures descended on Amanda Stevens right away. Brenda Dean, chief anchor for the Legal News Network, was the first to air the photos that Amanda's friends had anonymously mailed in. Amanda blowing smoke from a joint into the camera. Amanda sucking tequila out of a friend's belly button. In a now infamous phone interview, according to Wikipedia, Brenda Dean ripped Amanda Stevens to pieces, catching her saying "I loved my daughter," as if Amanda's using the past tense had proved that Macy was dead.

The public was brutal to Amanda, but no one was quite as bad as Brenda Dean. Four years after Macy disappeared, Brenda's "Where's Baby Macy?" segments became so ruthless that the district attorney agreed to investigate Amanda Stevens. But they never got anywhere; if Amanda knew what happened to her daughter, she wasn't talking.

Years later, someone leaked chapters from Brenda Dean's book proposal about the case. Dean promised a bombshell that would prove Amanda was guilty: court documents showed that Amanda Stevens had petitioned the state court to have Macy legally declared dead less than a year after she had disappeared—in order to cash in on a life insurance policy she'd taken out on Macy.

Amanda cut her wrists in her parents' bathtub after the segment aired.

In 2006, Amanda's parents brought a wrongful death lawsuit against LNN and Brenda Dean, claiming that the leaked information had driven the public to harass Amanda until she killed herself. The two parties settled for an undisclosed sum believed to be in the mid-seven-figure range.

Macy was officially declared dead in 2008. The Stevens family offered up a $100,000 reward for information leading to the identity and arrest of her killer. But by then, most people agreed that Macy's killer was really her dead mother.

Except, perhaps, my father.

He had the number for the tip line. Did he ever call? Knowing my father, he probably made a desperate attempt to get the reward, even though he'd never have been able to enjoy that kind of money from his cell block.

But I don't know my father, not really. I knew him for only eight years—my entire existence before he went to jail, but only a small percentage of his life. I didn't know about Bear Creek. I didn't know about him turning religious.

I know nothing about my father's life before he met my mother. I don't know where he lived back in 1994, when Macy Stevens was kidnapped and murdered. It could have been Tennessee, for all I know.

There's a nervous humming in my body. Ugly, ugly thoughts forming in my head.

One murder—now two. That was what I thought this was about. Now I feel like I've fallen into a rabbit hole, one where Lori and Ariel don't even factor in, and all I'm going to find at the bottom are terrible, awful truths about my own family.

Next door, the dogs go berserk. A car door slams in the driveway, and I know Maggie and Rick are home. I delete my search history and open Rick's tabs. He was buying more credit to play poker with.

I'm in the kitchen putting away the cold cuts when they walk in.

"Hi, honey," Maggie says. Her voice has a nervous edge to it. She shoots a glance at Rick, and I know exactly what's going on.

She doesn't want him to find out about last night. And since Rick rarely leaves the house without Maggie, except to go to work, she can't bring up what happened until he leaves Monday morning.

It buys me some time. But probably not enough.

• • •

After I call the Fayette prison and leave a message for Wanda saying I need to speak with her about my father's phone records, I knock on Callie's door. She calls for me to come in, and I quietly crack the door. She's sitting on the edge of her bed, pulling a brush through her wet hair. I didn't even hear her wake up or start the shower.

"How much trouble am I in?" Her voice is gravelly.

I shrug. "Your mom hasn't said anything."

"Shit." Callie stops brushing her hair. "That's bad."

Maggie's voice carries up the stairs.

"Callie! Someone's here."

"Crap." Callie wipes the inside corners of her eyes. She twists her wet hair into a bun. There are footsteps on the stairs. Whoever is here, Maggie sent him or her up.

Ryan stands on the other side of the threshold, uncertain whether he should stay there. "Uh. Wanted to make sure you're okay."

"I'm fine." Callie's voice is frosty.

Ryan scratches the back of his neck, stretching so his toned biceps is on full display. "Can we talk or something?"

"We can talk in front of Tessa." Callie puts her brush down, to show that that's final.

Ryan glances at me. "Yeah, sure. Okay."

I sit on the side of the bed opposite Callie, and Ryan sinks into the purple bowl-shaped chair in the corner. It's entirely too small for him.

"I know you're mad I followed you," he says. Callie scowls, and I can tell this is as close to an apology as she's ever gotten from Ryan for anything.

"You're going to tell your uncle where Nick is, aren't you?" Callie says.

"That's really what you think of me?" Ryan lets out a low whistle. "I was friends with him before you were."

"Okay, so then, as his *friends*, what do we do?" Callie asks.

"Captain," I say. They both turn their heads toward me. "Nick said the guy Katie told us about, the one who didn't have sex with Ariel, his username had 'Captain' or something in it. Nick told the police about him, but they didn't take him seriously."

"We don't know that," Ryan says, defensive. "They could be following up on that lead."

"What do we really have to lose by going to some truck stops and asking around?" Callie asks. "We could start with

239

Buckstown. It's outside Mason, and I think one of the first victims was last seen there."

Ryan looks speechless. "This isn't about Nick at all, is it? You really think it's the Monster."

Callie's chin quivers. "I don't know. But if it is, the cops aren't going to admit it."

Ryan covers his face with his hands. "Callie. You cannot go looking for this guy on your own."

"Fine," she says stubbornly, with a sidelong glance at me. "Then you can come with us."

Ryan sighs. I don't want to spend my day driving up and down the interstate with him either. I want to tell Callie about the bizarre phone call with the FBI agent, and the possible connection between my father and missing Baby Macy Stevens.

But Callie has made up her mind that she trusts Ryan and that he can help us. So now I have to keep my mouth shut until I decide if I feel the same way.

• • •

The Buckstown Travel Center is forty-five minutes south on the freeway. Another half hour and we'd be at the Ohio border. We decided to start here because it's the last place anyone saw Rae Felice before she disappeared. Ari could have met the Monster here as well.

Ryan parks in the rest area. "If there's any girls working here, they're probably afraid after what happened to Ari. We have to be careful what we say."

"Pretend we're looking for someone," I say. "Callie's sister. She ran off, and no one's heard from her in weeks, and we think she's hanging around one of these stops."

Callie's quiet; her eyes meet mine in the side mirror, and I know she's thinking about Joslin. That she could have gone to one of the stops after she ran away, looking for a ride out of the state. She could have fallen into drugs, or prostitution. Or worse. It's just what everyone assumed happened to her, because there are no happy endings for runaways.

"That's good," Ryan says. "But they still might not talk."

"Well, we're going to see, I guess." Callie opens the door and hops out of the truck.

The rest area consists of a cafeteria with a Burger King, a Dunkin' Donuts, and a Subway. Off to the side are the bathrooms and a newsstand selling snacks and maps of Pennsylvania. Everything looks too new, too family friendly. No truckers pissing in the parking lot and girls in leather skirts haunting the cigarette kiosks. It's nothing like some of the places off the interstate that I remember from when I was a kid.

Ryan can tell too that this is a lost cause. "We should at least ask around."

Callie stops walking and pulls out her phone. Over her shoulder, I see that she's on someone's Facebook page. Emily Raymes's.

Dunkin' Donuts has the shortest line, so we fall into it, and we wait until an older woman, around Gram's age, asks if she can help us.

"We're looking for a girl," Ryan says. "It's her sister."

He nudges Callie, who shows the woman Emily's picture. The woman blinks.

"She ran away," Ryan explains. "We're worried she's in trouble. Maybe hanging around here . . . with the wrong crowd."

"You've come to the wrong place, baby," the woman says. "They cleaned up this stop years ago. We don't get folks like that

241

anymore. You know, like hitchhikers," she continues, taking our lack of response as confusion. She lowers her voice. *"Pimps."*

Her accent is strong, maybe Georgia. She says it *peemps*.

"Thanks," Callie says, looking so dejected, I almost believe that she actually has a sister.

"If I was you, I'd check out Midway Truck Center," the woman says. "But don't go after dark, and definitely don't go without him." She points a pudgy finger at Ryan. We thank her and move so she can help the customers behind us.

"Hold on," I say as Callie and Ryan make their way toward the exit. "I'll meet you outside."

Five minutes later, I emerge with a bag of fries and a Diet Coke from the Burger King. Callie makes a face as I climb into the truck.

"What?" I stuff a fry into my mouth and offer the carton to Ryan and Callie. "May as well not waste the trip." And besides, all I've eaten today is half a bite of turkey.

Ryan grabs a handful of fries, and Callie gags and rolls down her window. I take a sip of my soda. I feel bad, but it's not my fault she's hungover.

It doesn't get better for her; according to the GPS, Midway Truck Center is an hour east. Even *I* start to get carsick in the back of Ryan's truck. We spend the ride in silence, watching the sky turn shell pink.

The Midway Truck Center looks like the blueprint of a nightmare. Next to a truck with Oregon plates, a man pisses right onto the curb, barely lifting his eyes at us as Ryan pulls into a parking spot.

There's a convenience store and a Dairy Queen. We get out of the truck and head for the convenience store. Callie and I hang back and let Ryan go up to the counter with the photo of Emily.

"He said check out the DQ," Ryan informs us. "Says 'lizards' hang out there."

Callie frowns. "Lizards?"

"It's what the truckers call the prostitutes," I say.

"I don't want to ask how you know that," Callie mutters on our way out the door.

The term always seems to pop up when people talk about Kristal Davis. A lizard usually trades sex for drug money. Before the police connected all the murders, a lot of the people who knew Kristal Davis assumed that she was killed after trying to rob the wrong trucker.

I spot them at a booth by the bathrooms—three women. They're clearly not a family; one is Hispanic, one black, and one white. There are balled-up burger wrappers on the table in front of them.

The white woman's face is pockmarked, her arms stained with spots of purple. Heroin track marks.

Over the lid of her soda, her eyes narrow at us. She nudges the woman next to her, and their laughter subsides.

"There a *problem*?" the black woman demands. A thorny rosebud vine is tattooed on her neck, encircling the name *Micah*.

Callie and Ryan are useless, so I open my mouth, despite the fact that these women intimidate the crap out of me. "We're looking for someone," I say.

"Yeah, well, we don't know someone." The woman with the heroin tracks is also missing one of her front teeth. Next to her, the youngest-looking woman of the bunch—the one who's been quiet so far—shifts in her seat, eyes trained on her soda straw.

"Maybe we can show you her picture," Callie offers in a meek voice.

The black woman sets down her drink. "Maybe you can fuck off, because for all we know, y'all work for the cops."

"Look, we don't want trouble or anything," Ryan says. He sounds so much like a cop that I'm embarrassed for him. "We're just worried that our friend is hanging around a guy who may hurt her."

"Then you're not doing her any good by looking for her," the white woman grunts. "Do yourselves a favor and get home before your bedtimes."

"Yeah, the bad men are gonna come out soon." Micah wiggles a penciled-in eyebrow. The two of them laugh and smack the table, jolting the younger girl.

Ryan mutters "Let's get out of here," and we turn around, heading for the exit. Just before we get to the door, the white woman calls after us, asking if we've got a cigarette.

I clench my fists at my side as I push open the Dairy Queen door for Callie and Ryan. I'm not deluded enough to think I have any street cred, but I might have gotten those women to talk without Small Town Barbie and Ken with me.

"Well, that went well," Ryan says darkly when we're in the parking lot. Callie looks like she's stepped out of an episode of *Beyond Scared Straight*.

"You should have let me handle it," I mutter. "They felt like we were ganging up on them."

Callie clears her throat and nods over my shoulder. The youngest girl from the table is standing behind me.

"They act like that when they're scared," she says quietly. "Shanice got busted trying to buy from an undercover cop, and then that girl got killed down in Mason . . ."

The girl wraps her arms around her body. "I'm Pam."

There's the slightest hesitation in her voice, like it's not her real name. She doesn't look like she's much older than us. No doubt this girl's on a missing persons poster stuck to a pole somewhere.

"Do you have that picture?" she asks. "Maybe I can help."

Callie pulls out her phone and shows her Emily, and Pam shakes her head. "Nah, I don't know her. But it doesn't mean she hasn't been through here. Lots of girls come through here."

"What about the girl who got killed?" I ask. "Did you ever see her around?"

Pam shakes her head. "She wasn't one of us, you know? From what I been hearing, she used Connect. Sometimes those girls meet men here, but I never seen her."

"Do a lot of truckers use that site?" I ask.

Pam looks uncomfortable. "No. Using the site to find men ain't smart at all. We don't do it. I mean, I've heard horror stories."

"What about a guy who calls himself Captain?" Ryan chimes in. "Our fr—her sister met a creepy guy on Connect. He didn't want sex from her."

Pam's expression changes, and a flicker of hope lights in me.

"We look out for each other," she says. "We got, like, a list of guys to stay away from. You can't tell nobody about this, okay?"

Callie and I nod. Ryan doesn't. I glare at him.

"Okay," he says.

Pam hesitates. "So, like, I used to work the Penn Welcome Center off 81, before they shut it down. It was rough, like rougher than here. This woman kind of took me in. I can't tell you her name or nothing 'cause she asked me not to. But she also danced at a strip club that used to be across the highway."

Pam lowers her voice. "So one night we're talking about johns to stay away from, and she tells me that four years ago, she met

245

this guy while she was dancing. She brought him in her car to the stop. And it was just like you said—he didn't want to touch her or nothing. She got real frustrated and made a move, and he hit her in the face. She tried to fight back, and he *choked* her."

Callie stiffens next to me.

"So she, like, passed out and stuff, and when she woke up, they were parked in the woods and the man was going through her trunk. But she always carried a box cutter, and she played like she was still passed out." Pam pauses for effect. "When he opened the door, she cut him in the face. He had her keys, so she had to run screaming for help, and he chased her for a while, but eventually he gave up and she got away.

"Anyway," Pam says. "It reminded me of your Captain guy, because she said he was in like a uniform of some sort. She didn't talk about it for years, 'cause she thought he was a cop and he'd find her and finish the job, you know?"

I swallow to clear my throat. "Did she tell you anything at all about what he looks like?"

"Like they all do." Pam rolls her eyes. "In his forties, maybe. Average height, balding. She told me to look out for two things, though."

The three of us practically lean forward.

"His eyes," Pam whispers. "She said his eyes are friendly."

Callie glances at me. I know what she's thinking. If this is Captain, he sounds nothing like Daryl Kouchinsky.

"What's the other thing?" Ryan asks. "That she told you to look out for."

"Oh, well, she got him real good on the face," Pam says. "So he's got to have a scar."

Pam looks down at her nails, which are bitten to the cuticle. "I don't know. I just been thinking of him lately since that girl got killed. He's probably not who your girl is hanging around with," she says quickly, her eyes sympathetic.

I almost want to tell Pam that we don't have a missing friend at all, but under her innocence I sense a woman who knows how to take care of herself. A woman who wouldn't like being lied to for information.

We thank Pam and head back toward the truck. Callie stops, like she forgot something. Ryan and I turn and watch her take a twenty from her wristlet and give it to Pam. I feel my eyes narrowing as Callie says something, and Pam nods.

"What did you say to her?" I ask when Callie catches up.

"Just to be careful." Something in Callie's demeanor has changed since we got here—as if all her bravado had been stripped away. She's silent as we climb into the truck and start the hourlong journey home. From the backseat, I watch her reflection in the side mirror.

She barely blinks the entire ride, like she's afraid to fall asleep now that she's finally awake.

CHAPTER TWENTY-FOUR

Somewhere around exit forty, I break the silence in the truck.

"I think the guy Pam described is Captain, and I think he's the real Monster."

Ryan says nothing.

"Tell me you think I'm wrong." I find his eyes in the rearview mirror. "You risked getting your uncle in trouble by telling us how Ariel was killed, you didn't rat Nick out, and you came with us tonight. You believe that they got the wrong guy for the Monster murders too."

Ryan's quiet.

"And if you didn't know already, Callie and I didn't see Stokes in her yard that night," I say. "We were just kids, and they manipulated us to get the statement they wanted."

Callie leans her head against the window. I can't tell if she's mad at me for telling Ryan. Maybe he already knew. Either way, his face is expressionless. Some people are impossible to read.

Ryan finally speaks after a loaded pause. "If the Monster murdered Ari, why did he start again? Why risk being caught after all these years? It doesn't make sense."

"He tried to kill another girl. He would have killed Pam's friend if she hadn't gotten away," I say. "He probably figured he had to lay low for a while in case she told someone about him. He's smart enough to have stayed hidden all these years. Obviously, he knows law enforcement. Maybe he's even—"

"Don't say it," Ryan says. "That he could be a cop."

"Why? The man Pam described sounds nothing like your uncle."

"Tessa." Callie's voice is sharp. "Just stop."

There's quiet for a beat, until Ryan speaks up. "Cop or not, no one's gonna believe the word of a prostitute. Nick is the only one who can corroborate that this Captain guy exists, and without the chat history on Ari's phone, his word is as good as nothing."

"He's going to do it again," I say quietly. "If he thinks he can get away with it, he'll do it again."

"I have an idea," Callie says, so firmly that I suspect she's been thinking of it this whole time. "Of something that we can do. To draw him out."

"No way," Ryan says. "I know what you're probably thinking, and that's nuts—"

It dawns on me, what they're talking about.

"It could work," I interrupt, my toes tingling. "We create a fake profile on all the escort sites and see if we can bait him. We know his type. Skinny, big eyes. Lonely."

"It's dangerous, and it *won't* work." Ryan grips the steering wheel. "This guy has gotta be on high alert right now. If he's smart enough to stay hidden for ten years, he'll sense he's being set up."

"So we make him think we're legit," I say. "He won't smell a cop, because there aren't any."

"If he contacts us, we'll see where he wants to meet up," Callie says, excitement in her voice. "But instead of meeting him, we stay in the car and scope it out. See what he looks like, and get a picture to show the cops."

We're almost at the exit for Fayette. Callie puts her hand on Ryan's knee. It's the first remotely affectionate gesture I've seen her make toward him.

"If it were you—if you were so wrong about something and it wound up hurting someone, wouldn't you do anything to make it right?" Callie says.

Even though she's not looking at me, I know she's talking to me. I know that in her own way, she's saying she's ready to be wrong, and for everything it means. That even if we'll never know what really happened to Lori that night, we can undo some of the damage we caused if we can just find the Monster who killed Ari.

There's an uneasy feeling in my gut. *Anything to make it right.*

Gram always says that people get what they deserve in the end. But could ending everything be as easy as finding Captain?

If making things right isn't the end of this ten-year nightmare, then what is?

• • •

Ryan drops us off at the bottom of the Greenwoods' driveway.

"You can't tell your uncle about any of this," Callie says through the window once we step out.

"You do realize that eventually we're gonna have to tell someone?" Ryan says.

Callie is stone-faced. Ryan snorts. Shakes his head.

"What?" Callie demands.

"I don't know why you do that," he says quietly, as if only she could hear.

"Do what?" she says, and I step back, wishing I could disappear.

Ryan just shakes his head again. "Act like you don't need help, when everything about you is crying for it."

So maybe I underestimated Ryan Elwood. Callie's lip twitches, but she doesn't say anything. Neither of us says anything as Ryan pulls away, his headlights disappearing down the street.

"He's right," I say. "About telling someone. We're running out of time, and I can't stay forever."

I don't get to see Callie's reaction, because she screams. There's someone crouched behind the minivan. Daryl Kouchinsky emerges from the shadows and blocks our path up the driveway.

It all happens too fast for me to react. Before I can even move, Callie's shrieking and Daryl's cursing and has her by the throat, lifting her off the ground by one hand. He slams her against the minivan, her head bouncing against the window.

"Heard you visited my daughter yesterday," he grunts. "You trying to put ideas in her head, you little bitch?"

Callie tries to shake her head, but Daryl is pressing his thumb into her trachea, and she can't move.

I run for one of the potted plants lining the driveway and lift it up. It's heavy, and it teeters as I raise it as high as my arms will allow. I come up behind Daryl and smash it into the back of his head.

He sways backward. I freeze, afraid that I've killed him. Callie crumples to the ground, crying. Daryl's on his feet again, and he turns to me and blinks, stunned. He steps toward me, but there's yelling across the street and he freezes.

"Callie? What's going on?" a woman screams from her porch, clutching a phone.

Daryl takes one look at her and makes a break for his truck, which is parked in front of the next-door neighbor's house. We didn't even see it.

The woman across the street runs toward us, but I'm already on the Greenwoods' porch. I throw open the door and scream for Maggie. Footsteps thunder on the stairs as I turn and run back down the driveway.

Callie is slumped against the minivan, gasping for air, hands clutching her throat. The woman from across the street is on the phone.

"Yes, she's been attacked," the woman says, and gives the operator the Greenwoods' address. I'm shaking as I sit beside Callie, and I think I've peed myself a little. Maggie and Rick round the corner of the minivan and gasp.

"What happened?" Maggie shouts. "What the hell happened?"

"Daryl," Callie says, her voice hoarse.

Rick slams his hand against the car and says he's going to get his keys. I catch "I'm going after him."

Maggie grabs Rick's sleeve and shrieks that no he's not, and the neighbor shushes them because she's still on the phone with 911. Maggie sinks down next to Callie and holds her face in her hands.

"I'm okay," Callie says. She repeats it and turns her head toward me. "Tess . . ."

"What?" Maggie snaps her head toward me. Her eyes drop to my filthy hands, the broken flowerpot on the driveway.

252

She lets out a sob and pulls me to her chest. Maggie holds me so tightly that a single word materializes in my head. *Safe.*

I break away as an ambulance pulls up to the curb and stops, a police first responder SUV right behind it. Two EMTs throw open the back doors of the ambulance and roll out a stretcher. Red light and blue light spill over the driveway.

"For Christ's sake," Callie says. "I'm *okay*."

Maggie isn't hearing it. She makes them load Callie into the ambulance. By the mailbox, Rick is raising his voice at the police first responder, a guy who looks barely old enough to drink.

"—*u-c-h-i-n-s-k-y*," Rick spells. "I'll drive you to his house right now—"

"Sir, that's really not necessary." The guy holds up a hand. He presses the radio mic on his belt and tells the person on the other end to send another unit to the house. He points a pen at me.

"You were here?"

I describe what happened—that Daryl was waiting for us, I hit him over the head with the flowerpot, and he took off when the neighbor came outside. When the first responder asks if there's a reason why Mr. Kouchinsky would want to attack Callie, I hesitate, stealing a glance at Rick.

"We saw his daughter in the hospital yesterday," I say. "Someone beat her up, and it's not exactly a secret that Callie thinks it was him."

Rick's mouth forms a line. The first responder writes something on a notepad. A police cruiser pulls in as the ambulance pulls away, taking Callie and Maggie with it. Rick tells me to wait inside and says he'll call me out if the officers need to speak with me further.

My knees wobble as I pick my way up the stairs. I change into my pajamas and lock myself in the bathroom. I vomit into the

253

toilet—sour, nasty, adrenaline-crash vomit. I brush my teeth and head back downstairs. The flashing lights of the police cruiser have lit up the living room.

I have to talk to someone about what just happened, *everything* that's happened in the past eight hours. But if I tell Gram I spent the day chatting with escorts at a truck stop before assaulting a man with a flowerpot, she may get on a plane and come up here.

I have to get away from the lights in the living room before my head explodes. I slip into the family room and sit at Rick's desk, forcing myself to do the breathe-in-through-the-nose-and-out-the-mouth thing. It settles me enough that my fingers stop trembling, and I shake the mouse to wake the computer up. With Callie in the ER, I might as well read up more on Macy Stevens and try to make sense of the phone call.

In the most popular photo, Macy is holding a stuffed frog. Her light brown hair is in a stubby little ponytail on top of her head. I click through the other photos: Macy in long johns, a Christmas gift on her lap. Macy in a high chair, her mouth circled with something sticky and orange.

An age-progression picture, showing what Macy might look like now, at twenty-seven. The face is unsmiling, but the girl is striking. She looks like Amanda Stevens, who had enormous green eyes and milky-white skin. I make the image larger, and my blood chills.

I missed it earlier when I was looking at the photos—the small, angry pink gash on Macy's chin. One that would have turned into a scar in a few years.

I enlarge the photo more and zoom in, my pulse thrumming in my ears.

Is it on the same side?

No.

Yes.

I zoom in on the age-progression photo of Macy. They got her mouth wrong—she didn't get Amanda Stevens's full upper lip. But her eyes, the slight point of her chin—there's no doubt in my mind that it's her.

Joslin.

That son of a bitch. Did he know?

My father didn't kill Macy Stevens and hide her body. She lived in Fayette with him for most of her life.

CHAPTER TWENTY-FIVE

I need someone else to look at the photo. Someone who will tell me I'm certifiably batshit for even thinking that Macy Stevens is my sister.

Gram doesn't pick up the house phone, even though I call twice. A quick glance at the time sends a sliver of panic through me. It's almost nine. Gram never goes out this late.

I try her cell phone, and I'm as surprised when she picks up as she is to hear from me.

"Tessa?"

"I called the house twice," I say.

"I went for a walk," Gram says, crabby like she gets when I do my worrying thing. This time, I don't give her my usual speech, which is that stories where the woman goes for a walk alone at night end with her waking up chained to a water heater in some creep's basement.

This time, I say, "You need to tell me who Joslin's father is."

Gram wheezes. I imagine the humid Florida air choking her, slowing her heart to a stop. "I told you, Tess—"

"You *lied*." Something is unwinding within me, turning my

insides into a mess of live wires. I'm a pile of dynamite waiting for someone to say the wrong thing. "I'm goddamn sick of being lied to."

"*Lied?*" Gram sounds angry. "The only person who's lied to you is your mother, Tessa. She kept you from me. I've never even met my other granddaughter."

She's not your granddaughter. I can't say it. Won't say it. Gram will think that being in Fayette has pushed me over the edge.

And if I say it out loud—that I think Joslin is a kidnapped girl—it means I think that she's not really my sister. Even after all she's done—the lies, running away, not coming back for me—I would still feel like I'm betraying her.

I blurt out the first thing that pops into my mind. "I have a birth certificate, right?"

"What? Of course you do. You needed it to get your driver's license. Remember?"

Vaguely. Gram took care of the paperwork since I was so nervous that I wound up failing the driver's test twice. But then, *of course* I have a birth certificate. I was born in Fayette, on December 18. It was snowing that morning. Even my father remembers, when by his own admission most of his days after 1994 were spent in a Jameson haze.

But what about Joslin? There's no way that she has a birth certificate if she's really Macy Stevens.

Did Joslin find out? She must have, and that was why she left. But why wouldn't she have contacted the Stevens family? *Hi, I'm your dead granddaughter. Today* show reunion, that kind of thing. As far as anyone knows, Macy Stevens is a heap of baby bones, forever the grinning two-year-old with a plush frog.

"Tessa, what's this about? What's wrong?" Gram sounds panicked. I breathe in through my nose.

"Nothing," I say. "Nothing is wrong. I just . . . I need to prove that Glenn wasn't Joslin's father, in case she comes back and wants his money. I can't find her birth certificate without her father's name."

Gram chews on this; she must hear the lie in my voice. My father died without a pot to piss in.

"Tessa," she begins. "I've only ever kept things from you to save you pain you don't need."

"Gram. Please tell me his name."

"Alan Kirkpatrick," Gram sighs. "I never liked him. Some people just aren't good, Tessa, and I knew any kid of his and Annette's would be the same."

There's the sound of a siren, but it's on Gram's end, not mine. Her voice gets shaky. "I never looked that hard for your sister because I was afraid of what I'd find."

She has no idea. I can hear it in her voice.

It means that Gram wasn't in on it, the twisted string of events that lead to my mother and father raising a stolen child as their own.

I hate myself for even considering it.

• • •

Rick comes back inside. Tells me that Maggie called, and they're seeing Callie right away in the emergency room. The police have already sent out officers to pick up Daryl Kouchinsky. I nod, throw in an "Oh, okay" here and there. As soon as he sighs and heads into the family room, I call Callie.

Voice mail. I hang up without leaving a message, wondering at what point I decided I was going to tell Callie about my sister and Macy Stevens. I have no reason to think she'll actually believe me, and I realize that not many people would. Decker, maybe.

Maybe the FBI agent who called me earlier to scold me for dialing the Stevens. Don't they have to follow up on all the tips they get, even if it's one as far-fetched as an eighteen-year-old who thinks the sister she hasn't seen in ten years is Macy Stevens? The sister I don't even have a picture of.

I go upstairs and shut myself in the guest room, and I stay there even when I hear the front door open after midnight, and then footsteps on the stairs. There's murmuring. Someone flips the light in the hallway on. Off. Someone uses the bathroom.

My door creaks open. I squeeze my eyes shut and throw in a twitch for good measure. I'm a pro at pretending to be asleep. On those nights when my father brought me to the Boathouse with him, I'd lie in the backseat on the way home, acting like I was out cold so he'd carry me into the house.

Maggie doesn't flip my light on. She sits on the edge of my bed.

"I wish you'd been here," she whispers. "All these years . . . Everything would be different if she'd had you."

I can't tell if she knows I'm awake, or if she's saying it only because she believes I'm asleep.

I don't go to sleep after she leaves. And neither does Callie. In my head, we're playing a game: who can stay up the longest. I hear her padding around her room, the rolling of her desk chair against the hardwood, until I slip into nothingness sometime after four.

•   •   •

I wake up to knocking. Callie steps into my room, holding her laptop. I sit up.

Her hair is down, a mess of unspun silk. The sun catches on

three different shades of blond. Callie has always been one of those girls who can simply wake up and be beautiful. It makes the purple bruises on her neck all the more noticeable.

She touches her throat, catching me staring. "Is it that bad?"

Her voice sounds like it's scraping the side of a tin can. She winces.

I pull my knees up to my chest. "Are you—"

"It's fine." Callie sits on the bed with me, and not on the rocking chair like she usually does. "I have a really small concussion, so of course my mom is freaking."

"Daryl Kouchinsky tried to choke you. I think you can give her a pass this time."

The corners of Callie's mouth twitch. Her smile fades before it fully forms. "They picked him up for a DWI. They're holding him for that until I decide whether to press charges."

"Decide?"

Callie shifts so she's sitting butterfly-style, the bottoms of her feet touching. Her knees bounce. "You saw what he did to Katie just for talking to me. I'm only gonna make it worse for her. I'll get a restraining order." She lifts her eyes to meet mine. "I don't think it's him anymore."

"Me neither." Pam said Captain was average height. No one in her right frame of mind would describe Daryl Kouchinsky as average. He's the type of man who has to duck to pass through a doorframe.

"Anyway." Callie sighs. She opens her laptop and turns the screen toward me. "I did this last night."

I'm looking at a page on Connect for Sasha, a twenty-year-old happy to offer her services to gentlemen in Fayette and Westmoreland Counties. Willing to travel farther.

Sasha was an American Girl doll Callie had when we were

little. Not one of the cool dolls from a different period in history with her own set of chapter books, but one of the dolls custom-made to look just like you. Sasha even had soccer and twirling uniforms like Callie's.

"Nice name," I tell Callie as she scrolls down the page. My heart flip-flops. There's an over-the-shoulder mirror-selfie of a girl. She's in a bikini bottom, long blond hair spilling down her back. I recognize Callie's cell phone case—it's mint green with the outline of a dandelion, the flower's seeds scattered by an invisible breath.

"I left my face out," Callie says. "On all of the pages of the other girls I visited, no one shows their face. There are a ton of other sites too—it's pretty gross how many, actually—so I posted on all of them."

I have to look away. "I don't like this. I don't think we should do it."

Callie closes her laptop. "You know we wouldn't even consider it if there was any other way."

I swallow. "So what next?"

"We wait," she says. "And see if he's interested."

• • •

I tell Callie I might have a lead on Joslin, so she'll give me the van keys while Maggie and Rick are out. Callie wants to come with me, but I remind her that Maggie will flip her shit if she catches Callie out of bed.

My first stop is the library computer room. I enter in the number from Callie's card, and a gray box pops up with an hour timer for my Internet session.

I search *birth certificates* and get a hit for an archive site that boasts more than 4.6 billion records in its database. To test whether or not it works, I type in my mother's maiden name: Annette Mowdy. Place of birth: Florida.

2 records found. I can't view the full image of the scanned birth certificate without a paid membership, but it looks legit to me.

I search for Joslin Mowdy in Pennsylvania.

No records found.

I try Joslin Kirkpatrick, and when I get nothing, Joslin Lowell, even though my sister didn't take my father's last name until she was a few years old.

No records found.

I slip a finger through the hole in the knee of my jeans. This has to be a mistake. Or my mother lied about where Joslin was born; the story was that she left Joslin's father, moved to Pennsylvania, had a baby, met Glenn Lowell when the baby turned two, and Glenn and my mother married a year later.

But there are no birth records for a Joslin Mowdy or Joslin Kirkpatrick anywhere in the United States. The search engine asks if I meant *Justine Mowdy* or *Jason Kirkpatrick.*

I click out of the website. I glance over my shoulder, paranoid someone's realized I don't live here and is going to bust me for using Callie's card. But the people sitting at the computers around me are slack-faced zombies in front of their screens. I hope I don't look like that.

I do another search on Macy Stevens, browsing through a photo album *People* magazine posted five years ago. It seems as if she captivates people, still. Macy Stevens is America's Baby. The public wants answers as badly as her family does.

The thought that she strolled into the Fayette County Penitentiary last week as twenty-six-year-old Brandy Butler is insane.

I skim the article. One quote sticks out to me: *In a 2004 inter-*

view with Cynthia Chan, Robin and Bernie Stevens stated that they believe their granddaughter is still alive, and may have been sold on the adoption black market. Law enforcement has said they will continue to follow up on all possible sightings of Macy but cautioned that the trafficking of babies in the United States is extremely rare.

Cynthia Chan hosted *This Evening* on NBC before Diane Sawyer or someone else booted her from the spot. Gram watched her sometimes; Chan was a coiffed, monotone woman who nodded from her leather chair as her guests cried.

I find her interview with the Stevens family on YouTube and plug my earbuds into the computer. The video is forty minutes long. I skim the beginning, which seems to consist largely of Amanda's parents proclaiming Amanda's innocence.

Amanda got pregnant at nineteen. The baby's father was killed in a motorcycle accident. Amanda had a tough life. But she loved Macy and would never have hurt her.

At the twenty-minute mark, Cynthia Chan asks the Stevens what they think happened to their granddaughter.

"I think she was sold," Robin Stevens says, with all the gall of a woman who gets an idea into her head, and damn it if she's going to back down from it until she sees proof otherwise. I'm thrown. It reminds me of Joslin. In the back of my head, I hear my father's muttering.

Stubborn brat. Takes after her mother.

On my screen, Robin Stevens dabs her eyes with a handkerchief. Even sitting, she's half the size of her husband. Her hair is bobbed and dyed the color of cherry cola. She adjusts her black cat's-eye glasses. "Macy was a beautiful, healthy little girl. Do you know how much they'd pay for a healthy white baby on the black market?"

The video starts to buffer. I exit the screen. I've heard all that I need to hear anyway.

• • •

Wanda doesn't look surprised to see me. She sets down a sheath of paper and sighs, a heavy one that uses her whole body.

"Me again," I say.

"Honey, I don't know if I can help you." Wanda looks guilty, and I know she must have gotten my message and chosen not to respond.

I lean into the edge of the counter. "It's important. I found something in my father's things. I think he knew something about a missing girl."

Wanda swivels in her chair. Yells over her shoulder. "Bill, I'm taking my lunch now."

She stands up. I move toward the security grate.

"No, you stay right there," Wanda grumbles.

She meets me on the other side of the glass and motions for me to follow her outside. Off to the side of the building, there's an employee courtyard. Two long picnic tables where three guards eat from plastic trays.

Wanda and I sit at the unoccupied table. I notice she didn't bring her lunch.

"Is this about Macy Stevens?" she asks.

Something in me deflates. "I found a phone number. I called it, and something really weird happened. An FBI agent called me back and said the number was a hotline for a missing baby."

I expect Wanda to look surprised, maybe to ask me to go on. Instead, she sighs.

"Your father tried to extort the family of a famous missing

child," she says. "And he wasn't the first. Over the years, at least half a dozen inmates said they killed that little girl, Macy Stevens."

I blink.

"False confessions," Wanda explains. "They're serving life sentences, they get bored. Claim to know something about a high-profile murder, then say they know where the body is just to send police on a wild-goose chase and draw attention to themselves. Happens all the time."

"That doesn't sound like my father," I say. "He wasn't even in jail for murder. What if he really knew something?"

"He called the tip line saying he'd tell them where Macy is," Wanda says, "but only if they gave him the reward money first."

"And he never said anything more about it?"

Wanda shakes her head.

And there it is. The one thing I never thought could break me has left its first fissure.

Proof that my father was a piece of shit until the very end.

CHAPTER
TWENTY-SIX

As I turn onto Main Street, my phone begins to buzz in my pocket. The last thing I need is a ticket for talking on my phone, and there's nowhere to pull over on Main Street unless I do a risky parallel park. And damned if I'm going to let accidentally totaling Maggie's van be the thing that gets me sent back to Florida.

My phone stops ringing, and panic claws at me. If it's her, and I miss her, I may not be able to get her again.

My mother.

I squeeze into a spot in the post office parking lot just as my phone rings again. I dig it out of my pocket. It's Callie.

"Where are you?" Her voice is raspy, but better than it was yesterday. "I've been calling you."

"Yeah, I realize that." My heart is still pounding. I'm annoyed at Callie just for being Callie and not Annette. Until she says, "You have to come back. I think he messaged me."

. . .

When I get back to the house, Callie is sitting cross-legged on her bed, laptop resting in front of her.

"He didn't ask to meet up or anything." The words come out of her in a single breath. "But his username—"

I plop down on the bed and turn the laptop to me.

Private message from cpt818:

What's a nice girl like you doing on a site like this?

I look over at Callie. "*CPT* could just be fake initials or something to throw people off."

"Look at his picture." She points to the screen.

The profile picture is a man in a black hat and aviators. He's pointing a long-barreled shotgun at the camera. "This looks like a screenshot from a movie," I say.

"*Cool Hand Luke*," Callie says, excited. "That's Captain, the bad guy in *Cool Hand Luke*."

I look at Callie. "You've seen *Cool Hand Luke*?"

She shakes her head. "I emailed it to Ryan at work, and he recognized it. I told you he would be useful."

I ignore that. "What are you going to say to him?" The blood pounds in my ears. *This could be him. The Monster.*

Callie thinks for a second before she types: *What makes you think I'm a nice girl?*

Captain doesn't respond. The icon in the corner says he's signed off. She covers her mouth.

"Shit," Callie says through her fingers. "What did I do wrong?"

I get up and pace around Callie's room. Shit is right. I want to throw something, lean out her window, and scream *Shit, shit, shit!*

We had the son of a bitch. We had him, and we lost him.

• • •

The next morning, Callie insists that she's feeling better and up for the shopping trip to the Briarwood Outlets that she and Maggie have been talking about. I'm too defeated about our failed plan to lure Captain that I don't even fight when Maggie suggests I come along.

At Pottery Barn, Callie picks out navy-and-white sheets for her dorm room. We pass by Old Navy, where a sign in the window advertises two pairs of shorts for twenty dollars.

Maggie's face lights up. "Oh, I could use a pair."

Callie rolls her eyes, but Maggie drags us inside, to a table of shorts in every color you can think of.

"I only need one pair," she says, rifling through the stack. Callie stands in the corner on her phone, yawning. Maggie finds a pair of shorts in my size and thrusts them at me. "Why don't you try these on? Shame not to take advantage of such a good deal."

I know she just wants to buy me a pair of shorts so I'll stop sweating my ass off in the jeans I packed.

"Thanks," I say. I disappear into the dressing room with the shorts. I slip them on and check myself out in the mirror. My legs are pale, but I've picked up a couple more freckles on my nose from all the time I've been spending out in the sun. My hair falls in waves around my face, instead of being the crown of frizz I have to combat every day in Florida.

From the outside, it looks like being in Fayette has been good for me.

The handle of my door jiggles, and I jump back, feeling violated even though I'm dressed. Callie steps into the dressing room, her eyes frantic.

"Look." She shoves her phone into my face.

She's on Connect, her private message box pulled up.

Got any plans tonight, sweetheart? —CPTN

"Holy shit," I say.

There's a knock at the door. "How do they fit, Tess?" It's Maggie.

"Fine," I croak out. "Think I'll get them."

When Maggie pads away, Callie starts typing a response to Captain. I grab her fingers.

"What are you doing?" I hiss.

Callie shrugs away from me. "I *have* to respond. He'll suspect something's up if I disappear."

"Can't you ask him more about himself? Something we can use to figure out who he is?" I ask. Suddenly there's not enough air in the dressing room.

"If he's the Monster, he's too smart for that," Callie whispers. "You know we have to do this."

I force my trembling hands into the pockets of the jean shorts, and I watch Callie type a response back to Captain.

I get off work at 10. What kind of plans did you have in mind?

• • •

Rick is in bed by ten-thirty. Callie and I are watching a movie in the family room, each of us tucked into opposite corners of the couch. Maggie putts around in the kitchen. Starts up the dishwasher. At eleven, she pokes her head in to tell us to have a good night.

We've just started another movie. "We'll go to bed when it's over," Callie says, with a yawn added for flair.

"Okay." Maggie kisses us both on the head. I hear her wiggle the front doorknob three times to make sure it's locked, even though Daryl Kouchinsky is spending the night in a holding cell.

Maggie heads upstairs, and Callie and I are quiet. We watch

forty-five minutes of a Fast and Furious movie before her phone buzzes with a text.

"Ryan's down the street," she says.

We leave the TV and lights on, since Maggie thinks we'll be up for another couple hours watching the movie anyway. The Westfield Plaza is twenty minutes from Fayette. If Captain is on time and everything goes according to plan, we'll be back in an hour.

Said plan is, in Callie's words, "simple." We wait in the dark in Ryan's truck until Captain arrives. We get his license plate number and a photo, and we get the hell out before he realizes that Sasha's not coming.

Like lighting a Roman candle, if we mess up the timing, it'll blow up in our faces.

Ryan's truck is parked two houses down. Lights off. He nods to us as we climb in, his eyes two worried orbs in the dark.

"Can't believe we're doing this," he mutters as he turns the key in his ignition.

The truck engine stalls, and we all take a collective breath. But the engine starts as soon as he turns the key again, a firm rumble beneath us. In front of me, Callie grips the handle on the passenger door, her knuckles white.

We get to the shopping center fifteen minutes early. All the stores are dark, except for a seedy-looking bowling alley on the far side of the parking lot.

"There." I point to the bowling alley lot. "It's darker over there. We'll wait there so he can't see the truck."

In the side mirror, I see Callie open her mouth to protest. "We said Sasha would meet him in front of Target."

"Tessa's right," Ryan says. "We have to keep our distance till the last possible minute."

"So he can realize there's no Sasha and get away?" Callie frowns. "One of us should hide behind the Dumpster over by Target so we get a clear shot of his license plate."

"That's how you wind up *in* a Dumpster," Ryan says.

I'm quiet, considering Callie's point. Ryan turns in his seat to look at me.

"What?" He furrows his brow.

"She has a point," I say. "He might leave before we make it across the lot, and then we won't get his plate number. I could hide behind the Dumpster and run around the back of the store to Best Buy once I memorize it. You can pick me up from there."

Ryan grips the steering wheel. "No one is getting out of this truck."

"We've already risked a lot. I'm not risking him getting away." Callie has on her stubborn face. Ryan sighs and puts the truck into drive.

"You get the license plate, and you get the hell out of there," he says to me.

Thanks. I was planning on hanging out, I want to say. I know he's only agreeing to this in the first place because it's me and not Callie.

We have fifteen minutes until Captain is supposed to meet Sasha. Ryan drives over to Target, and I hop out of the truck.

Ryan drives off to the bowling alley across the parking lot. Above me, the lampposts cast an orange glow on the pavement. I duck out of their way, to the side of the building where the Dumpster is.

I crouch next to a discarded, wet plastic bag. My bladder constricts, and I remember having to pee every time I played hide-and-seek as a kid. I consider the mechanics of going back here, but it's ten minutes before twelve, and Captain might be early.

I flip my cell phone open. There's a text from Callie already. *Your feet are showing.*

I shift and look at the clock on my phone. Only a minute's passed, and I swear, time is moving more slowly. I run through every disastrous scenario in my arsenal. Captain isn't the same man who attacked Pam's friend. Captain *is* a cop, but the good kind, and he's coming to arrest Sasha.

11:56. Headlights wash across the pavement. I crane my neck to get a better look.

A silver Subaru Forester idles by the streetlamp farthest from the store, fifty feet away from me. The car parks and turns off his headlights but leaves the engine on, just like Captain told Sasha he'd do when he arrived.

Captain is early. Of course he is. My breathing becomes shallow, and I can't move.

Come on, Tessa. I crane my neck slightly, but I can't see the license plate from here. He's too far away. It's too dark. A red light blinks against the brick wall next to me, and I freeze.

I look up; a camera is pointing toward the front of the store. I didn't notice it before. That's why Captain parked so far away; he knew his plates would be out of range of the security feed. Goose bumps ripple down my back.

I text Callie. *Can't see. Stay where you are.*

I eye my options to the side; there's a row of shopping carts by a cluster of trees, about twenty feet from Captain's car and away from the lampposts. If I'm fast, I can dart behind the carts without him noticing. It should be close enough to make out his plates.

Just stay away from the light.

I suck in a breath and get to my feet. And I run.

I duck behind the shopping carts at the same time that the Subaru's lights go back on. It's bright enough that I can see the back license plate: CRK-1841.

"Shit," I say as Captain starts his car up. The driver's window rolls down, and an arm in a denim shirt hangs out.

Captain pokes his head out the window, surveys the parking lot. His gaze skates over the shopping carts but doesn't rest on where I'm hidden.

I see his face through the carts. He's bald, with a beard, and my breath catches.

It's *him*.

I know who the Monster is.

Lights wash over the Target lot. Not Captain's—Ryan's truck. Captain turns his head, sees the truck pulling up behind him. It looks like he mutters something, and then he gasses it. He's tearing across the parking lot without rolling up his window.

I run out into the lot, in front of Ryan's truck as he skids to a stop. Through the windshield, Callie's face is ashen.

I yank open the door and crawl over Callie to get into the backseat.

"Did you get the license plate?" Callie says, breathless, at the same time that Ryan shouts, "You got WAY too close. He could have seen you—"

"I saw him," I say. "I saw his face, and I know who he is."

They're silent.

"He works at the prison," I say. "He's a goddamned prison guard."

CHAPTER TWENTY-SEVEN

He handed me the bag of my father's things. He smiled at me, and I thought, *He looks like he has a daughter.* And I left and never thought about him again.

"Captain is the warden in *Cool Hand Luke*," Ryan says quietly. "Damn."

"What did he look like?" Callie whispers.

"Like Pam said. Bald, but he had a beard. Average build."

"What about the scar?"

I have to put an arm on the door handle to steady myself. "I couldn't see. But I wasn't close enough, and his beard might've covered it."

"I'll get my uncle to run his plates," Ryan says. "We can get a name."

"You don't have to." Callie turns and shows me the screen of her phone. She's on the Fayette County Penitentiary website, on a page titled "Our Staff."

"Is that him?" She points to a white-haired man in a navy police jacket. Captain Phillip Swain, head of corrections.

I shake my head and scroll down the screen. He's smiling in his photo.

He had friendly eyes.

Correctional Officer James "Jimmy" Wozniak.

The son of a bitch isn't even a captain.

• • •

Jay Elwood doesn't have a doorbell. Ryan raps on the door until a dog starts going berserk inside. A light flips on in the hall, and a male voice soothes the dog.

Ryan's uncle opens the door and blinks at Ryan. "What did you do?"

He thinks we're here for him to get us out of trouble. I don't know why, but that comforts me.

"Nothing," Ryan says as a giant white shepherd pushes past him and bumps its nose into Callie's crotch. Then mine.

"Sammy, down." Detective Elwood tugs the dog's collar. "That's not polite." He turns back to Ryan once Sammy is lying down at his feet, and angles himself so we can step inside the house. "Your mom know you're here?"

I cross the threshold and wince at the smell of dog and old Chinese food. Off the hall is a laundry room with socks spilling across the hardwood. Ryan's uncle kicks them out of the way and leads us into the kitchen, where he stops.

"Okay, what's going on?" He crosses his arms in front of his chest.

Callie looks at Ryan.

"Are you looking at anyone besides Nick for Ari Kouchinsky's murder?" Ryan asks.

Jay Elwood grabs a half-empty bottle of orange juice from the fridge. He sinks into one of the kitchen chairs, spreads his knees. "You know I can't answer that."

Ryan holds his uncle's gaze. A staring contest. "If you were, would it maybe be Jimmy Wozniak?"

Jay leans back in his seat. Eyes Ryan skeptically. "Guy who works at the prison?"

Ryan nods.

"He's a nice guy," Ryan's uncle says. "Does a lot of court transfers."

Ryan drags a chair closer to his uncle and plops himself onto the seat. "We think he met up with Ari. Nick described this weird guy she found on Connect, and he sounds just like a man who tried to kill a prostitute in Ridgefield."

Jay sits upright. "Whoa, hold up. Where did you get all this from?"

Callie's eyes flick downward. Jay doesn't miss it. He sets his juice down on the table with enough force to jolt me where I'm rooted in the kitchen doorway. "Have you guys been *talking* to prostitutes?"

"You gotta believe us," Ryan says. "Jimmy Wozniak uses Connect to find girls to kill."

"He could be the Ohio River Monster," I say. "He killed Ari just like he killed those other girls."

Ryan flinches.

"Who told you how Ari was killed?" Jay's voice is eerily calm. "Did Elliot Banks the *coffee boy* tell you that?"

Callie stares at Ryan. "You said your *uncle* told you the details."

Ryan looks like a dog that just got spanked. "I didn't want to get Eli in trouble."

"Unbelievable," Jay mutters, making a fist on the table. "Kid's ass is grass. This is how shit gets to the media."

"We didn't tell anyone else," Ryan says in a rush. He points to Callie and me. "Don't you think they have the right to know? They testified against the guy *your department* says is the Monster. Even if there's the smallest chance they were wrong, they should know."

Officer Elwood wipes his hand down his face. "Go home, Ry."

Ryan's bottom lip twitches. "You have to look into Jimmy Wozniak. *Please,* Uncle Jay."

"I'll pull his file, see if there are any red flags," Jay says, leading us to the door. "That's really all I can do."

Jay whistles as he holds the door open for us, prompting Sammy to stand up to her full height. She jumps up and rests her paws on Ryan's chest. "I can't believe you've been digging around behind my back," Ryan's uncle says. "What were you thinking, Ry?"

Ryan flushes and gently removes Sammy's paws from his chest.

"You stay far away from this guy," Jay says. "If he *is* involved, and you tipped him off . . ."

I stiffen. Next to me, Callie looks like she's going to faint. Jay shakes his head and shuts the door.

None of us speaks the entire way home.

• • •

Callie goes straight to bed after Ryan walks us up to the house. I lie under the bed in the guest room, unable to sleep. The ticking of the cuckoo clock is like someone rattling the sides of my brain. I crawl out, grab the afghan, and head downstairs.

While the computer starts up, I watch the muted TV. I wonder if Jimmy Wozniak can't sleep either, now that he suspects Sasha was never real. Does he realize someone is onto him?

I pull the afghan tight around my shoulders. When the Internet browser loads, I search *Macy Stevens scar*.

I get a hit in the Cyber Sleuths forum and comb through the chatter. Apparently when the police questioned Amanda about it, she said Macy had hit her chin on a glass coffee table. But when they talked to Amanda's friends, some of them remembered commenting on the scar, and what Amanda told them. *When she grows up, it'll be a reminder not to be such a little pain in the ass.*

Years later, everyone seemed to agree with Brenda Dean that Macy's scar wasn't from an accident.

My mother's voice fills my head. I see her, hovering by the TV, two fingers propped gently against her chin as she absorbed the atrocities of the evening news. Something about a woman who had drowned her newborn.

"There's a special place in hell for people who hurt their own children," she said.

Above me, the floorboards creak. I shut the computer down and plop onto the couch, afghan over me to pretend I'm sleeping.

Footsteps on the stairs. Callie's voice. "What are you doing down here?"

I sit up. "Couldn't sleep."

Callie sits on the opposite end of the sofa. Tucks her feet beneath her. "Me neither."

After a beat, Callie says, "Did you know there were gray fibers on two of the victims?"

I nod. The judge didn't allow the fibers to be introduced into the trial, since they'd been ruled "inconclusive." Some of the Cyber Sleuths say the fibers couldn't have come from Stokes. They were polyester, and a search of Stokes's trailer didn't turn up any clothing made from that material.

The judge said the fibers could have been from anyone the victims had come into contact with, and besides, Stokes could have gotten rid of the clothes he'd been wearing during the murders.

"The state corrections officer uniform is gray," Callie says.

I know she's waiting for me to say it. So I do.

"We have to go to the DA's office tomorrow morning."

Callie closes her eyes. Her face is awash in white and blue from the TV. "My mom will never forgive me. Us."

I can't tell her what she wants to hear, that Maggie will eventually accept that we're doing the right thing. "I know."

"Do you think we'll ever find out what happened to her?"

I know she's talking about Lori now. I hear the defeat in her voice, the fear of seeing Stokes walk free without Lori's real killer to take his place.

"I don't know," I admit. "But maybe this is the first step. They'll open a new investigation, and it'll be something."

Callie yawns into the dark. She shuts the TV off and curls onto her side, stretching her legs across the couch so they're grazing mine. I do the same.

Neither of us falls asleep, but we stay this way, sharing the couch and the blanket like we used to back when we didn't know that monsters were real.

CHAPTER TWENTY-EIGHT

Callie shakes me awake. The afghan is tangled around my feet. The cable box says it's seven a.m.

"I left a note for my mom saying we're getting breakfast at the deli and going to the pool," she says.

I'm still in the pants and T-shirt I was wearing yesterday. Callie hands me the pair of shorts we bought at the outlets, and I take them into the bathroom in the hall, tear the tags off, and wriggle them on.

"Is the courthouse even open this early?" I ask Callie when I step out into the hall.

"Eight," she says, "but I want to be the first ones there."

And she wants to slip out before Maggie wakes up. I don't think I could look her in the eye either.

I read up on the new district attorney on Callie's phone while we're in the car. She was a public defender for fifteen years before being elected DA three years ago. That's good; she's been on the other side of the law and may be empathetic to Stokes's case.

She also supports the death penalty. Not surprising, since this is Pennsylvania. But also not so good.

"What is it?" Callie is looking at me.

"I just realized something. If Stokes gets a new trial, and he loses, they won't reopen the murders." I swallow. "Then Wozniak gets to stay free. He gets to keep working in the prison where they're going to kill Stokes."

"Don't say that." Callie's knuckles twitch. I know she's trying to stop herself from pulling at her hair. Her fingers stay wrapped around the steering wheel, leeched of color, for the entire twenty minutes it takes us to get to the courthouse.

There are two news vans parked across the street. Outside the courthouse, there's an armored truck marked FAYETTE COUNTY PENITENTIARY.

A pit of dread opens in my stomach. I know Callie can sense it too. Something is going on.

A security guard stops us as Callie tries to pull into the parking lot. She lowers her window, and the guard bows his head to check us out.

"You ladies have an appointment?"

Callie glances at me. "No," she admits.

"No entry today," the guard says.

"Why? Is something going on?"

"Hearing for a high-profile inmate," the guard says. "So unless you're authorized personnel, I'm gonna have to ask you to turn around."

"A hearing?" Callie looks at me, as if I knew about this. *High-profile inmate.*

It can't be. The judge hasn't set a date yet for Stokes's first appeal hearing.

We can't already be too late.

Callie's already opted for another tactic. "Sir, this is an emergency. We really have to talk to someone in the district attorney's office—"

"Emergencies are for the police." The guard taps the top of her car, as if to say, *Get on out.*

Twenty feet from us, in the fire lane in front of the courthouse, two guards lead a man in a jumpsuit out of the armored truck. He's Hispanic, and his hands and feet are chained.

"Callie. It's not him," I say, relief rising in me like a tidal wave.

"Sorry," Callie tells the guard. I can tell from her voice that she feels it too.

"S'okay. Pull over to the side and make a U-turn when it's clear," the guard tells us. Callie pulls over to let another van from the prison through, and she's already on her phone when the security guard stops it.

"Who are you calling?" I ask.

"Ryan," she says. "He's not picking up."

A door slams next to us. I watch a man climb out of the van from the prison. He opens the back for the security guard to inspect, whistling and looking over his shoulder.

The man notices us idling. He smiles at me, and my legs go numb.

It's him.

I look away, quickly, and Callie hangs up and turns her head.

"Don't do anything," I whisper. "Don't stare at him."

Callie's silent. I look up; Jimmy Wozniak is watching us, more intently now. The guard says something to him, and he nods. Gets back into his van and drives into the parking lot.

"We have to get out of here," I tell Callie. She puts the car in neutral by mistake. Corrects it to drive, then hits the pedal too hard and drives into the curb. The security guard is walking over to us, annoyed.

"Oh my God," Callie whimpers as she pulls herself together for long enough to make the U-turn. I wave a *Sorry* to the security guard as we speed out of the parking lot.

"It's okay." I dig my nails into the door handle. "There's no way he could know—"

"My case," Callie blurts. "He saw me on the phone, and my cell phone case—"

She doesn't have to finish.

Her cell phone case is in the photo we used to lure Jimmy Wozniak to the Target parking lot last night. I swallow.

"It's fine, we're fine," I say, as if repeating it would make it true. Callie's already tugging at her bangs.

"What are we supposed to do now? I don't want to wait until tomorrow to talk to the DA."

"We can call and leave a message," I say, trying to stay calm. As if by doing that I could hold everything together. "There's still time."

Callie exhales, but the pit in my stomach grows. I don't know if there's still time, but I just need her to believe that there is for now.

• • •

Callie calls the DA's office from her cell once we get home. She sits in the armchair, rolling her eyes every time she gets transferred. "There's seriously no one I can leave a message with right now?"

The ball of anxiety in my stomach, the one that's been growing since our trip to the courthouse this morning, finally explodes. "Let me talk to them."

Callie leans back in the chair as I try to wrestle the phone from her hand. She covers the receiver, eyes wild. "What the hell? Get off me."

I look down and realize I have my other hand wrapped around her free wrist. I pull back, suddenly unable to breathe. I run upstairs and shut myself into the guest bedroom.

Maybe it's a panic attack, or worse. Maybe I've really, truly lost it. Who is going to believe us about Jimmy Wozniak being the Ohio River Monster? The only reason they listened to our story as kids was because they needed it.

No one was ever really listening to us at all.

I close my eyes, and I see Lori. I see Baby Macy Stevens and I see my father, shriveled and spitting blood onto his cot in prison.

The guest room door swings open, and I yelp. Callie looks at me, confused.

I put a hand to my chest. "You scared the shit out of me."

"Sorry." Callie walks over, sits next to me on the bed. "Are you okay? You look like you're gonna pass out."

"Fine." But I can hardly get the word out. My heart is hammering in my chest, and my chest is so tight, I can't breathe. I lie on my side on the bed, blinking the light spots away from my eyes.

"You're freaking out." Callie hovers over me, her face concerned. "You want a Valium?"

I nod. Callie disappears, and I pull my knees up, hug them close. The minutes tick by, and my heartbeat slows. I don't even really need the Valium anymore. I sit up and wait for Callie to come back; my knees feel wobbly.

I watch the clock overhead. Callie's been gone almost ten minutes. She must have gotten distracted by something. I lift myself off the bed and head downstairs.

"Callie?" I call out.

She doesn't respond as I pad into the living room. From the hall, I see a glass of water on the kitchen island. Next to it is a bottle of Valium prescribed to Margaret Greenwood.

Also, Callie's cell phone.

I stick my head out the back door and call her name again. Nothing except the dogs going nuts next door.

I run into the living room, push the curtains aside. The mini-van is still in the driveway. I open the front door and call Callie's name. Then Maggie's, because I haven't seen her since we got back from the courthouse.

Callie would never go somewhere and leave her phone behind.

He followed us back, I think, my stomach folding into itself.

I look at the kitchen island. I picture the Monster coming to the back door, telling her to drop everything and come with him. She didn't scream; maybe he had a gun. But the dogs next door definitely heard his car.

I dial 911 from Callie's cell and tell them I need to report an abduction, and to please send Jay Elwood.

CHAPTER
TWENTY-NINE

A police cruiser with its lights on and siren off pulls up to the curb. Two uniformed officers step out and survey the house. The one who was in the passenger seat—a woman—says something into her radio.

"Where's Detective Elwood?" I ask.

"Are you the one who put in the call?" the other officer asks. I recognize him from the night Daryl attacked Callie.

"Yeah, and I asked them to send Jay Elwood—"

He holds up a hand. "I need you to calm down and tell me what happened."

I know how this looks. There's no sign of a struggle in the kitchen. It looks like Callie just wandered off, and I don't have time to explain why I know she wouldn't do that. Not now.

"She didn't come upstairs when I called her, so I ran to the front of the house, and I saw a man forcing her into his van," I lie. "He had a gun."

"Tessa?"

I turn to see Maggie at the end of the driveway, in shorts and a sweat-soaked T-shirt. She takes off her headphones; her eyes are saucers as she takes in the police officers. "What's going on?" she calls to me. "Where's Callie?"

"Ma'am, let's go into the house," the woman officer says.

"No, I want to know what the hell is going on." Maggie steps onto the lawn, coming toward me. An officer steps in front of her, putting an arm across her chest.

"Tessa, what happened?" Maggie shouts.

I can't make my mouth form the words. Down the street, a siren blips. Two more cop cars. A blue Ford Escape is behind them. Jay Elwood is at the wheel.

Maggie's shouting at the female officer now. I take the opportunity and run for Jay Elwood's SUV. He hops out and heads straight for me.

"What happened?"

"He took her," I say. "We saw him at the courthouse this morning, and he must have followed us home—"

"Who?" Jay barks, quieting his radio.

"Jimmy Wozniak. He had a gun," I lie again, because the truth won't buy us enough time to find Callie before he kills her.

"What was he driving?" Jay barks.

I hesitate, and Jay looks like he wants to throttle me. As though he can tell I'm lying. I think fast; there's no way Wozniak had time to go get his Subaru if he followed us here.

"A white van," I blurt. "From the prison."

Jay wipes a hand down his chin. The officer who was interviewing me trots over, confused.

"Put an alert out on a white prison transport van. I want units out looking for her," Jay tells him. He rounds on me. "You, get into the car. I need to put you with a sketch artist."

"I told you, it was Jimmy Wozniak—"

"I can't release his picture, but I can release a sketch. Get in the car."

I look back at Maggie. One hand holding her cell phone to her ear, the other covering her mouth. I imagine her begging Rick to come home. Another screw loosens in me.

I nod mechanically and get into Jay's car.

Jay backs the SUV away from the curb with one hand and uses the other to radio a message to the station. We hit a pothole, and my stomach rockets into my throat.

"We're not going to get to her in time," I say, my voice a choked-up warble.

Jay mutes his radio. "The next couple hours are critical. So if I were you, I'd try to be helpful instead of arguing with me."

I clench my jaw, grinding my back teeth against each other. I repeat my lie about Jimmy Wozniak forcing Callie into the prison van.

Jay's police scanner blips midstory. "Got reports of an abandoned vehicle. Wooded area off 74."

Two drops of rain glide across the windshield, and Jay turns his wipers on, but I can tell the scanner has his attention. "Sending highway patrol to check it out . . ."

I stare at Jay until he looks at me. "I-74 is where he dumped his victims."

Jay pinches the bridge of his nose. Mutters something under his breath. He holds his radio to his face. "Wait for backup. Officer en route."

He slaps a blue orb onto his dashboard. The light revolves around its center. Jay glances at my belt buckle and hits the gas. He passes the turn for the police station and gets onto the highway.

"You stay in the car," Jay says to me. "No matter what we find up there, you stay in here, understood?"

He thinks she's dead already. The scene blurs around me. Green and brown trees, blue light, gray highway—they spin into each other like paint on an art wheel.

This is not how any of this was supposed to happen.

The police dispatcher radios in the exact location of the car. I glance at Jay's speedometer. He's doing ninety. I dredge up an old physics formula from the place where I store information I'm not sure I'll need again. The force of this moving car is equal to one half its mass multiplied by its volume, squared.

I don't know how much this car weighs or how to convert it to kilograms anyway. The force is enough to kill us if we hit anything, I decide.

It would probably be fast. Painless. At least less slow than hearing the police explain to Maggie how letting me into her home could have destroyed so many lives.

Jay slows when we reach a break in the guardrail. Wooded area on each side of the highway. Miles until the next rest stop. He gets out of the car and locks the doors. Surveys the embankment.

There's a white van at the bottom.

Jay gets back into the Escape and starts the engine. "Hold on," he says.

The engine revs. Branches scrape against the windows as Jay drives us to the bottom of the embankment. He parks next to the van and leaps out of the car. He approaches the back window, his gun drawn.

The look on his face says it's empty.

A scream rips through the air.

Jay raises his gun and spins on his heel; I see her first.

Callie, pressed against Jimmy Wozniak like a shield. He has one arm wrapped around her body, the other aiming a gun at her temple. Twenty feet away from the van.

"Get back into the car," Wozniak barks at Jay, loud enough for me to hear through the window. His face is calm, like someone who is used to giving orders.

"I can't do that," Jay calls back. "Jimmy, is it? Let's talk about this, Jimmy."

Wozniak jerks Callie upright. From here, I can tell she's crying. "I can't go to prison," he says. "I'd rather die than eat and shit with those animals."

"Put the gun down, and we'll talk about it," Jay yells. "Come on, Jimmy. You got a wife? Kids?"

"I know what you're doing," Wozniak shouts back. "You have any idea what they'll do to a guard in there?"

"You won't have to go there." Jay's arms waver as he holds up his gun. "They'll transfer you somewhere no one knows who you are—"

Wozniak smiles. "There isn't a place in the world where they won't know who I am."

Wozniak's cheek is pressed to Callie's—even if Jay were a sniper, he wouldn't be able to shoot Wozniak without hitting her too.

Wozniak knew it would end like this. He knew we knew who he was, and that they'd find him after all these years. The Monster came here to die, and he brought Callie with him.

"Don't do this, Jimmy!" Jay shouts. "Think of your family."

Callie jerks under the Monster's grip. She says something to him that I can't hear. He looks down at her.

Wozniak's finger moves on the trigger. A gunshot. I scream and lunge at the dashboard.

The Monster crumples. Callie backs away, presses against a tree. Her mouth is open in a silent scream. Blood and brain matter in her hair, on her face.

Jay Elwood looks at the gun in his hands, stunned. I stop shaking for long enough to stumble out the passenger door.

"You could have killed her," I scream.

Jay turns and looks at me, stricken. "I didn't fire."

Callie is still pressed against the tree. "I . . . I asked him if he killed Lori."

She lowers her eyes to his body. I can't look. And I already know the answer, because Wozniak's lips didn't move before he blew his brains out.

If the Monster killed Lori Cawley, the truth just died with him.

CHAPTER
THIRTY

It's dark by the time an officer drops me off at the hospital. They won't let me see Callie until they process both of our statements separately. The receptionist tells me that Maggie and Rick are in the room with Callie. An officer hasn't interviewed her yet, but they'll send someone down to talk to me.

I sit in a chair outside the gift shop. I'm cold, and my cell phone is dead.

I'm not alone. A little girl prances in front of me, arms out, spinning semicircles with her torso. Her braids spin along with her, the beaded ends thwacking against each other. She watches me from beneath her hair. I wave to her, and she scampers into the gift shop.

I tell myself that if Maggie comes down to see me, everything will be okay. If she sends Rick, it means she's angry with me for almost getting Callie killed.

The little girl with the braids leaves the gift shop, clinging to a woman on her cell phone. I watch other people file out after them, and I rank them from least serious reasons for visiting to most serious. A woman with a balloon and a teddy bear. Least. A man with two children and a ghastly look on his face. Most.

They all make their way to the elevators. There's no sign of Maggie, or Rick.

It's been fifteen minutes. I can't bring myself to ask the receptionist to call up to Callie's room again.

Twenty minutes. Two police officers enter through the sliding doors. They walk right past me as if I weren't even here.

Half an hour. I watch a woman approach the reception desk and wrap her arms around her body, like she's cold.

"Is Tessa Lowell here?" she asks.

I sit up straight. That voice . . . I'm transported back to the night of the gas station.

Tessa, baby, get into the car.

Where are we going, Mommy?

I stand up. Stare at the woman's back. "Mom?"

She turns to me, her eyes going wide. She hurries over to where I'm standing. Stops in her tracks, as though she were looking at a ghost.

"Tessa," she whispers. She throws her bony arms around me. Even if I wanted to, I couldn't hug her back, she's squeezing me so tightly.

"You're hurting me," I croak out.

My mother lets go of me. Smiles and runs a hand through my waves. I was in such a hurry when I discovered that Callie was gone that I didn't even put my hair up. "You cut it," my mother says in a single sad breath.

"How—how did you know I was here?" I can't believe *she's* here. "Did you get my message?"

My mother nods. "This morning. I've been calling you for hours," she says. "I kept getting your voice mail, so I drove down here. I went to the Greenwoods, and a neighbor said everyone was at the hospital—Tessa, I was so worried." My mother grasps my forearms. She lifts a hand to my face. I turn away.

"Look at me," she whispers. "I can't believe it's you."

I can't form a response. I want to look at her, to press my face into her shoulder and see if she still smells like old leather and the peppermint oil she took to calm her stomach.

She's my mother, but she's a stranger.

"Is Joslin here?" I ask her.

Annette blinks. "Why would your sister be here?"

"She came to see Daddy," I say. "Right before he died."

My mother's face falls. "Glenn is dead?"

I can't help it. I grab her forearm and dig my nails in. "Where the *hell* have you been? Where's Jos?"

"You're making a scene," my mother hisses. "Let's talk in the cafeteria."

I want to say that I'm not going anywhere with her until she tells me the truth about my father, Joslin, and Macy Stevens. But a hospital cafeteria is as public a venue as I'll get, and if there's one thing my mother hates, it's a public scene.

I find us a table as she buys a coffee for herself and a hot chocolate for me. I keep my eyes on her back as she moves down the line, as if she might disappear again if I look away for even a second. As she's paying, she glances over her shoulder. Like she's afraid I'm not still here.

She smiles as she collects the cups and makes her way toward me. I look away. Pretend to be fascinated with the man in scrubs next to me as he dumps hot sauce onto his burrito. I wonder how the doctors can eat in a place like this; how they can go from stitching someone's skin back together to cutting through a slice of roast beef.

"Here you go—hot chocolate." Annette places a Styrofoam cup in front of me. She sits and watches me expectantly as I lift the cover off to let some of the steam out.

"Thank you," I say. Annette looks pleased, as if I'd done her a favor. She watches me blow and sip, her hands knitted together on top of the table. "I couldn't get you to stop eating the dry mix with a spoon. I had to hide the container above the fridge."

And Joslin would climb on top of the counter to be able to reach it for me. I burn my tongue on the hot chocolate.

Annette eyes me over the rim of her cup. "How is she? Your grandmother." My mother swallows. "Maggie brought me here that night, you know."

"Here?" I ask. "The hospital?"

Her eyes flick downward. "The psychiatric unit. I stayed for a week. I was so low, Tessa, after your father, and your sister . . . I failed you. But as soon as I got better, I wanted you back. Only, by then, your grandmother had already come to get you."

I'm quiet. I never knew that Maggie went back for my mother that night. How come she never told me?

"How is she?" Annette asks. "Your grandmother."

"She's fine," I say.

Annette hasn't touched her coffee. "She probably told you things about me—lies—"

"Don't talk to me about Gram," I say, anger igniting in me. "She's the one who was there for me for the past ten years."

Annette's eyes flash. "Has she told you once in all that time that she loves you?"

I can't look at her.

"She never, ever told me she loved me." Annette's eyes glisten. "Never—"

"I said I don't want to talk about her."

Annette seems to shrink in her seat. "Even if I'd had the money to get to Florida, I wouldn't have been welcome in my mother's home. She wouldn't have let me *see* you."

I slam a hand down onto the table. "You didn't call. Not once. You could have been dead, for all I knew."

"Tessa, I was dead inside. I'd lost both my daughters—"

"Don't say that." My head is cloudy. "You don't get to pretend that we died, when I'm right here."

Nausea hits me, swift and hard. I force myself to look my mother in the eye. "Did Joslin run away because she knew the truth about who she was? That you *took* her?"

"What are you talking about?" My mother sounds nervous. "Tessa, are you feeling okay?"

My head feels like it weighs nothing. Black spots dance in front of my eyes.

"I'm fine." The words stick in my mouth. "I want to talk about Jos. About *Macy*."

Annette takes my hand in hers. Her face blurs. "Macy? Who's Macy?"

I'm slumping in my chair, and my ears are ringing. "I think—I think I'm gonna pass out."

"Let's get you to the lobby. I'll find a doctor—"

I turn my head to the side, where the man in the scrubs with the burrito was, but he's gone. Annette helps me to my feet, and the blood rushes to my head.

"You're okay," Annette whispers into my ear. I'm fading, and I think people are looking at me.

"We have to go out to the ER," my mother says. She leads me through the visitors' entrance. A cold blast of air in my face, then thick humidity on my skin. *This isn't the way to the ER. We're* outside. I double over, and Annette helps me so I'm standing, tells me it's just a bit farther—

A car door opens, and I'm crawling into the backseat, a pickup truck, I think, a hand on my back. A voice somewhere far off screams *No, no, NO,* but my limbs won't work.

The last thing I hear before everything goes black is my mother's voice.

"We were finally safe, Tessa. Why did you have to do this?"

CHAPTER
THIRTY-ONE

Wool scratches my face. The faint smell of rose cream, the kind my sister rubbed into her hands every night before bed.

I open my eyes, thinking I've been dreaming about my old house. My vision clears, and I can see a brown knit blanket hanging off me, grazing the wood-planked floor. My old house was carpeted.

The blood rushes to my head as I sit up. I run my fingers over the blanket. Hold it to my face and breathe in, even though just looking at it is enough. It's mine.

It *was* mine.

I get out of the bed and take small steps over to the only window in the room. Sunlight streams in, an assault to my blurry vision.

Sun. It's the morning. The thoughts swirling in my head start to settle.

Jimmy Wozniak is dead. He blew his brains out right in front of Callie and me.

Hours at the police station. Then the hospital. Hot chocolate with my mother.

The goddamn hot chocolate.

Rage rips through me as I find the door. I jiggle the knob. Locked. I slam my palm against the door and scream. "What did you do to me?"

She doesn't come. I alternate between banging on the door and yelling, "What did you do to me, WHATDIDYOUDOTOME?"

When the flesh on my palm is red and raw, I throw myself onto the bed and scream. But I know it's no use—I knew it the second I looked out the window and saw nothing but sky and trees.

My mother has brought me to Bear Mountain, where no one will ever find me.

• • •

When I wake up again, I smell baked beans. I lie still on the bed until the lock in the door stirs.

"Are you hungry?" my mother asks.

I say nothing.

"I just wanted you to calm down." She sits at the foot of the twin bed, balancing a glass bowl on a pot holder. "We're going to figure everything out together."

She slides a plastic fork into my hand and holds the bowl in front of me. It hits me, how long it's been since I've eaten.

"What did you put in my drink?" I set the fork down and glare at her.

"Tessa—"

"I'm not eating shit until you tell me what you did to me and why you did it."

My mother opens her mouth and closes it. She forces a smile. "How about you come into the kitchen and I'll make you something else. I promise I won't put anything in it. You can watch."

I follow her into the living room of the cabin. Everything is made from flimsy-looking wood, as if one of the Three Little Pigs had constructed it. There's a kitchenette off the sitting area with a fireplace. A closed door on the other side of the room, adjacent to the front door.

"It's locked, Tessa," my mother warns me. "And there's no one around for miles."

She deposits me on the couch, within full view of the kitchenette. I watch her open a can of beans and heat it over a wood-burning stove. I notice that my mother's arms look firm, healthy, and I imagine her chopping the wood herself.

There's a lock on one of the drawers, where I can only assume that the utensils are held. A sick feeling washes over me. Has she been planning this since she found out that I was back in Fayette?

Annette places the beans in front of me, on a coffee table made from a split log. I ignore them.

"If you don't tell me who killed Lori, you'll have to carry my starved corpse out of here."

"Wyatt Stokes killed Lori," my mother says. She doesn't look at me when she says it.

"No, he didn't," I say. "Was it Joslin? Did Joslin kill her?"

Annette stares out the window. She doesn't deny it, but why protect Joslin now? Why lie to me now, when I'm trapped here with no one to tell?

My mother presses a palm to her cheek. Her hands are tanned, calloused. I picture them wrapped around Lori's neck.

Stay the hell away from me.

300

My mother isn't protecting Joslin. She was never protecting Joslin.

"Oh my God. Lori knew," I say. "Amanda Stevens killed herself that spring, after Brenda Dean's book proposal was leaked. Macy's picture was all over the news—that's how Lori figured it out. You had to kill her to keep her quiet."

My mother's gaze snaps to me. "Stop it."

"That's why you didn't fight Gram for me," I say. "You didn't come after me or call the cops because you couldn't risk everyone finding out you're some lunatic baby stealer—"

Annette is on me in a flash, stopping my words with a hard slap across the face. She aims too low and gets my jaw. I taste my lip, but she didn't draw blood. She stares at me, flinches, like she can't believe what she's done.

She never, ever hit me or Joslin.

I lunge for Annette, but she blocks me with her forearm. She forces me onto the couch. I try to yank my arms free from her grip, but she's stronger.

My father was wrong. I'm the weak one.

Annette grabs my jaw. "Open your mouth."

I clamp down, but she applies pressure on my face until my eyes water. I open my mouth, hating myself for letting tears escape. Annette reaches to the back of my throat and sticks a pill at the back of my tongue. She marches me into the kitchen and makes me drink a glass of water. Her hand is on the back of my neck. I jerk to shove a finger down my throat, but she catches my arm.

"If you throw it up, I'll have to do it again," she says gently.

She makes me sit on the couch, and she sits down on the other end, watching me. I return her stare until she grows another pair of eyes and her head splits into two. I close my eyes, fighting off another wave of nausea. Even if I could throw up what she just gave me, it's too late. I feel worse than I did when I woke up; the effect of whatever she's drugging me with must be cumulative.

It can't have been more than a day since Annette took me from the hospital. Maggie will have to wait at least forty-eight hours until the police allow her to file a missing persons report. It'll probably be longer before anyone realizes that I didn't leave with my mother willingly.

I touch my pocket, where my phone was last night. No doubt Annette took it, even though I'd have no use for it anyway. The battery has been dead since the hospital.

I drift into that fuzzy place between consciousness and sleep, and I find myself in the front seat of my mother's car ten years ago. I scramble out, my little legs getting tangled in fast-food wrappers, and I run across the highway.

She let me get away once, and the look on her face now says she'll never let it happen again.

CHAPTER THIRTY-TWO

I wake up on the couch. I raise my hand to wipe the drool crusted in the corner of my mouth, and curse. There's a zip tie around my wrists. I lift them both to my mouth and try to chew through the plastic. My jaw is sore, like I've been clenching my teeth in my sleep. Or maybe it's a side effect of the pills.

The sound of the front door being unlocked makes me drop my arms. The door swigs open, and Annette shoulders her way in. She's carrying split logs in her arms.

"I'm thirsty," I croak out.

Annette nods and sets the logs down. "I'll put some water on."

I watch the curve of her back as she stoops over the wood-stove. She lights a match and drops it onto the kindling. Sets up a pot over the grate.

"It's a little hot for tea," I say.

She looks over her shoulder at me. "The water is from the stream. I boil it to make it safe to drink."

"You drugged and kidnapped me, and you're worried about me getting a bacterial infection?"

Annette strides over to me. She sits on the opposite end of the couch, her eyes flicking to my wrists. "You're my daughter. You belong with me. *Do not* use that word."

"Kidnap?" I shimmy so I'm sitting up against the arm of the couch. My ankles are bound with a zip tie too. Annette's eyes focus on me. They're brown, like my father's and mine are. I never thought it was weird that Jos was the only one with green eyes.

"Daddy didn't know she wasn't yours, did he?" I ask. "She told him who she really was, in prison, years ago," I say. "And you know what he did? He tried to get the reward money from Macy Stevens's family."

Annette stands up and goes over to the stove. Checks on the pot of water.

"Gram told me about the baby," I yell, hysterical and desperate to make her answer me. "The one that died."

Annette flinches with her whole body.

"Is that why you stole Jos? Alan wouldn't have another baby with you?"

She's silent as she opens the cupboard and removes a glass, one of the jam jars with Tom and Jerry painted on the side that we used to save and wash out so we could drink from them.

"This was your favorite," she says with a wry smile.

"Answer me!" I scream. "Why did you take her?"

She closes her eyes, drifting off to some private place. "You never truly understand what fear is until you have a child, Tessa. Do you know what I saw in that woman's face, on TV, after she realized her baby was gone?"

Annette stokes the fire and looks back up at me. "Relief. Not fear. Joslin was safer with me."

"That's not her goddamned name!" I scream. "Her name was Macy!"

My stomach turns as she checks the water, as if she hadn't even heard me.

"We need more wood," she says. "I'll be right outside, chopping it."

There's a warning in her voice, as clear as a bell. Annette—ax. Tessa—drugged and incapacitated. When the door closes behind her, I shut my eyes. I won't allow myself to cry; she'll only give me more of the sleeping pills. Or worse, she'll try to comfort me.

I watch the flames in the stove sputter pathetically. The wood must be damp, from last night's rain. I scan the kitchen; the same zip ties are on several of the cabinet handles.

I wait until I hear the *thump, thump* of the ax outside before I sit up. I inch forward in my seat and rest my feet on the ground; slowly, tentatively, I stand. I sway a bit but regain my balance.

I press my zip-tied ankles closer together and hop into the kitchen.

Annette has left one drawer open, but my stomach sinks when I see the contents. Plastic forks, knives, napkins, all packaged together from different fast-food places.

I glance at the stove, feeling a surge of adrenaline when I see what Annette has left next to the pot.

A book of matches.

I struggle to get them into the front pocket of my shorts with my bound hands. I yank my T-shirt down as far as it will go and shuffle back over to the couch. Moments later, Annette comes in, empty-handed.

"The wood needs to dry out," she says. "I'll take a ride to the store and get some bottled water."

She comes over to the couch and helps me to my feet.

"What are you doing?" I ask.

"I can't leave you out here," she says. "I'm sorry, Tessa."

Annette puts a hand on my hip to guide me into the bedroom. A lump lodges in my throat as she sets me down on the bed and lifts my bound ankles onto it.

My shirt rides up. Before I can yank it back down, Annette's gaze lands on my pocket. Her face is emotionless as she pats it. Pulls out the book of matches.

She slips them into her pocket and locks the door behind her. I scream until I'm hollowed out and my voice is gone.

• • •

I wake up with a full bladder and pulsing behind my eyes. I lift my arms up; Annette cut off the zip ties while I slept. I check my ankles; they're free too. She probably thought she was doing me a favor by snipping them off.

Outside the window, an owl calls out to something in the dark. I pad over to the window and pry at the lock. It doesn't budge.

I tap on the glass, scaring a smattering of birds in the tree outside. It's thick glass, impossible to break with my bare hands. Nothing in the room except for the bed.

I pound on the door. "I need to pee!"

Nothing.

"I NEED TO PEE!"

I could keep screaming. I could try to kick the door down with my bare feet. Both will probably get another pill shoved down my throat, or more zip ties. I drop my pants, pee in the middle of the room, and get back into bed.

• • •

Annette sees what I've done in the morning. She says nothing as she mops up the mess with a dishtowel. When she finishes, she grabs me by the shoulder and drags me into the other bedroom.

Before she shoves me into a squat, square bathroom, I spy a series of pencil drawings hanging over the twin bed pressed against the wall.

"Did he do those?" I ask. "Daddy?"

"Your father built this whole place." Annette sits me on the toilet and turns the faucet on in the tub. "There's fresh water from the top of the mountain."

I eye the water as it drips into the basin. "Why didn't you bring us here, when we got evicted?"

"We had a tenant," Annette says. "Made a couple hundred dollars a month renting this place for years, but you don't get good people up here. Daddy let in a man I didn't trust. He stopped paying rent, and there was nothing we could do about it. Came up here to collect the money, and found him on the porch with a shotgun. Had no choice but to wait until he moved on."

Annette sticks a finger into the water. The tub isn't even a quarter full. "Get in."

I fold my arms against my chest. My mother yanks my shirt over my head and wriggles my shorts off. I step into the tub, ice-cold water coming up to my ankles.

"Sit." Annette grabs a cup from the vanity and proceeds to pour water on top of my head. "I haven't been able to pick up shampoo in a while."

I bring my knees up to my chest, shivering. Water drips into my eyes.

"I'm glad you're so calm now," Annette says, dragging her fingers through my wet hair.

Only because I'm picturing killing you in your sleep, I think.

. . .

I eat the beans, and the canned carrots. I don't complain at the bitter taste that obviously came from the white powder I saw her sneak into the saucepan.

All I want to do is sleep. Annette is content to let me. I hear her outside, chopping wood while I'm in bed. She comes in, sweaty, and washes herself before preparing vegetables from a can for her own dinner.

On the third night, she brings me a bowl of corn. I'm too tired to lift my head off the pillow. She feeds it to me with the plastic fork, a few kernels at a time. I store every one in the fold of my cheek like a hamster.

"I can do it myself," I say.

Annette gives a thin-lipped smile. Hands me the fork. "Last time I saw you, you still needed help zipping up your winter coat."

Because I'm pathetic, I want to say. *I have trouble ordering a sandwich because of you. Because you wanted us to be this way, so we'd always need you.*

Except Jos didn't. She never needed my mother, unlike whiny little me, who got stressed about everything. A stuck zipper. Gum on the bottom of my shoe. *MommymommyJos. Someone help me.*

She leaves without noticing that I slipped the fork beneath the sheets.

CHAPTER THIRTY-THREE

I wait until the faint glow from the oil lamps in the living room disappears from beneath my bedroom door before I crawl out of bed.

There's only half a moon tonight, so I have to feel around for them—the screws holding the metal bar beneath the bed in place. One wiggles under my finger. I silently thank my father's proclivity for cheap pieces of shit, this one most likely taken from someone's front lawn.

The bottom of the fork doesn't slide into the top of the screw like I convinced myself it would. I break into a flush, sweat beads on the back of my neck. It would help if I could see.

I tilt the fork so it sticks into the screw. I hold my breath and turn. Too forceful—the plastic is going to snap. I angle myself so I can turn the fork gently and push the screw from the bottom.

It takes a few minutes, but the screw starts to wiggle free. Maybe I wouldn't do so badly in jail. I've broken out in a full sweat by the time the screw pops out. And that was just one of them. I repeat the process, the back of my shirt soaking through with sweat and my face red-hot.

The bar comes loose once I undo the second screw. The bar feels hollow, but it'll do. I hope. I try to wedge the bottom between the windowsill and the lock, but it keeps slipping. I need a real crowbar, I realize with an ache of defeat.

My eyes prick. I stifle a sob as I force the bar behind the lock. I yank it toward me until it feels like the bones in my arms are going to snap.

The lock gives out first. It pops right off the window; a crack splits across the glass. I push the bar into the crack until the window gives out, taking the screen with it, and I hoist myself up onto the ledge. The top of the window scrapes my back, but I'm so elated that it barely hurts.

I'm out. I got out of the damn cabin.

I run. *Stumble* is more like it. Rocks, twigs stab the soft, fleshy part of my feet, but I don't stop. Even though it's dark and I can't see. I can't even tell if I'm going up the mountain or down it.

So, so tired. I see a light; an orange bulb on someone's porch. I keep going, past the cabin. No one is going to help me out here, even if they had cell phone reception. I'd rather be back with my mother than knocking on the door of someone like the skinhead Decker and I met outside the store in Bear Creek. Better the devil you know than the one you don't, and all that.

I keep going until my feet are bloody and my body can't carry the weight of my sobs. I've been walking for almost an hour, I figure, and the town is nowhere in sight. Hours of darkness are ahead of me.

I find a dark spot between two trees, where the moon can't reach, and I curl up on my side and I sleep.

• • •

The sun hangs in a sea of orange, yellow, and pink when I wake. The first thing I hear is a dog barking. And voices. Two of them. Men.

I shell up like a box turtle. Convince myself this is the end.

Until one of the men emerges from the trees. He's in a tan uniform, a badge over his shirt pocket. The German shepherd he's leading spots me and starts barking.

"Hey, Ed," the man calls out, not breaking eye contact with me. "Over here."

Someone was looking for me.

The officer extends a hand to me as I hear the crackle of a radio in the trees behind him. "Are you Tessa?"

The blood pounds in my feet, dirt and dust caked in my cuts. My bare legs are cold, and my neck aches from sleeping on the forest floor, but I manage to nod and croak out two words. *Help me.*

CHAPTER THIRTY-FOUR

I don't know what day it is when I wake up, or where the men from the mountain brought me. But I feel like I've been here for a while, sleeping.

The walls are white, the floor piss-yellow. Cool white sheets beneath me, and a remote tucked under my arm. I press the red button that says CALL NURSE beneath it.

A man in scrubs hurries in, followed by the sheriff who found me on Bear Mountain. I wonder if they were outside my door the whole time, waiting.

"How long have I been sleeping?" My throat is dry. The nurse lifts a paper cup of water to my lips.

"About twenty hours," the sheriff says. "The doctors found thirty milligrams of Ambien in your system. That's three times the normal dosage."

While the nurse siphons blood from my arm and gives me antinausea medication, the sheriff tells me that my cell phone pinged five miles from Bear Creek. Annette tried to turn it on to text Callie that I was fine and with friends, and the battery survived just long enough to make contact with the closest cell tower.

"Friend of yours told the Fayette police you may have been headed up here," he says. "Dexter Something-or-other?"

I make a mental note to get Decker Lucas the biggest bag of Twizzlers I can find.

The sheriff tells me that I slept through the rangers picking up my mother. I slept through Maggie arriving at Allegheny Valley hospital and yelling at the doctors until they let her in to see me.

"When did she leave?" I ask.

The nurse shakes his head and puts a blood pressure cuff on me. "She didn't. She's downstairs getting something to eat."

• • •

Callie wanted to come with Maggie to bring me home from Linesville, the nearest functional town to Bear Creek, where I stayed in the hospital, but she's only three days into her month-long stay at Healing Horizons Center for Youth Addiction. She tells me that after Jimmy Wozniak blew his brains out all over her, she locked herself in her room and drank half a handle of vodka. Maggie and Rick drove her to the rehab center that night. She calls to tell me all this as they're getting ready to discharge me from the hospital.

"We searched for you when we were leaving the hospital that day. My dad called the cops when your cell went to voice mail," she says in a hushed voice. "We thought maybe you were still at the station, but the receptionist at the hospital showed that you signed in. . . . She called the wrong room, that's why no one came to get you."

Callie lowers her voice even further, like maybe someone's listening to her. "The police didn't take us seriously. They said you'd come home soon. . . . If I hadn't freaking lost my shit, I'd have been able to help look for you."

"Don't blame yourself," I say, and add a feeble attempt at a joke: "The doctors say the psychological trauma shouldn't be permanent."

Callie breathes, a small *heh*. "You just had to one-up me by getting kidnapped too, huh?"

"You still win," I say softly. "She wouldn't have killed me."

Callie's quiet, and I know I've said the wrong thing. It's enough that she has to live the rest of her life with the memory of Jimmy Wozniak's gun barrel pressed to her head.

"You know what the worst thing is?" she whispers. "Stokes is still in jail."

"I know."

I guess we thought it'd be that easy—that we'd find the real Monster, find Lori's real killer, and Stokes would walk free. But overturning his conviction based on the new evidence against Wozniak is going to take time, even though Lori's killer is in custody at the Bear Mountain police precinct. Even though preliminary tests confirm that the partial DNA profile found on some of the victims matches Jimmy Wozniak's.

That was the "new" evidence Stokes's lawyers had, advancements in DNA testing that proved the partial profile could have come from one of thousands of men.

The DA said she's willing to consider a conditional release so Stokes can go free pending the decision from the judge. That will take time too.

But he won't be executed.

"Hey," Callie says quietly. "Did you have any idea—about

314

your mom? I mean, Annette. I just . . . She always seemed like she loved you guys so much."

I swallow. "No. I had no idea."

"Of course not," Callie says. "I'm sorry I even asked. Hold up."

There are voices in the background. A rustling sound like Callie is covering the receiver.

"My phone time is up," she says. "Can I call you again?"

I nod. Catch myself. Callie wants to call me, and not because she has to. "Yeah. Of course."

We hang up, and I look around the hospital room for the last time. My throat is tight, and my heart feels heavy. My flight back home takes off at five-forty-five tonight.

I knew this moment would come. Leaving Pennsylvania. I just never expected to be leaving with more than I had when I came.

• • •

After four hours of insisting that I was her daughter and had gone willingly with her to Bear Creek, Annette broke down and gave the following account to detectives:

Twenty-five years ago, Annette Lowell was at a gas station in Tennessee, where she'd been living for the past year. A young woman at the pump next to her left her two-year-old-daughter in the car while she went inside the convenience store to buy cigarettes. When she came back out, Annette told the woman she had a beautiful baby. The woman thanked her. Annette would later learn, from the news, that her name was Amanda Stevens.

Annette followed Amanda to find out where she lived. Later that night, Annette came back and saw that the woman's car wasn't in the driveway. She walked around the back of the house, where she heard a baby crying through a window opened a crack.

315

Annette found a spare key under the back door mat, waltzed into Amanda Stevens's house, and stole Macy Stevens from her crib. She made it all the way to Pennsylvania before anyone reported the baby missing.

When the police asked Annette how she'd left Tennessee without being concerned that someone had seen her kidnap Macy, she said that no one really noticed her to begin with. When she settled in Fayette, Pennsylvania, and introduced herself as the mother of two-year-old Joslin Mowdy, no one really noticed her either.

Then, shortly after, she met Glenn Lowell. Eight years later, Annette Lowell announced to her husband and friends in Fayette, Pennsylvania, that she was pregnant. She put on twenty pounds and claimed that her doctor had put her on mandatory bed rest until her due date. During this time, she went to the library once Joslin was at school and Glenn was at work. She spent her days in an online chat room for expectant mothers. There, she met a woman named Taylor from Warren, Ohio. Taylor, also four months pregnant, revealed that she worked at an OshKosh store half a mile from her house, and in her free time rescued retired greyhound dogs.

One week before Taylor's due date, Annette left Joslin with Glenn and drove to the OshKosh in Warren, Ohio, and waited for Taylor Lesley to close the store. She followed Taylor onto the highway and rear-ended her. When Taylor got out of the car, Annette pepper-sprayed her and forced her into the back of her car. Taylor's car was found burned at the bottom of the overpass a week after she was reported missing.

By the time the car was found, Annette was already in Bear Creek with Taylor, where she kept her hostage in the cabin until she gave birth to a baby girl.

Annette returned to Fayette one week before the due date she'd given her family and acquaintances. She told her husband she'd been visiting a relative in Philadelphia. She hid Taylor's child in her shed for two days, until nine-year-old Joslin came home from school and found Annette cradling a newborn baby in the living room. Annette said the midwife had come and gone in the early-morning hours. Glenn Lowell rushed home from work, and they named the baby Tessa. Glenn hadn't had a clue that Annette had faked the pregnancy—stupid Glenn Lowell, who would stumble into the house drunk every night, smelling of the women in bars who could give him what his frail, bedridden wife couldn't.

I had to stop listening when the detective described what Annette had done with my mother after she'd given birth. What I do know is this: Taylor and her unborn child were declared dead several years ago, her estranged husband the only person of interest in the case. Taylor's husband had been arrested for assaulting her before, and he didn't have an alibi for the night his pregnant wife went missing.

Authorities are mystified that a five-foot-six woman in a Toyota Camry was responsible for two of the highest-profile kidnappings in the past twenty years. When they asked Annette why she'd killed Taylor Lesley, Annette simply said that she'd lied about being pregnant and had had to come up with a baby somehow.

She said the police would find Taylor Lesley's remains buried beneath the porch at the cabin in the woods.

Two days after I was rescued, the police discovered a jewelry box in Jimmy Wozniak's bedroom. Inside were the following:

Rae Felice's locket,

Kristal Davis's watch,

Marisa Perez's gold bracelet,

And Ariel Kouchinsky's bracelet, identified by Nick Snyder as having belonged to his dead mother.

It was enough for the district attorney to announce plans to reopen the case of the Ohio River Monster.

A day later, Annette Lowell confessed to killing Lori, in exchange for the DA's office promising not to seek the death penalty.

In an attempt to get Joslin to listen to her theory, Lori had printed a picture of Amanda Stevens and pointed out all the genetic similarities. Attached earlobes. Green eyes.

Annette found the photo in our bedroom. When Joslin didn't say anything, Annette was sure that Joslin knew only one person smart enough to have figured it out.

Annette claims she only wanted to talk to Lori that night. She drove to the Greenwoods' home and parked in the woods behind the house, then turned the shed light on so Lori would come out to turn it off.

Lori threatened to call the cops when she saw Annette.

Annette says it was an accident. She didn't mean to kill Lori. She panicked once it was done, and remembered what she'd seen on the news about the Ohio River Monster.

Annette cut the bedroom window to make it look like Lori had been abducted.

People are saying Annette Lowell will never see the outside of a prison again.

People are calling her a monster.

I know it's true. But I don't know how to be angry with her for taking me when I still haven't forgiven her for leaving me.

CHAPTER THIRTY-FIVE

Now that I've been to hell and back, Atlanta airport doesn't seem all that bad. But this time I have a direct flight to Orlando.

The FBI has arranged for an agent to pick me up from the airport to bring me to Gram's house. I'm not allowed to be alone with her until she's cleared of any involvement in my kidnapping. DNA confirmed that I'm Taylor Lesley's daughter. The press conference was supposed to go down while I was thirty thousand feet in the air.

There are no news vans outside Gram's house. No men in pit-stained suits shoving microphones into my face. Just a black SUV in the driveway, with Virginia plates.

"Who is that?" I ask the agent driving me. He's beefy, but kind of soft in the middle. The type of guy probably assigned to paperwork and airport pickups.

"Another one of our people." The agent unlocks the door for me, and I climb out of the SUV.

Gram answers the door. She doesn't have her face on, as she

would say. Her eyes are red-rimmed, mascara-free. She stumbles toward me and presses me to her chest.

Over her shoulder, I spot a blond woman in the corner. She waits for Gram and me to break apart before she clears her throat and steps toward me.

"It's nice to meet you, Tessa," she says. "I'm Morgan Doherty. I believe we spoke on the phone."

Dread pools in my stomach. "You're assigned to the Macy Stevens case."

Agent Doherty nods, a twinkle in her eye.

Joslin steps into the living room from the kitchen. Her eyes and the tip of her nose are red. She balls up a tissue in her hand and smiles at me.

I run into my room and slam the door.

. . .

When I first moved down here, Gram took me to Disney World. I hadn't outgrown my Cinderella obsession yet. Two years before that, the Greenwoods had come back from Disney World and Callie had shown me her autograph book. That was the moment when I decided I *had* to meet Cinderella. I knew she wasn't *the* Cinderella, obviously, like the Santa Claus at the mall wasn't the real Santa, but still. I had to meet her.

In those moments when I got pissed at my mother and Joslin at the same time, I'd lock myself in the closet and pretend that I was Cinderella. My real father had died, leaving me with an evil stepmother and stepsister. I was the orphan princess. I'd never thought in a million years that I was *right* the whole time.

Anyway. When I finally spotted Cinderella at Disney World, Gram asked if I wanted a picture with her. And I froze. I just couldn't make my little feet propel me up to her. Cinderella spotted me, probably figured I was one of those shy kids, and smiled. I begged Gram to take me home.

I never thought seeing my sister again would be like that. But I also never thought that my sister wasn't really my sister.

No one comes after me when I storm into my room. Maybe they figure I've earned a tantrum after all I've been through.

I press my cheek to my pillow and inhale its scent. The full weight of what I stand to lose hits me. I can't let them take me from Gram.

There's a knock at my door a little while later. Gram comes in and sits on the edge of my bed. She smooths down the bedspread by my feet.

"You're probably wondering what kind of mother I was," she says, "to raise someone like her."

I don't say anything. Gram sighs.

"I keep going over everything I did, trying to find a reason. But I just don't know, Tessa." Gram wipes the area under her eyes. If she starts to cry, I don't think I'll be able to stand it. "I fed her. I changed her. I picked her up from the bus stop. I did everything you're supposed to do to care for a child."

Over Gram's shoulder I can see that we're not alone. Joslin is in the doorway, one hand on the doorframe. She's in a yellow sundress. If you looked at her, you might call her pretty, soft. If you looked hard enough, you'd see the eyebrow ring. The creases in her forehead that she's too young to have.

"I never got to know Annette," Gram says. "I never asked what she liked or what she wanted. I didn't have room for all that information, not after her father died. I did what I had to do to survive and tuned out everything that made the surviving worth it."

She pats my feet. "I see so much of myself in you, Tessa. And sometimes I can't bear it."

Gram gets up. Slips past Joslin, who steps into the room. We watch each other, an awkward staring contest that burns me up inside.

"I know you probably hate me," she finally says. "Ten minutes. Just give me that."

I sit up, and I make room on the bed for my sister.

• • •

Jos never knew that Annette and Lori argued on the phone that night. She was distracted by Danny calling her in a panic, saying he needed her to do something for him. She lied for Danny when the police came looking for him, and it wasn't the first time. It was just the first time he'd been stupid enough to blow something up.

Joslin didn't believe Lori could possibly be right about her crazy Macy Stevens theory. They argued about it a few days before Lori was killed—Joslin accused Lori of buying into the media frenzy over Baby Macy.

It wasn't until after Lori was gone that Jos started to feel guilty about not listening to her. Jos went through Annette's bedroom and found a birth certificate issued to Joslin Mowdy. The father's name was Alan Kirkpatrick.

Joslin saved up for months for a ticket to New Orleans. She slipped out of the house the night she ran away, got a Greyhound to Philly to catch the train. Once she was in Louisiana, she hitchhiked to the address she'd pulled up for Alan Kirkpatrick with a ten-dollar background check.

Alan, a leathery man who smelled like fish guts, was shocked to find Joslin at his front door. Jos said she took one look at him and knew he wasn't her father. Alan told her Annette had been pregnant when they'd been together. The lost baby was real.

But Annette moved out a few months after the miscarriage. She and Alan couldn't stop fighting—about children. Annette wanted them. Alan didn't.

Joslin called the Pennsylvania hospital on her birth certificate; they'd never had a record of her, or Annette Mowdy. The birth certificate was a fake.

Jos headed back up to Pennsylvania to tell Annette what she'd found. She showed up at our door in the middle of the night; realizing the truth was catching up with her, Annette played the only card she had left. She used me against my sister. Annette told Joslin that if she breathed one word about the Macy Stevens story, Annette would kill me before the cops could even get to our doorstep.

Jos came back for me when she turned eighteen, but I was already down here with Gram. She eventually tracked Gram down and called the Florida house while I was at school. She told Gram she wanted me to come live with her. Gram calmly told Jos that the next day was swimming day at school. I was so excited about it, I wanted to wear my bathing suit to bed. That weekend, we were going to Disney World.

Jos hung up and never called back.

Five years ago, Joslin went back to Fayette; she visited my father in prison and confronted him about Macy Stevens. He said he didn't know anything, and Joslin believed him. She made him promise not to tell anyone. She was waiting until I was safely in her possession before contacting the police with her suspicions.

That was when my father called the Stevens family. Tried to extort the reward money from them. Joslin didn't know until she emailed them through their Find Baby Macy website, saying she suspected she was their granddaughter. The Stevenses took one look at the name—Lowell—and told Joslin never to contact them again.

Jos was angry at their rejection. She started to doubt again that Lori was right about her being Macy. So Jos stayed in Allentown. She bought a new identity, Brandy Butler, so she could go to nursing school part-time.

Four years ago, she and her boyfriend had a baby girl. That was when she realized that she didn't just have herself to look out for anymore. She had to do everything in her power to keep her daughter safe, even if it meant letting Annette get away with what she'd done. Jos was afraid if she went public, no one would believe her, and that Annette would come after her and her daughter.

"I was so stupid." A tear streaks down her face. "I believed it when she said that no one would believe *me*. That my real mother never wanted me, and that my real family would never accept me."

"How did you know Daddy was dying?" I ask her.

"I had a Google alert set up on his name," Jos says. "A local news station found out he had cancer. You're too young to remember, but his case was a big deal at the time, someone getting a life sentence for armed robbery."

Jos reaches into her purse, pulls out something. A photo.

"He was going to give you this," she says, setting it on the bed in front of me. "I said I'd take it and keep it safe until I saw you again."

I've never seen the photo before. I'm lying on my back, a swaddled pink thing with no hair. Joslin is bent over me, clutching her own baby doll to her chest. In the corner, my father is in his armchair, laughing.

"I used to pretend you were my baby." Jos grins. "She—she

never let me hold you, really. So he came home one night with the baby doll."

My chest tugs. My father was surprising like that.

"He loved you so much," Jos says. "You were the only thing, I think."

"But it was all a lie," I whisper. "We're not even really sis—"

Jos takes my face in her hand. "Stop. You are my *sister*. Got it?"

I close my eyes and lean my forehead so it's touching hers. Even though I doubted her, even though I suspected her of the worst thing imaginable, even though I convinced myself I didn't love her anymore, I get it.

She gave up so much to keep me safe. I'll never unlearn everything she told me about those years we were separated.

I meant it when I told Callie there are some things we can never forget, no matter how much we want to.

But for the first time in a long time, I want to remember.

EPILOGUE

I meet Joslin's daughter, Alexa, a week before I have to start classes at Tampa. We go to Disney World, and she insists on holding my hand when we're in the lines for all the rides. When she spots a princess in blue with a long blond braid that falls to her waist, Alexa clams up, her little preschooler cheeks morphing into two plump strawberries.

We wait in line to meet her, Alexa humming along to the movie sound track and cowering between my legs every time the princess moves into our line of sight.

"I have to hear this song twenty times a day," Joslin says beneath her breath, rolling her eyes at me. "It's like waterboarding for mothers."

I flinch inside at the word, not quite ready to share my sister. Not after I've waited so long to get her back. But she looks the way I remember, now that she's dyed her hair brown again. We're both wearing sunglasses and baseball caps in case anyone recognizes us.

The media has been relentless—four ambushes, two changed

phone numbers, and one creepy-ass woman who followed me down an aisle at Walmart—but Joslin says she's never felt so free.

Think about it, she said. *We can get passports now. See the world.*

They're already writing books about my mother. When the story broke, the *New York Post* printed her mug shot with the headline WOMB RAIDER. Brenda Dean announced her two-million-dollar book deal for an account of the Monster murders and Lowell kidnappings, to be titled *Stolen Lives*.

I declined to be interviewed for it. I'm starting classes at Tampa soon, and I really don't need to draw any more attention to myself.

Besides. No one stole my life from me. It's always been mine. I just have to figure out what to do with it next.

• • •

They found her when they started to tear down the cabin in the woods. They'd missed the cellar door in their initial raid, since Annette had covered it with leaves.

The girl was about six or seven, obviously well cared for. They found her on a sofa bed, the floor littered with snack wrappers and stubs of crayons.

Drawings of her and a brown-haired woman, holding hands and picking daisies.

She said only one thing to investigators.

"Mommy said to stay down here and not come out for anyone but her."

ACKNOWLEDGMENTS

This is a story I didn't think I had the guts to write. I might not have if Suzie Townsend hadn't said, "Do it!" Thank you, Suzie, for always getting it.

This book wouldn't exist without a huge leap of faith from Krista Marino, who is an editorial wizard. Thank you for helping me build this story from the ground up, and for loving it as much as I do. I feel like the luckiest author in the world to get to work with you.

To the team at Random House Children's Books—Beverly Horowitz, Monica Jean, Kimberly Lauber, John Adamo, Mary McCue, Dominique Cimina, Adrienne Waintraub, Rachel Feld, Laura Antonacci, Aisha Cloud, Anna Gjesteby, Sonia Nash Gupta, and Stephanie O'Cain—thank you for the warm welcome and for your endless enthusiasm and support.

I am so lucky to have the support of the Dream Team at New Leaf Literary and Media—Kathleen Ortiz, Joanna Volpe, Pouya Shabhazian, Jess Dallow, Danielle Barthel, Dave Caccavo, Jackie Lindert, Jaida Temperly, and Chris McEwen.

This book was inspired in part by the West Memphis Three and their willingness to share their stories. To Margaret Riley, thank you for the encouragement, and for steering me toward the *Paradise Lost* documentaires.

Thanks also to Larry Salz and Lucinda Moorhead at UTA; to Kathy Bradey and Lindsey Culli, for tirelessly reading all my drafts; and to my family, for their endless support and patience.

ABOUT THE AUTHOR

Kara Thomas has written for everything from her high school newspaper to Warner Bros. Television. She is a true-crime addict who lives on Long Island with her husband and rescue cat. To learn more about her and her books, visit her at kara-thomas.com and follow @karatwrites on Twitter.